M. L. WHITE

Shifter Deliverance

First published by White Wolf Publishing LLC 2025

Copyright © 2025 by M. L. White

All rights reserved. No part of this publication may be reproduced, stored or transmitted in any form or by any means, electronic, mechanical, photocopying, recording, scanning, or otherwise without written permission from the publisher. It is illegal to copy this book, post it to a website, or distribute it by any other means without permission.

This novel is entirely a work of fiction. The names, characters and incidents portrayed in it are the work of the author's imagination. Any resemblance to actual persons, living or dead, events or localities is entirely coincidental.

M. L. White asserts the moral right to be identified as the author of this work.

M. L. White has no responsibility for the persistence or accuracy of URLs for external or third-party Internet Websites referred to in this publication and does not guarantee that any content on such Websites is, or will remain, accurate or appropriate.

Designations used by companies to distinguish their products are often claimed as trademarks. All brand names and product names used in this book and on its cover are trade names, service marks, trademarks and registered trademarks of their respective owners. The publishers and the book are not associated with any product or vendor mentioned in this book. None of the companies referenced within the book have endorsed the book.

Second edition

ISBN (paperback): 9798899713286
ISBN (hardcover): 9798896926603

Cover art by SeventhStar Art

This book was professionally typeset on Reedsy.
Find out more at reedsy.com

*To my mom and dad,
Thank you for all your love,
support and endless encouragement.
– Love,
Your favorite child*

I

Part One

*"Sometimes your destiny isn't your first choice.
No. Sometimes the path meant for you
isn't the path you would have taken,
but once you go... once you start down that path,
you realize it was the best thing you
could have ever done."*
— Shanely Fenrir

Chapter 1

The entire pack was at the lodge by the time Bastian and I got back from our run. We both shifted, and I immediately looked for Aerith. All of the members of my pack stepped in my path though, either to congratulate me or shake my hand. It seemed like everyone was a little star struck finally seeing the White Wolf that they had all heard about from their legends and stories. I don't think anyone really thought they'd see the White Wolf in their lifetime, and everyone was near giddy that it came from their pack. Cain, Ash, and Aspen thankfully made a path to us and guided us through the small crowd.

"Guys, give her some space! Let us through!" my Uncle Cain shouted.

Everyone still respected him as Alpha and listened right away, backing away from Bastian and I. We made our way to the steps where Aerith ran and jumped into Bastian's arms. She snuggled in close before reaching for me, and I hugged her tightly. My poor baby had been through quite an ordeal this summer, and I honestly didn't think I'd see her again. Bastian pulled me into his arms and just held the both of us close. The crowd grew quiet, giving us a brief moment of calm.

"My girls," Bastian whispered as I leaned my head on his shoulder. We were all alive and safe. I let out a huge sigh of relief and relaxed in my mate's arms.

"I hate to interrupt this moment guys, but we need to address a few things," my Uncle Cain said.

I lifted my head, but stayed in Bastian's arms as I listened to my uncle address the crowd. Our pack had become a lot smaller than it was when I first joined, but we still had a decent number here. They all looked a little unsure and excited at the same time. Everyone felt the change in leadership and the White Wolf's appearance. This was all happening whether I wanted it or not. I was way more connected and in tune with my wolf than my bear, and she seemed as uneasy as I was.

"Everyone, I know you felt the Alpha status shift from myself and my mate Cassia, so I would like to formally introduce your new Alpha and Alpha Female, Bastian and Shanely!"

Everyone cheered and clapped then. No one seemed too upset that Cain wasn't their leader anymore. I on the other hand had butterflies in my stomach. Cain ran this pack with so much ease. How was I supposed to do this?

"Now, we all have suspected this for some time now, but Shanely confirmed it when she shifted into our legendary White Wolf!"

They all cheered again, but Cain held his hand to silence them faster than the first time.

"This changes everything, as you all know. We have been changing things within our pack over the last few years, but it has all been done without the World Council's knowledge. We've kept Shanely and Aerith hidden from the other packs to ensure their safety. We did what was best for everyone in our pack but now that the White Wolf is here, the Wolf Shifter Summit will have to be called early. We cannot hide her anymore. This means we will have to go and inform the World Council that they will no longer be ruling. Shanely will be taking over."

I whipped my head to him. "I don't know about this Uncle. I never agreed to take that job, and you know that."

"Shanely, we will discuss this in a moment," he said, giving me a firm look that shut me up. "Now not to alarm anyone, but we had an unfortunate incident tonight, so I want you all safe inside your homes for the remainder of the evening. We're locking down tonight. No one comes near the lodge or in the woods. Enforcers get to your patrols now. Dismissed."

The crowd murmured as they scooped up their children, and the families spread out in different directions. Brody gave me a small wave before leaving

CHAPTER 1

with the other enforcers. I was going to have to find him later. I didn't want him to blame himself for what happened.

Frustrated with everything, and not wanting to wait around anymore, I turned without a word and went straight for the conference room where I met the pack's council all those years ago.

My family followed me into the room with everyone taking their normal places. I know I radiated tension, but thankfully no one said a word about it. I was a little out of control with my emotions from my wolf's awakening. I was trying my best to keep a lid on my temper, but man was it difficult. I didn't realize how emotional wolves really were. I took my normal seat, where Cain always put me when I was apart of pack meetings, and quietly watched everyone file in.

The members of the council came in as well. Kyle, Gregory and Nathan walked in behind a tall women named Alice. They were all that was left of the original council since Derek left. They took their seats as Elijah and Cade walked in and took their places behind the Alpha's chair. My aunt finally walked in last followed by Cain. She shook her head at me frowning. What did I do wrong now?

"You two are at the front. Not here," she said while my Uncle Cain stood behind my seat. I slowly stood up, looking around. Everyone smiled at me, waiting patiently for me to accept the Alpha's seat, but my feet felt like lead. I didn't like this. It felt wrong taking Cain's seat. Cade pulled out the head chair and gestured to me.

"This one Baby Girl," he said as he helped me into the large chair. He and Elijah beamed back at me, standing proudly behind us as Bastian sat in the seat to my left with Aerith on his lap. Bastian held her close, whispering something in her ear, when Brody suddenly appeared at the door. My mate motioned him forward, and the enforcer looked at everyone nervously.

"Take her upstairs to the movie room, please. Don't let her out of your sight or out of that room Brody. I'll come fetch her in a little while."

Brody honestly looked shocked as he knelt down to our level. "You want me to take her?"

Bastian looked puzzled and asked, "Yeah, why wouldn't I? You're the top enforcer in your class Brody. I trust you to watch my daughter."

Brody looked to his feet in shame. "But I lost them."

"Brody..." I replied as my voice trailed off. My heart broke at the look he gave me.

"I'm so sorry Shanely. I failed you and your daughter. I..." Brody said quietly, but Bastian cut him off.

"Brody, you didn't fail anyone. You were ambushed, and honestly I'm amazed that you were able to fight through that tranquilizer as quickly as you did. The amount you received should have knocked you out for the rest of the day, but you fought through it and saved my family. You did everything you could for them, and I'm grateful for that. You have to understand, sometimes bad things happen even to the best enforcers, but you can't ever give up even when it seems like you've lost already. My family is alive and with me today because you were smart and never stopped trying to save them. You are officially graduated from training, Brody. You are a full enforcer, and I want your first job to be protecting my daughter. You will be her personal bodyguard until further notice. Can you do that?"

Brody actually looked emotional, and I was incredibly proud of both Brody and Bastian. He built Brody back up even when Brody felt he failed in his mission. I can see why Ash and Aspen wanted my mate to take over training. He was an amazing instructor and friend to the enforcers. They needed more than just a drill sergeant. Bastian was meant to lead. Myself on the other hand... I wasn't so sure about that.

Brody gave Bastian a nod. "I can do that Alpha. I'll protect her like she were my own."

"Good. I trust you Brody. Go and have fun you two," my mate replied as I whispered a thank you to Brody. He smiled wide at me before leaving with Aerith in his arms.

"I'm proud of you mate," I whispered before kissing Bastian's cheek. He scooted his chair until it was right up against mine before taking my hand.

"I'm proud of you too, Shanely. Are you ready for this?"

"In ways I am, but mostly I feel like I just stole my Uncle's place," I replied quietly. Everyone was talking among themselves as the meeting

CHAPTER 1

hadn't officially started yet. I apparently wasn't quiet enough as my uncle interrupted us.

"Shanely, I don't want to hear anything like that. The Alpha's position would have been yours anyways if your mother and you had lived here all along. It's in your bloodline, and we merely filled in until you were ready. And you are ready for this."

I sighed before gently rubbing my face. "Let's just start small. I don't think I'll be able to change how I feel just like that. How do we proceed Uncle?"

"Well let's just officially start the meeting. Now that the shift in power happened, because of Shanely unlocking her wolf, we don't need to have any ceremony. It's already done, but we can have a celebration if Shanely wants one. Now that you are the new Alpha pair, you need to pick your new council members," Cain continued.

I looked confused before giving my mate a sideways glance. "Wait, it doesn't stay with the current members?

Kyle decided to answer me instead. "It stays within the family usually, and each Alpha chooses who they want on their team, but you are the White Wolf. Traditional rules no longer apply. You need to pick those on your team that can handle dealing with worldly conflicts."

"How did Derek get a seat then?" I asked.

"He was the only one from that family that offered. The other man that could have taken it flat refused, so I chose Derek to fill that seat. He wasn't that bad back then," my uncle responded.

"Your first decision is to pick your new team. We're only here as a formality and a passing of the torch, so to speak," Nathan said with a smile.

"And to show our support to our White Wolf as well," Alice chimed in. I internally cringed. I didn't want anyone to treat me differently than before. I wasn't anything special, and I felt uncomfortable with all the attention.

"Now Shanely, every wolf in the world felt you emerge. They know exactly what has happened including the Council members. You became Alpha of the McCoy pack, but now it's time for them to pass their power to you, so you can take your rightful place as Head Alpha," Cain continued informing me, but all it was doing was making me nauseous.

"The World Summit. The packs will not have a choice whether to attend or not for this one, correct?" Bastian asked.

"Every pack will need to be called by the end of the week. We will call the World Council tonight, and they choose the date and inform the rest of the packs, but you are right. This isn't a normal yearly Summit, so attendance is mandatory," Aspen answered.

"Which means Derek will be there right?" Bastian asked again. I closed my eyes, taking in a deep breath. I hadn't thought of that when the Summit was mentioned before. How will I face him again?

Cain nodded slowly. "But he has a bounty on his head, and the Council will be forced to deal with it. Derek will be brought to justice, especially when it comes out that he tried to kill our White Wolf. The World Council cannot ignore that."

"You say White Wolf like I'm royalty or something. That's not me!" I practically shouted. I didn't mean to raise my voice, but this has to stop. Everyone looked at me now wide eyed, but my aunt broke the silence.

"Shanely, you basically are royalty to us now. We've all heard the prophecy and legends surrounding the White Wolf since we were children, but you are even more unique because you're a White Bear as well. That comes with a whole other set of legends and prophecies. It was always thought to be two separate shifters but we were all wrong. It means so much more because it's just one. We all feel like you are meant to bring the entire shifter race together. All of us together like it used to be. Not just reconnecting the wolves."

I sunk in my chair. I barely could protect myself and my family. How was I supposed to bring about that kind of change? I didn't want to be shifter royalty. I mean sure I wanted to help improve life for shifters, but this was a bit overwhelming. Bastian grabbed my hand, pulling me from my thoughts.

"We can do this Shanely. Together. Everyone knows what you are now, but this is our chance to show them who you are, and I want to take it. You are an amazing, loving and beautiful person inside and out. You are helping heal our lands and issues within our kind already. I mean look at the bear and tiger shifters around here. Everyone is happy and safe because you have united us all. We're stronger for that, but imagine what you could do with the world. This is also your opportunity to shine a light on your mother, Shanely, and what she did just to keep you safe. You're giving her a legacy for everyone to remember, not just us. The mother of the White Wolf, who defied ancient and stupid laws, to keep her family safe. It's why it's you. Don't you see?"

I leaned against him and took a deep breath. I had never thought about it with my mother before. She broke many laws to stay with her mate, and then again to keep both of her children safe, and here I was cowering in the corner when my mother was bold. She faced everything alone while I have so many by my side. If I can make a change, then maybe others won't have to go through what she did. I wouldn't have to hide away with Aerith either if the old laws weren't a thing anymore. Mixers won't be looked at as abominations but a valued part of our community.

I was terrified, but I wanted to help others outside of our pack find and keep their mates. I looked up at Bastian, knowing he was listening to my internal monologue. He smiled, and I kissed his cheek. If I was going to do this I definitely needed him, and I'm glad he was made an Alpha as well.

I turned back to those at the table. "Okay. I will do my best to be the White Wolf and all that it entails."

Everyone smiled before bowing their heads to me. I think they were all relieved I didn't just up and run away, but one thing's for sure I did not want to be put up on a pedestal, especially by my own pack.

"Okay, okay, please no bowing or anything. Just treat me like how you'd normally treat your Alpha. I don't want to be royalty or anything. Just Alpha Female, especially here in pack lands. I need a sense of normalcy, and I still want to be Shanely, alright?"

Everyone chuckled when Kyle replied, "We will all do our best. We will help spread the word to the pack here if that is truly what you wish."

"It is, and thank you all," I replied with a smile. Okay, maybe this won't be so bad then, I thought to myself.

"In my opinion, I think we need a new council here. Not to disrespect any of you, but if Shanely agrees I would like to pick a whole new panel," Bastian chimed in, moving the meeting right along.

I looked around the room unsure what to say. I felt horrible taking their seats, and I didn't want them to feel undervalued. Alice chuckled when she noticed the look on my face.

"Shanely, we are all getting older. Like Kyle said earlier, traditional rules don't apply here anymore. You need to go with what feels right, and none of us will be offended if you choose another."

They all nodded in agreement, and Bastian looked at me, waiting to see how I'd feel.

"Okay well..." my voice trailed off. How was I supposed to choose?

"Trust your wolf, Shanely. You need to rely on her to give you direction. She will tell you who to choose," my Aunt Cassia said.

I sighed.

Okay, listen to my wolf then. Seems easy enough.

I took a few deep breaths, and I let her guide me. My wolf seemed so sure of herself now, and we were in sync with each other. It was an incredible feeling. Soon, I was rattling off names I felt she was whispering to me. "Cade, Elijah, Ryder, Johnny, Caleb, Abraham, and Bay."

I opened my eyes, and Bastian was smiling at me.

"Some you mentioned are not wolves Shanely," Gregory pointed out.

"I felt those names too. Our wolves are in sync Shanely," Bastian replied.

I smiled. "It's what my wolf is saying is right. These few are who she wants apart of our team, and I think having a blend will enforce our new way of thinking."

"It seems fitting," Cain said.

"You want us though? Really?" Elijah asked with nervous smile.

"Of course! You two are my best friends as well as my family. You've saved me more times than I can count, and I can't imagine having anyone else on my council. My wolf and I trust you both completely," I replied as I smiled to them both.

"Our first pick honestly," Bastian chimed in.

"I think Cade and I assumed we would just be your personal enforcers like we were with Cain," he replied sheepishly.

CHAPTER 1

"Absolutely not. My brothers will help run this with us not just be enforcers," Bastian agreed, and Cade clapped him on the back.

"We're honored guys," Cade answered.

"Well, I think we should excuse ourselves now. It's time to call your new council in and figure out the next steps," Nathan said, and they all stood. They gave a small bow before retreating to the door.

"Thank you all for everything you've done for this pack," I said, and they gave me a smile before leaving.

"I will go and retrieve Ryder and Johnny. You will have to call Caleb and Abraham. They should make it for the call if they can leave fairly quickly," my aunt said before leaving the room herself. Ash and Aspen congratulated us once more before making their way out too.

"You won't stay?" I asked my Uncle Cain who stood as well.

My uncle replied, "I will be here merely to address the switch. We will always be here if you guys need insight or help with anything, but after tonight I will only attend if summoned. You all must be able to function together and to trust one another. Don't forget to choose your personal Betas as well. You will each need one since you will both be Head Alphas soon."

We looked at one another before Bastian nodded in response to Cain.

"Shanely, I'm not sure who you were planning on choosing, but I'd like to pick Elijah as my Beta. Are you alright with that?"

I grinned back at him and gave him a nod. I loved that idea. Elijah and Bastian would be an incredible and intimidating team, and knowing Elijah would always be with Bastian made my wolf and bear happy.

"I love that idea Bastian. I think he'd be perfect as your Beta. I would like to choose Cade. Are you okay with that?"

"Really?" he said, grinning. His brows rose ever so slightly that I wondered if he didn't want that. *"You want my brother as your Beta? Not one of the girls?"*

"Do you not want him as my Beta?"

He gave me a pointed look.

"No, Shanely I love the idea. You two are best friends, and I feel better knowing my brother will be there to assist and protect you if I cannot be. I'm just surprised is all, but you have no idea how happy it makes me. I love knowing you are as close to my brothers as I am."

I smiled back at him. *"Good, then it's settled. Let's tell them."*

"Give your brothers a call Shanely before the World Council gets impatient and calls us," Bastian said to me before turning around, "Brothers take a seat."

My Uncle Cain moved down a seat to make room for the Fenrir brothers. I think he already knew who we were choosing as our Betas and gave us a knowing smile. Cade and Elijah started to take chairs side by side by one another when Bastian interrupted.

"No, Elijah you're seat will be on my left," he said as he gestured to the available seat.

"And Cade you will be on my right," I continued on.

They both looked to one another before Elijah spoke. "Aren't those seats for your Betas? We should probably wait until everyone is here, and then we can all get our permanent seats. Cade and I can sit down here until then."

"No, we know who belongs in those seats already. Cade, I would like you to be my Beta. I choose you," I countered, and his eyes widened.

"Really Baby Girl? You want me?"

I nodded my head as Bastian continued on.

"And I asked Shanely if she would mind if I chose you, Elijah. I want you as my Beta, brother. Do you accept?"

Elijah gave a soft smile. "I'm honored to be your Beta, brother."

"You must say it in a specific way for the connection to snap in place. It must be official with our wolves," Cain chimed in. I did not know that.

Bastian gave a slow nod before addressing Elijah, "Elijah Fenrir, will you accept the position of Beta to myself as your Alpha?"

He stood proudly and said, "I accept Bastian. I choose the position of being your Beta."

I felt a snap in the air as Elijah and Bastian took in a deep breath. Bastian gave an unrestrained smile before he stood and clapped hands with his brother.

"Thank you brother," Bastian replied before hugging him.

I turned to Cade who looked excitedly at his brothers. "Cade Fenrir, will you accept the position of Beta to myself, your White Wolf and Alpha?"

Cade beamed back at me. "Baby Girl, of course I'll be your Beta! I accept the position of Beta to the White Wolf, Shanely Fenrir."

Another snapped filled the room, and I felt connected to Cade more than with just the sibling bond. We were more in sync with one another as he became my right hand man. I gave him a hug, thanking him for being there for me again, before I pulled his chair out. I grinned when he laughed at the gesture, but I didn't care if it was cheesy. He acted like a girl on a date when he sat down, and my uncle rolled his eyes. We all laughed, and everything just felt right.

I was actually excited about my new team, and this was the first time I genuinely felt this way since becoming the Alpha. With our brothers at our side, I honestly felt pretty good. Uncle Cain smiled softly, shaking his head before he pushed a button on the table, and the screen lowered from the ceiling. Prepping for the call, I guess. I took out my phone to dial my brother's number when I had a thought. I pushed my Alpha power out with the mind link to see how far it could go. I tried Abraham first since he was the farthest away.

"Abraham?"

"Well hello, Shanely. I didn't expect to hear from you today. Stopping by then?"

"No, I'm actually still at the pack lodge, but we do need to talk," I replied.

"Wait..." Abe said, and I could hear the confusion in his voice. "How are you mind linking me then if you're still at the lodge? I'm home right now."

"That's part of what I need to discuss. Can you and Bay come to the lodge? It's really important."

"Of course. She's somewhere on streak lands right now, but I'll find her. We'll be there soon."

"Abraham is on his way now," I said to the small group.

I called Caleb the same way at Abraham, who was just as surprised to hear from me from this far away. He said he was leaving right now, and it wasn't long before Ryder and Johnny strolled in. We informed them of our decision to make them apart of our council, and they were excited. They each took a chair while we waited for the rest of the group to get here, but the call came in before my brothers made it.

"The World Council doesn't mess about," I whispered as my uncle answered it. Five men sat at a table much like ours. They wore expensive suits and looked cross. Oh boy, here we go, I thought to myself. It just can't be easy, can it?

"Hello Council members. We were getting ready to call you ourselves," my uncle said with a fake smile. I almost snorted. These were our favored leaders? Five overweight, stuffy looking men in suits all glared down at us. They didn't look very amused to be talking to us.

"Hello Cain. It seems the White Wolf is among us finally. Who might it be? All that was made known to us was it was here and at your pack," one of the stuffies said.

Cain motioned to me as he replied, "My niece Shanely Fenrir, the White Wolf and newest Alpha to the McCoy pack."

Another member scrunched his nose at that. "The White Wolf is a female? That seems unlikely it would be her. Are you sure it is not the young man next to her instead?"

I bristled at that comment, but Bastian gripped my hand fiercely under the table. I gave him a look, but his face was stoic.

"It is not to control you, my love," he said softly. *"I need your touch to control myself."*

I sighed before rubbing his thumb with mine. This was not going to be easy on either of us.

"I promise you it is not wrong. I have seen her wolf myself," Cain countered in annoyance.

"She cannot continue to stay Alpha of the McCoy pack. You'll need to find a replacement Alpha or step up again Cain. She will be far too busy once

CHAPTER 1

she starts handling the White Wolf's responsibilities," another man said, looking down past his glasses to us.

"Silas, I did not transfer my Alpha rights, the shift took them. When she discovered her wolf, it pulled the power from me to her. Best not to mess with what's been chosen, don't you think?" Cain countered again.

Silas didn't look to happy with that. "How do you expect her to run your pack when she lives here?"

"Excuse me?" I asked. They all turned to me like I spoke out of turn or something. "I never said I was moving."

"Child, it was not a invitation that you could say no to. It is how it is meant to be. You will live here among us where we can guide you in your journey," Silas responded.

Bastian tensed up, and I was floored. Everyone looked to one another. This was not how I thought this call was going to go.

"Silas, Shanely has a Fated Mate as well as a child. You can't expect her to leave and move to Canada away from her family. Besides once the White Wolf appears, the World Council is no longer needed according to the prophecy," Cain countered again. They scoffed at that and started murmuring among themselves.

"You really cannot expect us to just hand over the entire Wolf Shifter community to a girl we've never met before? No, we must determine she is ready first, but we can discuss this further at the Summit. It's being held here of course, in two weeks. We will see you then."

The screen went black then. They hung up on us. Bastian was fuming next to me, and I was ready to tear their heads off. My wolf agreed.

"Could they be anymore arrogant? God, the nerve of those guys! They have no idea what's coming their way!" I shouted as Bastian rubbed my back, but then a scary thought popped in my head. "Can they really force me to live there?"

Bastian replied firmly, "Absolutely not. The White Wolf is meant to change things, and they're simply afraid of losing control. You will not be forced to do anything you don't want to, and I'll make sure of it."

"We need to convince the masses when we get there. The Council will fight us ever step of the way it seems. Here, talk among yourselves while I inform the pack and make the travel arrangements," Cain said before leaving.

Cade whistled before running his hand through his hair. "We cannot catch a break, can we?"

Elijah shook his head. "How are we going to do this?"

Bastian looked to me and asked, "What does your wolf tell you?"

I leaned back and gave her a chance to tell me. "She wants to be bold, yet kind. She doesn't want to follow their command blindly, and she feels ready to use her power to make them yield if necessary. We need to use it wisely or everyone may see me as a threat, especially with the changes I am bringing."

"What changes?" Caleb asked as he strolled in with Abraham and Bay on his heels. We all said a quick hello before filling them in on everything that had happened so far with Peter.

Abraham gritted his teeth. "We should of killed Peter a long time ago, if you ask me."

"We're really glad you're okay Shanely," Bay stated as she squeezed my hand.

"At least he will never be in your life again. Why are we here though? We aren't wolves, and this seems like more of a pack meeting right?" Caleb asked.

I eyed Bay who just grinned at me. I asked, "You didn't say anything to them coming in?"

"I figured you'd rather tell your brothers yourself," she replied as Abraham gave her a funny look.

"Keeping secrets, my love?" he asked, poking her sides. She giggled before giving him a playful shrug.

"What's going on Shanely?" Caleb asked.

"We've called you here because when Shanely was attacked the only way to save her was to force her shift. She shifted into a beautiful White Wolf. Bay would have felt the call because she is a wolf, which is why she knows already. During that shift, the Alpha power left Cain and Cassia and came to us. According to custom, Alphas choose their own council and Betas, and we've asked each of you here to be apart of ours," Bastian stated matter of

CHAPTER 1

factly.

Caleb laughed and replied, "We can't be part of the council. Abraham and I are aren't wolves."

"I know that Caleb, but those rules don't apply to the White Wolf. You know that to wolves and bears the color white means something. Uncle Thomas always said it signified great change, and well this is part of it. I'm going to abolish the laws that shifters across the world have. I want to start mixing us together again and to make us stronger against the Division if need be. What better way than to have my non-wolf brothers apart of my council, plus I need you all there. I need people I can trust and that my wolf and bear trust completely," I replied.

"Elijah has become my Beta while Cade is Shanely's," Bastian chimed in while his brothers looked ahead proudly.

"The World Council isn't thrilled the White Wolf is a female, and they're aren't ready to relinquish their power," I continued on.

"They are a bunch of old fools. They're trying to insist Shanely live there at Summit Hall rather than here with her family. They don't want to give up the control, so this will end up a fight I'm sure of it," Bastian added before gripping my hand hard again.

"The Summit's in two weeks, so not a lot of time to prepare," Elijah chimed in.

Abraham bit his bottom lip nervously. "Two weeks? How long does it last?"

"It's a week long event," Ryder answered.

"First things first though, will you all be part of my council?" I asked. I needed a concrete answer.

"We're in," Ryder answered as he gestured to Johnny.

"We're honored you guys chose us," Johnny replied.

"I'm in too little sis," Caleb replied with a soft smile.

I looked to Abraham who just looked stressed. "How about you Abey? Are you and Bay accepting?"

He sighed and leaned back in his chair. "I'm always in with whatever you are planning. I will stand by you and protect you always, but I'll be honest this Summit makes me nervous. The Blackwood pack will be there correct?"

I shook my head yes. "As will Derek."

That got everyone's attention. We haven't gone to a Summit since I came to the pack, and now we were finally going to catch him. I got my brother's hesitation though. He was going to have to face many demons by joining my council and coming to the Summit with us. He had an entire pack while I simply had one vile man to face.ABraham seemed to get he wasn't the only one that was nervous, and nodded his head.

"Then we accept. Let's change the world Shanely," he replied, grabbing Bay's hand.

"We won't just be the council for the McCoy Pack, but we will also need to take over for the World Council. Is everyone okay with that?" I asked. I wanted to give anyone who wanted an out a chance to say no. I didn't get one, and I wasn't going to force anyone to do something they didn't want.

"Everyone has the chance to walk away from this without any repercussions. Shanely and I won't be upset if anyone doesn't want this kind of responsibility."

We looked around the room but no one moved or replied. Cade gently kicked my foot from under the table.

"I think there's your answer, Alpha."

I smirked at Cade before I stuck my tongue out at him.

"Alrighty then. I just wanted to make sure before we proceed. This wasn't exactly what I wanted, and I don't want to make any of you feel like you have to be apart of the council if you really don't want to. Things won't be easy going forward."

"We'll be ready guys," Ryder said confidently.

"The World Council doesn't scare me. I'm ready for this change and a chance to finally deliver on my promise," Bay replied.

"Speaking of Derek, he is to be brought forth when found at the Summit. He won't be able to ignore the call to go," Bastian said sternly.

Everyone nodded in agreement.

"Good. Now that everyone's on the same page, and we are officially a team, I say we start this meeting then. I know Caleb and Abraham need to make

CHAPTER 1

other arrangements to keep your own streak and clan running smoothly while we're gone at the Summit. We have two weeks to finalize everything before we go, and I want a solid plan with how to handle everything. The World Council is going to be scheming as well, and I don't want to be caught off guard. They will make a fuss out of Shanely being a mixer and us for not reporting her all those years ago. We need to be prepared for that. Cain said we needed to trust one another. We can call him if we need assistance, but I feel confident we can handle this ourselves," Bastian addressed the group.

I was amazed by my mate. He was meant to be an Alpha, and his confidence was something I wish I had more of. However, looking around the room and seeing my family on my side, made me feel so much better. I know we can figure this out and handle whatever happens at the Summit.

"You are all welcome to stay here tonight as well because I know it's getting late. Cain is informing the pack of the Summit's date, so for now let's fill in Caleb and Abraham what normally goes down during these events. Oh, and guys? Thank you. We couldn't do this without you," Bastian said appreciatively.

"Not a problem, guys. Now, let's get started. Fill us in, and we can start planning," Caleb replied, and I grinned.

This might not be too difficult after all.

Chapter 2

The next two weeks passed by so fast. I think it was because I was dreading the Summit. The pack was furious with how the Council handled the call with us. Most were coming to the Summit, but a few families with very young babies or mothers about ready to give birth asked to stay behind. When I gave them permission, it seemed to abolish the pull they felt to go, and they were able to miss it. I didn't know I could do that, but I was happy to give them comfort over all this mess. They would keep the pack lands running smoothly, and my father said that Thomas would help maintain order and keep an eye on everything as well. My dad was coming with us though because in his words, he would not allow all his kids to face these pompous arrogant men alone.

His exact words.

So we were finally all together at the pack lodge the night before our flight. My uncle hired a private plane for all of us, which I could not even imagine how much that cost.

Cain handed everyone their passports before explaining the car service, and what to expect at the Summit for the non-wolves. I know most of the group had been here many times before, but this was my first time. We went over everything with Caleb and Abraham during our first meeting, but I wasn't against listening to everything again. Everything would be different because now we were taking five bears and seven tigers as well. Which was a first and a big no-no, according to the World Council. *What they don't know won't hurt them, right?*

Henry and Darryl insisted on coming with Abraham and Bay, which I

CHAPTER 2

understood. Cade and Elijah, being our Betas, have also taken on the role of being our personal enforcers while we're away. Bastian and I don't go anywhere without them. No one was taking any chances, and Brody was coming along to assist with Aerith.

"Okay, so I recommend the tigers and bears hang back until we can get Shanely established in her chair. We need to convince the vast majority of wolves that our change will be good for the whole shifter community. It's a lot of hate to get through," Cain said matter of factly.

It just didn't sit right with me though, and I frowned at him. "I don't like this Uncle. I made them apart of my personal council. They're literally my blood relatives, yet I make them hide away?"

"I know, but if we push too hard too fast, we could close the hearts of wolf shifters before we even present our case. The World Council still has a lot of power and pull with the people. I don't want to go against them if they try to force something. If we can avoid war, we should."

He gave me a pointed look then, but my wolf and bear were just annoyed.

"I take it I won't be allowed to shift into my bear then?" I asked, clearly frustrated.

Cain sighed. "No, you and Bastian should remain as wolves. Most do not know that you are a mixer and throwing in a tiger and bear relation is going to rock the entire Summit. A great many have been waiting to see the White Wolf and to find out she's a mixer will be a lot to accept. I hate this as much as anyone else here, but we must tread cautiously."

Bastian pulled me back against his chest and held me tight. "It's okay, Shanely. It's only for the start."

I nodded my head, but I couldn't relax this time. His touch helped but not like normal. I was so frustrated and annoyed with this whole thing. *I didn't even want to be the White Wolf in the first place, and now I have to go through all these stupid hoops for arrogant shifters?* I should be able to do this my way, but I can't, and that didn't sit right with me.

"We'll be fine, Shanely," my father said. I looked to him and my brothers, who gave me half-smiles. They were trying, but I could see it was all weighing on them too. *How can they stomach being treated this way? As if they were less of a person because their animals were different.* I tried to smile back, but it was pitiful to say the least.

"Everyone get some sleep. We leave at 5 am to head to the plane, and it's a couple hour flight from there. We're supposed to check in when we get there, so the Council can announce Shanely to the rest," Cain said before grabbing my aunt's hand. Everyone split from there. One last decent night's sleep for awhile, I'm sure is how they all felt. Bastian led me to our room, where Aerith was already fast asleep in the other bed.

"Just try to get some sleep, my love. I won't let anything happen to you two," Bastian whispered as he pulled my jacket off. I kicked my shoes off and laid in bed next to Bastian. He wrapped his arms around me before kissing my forehead. He starting snoring within minutes though, leaving me alone with my thoughts.

And boy did I have a lot to think about.

My entire life completely changed when I unlocked my wolf. I felt stronger than ever, and closer to my mother than I had in my entire life, yet part of me wondered if it would have been better if I never unlocked my wolf. She bristled at that thought, and while I didn't mean to hurt her, it was so hard not to think about the way life used to be. Life would have stayed normal without all this pressure and responsibility. All I wanted was to be with my family, not the ruler of the wolves. I was incredibly nervous to be meeting so many new people tomorrow too. All eyes would be on Bastian and I, and that kind of scrutiny was unappealing.

I couldn't turn my mind off, and I ended up tossing and turning most of the night before finally crashing. 5 am came way too soon. I was already not a morning person as it was, and after the night I just had, I felt dead inside. I grumbled and groaned as I pulled my shoes back on, grateful that I just crashed in my clothes because it was surprisingly chilly this morning. I didn't want to change clothes now. Bastian had Aerith in his arms already, who thankfully stayed asleep. We made our way downstairs to the rest of the half-dead crew before making our way to the trucks outside. We had quite a few vehicles to take most of the pack to the plane.

The only ones who seemed truly awake was my father, Uncle Cain, and

CHAPTER 2

Bastian. I don't know how they do it. I climbed in between Aerith, who was passed out in her car seat with her mouth wide open, and Bastian. I snuggled back up to him, making him smile. He knew how much I hated waking up early, so he let me try to get as comfy as I could manage on him. It didn't take long to get to the plane, but I was out cold when we arrived at the airport.

I groaned again as we all hustled onto the plane. I just wanted to go back to sleep. Aerith was starting to stir now with the constant movement, but hopefully she'd be able to crash again when we were in the air. The last thing we needed was a sleep deprived toddler. We all piled inside, and it didn't take long to get everyone strapped in, and before I knew it, we were up in the air. The flight attendant had blankets and passed them out to our group, which was great. I covered me and Aerith in one and passed out before the attendant even brought around the snacks.

* * *

Bastian gently nudged me awake as the plane started to descend. I was sprawled out on him with my mouth wide open.

"I didn't drool on you, did I?" I whispered, embarrassed that I slept on him like that.

Bastian started to laugh. "No. I'm dry, baby."

"You did snore like a freight train though. No one else could sleep around you!" Abraham cried out as he rustled my hair. I smacked his hand away and turned in my seat. Bay was passed out asleep against the window still, but Abraham was grinning like a fool.

"Aww, did little Abey not get enough sweep?" I asked in a baby voice. He stuck his tongue out at me, and I giggled. Aerith was awake now and reached for me. I sat her on my lap and snuggled her close as we waited for the plane to officially land. It was my first time being in Canada, and I had to admit it was beautiful! *I get why the wolves' headquarters were stationed here, I thought to myself. There was so much wilderness around us.* As far as the eye could see really. It was never ending, and it grounded the animals within me.

Everything was just green, and I loved it. It was the perfect place for wolves to roam wild, without the prying eyes of humans.

We all filed off the plane, and I noticed a bunch of large SUV's pulling up into the airport. I looked back at Bastian, and he shrugged.

"Uncle Cain, is that our ride?" I asked. *A little flashy if you ask me.*

He seemed irritated. "It must be. Not the ride I had scheduled though."

There was a fleet of Escalades driving up, but the front two cars were limos. I rolled my eyes.

"What is the Council up to?" I asked my mate.

Bastian responded, *"I don't know. Just stay close."*

The drivers all exited their vehicles to wait for us. The first limo driver stepped forward and asked, "Is this the McCoy pack? We will be your drivers during your stay here."

"What happened to the service I hired?" Cain asked flatly.

"The Council canceled that. They said the White Wold would be present, so we are to escort her for safety reasons. The vehicles behind the limos will take your pack to their hotel. Your personal council and the White Wolf will be staying at the Summit Hall with the World Council," he replied as he inhaled deeply. His eyes shot from me to Abraham, who had slowly made his way off the plane and towards my bear family, dragging Bay along with him.

"Sir? I have to remind you this is the wolves' Summit..." he started, but I had had enough.

"Where am I supposed to go then?" I asked, stepping forward.

The wolf looked at me clearly confused and unsure what he should do. He scented the air again, his eyes widening as his jaw dropped open. I guess it's time to fill him in then.

"I am the White Wolf, and this is my family and my council. They will be traveling with me, so which car is mine? Or shall I be running there in my wolf form?"

He snapped his jaw shut before gesturing to his limo. "This one is yours, and the rest are in the other one."

"Wait, so I'm in a limo alone?" I asked. *God, this was going to be a long week.* He just nodded at me and opened the door. I turned to my group instead.

CHAPTER 2

"Okay Bastian, Aerith, Cade, Elijah, Abraham, and Bay in my limo. Ryder, Johnny, Alana, my sweet baby nephew, Caleb, Dad, Aunt Cassia, and Uncle Cain in the other limo. The rest of the pack, jump in the black cars wherever you will fit. Be safe and try to enjoy yourselves this week! If you need anything though, you contact me right away. Not the World Council but me personally!"

Everyone took off at my order not once questioning me. I was honestly surprised how easy I was able to just decide what needed done, but I knew I would not be riding alone like some princess. *The Council was about to get a rude awakening this week.*

"Ma'am, I have to insist. The Council will be upset..."

I cut him off again. "What's your name, wolf?"

"Luke, ma'am."

"Okay first off, I'm Shanely. Not ma'am, not your White Wolf, nothing fancy, alright? We are like the same age, so just relax. Second, I need you to know that I do not have to listen to the Council. I'm in charge here, correct?"

He nodded. "Yeah, I guess so... I mean yes. The White Wolf is the Alpha over all when they appear."

"Right. So here I am, and yet I'm just supposed to tuck my tail when the World Council starts giving orders? I don't think so, and I would hope you'd be smart enough to stand up for who's the rightful Alpha here."

Luke's face turned red, and he quickly nodded. "You're right, Alpha. Of course, please come sit all of you. I'll take you to the Summit Hall."

I smiled before reaching out to shake his hand. "Thank you for helping us today, Luke."

Luke smiled before accepting it. He had a kind smile, and it matched his uniquely hazel eyes. "It's an honor, Shanely. I'll be part of your security team here as well, so just let me know if you need anything."

I nodded and slid into the limo, my eyes widening. It was so comfortable and nice in here! Spacious and filled to the brim with drinks and snacks. It took me a solid minute of gawking before I noticed everyone staring at me. I was too busy admiring the ride.

"What?"

They all laughed before piling into the limo with me.

"Well, look who's embracing the White Wolf now?" Cade spat out as he smacked my knee, making me blush.

"Was it too much?" I asked sheepishly.

Bastian laughed. "No, it was perfect. I wasn't going to let you go alone anyways, but you just took charge. You did great out there, but I have a feeling we're going to have to do this a lot more once we get there."

I groaned as I reached for a bag of peanuts. I passed a bag of chips to Aerith, who ate them greedily.

"I'm really not ready for this. It seems like they have a lot more up their sleeve than we thought. They're trying to prove who's in control," I said.

Elijah sighed. "The Summit used to be fun, but now everything's different. We get to see dear old dad again, Bastian."

Bay tensed at that, and I watched Abraham put his arm around her. The idea of meeting Liam again just permanently killed my mood. This was all too much. Liam, Derek, Emma, who I'm sure would be there as well, and the World Council. There were too many people here that hate me or have tried to kill me. Yet, *I get to party with them all week! Yay me.*

The drive was sadly short, but good lord Summit Hall was huge! It was like a massive castle deep in the woods, and honestly looked liked it belonged in an entirely different time period than ours. *I wonder why the packs stayed at the hotel when this place could clearly hold a large crowd. Must be another power move,* I thought to myself. If that were true then it was just a stupid waste of money. There was nothing around for miles, which I assume was the point. Luke parked the limo at the main entrance, and we all piled out. Thankfully, no one else was here to greet us because I was not in the mood.

"The World Council said you are to report to them as soon as you arrived. They are in their chambers," Luke said, shutting the door behind us.

"They couldn't be bothered to greet their White Wolf in person?" Cain asked, annoyed by the whole thing.

Luke shrugged, clearly bothered and on the spot. "I don't know, sir. I'm just to be apart of your security team and to give you any and all messages."

I rolled my eyes. "This is all just another ploy to show who's in charge here.

CHAPTER 2

They want me to come to them on their time frame, and I'm not playing along. I'm exhausted Luke. When is the first event?"

Luke shifted on his feet again. "The first event is the ball in your honor, It's tonight at 6 pm."

I laughed harshly. "Really a ball? Okay, never mind. Please show us our rooms, and then you can inform the Council that I am exhausted from traveling but will see them like everyone else at the ball. Let's go everyone!"

I grabbed my suitcase and saw everyone smirking around me as they followed suit. I whispered shut up to my brothers as they passed by. Luke was starting to look a little pale though, and I worried I put him in a bad spot. Bastian straight up laughed though, pulling me from my thoughts.

"Pissing everyone off on day one, are we?"

"Uncle Cain's plan to lay low isn't going to work, I'm afraid. I'm doing things my way."

Cain rolled his eyes at me as he passed by before shaking his head. Luke led us to our rooms on the second floor, and that's about the point where I lost my temper.

"Everyone's names are on the doors, but you have some extra guests here we did not expect," Luke mentioned, looking towards my brothers and father. I looked at the first door on the left, and all it said was the White Wolf. I looked to the next door, and my temper flared. *It had Bastian Fenrir and Child on it!*

"They expect me not to sleep next to my husband??" I shouted, and everyone turned to see the door.

Luke ran his hand through his hair. "All they told me during the instructions was that you needed to get used to the room you will be living in. The sooner you learn to appreciate our traditions, the easier it will all be. Their words, I swear!"

Everyone started talking at once now. Bastian went straight for Luke, who was only caught in the middle. He was alarmed by the big guy in his face, but this wasn't his fault. I let my power out just a teensy bit, forcing everyone to notice me but not enough to hurt. Luke's eyes went big as he felt it harder than my family did. I ripped the name tag off Bastian's door and slammed it under my name.

"There. Now it's fixed. Abraham and Bay, you get this room," I said, pointing to the door. "There are other rooms right past ours that look like they have no names on them. Am I correct, Luke?"

He nodded but kept eyeing Bastian, who was seething mad now.

"Perfect. Dad and Caleb will bunk together, and Alana and Johnny, go ahead and take the other. No one leaves their room to explore. You may visit one another here, but do not leave without me. For everyone's safety, we will be staying together. Understood?"

They all nodded, and my aunt gave me a proud smile before following Cain into the room across from us. I nodded to Luke before dragging Bastian away. I locked the door behind us and leaned against it.

Bastian set Aerith down on the bed and turned on cartoons for her. I snorted as I took in the room they decided to give me. The room was like a hotel room and nothing more. One large bed in the center with a couch along the back wall. A TV and a dresser were against the wall on my right, and I saw another door that I assumed was the bathroom. I realized then the White Wolf really was just a formality they knew they had to deal with, but I was nothing special to them. They expected me to live my life in a hotel room, never feeling like I was at home. Away from my family and isolated enough for them to control me. They were not going to step down from their positions. *Not willingly at least.*

Bastian could hear my internal monologue and wrapped his arms around me, pulling me into a hug. He forced me from my thoughts before whispering, "You will never be separated from me, Shanely. The Council has another thing coming if they think they will be controlling you."

I leaned against him, trying to calm down. *They were infuriating! I didn't want the job of the White Wolf, but after seeing all this... All they had done.* I hated the idea that these people were in control of all wolf shifters. *They all needed to go.* Suddenly, my aunt's words filled my head.

If I gave up the position of the White Wolf then I needed to accept how things were right now. Would I be okay leaving, knowing these people were the ones left in charge?

CHAPTER 2

Could I live with myself if I ran?

Chapter 3

I awoke to an empty bed, and I missed the warmth Bastian had brought. I remember falling asleep next to him while my daughter watched TV, but looking at the clock I realized that was hours ago. I looked around and saw Aerith munching on a sandwich at the couch with Aunt Cassia.

"Hey," I said as I rubbed my eyes.

"Hey sweetie. Bastian went to his brother's room to discuss a few things. I told him to just shower and dress there, so us girls can get ready together. I thought it might be a nice little distraction, I suppose."

I smiled, leaning forward to stretch. "That sounds nice. I'll go jump in the shower then and thanks for bringing her something to eat too."

She just smiled and waved me off. I took a nice hot shower, letting the water just work against my sore muscles. I knew it was stress that made everything ache, but that shower was divine! I exhaled deeply, letting my anxiety go. *Tonight was the start of something good*, I told myself. *It just had to be.*

I wrapped up in a towel and started to dry my hair. After changing into my undergarments, I put on the robe that was left in my bathroom. It was comfy but a little short, just coming up under my butt. *Eh, not like anyone was going to see me in it anyways.*

I started to walk out, when I noticed a weird looking shadow. I stepped back, studying the wall. *What in the world was that?* I waved my arms around, but it wasn't me making the shadows. There was nothing behind me to cast a shadow like that. I realized it was coming from the light above me. I ran out of the bathroom and grabbed a chair. My aunt looked at me funny but said

CHAPTER 3

nothing. Bay and Alana were here already in their fancy ball gowns. They looked gorgeous, but I didn't have time to tell them yet. I needed to know what was in my light.

I stepped on the chair and unscrewed the cover to expose the light bulbs. Bay and Alana had come in the room as well, but thankfully didn't say anything because I found a small square device taped to the side of the light. I yanked it off, and my blood boiled as I realized what it was. It was a listening device. In my bathroom! They bugged my room!

I hopped off the chair and showed them all. They gasped, and I quickly shushed them. I shook my head no and started tearing the room apart. They seemed to understand, and everyone started unscrewing things to help me look. I found four more devices before we finally stopped.

"Aunt Cassia, stay with Aerith please."

She nodded, and I left my room, leaving the devices on the table with my aunt. I began banging on everyone's door, and they all started pouring out of their rooms looking concerned. Bastian immediately looked me up and down, and I realized I was wearing nothing but my short bathrobe. *Whoops.*

Bastian's eyes went wide before they started glowing. "Shanely what's going..."

"They bugged our room," I stated, pissed as ever.

"They what?!" Bastian asked, and I could feel his Alpha power spilling out now.

"What do you mean they bugged your room?" Elijah asked as he and Cade stepped closer to me.

"I found 5 devices scattered in our room. One was in our bathroom, Bastian!"

"That's it! I've had enough of this," Cain shouted as he turned around to leave down the hall.

"No!"

Everyone stopped to look at me. "Search your rooms quietly. Bring me all the devices, and I'll put them in a bag. Act and speak like nothing is wrong. Get ready like normal, and give them to me once we are all ready for the ball. I'll deal with the Council."

They all nodded before disappearing into their rooms.

"I cannot believe them, Bastian," I said as I started to pace in the hall.

"I have never seen something like this from them before. We'll fix this tonight, but *please* Shanely for right now, go get dressed. That robe is entirely too short, and it's driving me crazy. Plus, my wolf is getting pissed about you wearing something so little in front of everyone," he replied as he rubbed his hands over his face. I grinned before kissing him. He smiled down to me, and I nipped his lower lip, making his eyes flash. Bastian quickly looked up to the ceiling, and I grinned wickedly.

"Shanely... You are *killing* me here. You better go before I can't let you anymore."

Bastian's voice was gruff, and I slowly backed away. I purposely took slow steps, giving the tease of a chase. He took a deep breath, and I could see him struggle not to come after me. I blew him a kiss before disappearing back into my room.

"That was cruel, mate," he said through the link.

I gave him a kiss through our bond. *"I promise to give you a proper chase soon, love."*

"You better."

I giggled as I felt him retreat from my mind. We all quickly got dressed after that. I found an ugly old dress in the closet with my name on it. I rolled my eyes, showing everyone else in the room. Alana scowled, and Bay looked annoyed. *Did they seriously expect me to wear this tonight?*

Instead, I wore a white ball gown similar to my wedding dress. It was strapless and reminded me of Cinderella's ball gown. Just big and flowy at the bottom with simple white flats. I braided my hair to one side and curled the pieces I could not contain.

Feeling jittery still over our discovery, I exited the room with my small white purse filled with the devices I found in my room. My eyes immediately went to Bastian. He wore a white tux to match me, and boy did he look good in it. His hair was styled somewhat messy at top, and it looked good with his fade and beard. Bastian seemed to like the dress I was in too because his eyes traveled up and down me slowly. I grinned wickedly at him.

CHAPTER 3

"*See something you like, baby?*" I said, with a sultry voice.

His eyes flashed to mine.

"*A whole lot let me tell you, Mrs. Fenrir,*" he said, with a wicked grin. "*Can we just skip tonight and hide away in our room?*"

"*I wish! I'm ready to go home,*" I replied.

Bastian crossed the floor and kissed me hard. He broke the kiss and leaned his head against mine.

"*I so badly wish we could just go home.*"

I sighed, knowing where he was going.

"*But we have job to do, I get it.*"

"*I cannot believe this is where our life is right now. I miss the simplicity we had before. Well, what we had in moments,*" he said.

I laughed. "*Seems there is always something to keep us on our toes.*"

He kissed my forehead as Luke appeared at the top of the stairs.

"*Everyone looks magnificent. I'm here to lead you to the main room. All the packs are here already,*" Luke replied casually.

I gestured for everyone in my party to go on ahead of me. I opened up my purse, and they dumped a plethora of devices they found in their own rooms as they went by. Luke's eyes widened, and his jaw dropped open. He must not have known about them, or he didn't expect us to find them so fast. I really wasn't so sure which way he landed, but I guess time will tell. Bastian took two steps towards the young wolf and carefully closed his jaw shut for him. He put his finger to his mouth, and Luke paled slightly.

"*Careful, Bastian,*" I teased. "*You're going to make him wet himself.*"

My mate slowly turned around to face me, his eyes glowing gold. He stuck his tongue out before his brilliant blue eyes snapped back. I turned to Luke, winking at him. *The poor guy.*

Bastian extended his arm to me, and I wrapped around it. Aerith held my hand, wearing a pretty white, red and gold dress. Her hair was all curled and pinned in the back, matching her aunt Bay. *Now she looked like a princess!*

I tugged her hand, and she looked up to me. "Aerith, you belong here. Okay? Don't let anyone tell you otherwise."

She seemed confused, but the poor thing seemed determined to learn whatever was going on. She was always wiser than her age let on, but ever since our last encounter with Emma, she seems more aware of things than carefree. I hated part of her childhood and happiness was robbed from her then. It was never coming back either.

We all followed Luke towards the massive ballroom. I stole a peek around the corner to look inside, and they really outdid themselves. I mean a little over the top, but it was decorated in gorgeous blue and gold colors with white linen table cloths. Fresh flowers filled the room, and I noticed the World Council was seated up on the stage in the corner of the room. I could see there was one empty chair next to them, which I assume was left for me. There was a live band playing already, and everyone stood when they saw Luke enter.

"You sure about this, Shanely?" Abraham asked nervously.

"No going back after this," Caleb chimed in.

"I'm positive. Everyone will smell me anyways, but I'm not hiding anything. Things are changing tonight," I replied, holding my head up high. Bastian gave me one last smile before turning into the true Alpha I always knew him to be. His face darkened to the room ahead of us, and Cade stepped right behind me. I noticed Elijah on Bastian's left, and I gave them a grateful smile before we stepped into the room.

Everyone, and I do mean *everyone*, inhaled at the same time. Some women gasped, while others looked disgusted with me. A few just looked shocked to say the least, but no one spoke. It was dead quiet in here other than the clacking sound the girl's heels made. I walked on like nothing was wrong, hand in hand with my mate, even though my insides were screaming. Bastian and I decided to let our Alpha power out just a bit as we walked. While normally I did not want to ever be this kind of leader, I didn't want anyone to question whether or not I belonged. *Tonight I would do this, but after this point I wouldn't use it just to enter a room.* I could see everyone felt it and instinctively dropped their eyes.

The Council looked furious.

I ignored them and made my way to the head tables. I let everyone find their seats before Bastian and I made our way upstairs. My insides were screaming as anxiety filled my chest. I prayed no one could hear my heart race.

"Evening Council," I muttered.

"What do you think you're doing, child!?" one of the council members snarled.

"You disregard everything we requested of you today, and now you show up with tigers and bears!? This is for wolves only! We do not mingle with others not of our kind! This is against the law!" one shouted.

The one my uncle called Silas bellowed loudly, "And you are a mixer?! Why did no one inform us of this?"

"Because it did not concern you. I know exactly what you would have done had you known what I was prior to all of this. You all are lazy and old-fashioned in your traditions, and I have had enough of it," I snarled right back as I reached for the microphone.

Before I could grab it, Silas ripped it away from me. "This will need to be discussed between myself and the Council members. You are illegal just by existing and bringing those creatures here is against the law as well. I can scent you have a bear within you, so I take it that tall man with matching green eyes there is your father?"

I shook my head yes, and he scoffed.

"He broke the law then too! As well as the other two wolves there by mating with a tiger and bear."

Silas turned away from Bastian and I to whisper with the others. I looked to him, and he shook his head in shame. Suddenly, a dozen enforcers came into the room. Everyone seemed tense as they pushed their way through to the front. They grabbed Johnny, Bay and my father, shoving them all to the stage. My family was livid and started pushing right back as my eyes widened. I realized they were being arrested right now! The crowd gasped, and I bolted down the stairs.

"Stop!"

That's when one of them grabbed me by the back of the neck. Bastian roared as he pushed through the line of enforcers.

"Him too!" Silas shouted, and they tackled Bastian. He hit one of the enforcers, and I could see Cade and Elijah try to push past but there were too many. No one was getting through.

"Silas, what is the meaning of this! Let them go!" Cain shouted, trying to reach us.

"Bastian!" I shouted as one of the enforcers hit him hard. He dropped to his knees then, and they continued to hit him. I winced with every strike, my heart breaking.

"Stop it!" I shouted angrily.

Bastian was breathing hard as blood dripped down his face. I couldn't breathe. Fear gripped my heart as I scrambled to figure out how to fix this. I knew it would be trouble, but I didn't expect this. I would have never come if I knew it would be like this.

I turned to Cain and snapped. "Why won't he shift to protect himself?"

"Everyone quiet down! I apologize for the abruptness, but we had to take action!" Silas shouted as the enforcers pushed Johnny, Dad, and Bay next to me. We were all forced to our knees then, but they made sure Bastian stayed on the ground with a knee in his back.

"This has become a judicial matter, Shanely. If he or anyone of us shifts now, then they have every right to kill us. It's law," Cain whispered angrily. His eyes were fixed on Silas though.

"As you can see, we were not informed that the McCoy pack were harboring mixers! Ford grab Cain, and the little girl as well."

I screamed as one of the men grabbed Aerith forcefully from my family, decking Caleb as they did. My uncle was taken and shoved forward with the rest of us while the enforcer held Aerith. She was scared out of her mind, and I wished we never came here. I didn't want this power or rank in the first place. All I wanted was my family, not this trouble. Cain glared at Silas, who stood pompously on stage. He looked down at us before shaking his head.

"My, my, the McCoy pack has fallen into despair. Now, I'm going to ask a few questions, and you better tell me the truth," Silas said to us before turning to me briefly. He then looked to Johnny. "Is that your biological child, Johnny McGee?"

My eyes went wide, and I could feel Johnny's panic and fear from here. He looked to me for direction, so I turned and spoke up for him. "No. The child is Alana's, and she had him before Johnny mated her. Go ahead and scent him! He's not a mixer."

"She is right, sir. The child reeks of bear," one of the enforcers said, letting Alana go. She breathed a sigh of relief but stared down at her husband with fear in her eyes.

Silas grunted. "Too bad. We do not deal with their kind, only our own."

"Then why am I here!?" my father yelled.

"Because your mate was a wolf, and since she is not here to take the punishment, then it will fall to you," Silas said before turning away from us. He started whispering to the other Councilmen. Taking his sweet time while we all waited for his answer.

"Silas, this is ridiculous! Shanely is the White Wolf! You cannot do this to her!" Cain shouted, and the crowd started to murmur again. Everyone looked worried, but no one dared to step across the Councilmen. I was just pissed.

"Let them go right now!" I cried out, and Silas looked down to me.

"See, I knew you would not fully understand our ways child, but we have laws for a reason," he shouted that part to the crowd, and they all started to look to their feet. They were being shamed for feeling bad about this situation, and it only infuriated me more. "They have broke our laws and must be punished!"

"The punishment for being a mixer according to those laws is death! Are you saying you will be killing our White Wolf then?" Cain shouted back, and the crowd gasped. I watched Silas and the rest of the Council look upon us with worried expressions as the crowd of wolves around us grew upset.

"You can't kill the White Wolf!" someone finally shouted. It was enough to encourage everyone to say something. They all began shouting back at Silas. He was losing the crowds, and the council knew it. I felt his Alpha power stretch out over everyone.

"Everyone quiet down please! We have our laws for a reason!"

Everyone hushed, waiting on Silas and the rest of the Council to decide what to do.

"Silas, we all know the prophecy! When the White Wolf emerges, he or she will take their rightful place as Head over all. Shanely is to become a Head Alpha! You are not in charge anymore, and this is wrong!" Cain shouted, stirring the crowd once more.

"I am still in charge here! We are still your Council and have not actually passed the torch to her yet! The enforcers answer to us not some child no one knows! We are the ones you elected to run the entire wolf race as a whole, and we deserve some respect!"

You could hear the crowd murmuring again. I looked behind me, and they were torn. They didn't know me enough to trust me, yet the thought of just killing me appalled them. That was a plus, I guess.

"What's the punishment for mixing with non-wolves?" I asked loudly.

Silas turned back to me. "It depends on the offense and is left for the Alphas to decide. Since you are here, it becomes a Council issue."

"So, what are the punishments for mating with non-wolves, according to you?"

Was I deaf? Good lord dude, just answer the question.

Silas debated a moment with the other four before turning back to us. "For mating non-wolves, they will be banished from their wolves and from the pack. We cannot allow our packs to become tainted anymore than it already has."

"Okay, then give their punishments to me," I said, and the crowd started whispering again.

Silas studied me a moment before answering, "It's not that easy."

"Oh, but it is," I said confidently, "I am your White Wolf! I am meant to help the wolves, am I not!? What better way then to carry the burden for them? I will keep the inhibitor bracelet on instead."

"They would still be banished from the pack becoming rogues. That is not something you can take from them," Silas countered.

"You are right Silas. There is no way to banish the White Wolf from her pack is there?" Cain asked snidely, and Silas's eyes furrowed. He snarled, and I stood abruptly on my feet to look at the crowd. The enforcer stepped forward to shove me down again, but I gave him a murderous glare. He stopped in his tracks, and I looked to everyone.

"You all felt my wolf awaken! You know exactly what it means for all of us. Times are changing everyone, but if your precious Council would rather we be punished for the mates that fate chose for us, then by all means let's follow their direction blindly! Go right ahead, and punish me. Take a good look around though and imagine your mate down here with me. Handcuffed and waiting on judgment simply because the mate bond happened."

Everyone looked to the floor, and I glared back to the Councilmen.

"This is my pack! I will be the Head Alpha, and I abolish the law that says shifters do not mix!"

The crowd gasped as Silas glared at me.

"You cannot..."

"Actually, she can! She's the White Wolf! You cannot go against what she decides! You cannot pick and choose the rules that suit you best Silas," Cain shouted, and Silas fumed. You could hear the crowd agreeing with my uncle, and the five men on the stage took in the crowd as a whole. I could see their puny minds turning, trying to figure out what to do now.

"Rules are rules Silas," I said sarcastically. I took a good look around at the people behind me. My people. There were many that were happy and seemed to like the idea of banishing the law, but a great many still looked uneasy. This was all they ever knew, and no one questioned the Council like this before. No one ever challenged them. Even if they sensed who I was, it was still going to take some convincing. I needed to be something they looked up to not cower away from. If I was really going to make a change, then I needed to win their support. *This wasn't going to be easy*, I thought to myself. The Council were still discussing with one another, and I could see Silas turn about five different shades of red before he finally graced us with his presence again.

Silas raised his hands up to silence everyone. "Please everyone. Settle down! The Council and I all agree that punishment will still be handed out!"

My family roared, but I glared right at Silas. *Bring it on then.*

He lifted his hands again. "Even if the White Wolf changes the law today, the offenses were made in the past when the law was still in tact. There is nothing we can do about it. Rules are rules, right Shanely?"

"That's crap, and you know it!" Cain shouted angrily as I rolled my eyes.

Silas ignored him. "However, since the White Wolf has offered to accept the punishment for everyone else, we have decided to allow it. Do you still accept, Shanely?"

Everyone of my family members protested, but I said proudly, "I accept."

The grin Silas gave me made my skin crawl. An uneasy feeling hit me square in the gut. *What did I just agree to?*

"Good then you will hereby be forced to wear the band for the entire Summit Event, separated from your own personal bonds and your wolf. You will not be allowed to use the mind-link with anyone, and you must learn our ways from the five of us before we deem you ready to take on your role as the White Wolf. We will only pass the torch once we are satisfied you have learned everything properly. This means you must not allow distractions get in the way, so you will be staying in a separate room on another wing."

"Shanely, stop! We can take our own punishments!" Bastian shouted as they pushed his face harder into the ground. I wasn't about to let anyone here suffer because I unlocked my wolf. *No, this was my cross to bear.*

"Deal. Now let them go!" I shouted, but Silas just chuckled at me.

"They will still be banished Shanely, meaning they will now become rogues. We do not allow rogues within our manor, so you all will be required to leave immediately."

He gave the motion to his enforcers, and I was pushed to the side. Shock covered my face as the little loop hole Silas just made struck me. The enforcers let my father go, and he forcefully took Aerith back. Bastian, Cain, Bay, and Johnny were all forced to stand in a line when Silas came down the stairs.

"It's okay, baby. I'll find a way to sneak back in," Bastian said softly, "*just stay with Cade and Elijah. Promise me, you will be careful!*"

"Bastian, you can't be banished!" I bellowed through the link. "There must be some way!"

"We'll figure this out, my love. Just don't forget the Alpha you truly are," he said, giving me a firm look. "You will figure it out, I'm sure of it!"

"You four wolves have broken the law and are no longer true, untainted, wolves. That being said, since Shanely has accepted the other half of the punishment, you will be allowed to keep your wolves. Bastian Fenrir, Bay Fenrir..."

"It's Macan, you idiot," Bay mumbled to herself, but Silas ignored her.

"Cain McCoy and Johnny McGee, you are hereby banished from the McCoy pack as well as the World Pack."

I watched my family visibly shake, and Bay fell to her knees in pain. Abraham moved to catch her but was blocked by a line of enforcers. I felt their disconnect from the McCoy pack, and it killed me. This was wrong, so very wrong. Bastian's heart raced in my chest, and I could feel his pain. His agony. My mouth was wide open as they all were disconnected from the pack lines.

Silas grinned before turning to me. "You better say goodbye, child. They are to leave soon."

The enforcer holding my shoulders let me go, and I raced to my mate. I collided with him, needing his touch. *What was I to do?* I couldn't stand to watch him be tossed out like this.

"Bastian, are you alright?"

The color in his eyes had faded, and he looked different. He scented different too, and I hated it. I missed the deep, woodsy scent he used to have. Everything was just dull now, and my heart broke. He hugged me hard. "Promise me, Shanely. Promise me, you will be careful. Please stay with Cade and Elijah!"

Tears filled my eyes as Silas shouted, "Time's up! Remove the rogues from my presence."

I turned to block the enforcers moving in, throwing my hands up defensively. I released my Alpha power, grinding them to a halt.

"Don't touch them!" I snarled.

"Don't make this any harder than it needs to be Shanely. Now come here for your bracelet. It's time to start your punishment."

I turned back to Bastian, who gave me a sad smile. "Remember what I said."

Suddenly, I understood. *I was an Alpha, which meant I have the power to accept new ones in my pack. I could fix this.*

"Bastian Fenrir, do you wish to join the McCoy pack? Connecting you to the World pack by extension and no longer becoming a rogue?"

Bastian gave me an odd look before it clicked for him too. "I accept."

His chord forcefully snapped in place, and Bastian's beautiful blue eye color returned. Bastian kissed me hard then.

"You brilliant girl."

I smiled and turned to Bay, asking her the same question, while Silas screamed at me. He stomped his way down the stairs just as I accepted Johnny back into my pack, and when I turned he was in my face.

"What do you think you are doing?!" Silas yelled, but I wasn't afraid of this man.

"You punished them, Silas. Nothing in the ruling or law says they have to stay banished. I accepted them back into the McCoy pack, making them full-fledged pack mates. They are no longer rogues which means they stay!"

Silas turned red in anger, and his mouth opened wide, but even he knew there was nothing left to say. I had found my own loop hole, and there was nothing he could do about it. I felt rather proud of myself then as he snapped his jaw shut. Everyone clapped, happy not to see them all banished from Summit Hall after all.

Cain walked up behind us, putting his hand on my shoulders. "Can we be done with this nonsense now, Silas?"

He was fuming mad but stomped his way to the stage. He motioned for Luke, who stepped to me.

"Can I have your hand, White Wolf?" he asked, and I turned to Bastian, who was still angry over it.

"It will be okay Bastian," I said, extending my hand out. He clamped the bracelet over my wrist, and my shifter side disappeared. I gasped, forgetting how empty I felt when they were taken from me. Bastian rubbed his chest before clinging to me.

"Now welcome wolf shifters to our Annual Summit event!" Silas shouted as if nothing just happened. "Shanely, your White Wolf, simply does not

CHAPTER 3

know the ways of the wolf. Her other side seems to have emerged first and has gotten in the wolf's way. The Council and I will continue to stay here with her to ensure she has everything she needs to rule our kind. We will teach her our ways!"

The crowd started clapping, clearly approving of my new lessons, but I was fuming mad again.

"Shanely, he's just trying to get the upper hand here. Remember, you need to sway your kind in order to make it all blend. Whether they want to admit it or not, the Council fears the people revolting against them," Uncle Cain's voice whispered quietly to me through the noise of the crowd. He gave me a pointed look. I exhaled slowly at the new task set before me.

Silas raised his hands to hush the crowd. "Never fear, my friends! The Council and I all agree, it's in everyone's best interest that she live here at Summit Hall without the distractions in her old pack. She is in good hands, and we will make sure that she becomes the White Wolf we all need! We will also be keeping a very close eye on the guests she brought with her. Since the White Wolf wants to abolish the law, we will allow them to stay, but do not fear for your safety is our upmost concern. Now eat and dance! We have a wonderful week ahead of us!"

Silas motioned for the music to start up again as Bastian and I reached the center stage. Silas covered the mic, snarling at the two of us. "I suggest you heed our direction, *mixer*. This can only go one way."

I glared at him as he passed by, and Bastian snarled in response. I grabbed the mic, without letting my nerves get the better of me, and raised my hands to silence the band again. I could feel Silas's anger behind me, but Bastian blocked him from progressing any further.

"Hello, everyone! Seems our esteemed Council forgot to let me say hi to everyone. Silly them!" I waved my hand, pretending to be exasperated, and some in the crowd giggled. *Eh, not a bad start at least.*

"Well for one thing, I would like to express how happy I am to meet all of you despite our rocky start to the evening! I know I have only recently found my wolf, but I have actually been learning for the last few years about our kind. I promise, I'm not as dumb as they think I am!" More people laughed at that, and the crowd seemed to loosen up a bit with me.

"The thing is... They do have a few bits of information wrong. It happens to everyone so don't feel bad, Silas! We just got our wires crossed!"

Silas forced a smile to his lips, but Bastian still wouldn't let him or the other council members, who were now standing. Cade and Elijah had joined us on stage now and helped Bastian create a wall between us. I took a deep breath before continuing on.

"I will not be living here at the Summit Hall."

Everyone started whispering at that, but I didn't let that shake my confidence. "You see I have a mate, a Fated Mate actually, and a daughter sitting at the table right over here. I grew up without a family, and I just found them, so while I will be taking over for the Council like our prophecy has foretold... I will be running everything from my pack lands instead. That way my daughter can grow up in the safety of her pack with two loving parents at her side. I know all you parents out there will understand why I'm doing it this way, and I thank you for your support!"

Everyone clapped and some seemed to be nodding in agreement, while others still looked outright angry. I won't be making everyone happy tonight but that was to be expected.

"Please feel free to come and visit with me and my family! I understand this is the first Summit with non-wolf Shifters here, but I promise you we will still have an amazing time. Ask any questions you have, about myself or my family. I'm happy to clear up any misinformation I'm sure you all have by now, and I promise you that no one needs to fear us. Everyone within my party is an upstanding shifter and either on my personal council or working for those on that council. I can assure you that they are *just* like us. Now I will honor the punishment given to me during this week, but I am here to tell everyone that change is coming. As your soon to be new Alpha, I assure you all that it will be in everyone's best interest! I am here to help fix the problems weighing heavily on all the packs, not just with the McCoy's. The Council may continue to announce the events as this is their very last year to do so, but if anyone needs anything, you may come to me directly! Oh, and Council members?" I said as I turned to them behind me. "Enjoy this week.

CHAPTER 3

Soon, you all will be allowed to finally go home to your own families! Won't that be wonderful everyone?"

The crowd clapped even harder, excited at the idea that the Councilmen will get to return to their own families and packs again. They so tried to smile at the crowd, but I could feel their anger. It was thick in the air and felt gross against my skin.

"You little..."

"Watch it, wolf," Bastian snarled at the council member. I have yet to learn all of their names, but I knew enough about them to know they needed to go. *Every single one of them.*

"We will not stand for this, child! It is better for you to just accept your fate. This whole *White Wolf* business is just nonsense, and we are not letting you take over because of a formality. No mixer will run our wolves," Silas spat out.

I cocked my head ever so slightly with my hand on my hips. "Oh, Silas. You really do think you have a chance, don't you?"

I opened my purse, and his face turned an ugly shade of red in the corner of my eye. I didn't think it was possible, but if he didn't calm down, I was afraid his head would pop clear off his shoulders.

"Oh, and Councilmen? If I ever catch you bugging my room, or anyone else's rooms for our stay then I will banish you all, turning you into the rouge wolves you're acting like. Unable to rejoin a pack permanently. Is that clear?" I said, dumping my bag, and all the devices poured out onto their table. "I figured you'd like these back."

Their eyes went wide before murmuring amongst themselves. Silas was shaking now, trying to hold back his shift. I rolled my eyes, refusing to wait for a response from them.

The brothers followed me closely, and I was surrounded by my family the second I stepped off the stage. I watched the crowd around us all return to their seats, and the band began to play. I was baffled and just completely frazzled by what just happened.

"They just arrested me and my family in front of everyone less than 10 minutes ago, and now everyone's ready to party," I muttered to myself.

"It's not uncommon at these things, Shanely. The World Council has always been swift when dealing with issues. This isn't the first time judgment and sometimes execution that has happened in front of everyone. It's why they have the control they do," Cain answered, only causing my blood to boil even more.

"You abolished a law though, Shanely. Everyone, *including* the Council, has to accept it," Aunt Cassia chimed in, and while I was glad, it still didn't improve my mood.

"It isn't fair you took all our punishments though love," Bastian said, giving me a pointed look. I waved him off.

"I'd do anything for my pack and family," I said, and everyone gave me a grateful smile.

"It's why the White Wolf is you," Bay said softly, and I hugged her tightly.

"Thank you, Shanely," Abraham said, and I hugged him as well.

Johnny and Alana hugged me fiercely, and I knew why. Tommy and Abraham were mixers as well. They could be executed if the Council found out before I can clear house. The Council may not be able to kill me, but they would be fair game. The enforcers here are still loyal to them, and with this new bracelet on I wouldn't be able to stop it. It would be war.

"We need to get everyone to see the Council is wrong," Cade said quietly.

"They need to trust me. I won't use my Alpha power like Silas tried to do and frighten them," I said to the group, and Cain rubbed the back of his head.

"Proceed with caution, everyone."

"Dance with me, my love?" I asked, ready to not think about it anymore. *I honestly didn't want to think about anything.*

Bastian reached for my hand, kissing it gently before saying, "I thought you'd never ask."

Everyone watched us walk to the middle of the room, and Bastian wrapped his arms around me.

"I don't know how just yet, but I feel like the punishment they gave you is a trap somehow. They've never allowed something like this before. We need to be careful, baby," Bastian whispered in my ear. I nodded, letting him guide me around the floor.

CHAPTER 3

"I miss your heartbeat, Bastian," I whispered back. He kissed the side of my head.

"I miss yours too."

I leaned against his cheek, letting my emotions settle back down. Slowly, others joined us on the floor with their own partners. There wasn't a lot, but it was something at least. It wasn't long before Cade was cutting in. I laughed as Bastian rolled his eyes but let me switch partners. I soon saw him dancing with Aerith, teaching her the steps. She still seemed nervous, but at least the enforcer that held her wasn't harsh with her. She was slowly loosening up again. Cade thanked me for what I did for Johnny and Bastian, and promised to stay close as my Beta. While we danced and laughed amongst ourselves, something unexpected happened. A middle aged man tapped me on my shoulder.

"White Wolf?"

I smiled as I turned to him. "Shanely, please."

The wolf returned my smile. It was warm, and he seemed like a kind man. "Shanely, would you care to dance?"

I was surprised at the request, but I said yes. Bastian watched closely, and I could feel his tension as Cade let me go.

"Shanely, it is an honor to meet you," the man said as he led me around the room.

"The honor is mine. I didn't catch your name though?" I asked.

"It's Garrett Taylor. I'm from the Amber Pack in East Canada," he replied.

"Well, it's great to meet you. It's pretty incredible how many shifters there are in the world."

He nodded. "We would be a lot more if the Division never got involved."

"It seems we all have a mutual disgust for that group," I replied as I studied the man. His hair was a light brown, and he had no beard, but he seemed to take care of himself. He wasn't overweight, nor was he bad looking by any means. *I wonder if he has a family here with him tonight. It would be nice to make more friends during our stay here.*

"Yes, we do. We've all been affected by them sadly. It's what really helped split all of shifter kind honestly."

"It would make sense that we should all try to unite against our common enemy. What's that saying? The enemy of my enemy…"

"Is my friend," he finished for me. "I think you'd find you have a lot more on your side than you realize." The song ended, and he bowed before leaving me to my thoughts. I watched him head back to the far tables in the corner, when I felt a warm embrace.

Bastian pulled me close. "Seems like you made a friend."

I smiled. "Yeah, I think so."

He led me away from the dance floor to our tables so I could finally eat. Most here at the ball had completed their dinner by now and were finally on the dance floor. I was behind everyone else, but I didn't care. I was just starving and not worried about eating a cold meal. I dove into the basket of rolls, when I noticed the World Council never left the stage, and they eyed me the whole time. I rolled my eyes, and Bastian noticed my frustration. He must of said something in the link because all the men in our immediate group stepped in front of me, blocking the Council's view of me.

I turned to him and smiled. "Was that because of you?"

He smirked back. "You deserve to eat in peace."

Bastian kissed my cheek before adding another roll to my plate. My plate looked amazing. I was starving, and boy it was not disappointing! Mashed potatoes, turkey slices and an array of vegetables all smothered in gravy. It was divine! *If this was the first meal, I could only imagine what else was in store. Probably the only decent thing I would enjoy this week.* Bastian seemed amused with me, and I just nudged him playfully.

We enjoyed ourselves despite how the trip started. I knew this was going to be a battle every step of the way, but for tonight it seemed over with. As I stood up and crossed the room to use the restroom, someone grabbed my hand from behind.

Silas.

"It would be dishonorable for me not to dance with our White Wolf. Shall we?"

He squeezed my hand hard as his eyes bore into mine. I was on the opposite side of the room from my family and those around us were staring at us.

CHAPTER 3

Everyone watched our interaction, and he seemed to pin me into a corner. *I had no desire to dance with this man, let alone let him touch me, but if I refused in front of everyone how would it make me look?*

"Shanely? Are you still with us child?"

I gritted my teeth before forcing myself to answer, "Certainly, Silas. Lead the way."

He gave a triumphant grin and started to drag me back to the dance floor. His grip on my hand hurt, and I felt Bastian zero in on us. I could see the anger in his eyes from here, and everyone in my family grew tense.

"Better tell your mate to stop glaring at me," Silas commanded as we started dancing.

"Ah, Silas even if I could, you and I both know he won't," I answered back confidently. I felt his claws sharpen against my back as they dug in slightly. My head snapped to his, and he glared at me.

"I suggest you check your tone, child. You have not been behaving well as it is, and we are *not* happy with you or with the people you have brought. You are lucky we have not executed the judgment you deserve for being a mixer as well."

"Excuse me..."

I tried to pull away, but he dug his nails in further, causing me to wince.

"Ah, ah, ah, careful now. We are well within our right to do it too because mixers are illegal. That's a fact, and the only reason you are still alive is because you are the White Wolf. The crowd would be in an uproar over it, but this isn't just about you anymore, Shanely. No, you see while you've been dancing and acting so carefree, the Councilmen and I have had an interesting conversation with a poor young wolf who was recently banished from McCoy pack. We made a deal, and she told me some very important information about your child."

I snarled, but he pulled me closer to him. My body was pressed firmly against his, and he snarled back.

"I said hush!" he snapped angrily in my ear. Then he smiled and waved to a family nearby.

"She doesn't scent like anything, Shanely, which is strange to the rest of the Council and I. Even for being a mixer, you and Bastian both have strong wolves yet Aerith doesn't seem to have one. It's more than a rare recessive gene, isn't it? Our lovely wolf shed some light on that subject for us."

"Why are you telling me all of this?" I asked angrily.

"Because you are going against everything we've set up, and I will not have it. Unless you want your child to disappear, and I get the Division involved, I suggest you play by our rules."

My eyes widened as the song slowly came to an end.

"Oh, and I suggest you keep this to yourself for now. It will be the best for everyone, I assure you," Silas threatened before bowing to me. "Thank you, my White Wolf, for honoring me with this dance!"

He kissed my hand before leaving me shaking in the middle of the dance floor. Bastian, Cade, and Elijah were there in seconds though, and the wonderful dinner I just ate threatened to reappear. I let Bastian lead me back to our tables.

"Shanely, you look pale. What did that prick say to you?!" Bastian demanded as I sat down. I found Silas staring at me from on the stage.

I didn't know what to do. I looked to my dad, who had Aerith in his arms. I started to answer but snapped my mouth shut. Silas grinned from above, and I felt sick. I couldn't say anything to Bastian or anyone. I couldn't say *anything* for fear I'd lose my child forever. He knew exactly where he struck, and now he had found his way to control me.

"Whoa, Bastian look," Cade said, gesturing to my back. "Her dress has all these holes in it."

I felt Bastian's hands run up my back before he asked, "Is that blood?"

The moment he said blood, he had everyone's attention. I quickly pulled away. *I had to get away*, I thought to myself. *I couldn't let him know.*

"Bastian, it's nothing. He didn't say anything to me either. I have to use the restroom."

Bastian didn't look like he believed me, but I didn't stick around to have them question me any further. I moved as fast as I could with my heels on, trying to look happy amongst the many tables full of wolves. I refused to turn my head to look at Silas. I couldn't stand to see the smug expression on his face. Footsteps sounded behind me, but I made it to the restroom before they caught up to me.

I stopped at the sink, trying to get my composure. I felt jittery inside, and I was completely frustrated. *How did I not expect this?* I thought angrily. *I should have never brought Aerith here.* I stupidly *believed* everyone when they said the White Wolf was in charge. I thought I could step in and change everything so no one would be in danger, but I was wrong. *I was so very wrong.*

A stall door slammed shut, startling me.

"Well, look who it is," Emma snarled as she stepped out of the stall. This was the first that I had managed to see her since we arrived, but I was not in the mood. She stepped up to the sink to wash her hands and adjust her dress, and I saw *red*. I took two steps towards her, when she put her hand up, casually wagging her finger in my face.

"Ah, ah, ah. No closer, Shanely. Otherwise I'll have to get Silas involved. We wouldn't want that now, would we?"

I snarled at her but didn't move a muscle. She had me too, and I cringed watching her primp in the mirror. *I didn't like this. What else would she use against me now because of her deal with Silas?* I caught a whiff of her scent and shock rippled across my face. She was no longer a rogue without a pack. *Someone had taken her in.*

"Emma," I gritted through my teeth.

"Looks like your whole gang is causing trouble, it seems," she said, applying more lip gloss.

"Looks like someone actually accepted you into their pack. Pity," I countered.

She snorted. "It wasn't that hard, Shanely. I may not be the White Wolf, but it doesn't mean I don't have value."

"Hey, I never said you didn't. You diminished your own value by how you acted around everyone," I replied, and she bristled.

"You were just threatened by me! That's why I was forced to go to Blackwood," she said, stomping her foot at me.

"I banished you from the McCoy pack over how you treated my daughter and mate. She has never been the same since that night. You've taken something from her in an attempt to hurt me. You *hurt* a child, Emma, and now this with Silas! That's a new low even for you. God, you are pathetic, Emma, but I'm so glad you found a pack that values you!"

She scoffed in my direction as I passed by her.

"You know not everything is about you, Shanely, but no matter. You know Bastian and I used to dance nearly every song at these balls. For years, he always asked me to dance. Oh, we made such memories here! You'll have to tell him to save me a dance later, you know for old times sake."

I bristled at her comment, and she gave me a smug smile. I was already spent from everything today, and I didn't need to hear how much my husband danced with another. I know I wasn't being rational, and it was probably not true, but it just *stung*. I stomped by her and out the door.

And right into Bastian.

"Shanely..."

I put my hand up. "I don't want to talk, Bastian. Can we please..."

Emma walked out now and smiled seductively at Bastian.

"Good to see you again, Bastian," she said quietly, putting her hand on his arm before she left us. I glared at her, trying desperately to rein in my temper.

"Whoa, Baby Girl..." Cade started to say, but I put my hand up, silencing him. I stomped off towards the exit, when Luke stood in my way.

"White Wolf? Your presence is being requested," he said, pointing to the stage. I turned to see Silas gesturing to the open chair.

"Tell him not now, Luke. I need a break," I replied, when I heard Silas's vile voice fill my head.

"Don't even think about leaving," Silas snarled, and my eyes widened. *"Tell the Fenrir brothers to find their seats, and you march yourself up on this stage. You're not done yet."*

That wasn't possible, I thought to myself. I looked down at my bracelet before turning to Silas. He smirked at me, patting the seat again.

"I'm sorry, Shanely, but he is insisting," Luke countered, when Bastian stepped in front of me.

"She said no..."

I grabbed my mate's arm and said, "Bastian, it's fine. You guys just go take a seat, and I'll see what he wants."

"I'm coming with you," Bastian said firmly.

"No!"

He seemed startled by my abrupt reaction. I felt awful, but I wasn't about to make anything worse for my family. Not until I could get the upper hand here.

"Bastian, I will be fine. I am the White Wolf after all, so you can just take a seat with your brothers."

He flinched.

I had hurt him. I didn't mean to. I just needed him to sit with his brothers, but I didn't mean it like that. He looked like he was struggling with his wolf, and I stepped closer to try and fix it.

"Bastian, I didn't..."

"No, you're right. You're the White Wolf and not me, so we'll just take a seat where we belong," Bastian said dryly before stomping away from me. Elijah went after him, while Cade gave me a look.

"Baby Girl, what is going on with you?"

My eyes pleaded with him to understand. I struggled with my emotions and felt desperate to tell him without actually saying anything, but Cade just looked sad. He wasn't understanding, and I was so overwhelmed.

"Shanely, I must insist we move now. Silas is waiting," Luke said, pushing me forward. Cade watched me walk away, and he didn't come after me.

My family watched me walk up the steps before taking a seat at the table.

"That's a good girl," Silas muttered before smiling for a picture. I couldn't bring myself to smile. Bastian was sitting at our table and wouldn't look at me. Cade had made his way back and just watched the whole thing continue to play out.

"How did you do that?" I asked my captor.

He smiled. "Child, those bracelets do not work on the five of us. We engineered them that way, so we always have control."

I glared at him, crossing my arms angrily. *So the only ones I could link were them,* I thought to myself. *This is ridiculous!* But now I could see punishment they really gave me. Wolves were not solitary creatures. We belonged to a pack, and he just isolated me. The emptiness inside killed me, and now I didn't even have my family around for comfort. They were all below me and out of reach. *I hadn't felt this small since I was with Peter.*

Silas did not allow me to leave for the rest of the ball. I stayed up there with them as most of the hall left. It killed me to watch Bastian pick up a sleeping Aerith and walk out of the room.

He left me.

But what did I honestly expect from him?

Cade and Elijah stayed behind as the rest of my family went back to our rooms. Silas finally motioned for me to stand.

"I think this evening went by rather well, don't you? Have a good night, Shanely. Oh, and don't forget our deal," he said as he winked at me. I gave a small nod and watched them make their way down the steps. Cade looked ready to murder them as I finally made my way to them.

"You waited," I said quietly.

"What else did you expect from us?" Elijah asked, his voice a little gruff.

"Elijah, I..."

"I heard," Cade said, crossing his arms. My eyes went wide, and my heart stopped. *I forgot about Cade's ears. He heard everything Silas said.*

"What deal did you make with him?" Cade asked.

I tried to push passed. "I didn't make a deal, Cade."

He grabbed my arm. "I'm not dumb, Shanely. You have never put yourself above Bastian like that before. You have always made him an equal, but one dance with Silas has you doing exactly what they want, so what gives."

I fought back tears now. "Cade, I promise I didn't make a deal with him. Can you please take me to my room? I'm exhausted."

Cade gave Elijah a look, and they had one of their famous silent conversations. Cade finally turned to face me, and without another word, he gestured to the door. I sighed, knowing I had upset all three boys now and made my way out the door.

Luke appeared just outside the ballroom, and he stepped in our path.

Again.

"This way, Shanely," he said, making Cade snarl.

Luke took a step backwards. "Look, I'm sorry about this, but it's part of her punishment. There is nothing I can do!"

Cade threw his hands up. "Luke, this is stupid! This is her first time here, and after how the evening started, do you really expect us to just let her be all alone? I'm her Beta, and my wolf will not allow this!"

"I don't know, Cade. She accepted the punishment for everyone. I cannot change the outcome," Luke said sadly, and I turned to my Beta.

"I'll be okay. Just come get me first thing in the morning, so I can make things right with Bastian. Please?"

Cade gave me a look before his eyes narrowed in frustration. He turned to Luke. "The punishment doesn't say anything about me staying outside her room, does it?"

My eyes widened, hearing what Cade was asking. "Cade..."

"Does it, Luke?" he asked, cutting me off.

"Technically no. She just has to stay in the room alone," Luke finally answered.

"Then lead the way!" Cade said, gesturing to the hall. He turned to Elijah. "Let Bastian know what's going on. I'll bring her back first thing in the morning."

Elijah gave us both a nod before heading back to our rooms.

"Cade, you shouldn't sleep on the floor like this," I whispered, but he just pushed me down the hall.

"If you think I'm going to leave you alone on the same floor as our esteemed Council, you've got another thing coming," he snapped back angrily. He stared straight ahead, following Luke to the elevators. We went to the 5th floor, and Luke stopped at the first door on the right.

"Here we are," he unlocked the door, and I turned to Cade.

"Cade?"

His eyes met mine, and they softened a little. He pulled me into a hug now, one I desperately needed.

"Just get some sleep, Baby Girl. I'll watch over you," he whispered, and I stood on my tiptoes, kissing his cheek.

    I entered the massive lonely room before shutting the door behind me. I could hear Cade slide down to the ground now, and my heart hurt. I hated this for him. I hated being away from Bastian. I had to wait to fix things with him until morning, which was excruciating. This was cruel, and I was dreading the rest of the week. I shimmed out of my massive gown and collapsed in the bed. I had none of my stuff with me, but I didn't care. I was so tired that I was asleep by the time my head hit the pillow.

Chapter 4

I woke up completely stressed and exhausted. The beds were amazing, I'll give them that. The Council did not skimp on luxury, but after yesterday I felt like all I did was toss and turn all night long. I woke up and shimmed my dress back on. It was early, but I didn't want to wait anymore. I needed my mate.

I slowly opened the door and found Cade wedged between the door frame with his long legs sticking out into the hall. He peeked an eye open, giving me a smile.

"Morning, Baby Girl," he said groggily.

"Sleep well Beta?" I asked, chuckling. He grunted before slowly standing up.

"C'mon, let's get you to your mate, so I can take a nap," he said, taking my hand. Cade led me down to the second floor, dropping me off to my room. I quietly snuck inside, finding Aerith and Bastian still passed out asleep. I felt bad for waking them, so I quietly slipped away, choosing a hot shower instead. There was no way I was going back to sleep anyways.

I let the hot water melt away all my problems, trying to pretend nothing existed anymore, but everything that happened last night flooded my brain. *How was I going to get out of this? How could I get the upper hand without dragging my mate through the mud or risking my child?*

I groaned, knowing I was going to see Emma again today too. I'm sure she would have vile things to say just to get under my skin. With the Council on her side, there was no telling what she'd get away with. The only positive thing going for me was knowing that Derek and Liam weren't here yet.

They were late for some reason, but I didn't care. I can't deal with them all, especially if Bastian and I are at odds. I needed to fix things with Bastian this morning. I couldn't do anything if he was still upset with me.

The shower felt great, but my stomach rumbled loudly. *Breakfast was scheduled to be ready in about 15 minutes, so I better go wake them up.* I exited the shower and got dressed quickly. Just a simple pair of jeans and a pretty blouse before I dried my hair. Well half dried it. I was running out of time, but at least it wouldn't drip everywhere I went.

When I left the bathroom, I was surprised to see them both awake already. Aerith was already dressed, and Bastian was fixing his hair in the mirror out here.

"You could of come in to get ready, my love," I said, standing in the doorway.

"It's okay. This mirror works just as well."

"Yeah, but I was in the other room, getting dressed after my shower," I winked at him, and his eyes glowed.

"Well now I'm regretting every decision I've made this morning," he said, turning around. He held his hand out for me, and I ran to his arms.

"I'm sorry, my love. I didn't mean it the way it sounded. I don't think I'm better than anybody, especially you," I said softly, and he gently pushed aside my hair.

"I know, baby. I'm sorry too. I should have known that's not how you meant everything, but why did you sit by them for the rest of the evening? I thought we weren't going to play into their crazy demands."

I opened my mouth, but the words wouldn't come out. I didn't know what to do. If the Council suspected I said anything, they would do something to Aerith and get the Division involved. Silas would just pull the same crap he did last night, and I didn't want to risk her.

I pulled away slightly, trying to hide the emotion in my voice. "I was just trying to show everyone that I could play along with some things. I don't want everyone to be defensive because I'm stomping on their customs and traditions. I haven't actually taken over yet Bastian."

He gave me a look like he was trying to get a read on me. I knew this look

CHAPTER 4

well. I held my breath, hoping he couldn't read every worry running through my head right now. Bastian closed the gap between us, gently rubbing the side of my face with his hand. I leaned into his touch, needing the comfort badly. Not having our bond opened was awful.

"Shanely, you already took charge when your wolf emerged. They are the ones that need to understand that and pass it off to you," he said quietly.

I dropped my head. "If I don't make everyone like me, and I go on trying to change everything before they are ready, they could revolt against me. I'd have to force everyone to submit to me with my Alpha power, and I don't want to do that. Not like that."

His face softened. "I understand, my love. Just talk to me alright? We do this together."

Bastian pulled me in close, kissing my lips. *If only he knew how badly I needed him.* How badly I wanted to do things together, but I was stuck, isolated, and alone. Aerith squealed as our lips parted.

"Ew! No kissing, daddy! That's gross!"

I laughed as I pulled away. He swatted my butt before I got too far out of reach. At least we were on the mends, but I hated I only told him a half truth. Guilt wrapped around me then, and there was no shaking it.

I sat by Aerith, needing a distraction. "How are you doing with all this, baby?"

"It's fun, well fun now. There are a lot of kids here. I want to play with them today!"

"Yeah? I think we can make something work. What's on the itinerary today, baby?" I asked Bastian.

"I think today is all outside. We have the picnic today, and sometime this week we play the Hunt and also the Mate Run. Well, assuming they don't change anything."

"What's the Hunt?"

"Normally among the packs it's a game that is played to strengthen the enforcers, but here it's a different kind of mate game. Basically everyone gets to see how strong your connection is to your mate, without relying on the bond. The girls wear something that hides their location, and then they scatter in the massive woods beyond the Hall. The men get the go ahead, and they have to find their mate on scent alone. We all have matching tags, so those who are watching can see who finds their mate first. It's bragging rights till the next year."

"It sounds like hide and seek!" Aerith shouted.

"Kind of sweet pea, but only those who have their mate play that round."

"What about the Mate Run? Is that just a way to try and find a mate?"

Bastian nodded. "Wolves just need sight to make the bond happen, but the last few years before you came to town, the Council added the game to try and assist in getting bonds to happen. The thought process was maybe the bonds were changing, and you needed your own wolves to look at one another for it to snap in place. All single men and women have this like relay race in their wolf form. The venue is pretty big, so sometimes it is easy to miss one another, and the race pushes everyone together."

"Interesting. Do the World Council participate in any events?" I asked, curious about it all.

"Never. They sit back and direct the whole thing. Though there is one on the council that has never found his mate, but he has yet to ever participate in the Mate Run."

"Wait who? I assumed they all had mates."

Bastian shook his head. "No Silas, Harold, Paul, and Evan all have mates, but Xavier does not have a mate. He's the only lone Council member."

I mulled over that little tidbit of information. A knock on the door interrupted my thoughts. Bastian opened it up, and Bay and Abraham walked in. Brody hung back in the hall, and I gave him a smile. He waved back before leaning on the door frame. He was taking his job as bodyguard very seriously, and I was proud of him.

"Good morning, my sweet niece! You ready for today?" Bay asked as she scooped Aerith up. Aerith was so excited and practically leapt from Bay's arms towards the door.

"Yes! Let's go! We don't want to miss anything!"

Abraham laughed, his deep voice echoing throughout the room.

"Alright, squirt! Let's go. Everyone is already down in the main dining hall.

CHAPTER 4

We thought we'd walk with you guys," he said, hauling me off the couch.

We all left the room, and I saw my father and Caleb waited as well.

"You guys okay?" I asked nervously.

My father nodded, giving me a sad smile. "Not everyone wants us here. We thought it would remain peaceful if we entered with you at least for the first few days."

My heart sunk, but I understood their hesitation. I linked my arms with my dad, and we all headed down the grand stairs. I noticed Luke was waiting as well. I guess the Council still wants to keep their tabs on me, I suppose.

"Morning Luke," I said as we passed. He fell in line behind us but said a good morning in return. Thankfully, he didn't have another message to deliver this morning.

We turned left from the stairs and passed the entrance to the ballroom. Way down towards the back of the castle was a very large room where all the packs ate most of their meals together. *It smelled amazing in here! Someone could seriously cook,* I thought to myself. I could see my family had already gone through the line and had seats saved for us.

We quickly went through the line ourselves, and I filled my plate with pancakes. I grabbed peanut butter and syrup before making my way to the coffee. Bastian had Aerith's plate with him, and Aerith had somehow managed to find her way to Abraham's shoulders. Everyone seemed to quiet down as we passed by, and I heard nothing but utensils hitting plates. Some smiled, others frowned. It was difficult to get through everyone and this awkward silence.

We were soon eating and talking, pretending everyone around wasn't just staring at us, and the room soon grew noisy again. The man I danced with last night, Garrett, walked up with a small woman and two young kids behind him.

"Can we sit with you, Shanely?" he asked.

My mouth was full of food, but I gestured for them to sit. Bastian just laughed at me, and I nudged him playfully.

"Hello, I'm Shanely's Fated Mate, Bastian. She'd introduce you, but well you can see she's a little busy. It's nice to meet you."

They shook hands, and the woman smiled sheepishly at me. I hit my husband, making them both laugh.

"I'm Garrett Taylor from the Amber pack. This is my mate, Eliana, and our twins, Scotty and Hudson. They're almost five," he replied, and the boys waved before diving into their plates. Aerith was so excited to have someone her age to play with.

"I'm four!" she shouted.

I laughed, finally swallowing my food. "This is Aerith. She turns five herself real soon."

"That's perfect! Maybe she can play with our boys today?" Garrett asked.

"We'd like that! She's been itching to make new friends."

"Us too. We've been trying to branch out a bit among the packs. Sometimes everyone tends to stay in their comfort zone, but we'd like to meet new ones. Thank you for letting me dance with your mate too, Bastian. I know that probably wasn't easy."

Bastian laughed, waving him off. "It's fine. I know everyone is going to want to meet the White Wolf. You seemed like a nice enough guy anyways, plus I saw your own mate watching. If she knew about it and was okay with it, then I would be too."

She nodded. "I was. It was our way of welcoming you here, and a way to show support and acceptance of you to everyone else. We've noticed a line is being drawn, I'm afraid."

I groaned, thinking back to my conversation with Silas as Garrett studied me. He spoke, "It'll get better Shanely. We've always been told that when the White Wolf shows up, it's for a reason. We just want everyone to know we are not against whatever's coming. We can get onboard the change, whatever it may be."

"Thank you, Garrett and Eliana. Your support means the world to me," I said as I sighed. It really felt good to hear them openly say they support me and whatever change we will bring. It's been weighing on me since I discovered I was the White Wolf. I didn't realize how badly I needed to hear that.

"Can I ask you something, Shanely?" Eliana asked, pulling me from my

CHAPTER 4

thoughts again.

"Sure."

"What is up with the bear and tiger shifters you brought? And I hope that didn't come off rude or anything, but it's a huge difference than what we normally deal with during the Summit events."

I shook my head. "No it's fine! It's not rude and honestly everyone should know. Those two," I said, pointing to my father and Caleb, "That's my father and half-brother."

"We could all scent mixer when you walked in last night. We've never heard of this happening before."

I nodded. "My mother was a wolf, and she found her mate among the bear shifters. They were torn apart though, and it's why I didn't grow up in the shifter community. I grew up without a family because of the stupid shifter laws that were in place."

I let that bit of information sink in.

"And the tiger?"

"He's her brother," Bastian stated matter of factly.

I nearly screamed, "IN LAW!"

Everyone around me gave me a weird look as I quickly tried to gain some composure. I straightened out my shirt and said calmly, "That's my brother-in-law. He mated Bastian's sister, Bay."

Garrett set his fork down, processing everything we just dumped on him. Bastian and his brothers just gave me odd looks, but I couldn't look at them. I couldn't answer the questions I knew they had, and I prayed no one else heard Bastian's slip up.

"Shanely, what is going on with you?" Bastian barely whispered to me, but I ignored him. *What else could I do?*

"Your poor family! I can't imagine how your father must have felt with everything," Eliana replied.

"It's been hard, but I think it's been easier for him ever since we reconnected and blended the clan and pack. He adores getting to be a grandpa, and he seems fairly happy despite everything that happened. We're all one big family now," I said, picking at my food. I really wasn't hungry anymore as all I could think of was Abraham in Silas's clutches too.

"So, you all are together often?" Garrett asked, his surprised wearing off to show more of his curiosity.

"All the time. We gave the bears more land to use, and we share the roaming rights. Both Caleb and Abraham are on our council as well," Bastian replied, smirking.

"So, you have had a total of four mixed matings then? Including your parents, Shanely," Eliana asked.

"Actually, we have another back home. Her uncle Ash found his mate among the bear clan as well. He stayed home though to help some of the families about to have their littles," Bastian replied, making me pale slightly. *Please, please, don't let the council find out about them.* I sunk in my seat further, hoping I didn't have to do something else to cover up Uncle Ash's punishment. Hopefully, no one else heard my mate, and he can fly under the radar.

Garrett ran his hand through his hair. "Wow. Your pack is completely different than all of ours. How exactly were you getting around the laws, if you don't mind me asking?"

"Well, honestly we kept her hidden from as many shifters as we could other than our immediate area. If no one really knows anything, then there is nothing to report. It's not a Division problem but one within our own community. Now that she is the White Wolf, we want to do some real change here," Bastian answered before taking another bite of his breakfast.

I didn't chime in with him, and I pushed my plate away entirely. Silas's threat still loomed over me, and I wasn't so sure of our future. I wasn't so sure of the change I was hoping to bring.

"Maybe it's why no one can find their mates anymore, love?" Eliana asked, pulling me from my dooming thoughts.

"I heard about that. What's going on?" I asked.

"Nothing that's the problem. There are a lot of packs that haven't had new matings in a few years. The World Council even canceled the mating game we usually have. It's depressing when no one ends up with their mate, but even more than that everyone's been worried because it could mean a decline in littles."

"Mate Run's been canceled?" Bastian asked.

"It's what I've heard. Who knows what the Council is up to though," Garrett answered. I was lost in thought, and Bastian noticed.

"Hmm, well maybe next year we could bring the game back?" Bastian offered, but I just looked dejected. I couldn't hide it, and the stress was becoming way too much to handle.

Eliana put her hand on mine, seeing how I felt. "Hang in there, sweetie. You have more support than you realize."

Suddenly, a loud buzzer went off, making me jump. *I'm lucky I set my coffee down otherwise I'd be wearing it!*

Bastian laughed as he kissed my cheek. "It just announces that the festivities are about to start."

We threw our plates away when I realized something. I had a somewhat pleasant breakfast with no Council member in sight.

"Where is the Council?" I asked.

"They don't eat with us unless it's in the ballroom. They just meet us for the events later on in the day," Bastian replied as if it was no big deal.

"Seems in-personable, don't ya think?"

Bastian shrugged. "Can we really expect anything different? It's what they've always done."

I snorted, but he was right. They were pompous, and I could not wait to do things differently. Funny how a little anger got me on board with this whole White Wolf responsibility. *Now the only question left was how?*

I followed my mate out of the dining room to the massive backyard. Outside was decorated in fun colors and balloons for the kids. They had lots of games set up, booths for the kids to get their face painted, and plenty of seats for us adults to visit. It was almost like a baby carnival set up in the backyard.

Bastian and I went around trying to meet as many as we could from the other packs. Everyone seemed nice for the most part, but it was a little awkward. I was trying desperately to convince everyone that I wasn't a bad person, and that mixers weren't such a bad thing, which in hindsight was off putting. Bastian kept eyeing me funny, and I realized I was coming on a little strong. I couldn't help it though. I needed to get this done before the Council did something else.

I watched everyone's interactions with each other, trying really hard to get a feel for what was going on with everyone. For the most part, the packs were enjoying themselves. Aerith was having a ball, and I saw she already had a paw print painted on her face. She was playing tag with all the other kids. Not a care in the world. Caleb, Dad, and Brody all stayed close to her and the other kids, while Bastian and I continued going from pack to pack. It honestly seemed like everyone was adjusting fairly well to my non-wolf family too. Well, all except one. One pack seemed really upset by them, and when I saw Abraham standing off in the corner, I soon figured out why.

It was the Blackwood pack.

Abraham was almost shaking by the time I walked up to him. I pulled him into a hug, forcing his eyes away from the group staring at us.

"Abraham, why don't you stay with Bastian and I? We can put some space between us and them."

"Shanely, I don't know how long I can do this. They killed many of my people, and my parents..." he snarled, his voice trailing off as anger flashed through his eyes.

"Hey, chill out man. You snap, and they have all of us right where they want us. I mean look at them! They're looking for an excuse to throw you out and take what is rightfully Shanely's away. This sucks for everyone, but we need to keep a level head," Bastian said firmly as he stood in front of Abraham.

Abraham raised his head slowly before glaring back at Bastian, "And how are you going to feel when you see Derek or your father, Liam? Think about what you are asking, brother."

"I am!" Bastian snapped back before quieting himself, "and I'm going to need you to remind me of this very conversation when I do see them. I know my wolf will want to slaughter them all the minute they arrive, but you and my brothers need to make sure I don't snap. We don't do this right then we could lose everything."

Abraham eyed him for a moment before his face softened. "You're right,

CHAPTER 4

brother. My apologies."

They shook hands, and Bastian led him away from the Blackwood's view. They were smirking amongst themselves, and it pissed me off. I stalked over to their little group. They were not mingling with anyone, and I could see the kids and teenagers watching the fun longingly but not joining in. They looked uneasy as I approached them while the adults all looked disgusted.

"Hello, this is the Blackwood pack right?" I said as cheerfully as I could muster. *By the end of this week I was going to be an expert at lying and hiding my emotions, it seems.*

They all just looked at me before a lanky man, who I assumed was their Alpha, spoke. He didn't even bother to stand to shake my hand or anything. Just answered from afar.

"Yes, we are the Blackwood pack. Can I help you?"

"Nope! Just wanted to come say hi! We have a lot going on, and I wondered if the kids would want to have some fun?"

The kids all looked towards their Alpha anxiously, and he gave me a slimy smile in return. "They're okay. Thank you though."

They looked dejected, and some of the older teens looked pissed. I wish I had my wolf to call on, but I guess I was going to have to do it the old-fashioned way.

"Well let's ask them! They all seem so bored over here," I countered as I made my way through the pack.

I went to the angry looking teens first. "Hey! Do you want to join in the fun? All the other teens are playing some sort of game over there, and they have cotton candy in the far back booth. The younger kids are playing tag too."

I pointed to the field farthest away from this group. They shifted on their feet nervously.

"Umm... well it looks like fun but..."

"Then go! Have fun! Go enjoy yourselves. Call it a direct command from the White Wolf."

The Alpha looked furious but said nothing. *What could he say really? According to their own prophecy, I was above him even without my wolf. I* whispered to the oldest kid, "I'll deal with him. Go. Take all the kids and have some fun this week."

The oldest boy looked at me gratefully before grabbing the hands of the younger kids. "C'mon, we don't want to disobey our White Wolf."

He was smart, and I winked at him as he picked up a small child. They all scattered quickly, and I turned to find a very red face Alpha in my bubble. *He finally decided to leave his chair,* I thought to myself, and he squared up against me.

"What do you think you are doing? You have no right to decide what happens in my pack!"

"Actually, I do or did you forget because of the World Council here? I am to be Alpha over all, which *includes* Blackwood. This is my pack now, and I don't care for how it's being run. You have isolated this pack, and it's not healthy or fair for anyone. The kids seem almost afraid of you. Unless you would like me to personally visit your pack, which mind you is not far from my home, then I suggest you lighten up. Otherwise, I will chose a new wolf to be Alpha. Understand?"

"You have no right!"

"Were you not listening? I have every right, and I really don't think you want to go head to head with me over this. I have no idea why you run this pack like this anyways! It makes zero sense," I snapped back.

"You think I want anyone in my pack to mate with the others here?! No! I keep my pack close to ensure no one accidentally mates with someone outside our pack. No one shares the same rules that we have. It's better for us to stay separate!"

"Umm... first of all eww. No one accidentally mates with anyone. You just simply find your perfect mate, and it's not wrong. We all only get one, so all you're doing is keeping others from finding their other half. No one can possibly be happy with that decision! Mate bonds are sacred, and you have no right to interfere. Second, you need to start getting used to the idea of mixing with other shifters. Right now, there are mostly just wolves here but you need to find a way to be okay with this before more change happens. Your pack doesn't seem to be happy, and I intend to fix that."

CHAPTER 4

This man was disgusting and clearly needed to be removed as well. *One thing at a time,* I reminded myself. I started to walk away, when he sneered at me.

"Says the wolf that mingles with tigers. If you're so worried about my pack then why don't you take care of that tiger!? He's destroyed most of the Blackwood's numbers and stole our land away!"

I wanted nothing more than let them see my wolf right now, but it was locked, and I was pissed.

"I will only say this only *once*, wolf. I have lifted the laws about mixing, and you all need to get on board with it. That tiger will do you no harm, but I demand you all treat him and any other shifter with the same respect. Abraham is a member of my council, which according to wolf customs means he's over your head. I've heard of the stories of Blackwood, and no one believes your lies. Even other wolves tend to keep their distance from you all because you are violent and selfish shifters. I know you killed innocent tigers to take that land in the first place. Now I will not tolerate shifters destroying one another. We have bigger enemies to contend with. Do not speak to me like that again. You," I snarled, pointing to their Alpha, "are on thin ice. Fix your attitude this week, and I'll ignore what just happened, but choose to hang onto your anger and hatred, and see what happens when you stand against your White Wolf."

"Your wolf's locked, girl. What exactly do you think you're going to do to me right now?"

I glared at the entire group of wolves around me. They all lowered their eyes in respect for me but their Alpha. *I had enough to deal with at the moment, and now this?!*

"Want to be the first person I find once this comes off?" I asked, lifting my arm. His eyes narrowed, but he wisely kept his mouth shut. "This is my warning to you all. Let go of your hate and pride to unite with us or let it be your downfall. You all have the choice, even if it's different than his."

I pointed to the Alpha who was gritting his teeth in anger. He clenched his fists together so tight his knuckles were white. I left them to think about what I said, and I prayed the rest of the pack had better heads on their shoulders than that guy. Bastian was already making his way back to me, looking entirely stressed out. I met him halfway, and he pulled me close.

"I thought you were following us, Shanely!"

"I'm fine, Bastian!" I replied, chuckling as I gently pulled away from his suffocating hug. I took one last look at the Blackwood pack. Some of the adults had moved away from the group and were getting closer to the festivities but most sadly stayed.

"I just had a conversation with the Blackwood's Alpha is all. He's a grumpy guy."

Bastian glared in his direction, taking my hand to drag me further away from the Alpha's glare. I tried to relax in his arms, but a loud booming voice came from the stage, completely killing any chances of that.

"Welcome all! The Council and I decided to come to the festivities a little early today! We've missed seeing all your happy faces! Now first things first, where oh where has our little White Wolf gone?" Silas hollered as he pretended to scan the crowds. "Ah! There she is! Everyone please welcome her to the stage!"

The crowd parted, and everyone started clapping their hands. I looked to Bastian uneasily, and he rolled his eyes.

"C'mon, love," he whispered and started guiding me to the stage. The Councilmen all looked happy, which just seemed odd. Silas's eyes met mine, and it was like a slimy, icky feeling coated me entirely. I shivered slightly, wondering what in the world he was up to now. Silas covered the mic as we got close.

"That's far enough, boy. We only need her up here," he snapped before yanking me further up the stage. Silas's enforcers stepped in between Bastian and I, and he looked ready to kill them.

"Silas, you have another thing coming if you..." Bastian was livid, and I quickly spoke before he made everything worse.

"Bastian, it's okay. You can still see me, and I'll be down soon," I said, giving him a weak smile. Bastian stared at me with a blank expression then. My eyes pleaded with him to just cave and let this go, but I didn't know if he would. He was an Alpha male and letting something go like this wasn't

CHAPTER 4

easy. I breathed a sigh of relief when he finally stomped back to our family without another word.

Silas leaned into me, his breath reeking of stale coffee mixed with cigars, whispering, "Good girl. You make sure to put him in his place, and I'll stay quiet about the other mixer in your group."

My head snapped to his as fear gripped my heart. *Was he talking about Abraham or Tommy?* I gritted my teeth in anger. I was livid, but Silas wasn't worried at all. He merely smiled wide, knowing he only had more control now. I instinctively stepped towards the vile man, my fist clenched together.

"Ah, ah, ah. Don't even think about it. I have control here, and I run these laws. It's up to the Council and I to decide one's fate, and mixers shouldn't exist in my book. So get your temper under control before I have him executed in front of everyone."

My eyes widened. Knowing I was stuck obeying that vile man, I forced myself to stare out in front of me. *God, I wanted to kill him.* I wanted nothing more than to sink my teeth in his neck even without the push from my wolf, but there was nothing I could do. Absolutely *nothing*. Tears filled my eyes, but I forced them away. *Don't cry, don't cry, don't cry,* I told myself over and over again. *The triplets would see. They would see, and then there would be no hiding this from them.*

Silas turned to the crowd again. Once more becoming his cheery self. *How did he know?* I wondered. *Does he have the whole place bugged or something? Are there cameras everywhere just waiting to trap any shifter out of line?*

Silas must be talking about Abraham because of Bastian's mistake earlier. I stared at Bay, who was laughing with my family. She seemed so carefree and happy with everyone. I just put a target on her mate's back, and she has no idea. No idea the mess I caused. I quickly looked away otherwise I wasn't going to keep the tears from falling and then what a mess I'd be in. I needed to get ahead of this. As soon as I could run back I'd sneak Abraham out. I'd send everyone home if I had too. The less they had in their clutches, the less they could use against me.

I found my mate standing with his brothers off to the side watching me closely. They whispered amongst themselves, looking utterly angry. *I'm sure they were pissed with me, but if they only knew what was going on.* I wish I could send them a link right now while the Council was distracted. They'd save Abraham for me, but I was stuck up here all alone with no way to reach them. I felt sick inside as I listened to Silas carry on.

"Now, I know we mentioned before about canceling the Mate Run, but seeing how our White Wolf has emerged, we think this might just be our lucky year! Will all single male and female wolves please come to the front? And again this is for wolves only."

I clenched my fists together, and my mouth opened without thinking. "Would it be so bad if non-wolves played? I mean maybe that's a reason no one is finding their mates? Maybe it's because they aren't wolves!"

Only the wolves nearest the stage heard me, and they all looked to me shocked by my outburst. They started whispering amongst themselves again, and Silas glared at me.

He covered the mic again. "Shanely, take a good look around right now. Anyone missing?"

My heart stopped as I scanned the yard. I didn't have to guess who he was talking, but I searched my pack and family anyways, feeling sick to my stomach. Abraham. He wasn't around anymore. He was just gone and panic began to set it. *I couldn't find my brother!*

Silas smirked when I realized he was missing. I snarled at him, "Where is he?!"

His eyes flashed gold briefly before he adjusted his tie. "Did you really think I'd just let him run loose after finding out about him? I may have warned you last night, but I realized I needed insurance to keep you in line more than just with Aerith. When Bastian said he was your brother too, it was too good of an opportunity to pass up. You will be the White Wolf I tell you to be, got that? We may be stuck with you, and I may not be able to kill you myself, but I'm going to make sure things go my way. We are not having some great change, and by the end of the week you are going to insist to the wolves that you were wrong. That you need guidance and wish to remain here with us. I don't care how you put it, but you sell it or I'll bring down sentencing on your brother and child!"

CHAPTER 4

My heart stopped. I stood there dumbfounded as Silas turned back to the Councilmen. *Abraham was just with us,* I thought to myself. We walked down to breakfast together, and I just saw him not even 10 minutes ago. *How did I lose him in that short amount of time?!* I felt sick, and I didn't know what to do. All three of my boys were hyper aware of me right now, but my hands were tied, and I couldn't say a thing.

"Now correct the crowd, and tell them it's for wolves only!"

Silas smiled again at everyone before handing me the mic. I tried desperately to not let my voice shake as I said, "This is a wolves only game. Please all single men and women come forward, so we can start."

Caleb looked a little hurt and said something to my father. Everyone looked to me, completely lost at what I was doing. *I'm so sorry, Caleb. I'm so sorry everyone.* I blindly pushed my way through not fully knowing the kind of people I was up against.

"I said sell it, didn't I?"

"I'm trying!" I snapped back at Silas.

"Watch it child or I'll..."

"Sir, we're ready to start," Luke said, giving me a small wave. I looked to my feet, and he frowned.

"Good, good! Wait, what about those young men?" Silas asked, pointing to Cade and Elijah.

"They have decided not to play," Luke answered, and I looked to them gratefully. They were still taking a stand.

"Well that's not allowed, Luke. Bring them to me," Silas commanded, and Luke moved through the crowd quickly. I watched my boys grow even more and more upset, and it didn't take long for Cade to stomp over to us.

"Silas, I do not wish to play this year. It's not against the rules to skip out," he yelled.

"Not this year. This year it's mandatory. Isn't that right, White Wolf?"

I glared at Silas, but he held my stare. I caved, feeling entirely defeated right now. "It's mandatory, Cade."

His eyes narrowed at me. "What is going on with you, Shanely?! This isn't you!'

Those around us were starting to form a circle to watch everything play out. Everyone loves drama it seems. *I was so angry, but what was I supposed to do!? I can't risk Abraham and Aerith!* Not anymore than they already were, and God forbid he discovers Tommy.

"Shanely, command them," Silas demanded of me.

I lifted my arm in annoyance. "Can't remember?"

Silas rolled his eyes. "Not like that, child. You three are close, are you not? Make them play."

"Silas stop! This is ridiculous!" Elijah snapped at him.

I held my tongue instead. I didn't want to force them to play in this stupid game. Silas's eyes glowed at me before he pulled the enforcer standing behind me.

"Fine. Finn, I need you to do something for me," Silas said snidely. My eyes went wide, and I yanked on his arm.

"Don't you dare," I whispered. He jerked his arm away and straightened his coat out before gesturing to the boys. I clenched my fist before turning to my boys.

Elijah was shocked. "Shanely..."

"Cade, Elijah? As your Alpha of the McCoy pack, I command you to participate in the Mate Run this year."

They didn't move but looked furious with me. When nothing happened, I turned to Silas and in the most sarcastic voice I could muster I said, "Oh, right! I can't actually give them an Alpha command without my Alpha power. If you want them to play, you'll have to do it yourself, Silas."

"Don't be so dramatic girl. Cade, Elijah, since you won't listen to your White Wolf, I guess I'll have to get involved. You both are required to participate in the Mate Run," Silas commanded.

Elijah was pissed as the command hit him in the chest, and they started moving to the front, where the other males stood ready to play. Cade was yelling all kinds of things to Silas now, but it didn't keep his feet from moving.

I could feel Bastian's eyes staring straight into my soul, but I couldn't look him in the eye and see his disappointment. Everyone was mad at me already, and it was hard to stomach. Those participating in the Mate Run shifted now,

CHAPTER 4

and my boys were bigger than the rest. Cade and Elijah snarled viciously, but the gun went off, and they ran through the gates. We watched on the screen as they ran through the course, the boys mixing with the girls. Because of how the course was set up, all the wolves were forced to brush up against one another just to get through certain spots. Cade and Elijah took off past the pack though, running faster than the rest. I realized they were trying not to touch anyone. They refused to find their mate during the race. They stayed close together, grabbing the end marker and circling back.

Silas and the Council cheered along with the crowd. I didn't want to watch.

I hated myself for this. It didn't take long before Cade and Elijah shot through the gate, dropping their markers in front of the stage. They howled, and the other wolves in the woods met their call.

Cade still in his wolf form snapped his jaw at us. He was not happy.

"Oh, it looks like we have a bond forming everyone!" Silas cried out, and my head shot forward. There was a brown wolf slowly moving towards Cade. I looked to Silas.

"You can't be serious?!"

"See, everyone the mate bonds aren't dying! We just need our wolves to connect!"

Cade looked shocked and started backing away from the girl in front of him.

"Aww, he's nervous everyone!" Silas cried out, and the crowd aww'd.

Cade shifted back. "I'm not nervous, but that isn't my mate!"

The brown wolf shifted as well, and I thought I was going to be sick. Emma stood wide-eyed before him. Suddenly, I knew what Silas promised her. My eyes went wide, watching this unfold before me.

"Cade? I can't believe it's you!" she cried out, running towards him. She plowed into him, and our entire family looked shocked.

"Emma, let go! There is no mate bond!" Cade said, trying to tear her off of him. She seemed stuck to him like glue though.

"I can feel it, Cade! You don't have to be afraid! Shanely can't interfere with our bond anymore!"

I started towards them, when Silas grabbed my arm. He shook his head no, and Cade looked at us bewildered.

"You sell this bond Shanely or else," he snarled.

"What are you talking about?! Let go, Emma!"

I felt sick to my stomach. No matter which way I chose, I was risking one brother or another.

"Shanely hates me! It's why you're fighting the bond, Cade!"

He forcefully pulled away from her, getting much needed space. "I hate you! That has nothing to do with Shanely!"

She started to cry now, and I couldn't believe my eyes. She was acting ridiculous, but everyone surrounded them, eating it all up. Bastian pushed his way forward to defend his brother.

"Emma, Cade says there is no bond. It isn't something you can fake."

"It's the White Wolf's fault! She's interfering with a mate bond. It's because of her hatred of me that Cade is rejecting me!"

Everyone started talking at once and staring back at me with disgust in their eyes. *I couldn't interfere with a mate bond even if I wanted to! Didn't they know that?!* I opened my mouth to say something, when Silas gripped my arm tightly, warning me *again* to sell this bond.

"I... I um, don't hate you Emma," I said quietly, and Cade looked stricken. Like I just betrayed him.

"Now see! The White Wolf doesn't hate you, Emma dear. Cade, maybe you should give the girl a chance? Are you fighting the bond because of how the White Wolf felt about her?"

Rage filled Cade's eyes, and he barred his teeth. "No! There is no connection between us! We were pack mates for years everyone. The bond didn't happen then, and it sure as heck didn't happen now!"

Emma started losing it again as everyone looked to her with pity. The brothers all turned to me for help, but Silas was digging into my arm again.

"I... I..."

"I think what the White Wolf is trying to say is to give the girl a chance! Right, Shanely?"

If I opened my mouth again, I was going to throw up on this stage. He dug his nails into my skin, and I felt a small amount of blood trickle down my arm. This was my last warning, so I caved. There was no way I could get the words to come out of my mouth, so I slowly nodded, and the crowd started clapping excitedly as Cade looked feral. *He would never forgive me.*

"Shanely!" Bastian cried out, trying to push his way towards me again.

The rest of my family came forward now, trying to help. Abraham's few enforcers made quick work of it as no one wanted them to touch them. They guided Bay and the rest of my family through, but it put Silas on high alert. I could see Bay searching the crowds now, looking more and more alarmed. *She was searching for Abraham.*

"This is wolf business, tigers. No need to get involved."

Emma suddenly stopped crying. She narrowed her eyes in confusion and slowly turned to Cade. He glared at her, throwing his hands up angrily.

"You don't feel that?" she asked more seriously, and Cade laughed sarcastically.

"I feel plenty of things about you, but a mate bond isn't one of them, Emma! God, this is a new one for you! Are you that desperate and pathetic that you'd fake a mate bond?!"

Suddenly, one of Abraham's tiger roared loudly. It startled the crowd and all of us on stage. One of Abraham's enforcers, the one with dark spiky hair and orange eyes, pushed past Emma.

Wes.

"Don't talk to her like that!" he snarled. Bay looked panicked and bolted forward. She whispered in his ear, but he pushed his Queen away.

Cade turned to me baffled now, and I shrugged. I had no idea what was happening anymore than he did, but Emma looked frightened. Like more than the fake crap she always pulled. She was terrified, and suddenly it clicked.

"Oh my," I whispered, and Silas jerked me around.

"What did you do?!" he yelled but was drowned out by another roar.

"Apologize!"

Cade rolled his shoulders. "Nah, I don't think I want to man."

Bastian was at Cade's side in seconds, trying to calm him down, but Cade wasn't having any of it. He looked ready for a fight. The tiger visibly shook in anger and began pacing back and forth. *He was going to shift. This was going from bad to worse!* My eyes widened as Cade stepped towards him.

"You're acting like her mate, dude! Either prove it or sit down and shut up!"

The tiger's eyes went wide like he was warring within his own mind. He slowly turned to Emma, who backed away from him.

"No, no, no. This can't…"

The tiger yanked her towards him and kissed her. The crowd gasped and all started murmuring with one another at this brazen conduct. Emma sank into his embrace and wrapped her arms around his neck willingly. My eyes widened, but Silas was pissed.

"Guess her real mate wasn't a wolf at all!" Cade shouted, and the crowd started clapping and cheering. The two finally broke apart, whispering to one another and smiling wide.

"Settle down…"

I took the mic from Silas before he could stop me.

"How about a hand to our esteemed Council for bringing back the Mate Run! If the Council hadn't brought it back this year, then everyone would have missed this wonderful mating! Are we not thrilled to see a bond form because of the laws that are no longer in effect?!"

The crowd got really excited at that and cheered loudly again. I genuinely smiled and continued on before Silas could stop me.

"I think that's enough fun for one day, don't you agree? Let's end the festivities on a high note, and let the happy couple get to know one another better!"

The tiger immediately began dragging Emma away from everyone before I had even finished speaking. He wasn't wasting time, but the look on everyone's jealous face told me one thing. The packs must really be suffering. *Blending everyone was the right thing to do*, I thought to myself. Silas abruptly yanked the microphone away from me and got in my face.

"What did you do?!"

"I didn't do anything! That was fate not me. Now let my brother go, Silas!" I said it an hushed tone.

CHAPTER 4

"I don't think so, Shanely. You have made everything worse, and now he will pay the price! You better be on your best behavior for dinner tonight, and keep the non-wolves in their rooms! I don't want anymore accidental matings to happen. This goes against our better nature!"

"You so much as touch a single hair on his head, and I will…"

"You will what?! What could you possibly do to me child without your animals to rely on? Only I have the key, child. I *own* you! If I say this goes against our nature, then it goes against our nature!"

"The wolves are changing, Silas, and the law is no more. You're fighting against the core of who we are, and it's killing us!" I pushed again.

"Spend the afternoon knowing that the pain that tiger feels is all because of you!" he snarled before stomping away, leaving me feeling like the world's worst sister. My stomach twisted in knots as tears filled my eyes.

I felt my mate's familiar and normally comforting presence behind me followed by Cade and Elijah. Even without my wolf, I recognized their scents. I could feel their presence without having to look. They all waited patiently for me to turn around, but I just felt broken. *How could I face them?* I tried to wipe my eyes when I heard my mate's voice.

"We need to talk," he said firmly.

"I can't," I whispered, slowly turning around. My heart sunk as I had all three of the Fenrir boy's frustration pointed right at me.

Bastian pursed his lips together before nodding as if he understood everything. *He has no idea though.* No idea of the constant stress over everything Silas has threatened me with. No idea the pain and suffering I forced my brother to endure. No idea the threat against our baby girl. I exhaled slowly, trying to keep the tears at bay.

Bastian turned to his brothers and gave them each a look. I watched the brothers take off in opposite directions then without so much as even looking at me. *Had I really angered them so greatly that they were done with me?*

Bastian grabbed my hand firmly and forced me down the stairs. He was not letting me go either, and my mate started towards the manor behind everyone else. We passed under the archway, but instead of going through the doors, Bastian pushed me to the left abruptly. Startled, I turned to question him.

He put his finger over his mouth, and then pulled me along a small pathway that ran alongside the house. Bastian paused to look around the corner before dragging me further. We were around the far left side of the property now, and there was a large stone wall blocking our path. Long ivy hung from either end, and Bastian started feeling around in them. Suddenly, I heard a creak, and he grabbed my hand again.

"Bastian, what are we..."

He slammed his hand over my mouth, giving me a hard look. I gulped and stayed frozen until he finally let me go.

Quiet. Got it.

I kept my mouth shut as he pulled me through the ivy wall and out the other side. There was a gate beneath all the ivy, and we were in a secluded part of Summit grounds now. He followed a trail through the woods, and soon a large greenhouse came into view. Cade and Elijah were waiting there already, and the three of them pushed me inside.

It was abandoned in here as everything was broken or run down. There were no pretty flowers to look at it or anything at all for that matter. It was just dead inside, much like how I felt. Bastian spun me around, before picking me up and placing me on one of the tables. The three of them took a stance in front of me, all crossing their arms. They were not happy with me right now.

"Alright spill, Baby Girl. Right now," Cade demanded.

Chapter 5

"There are no cameras or anything in here," Bastian said, spinning his finger around the room. I looked around curiously.

"What is this place even?"

"My brothers and I found it years ago, and we've used it to escape everything when we needed to during these trips. Now spill. What is going on with you?" Bastian demanded.

"Yeah, like seriously you offered no help with Emma today!" Cade said frustratedly.

"You encouraged it!" Elijah yelled.

I sat there with my mouth open, unsure with what to do. *How do I answer them without hurting everyone else around me?* Silas had my brother somewhere, and if he found out the Fenrir brothers knew... *I have no idea what would happen to him!*

"Shanely..." Bastian said firmly, his voice warning me to answer him. I couldn't take it anymore. All the pressure, all the worry. I snapped.

"Bastian, I can't! I just can't, so *please* stop asking me!"

Tears filled my eyes as I buried my face in my hands, and the boys softened their stance.

"He's really got something over her, Bastian," Elijah said, his temper calming as my mate stepped forward. He gently lifted my chin up, and I saw love in his eyes. The anger was gone, and I felt like I could breathe a little.

"Did Silas tell you not to tell us something?"

I dropped my head in shame.

"Shanely, this spot is safe. I promise you. Silas doesn't even know it's here. They stopped using it before he even got into the job. Please just tell us," my mate pleaded with me.

I caved. I couldn't lie anymore, and I needed them. Everything I've been doing so far was only making it worse.

"He has Abraham," I whispered.

"What?!" Cade said as he and Elijah stepped closer.

"Silas threatened me during the dance. He wants to kill me because I'm a mixer, but he can't because of how everyone feels about the White Wolf. Emma told him about Aerith not being yours, and he threatened to take her and give her to the Division if I said anything to you guys or disobeyed his orders. Then he found out about Abraham being a mixer too, so he took him this afternoon."

"Oh, God. That was my fault, wasn't it? It's why you freaked out at breakfast!" Bastian said, rubbing his face. I slowly nodded.

"He's been manipulating me to look like we're on the same side, and today he admitted he took Abraham as insurance. I can't find him, Bastian! He's just gone! Silas said if I told anyone then he'd pronounce judgment because Abraham isn't anything to the wolves, and I'd never see Aerith again."

I collapsed in on myself completely overwhelmed. Bastian wrapped his arms around me tightly.

"Shanely, I wish you would have told me sooner," he whispered to me.

"I couldn't! He's been watching me like a hawk, threatening me through the link. It's like he knows everything going on at Summit Hall at all times. I was terrified he would hurt Aerith, and now Abey's gone."

"Wait, he can mind-link you even with that on?" Elijah asked, and I nodded.

"They designed these, so it lets them through but no one else. It isn't like the collars Abraham has," I answered.

"Good lord! I always knew Silas was a douche bag, but this takes the cake, don't it?" Cade asked angrily.

"He's threatened our Little One, Bastian," Elijah snarled, and Bastian's eyes flashed gold.

Bastian gripped my chin, forcing me to look in his eyes. "Shanely, we will find him I promise, and he ain't touching my child. If Silas wants a war then a war he's gonna get."

I slowly nodded before burying myself in his arms. "I'm so sorry guys. I didn't know what to do."

Cade pulled me from Bastian's arms. "It's okay, Baby Girl. We knew something was up, but we couldn't figure out what."

Elijah gave me a hug next. "Thank Cade's impeccable ears. I don't think Silas even knows how well they are. He picked up on some of your conversation the first night at the ball. We knew something was going on, but we just didn't know it was something like this."

"I've been a nervous wreck. I need to win the heart of the people, but Silas keeps getting in the way of everything and using Aerith against me. Now he has Abraham. He isn't going to pass the torch to me either. I'm going to have to take it, but I can't with this stupid thing on! I can't do anything without risking his life or Aerith's."

"Alright Bastian, how are we going to fix this?" Cade asked, crossing his arms.

"First things first, we need to discreetly let the rest of our team know, and then find Abraham. We need to take that hold over Shanely away from him. Until then we go on pretending like we don't know what's going on, and we triple up on Aerith's guards. Honestly, it would be better if we snuck her out entirely. We should send her to John's place at Abraham's."

"She'd be safe there," Cade chimed in.

"I think we need to start moving Shanely through the packs without Silas attached to her. You can't help but fall in love with her, and we need everyone to see they are not working together in this," Elijah chimed in.

"Shanely??? Where are you?"

My eyes went wide. "Silas knows I'm missing! He's trying to find me, Bastian!"

"What?"

"He's linking me right now! What do I do?!"

Panic swelled inside. *What if he figures out that I told my mate?!*

The boys all swore.

"Shall I take another visit to your brother, Shanely? We needed to have a meeting, but since I can't find you, I might have to find something else to do in the meantime. Shame, he was bloody the last time I saw him as it was."

"He's going to hurt Abraham again if he doesn't find me soon! Bastian, tell me what to do!"

His eyes were a bright gold now as he rubbed the back of his head. He started pacing back and forth, trying to figure out a plan, all while I was freaking out.

Suddenly, he stopped.

"That's it! Shanely, we fight."

"What?"

I didn't want another fight with him. I've been trying to avoid it at all cost, and now he wanted to purposely do it?

"Nothing major, my love, but enough to show we tried to get you to talk to us, and you refused. If we're all mad at you then Silas will assume you stuck to your word and didn't say anything."

"That's brilliant, Bastian," Cade said, giving me a wink.

"It won't be real then?" I asked nervously. Bastian grabbed both sides of my face.

"Not one word, my love. I love you, Shanely, and I promise I will find your brother. I'll take care of Aerith too. Now let's go before we can't sneak back in," he said before kissing me softly. I felt empty the moment his lips left mine. This was all becoming too much, and I needed him. Again, I was forced to wait.

"We need to fight somewhere secluded. We don't need everyone in the pack to know just the Council," Elijah said as we all filed out of the greenhouse.

"Just start in the halls, and we can blow up outside our rooms. Chances are our families are there, and their reaction will help sell it all," Bastian said as we went back the way we came. The boys were sure of their plan, while I hated it. *But they were right*, I thought to myself. *If Silas saw us arguing then he wouldn't question it.*

There was no one left outside now, and the boys covered our tracks well. One of the packs were clanging around in the back kitchen, preparing for

CHAPTER 5

dinner tonight, and no one paid us any mind as we went through the dining hall again.

The second we hit the halls the boy's demeanor changed. Even though it wasn't real, it still hit me like a ton of bricks.

"This is getting ridiculous, Shanely," Bastian snapped at me, and it felt like he struck me. Bastian briefly turned around to glare at me, and I had to remind myself it was just pretend, even though it felt so real.

I just dropped my head, choosing not to say anything at all. I don't think I had it in me to lie like they could. I was too heartbroken hearing Bastian use that tone with me.

"You're keeping something from us, Baby Girl," Cade said as his eyes bore into the back of my head.

"And we don't like it," Elijah replied firmly.

I groaned, feeling sick to my stomach. They guided me up the steps, and we were near our rooms now. I wasn't sure I was ready for this.

It isn't real.

It isn't real.

It isn't real.

Bastian whipped me around so fast once we reached our room, and his eyes were angry. No more than that. They were *livid* and blood red. Not gold like shifters usually show when their animal pulls through. His were red from his Alpha side. They narrowed on me, and he crossed his arms as if waiting for something. My mate finally snapped at me, when I looked confused, and I nearly jumped out of my skin.

"Well I'm waiting, Shanely."

His brothers came around to join him, and now I had all three of them directly in front of me, looking entirely pissed off.

"I told you before I'm not hiding anything," I said quietly.

"THAT'S A LIE!" Bastian bellowed, shaking the walls. Everyone's doors slammed open, and I was at the center of it all.

"What is going on here?" Cain asked, but Bastian put his hand up, stopping him from interfering more.

"Shanely..."

"White Wolf!" Luke shouted as he came into view behind me. I was startled to see him so suddenly.

"Not now, Luke," Bastian said gruffly, and Luke slowed his pace.

"I'm sorry, but she's is being summoned by the Council. I'm just here to escort her," Luke countered, giving us an apologetic look.

"I said..."

"Bastian, it's fine. I can go see what they want," I said quietly, and Bastian's eyes flashed. I know he said it wasn't real, but *good lord* he was a fantastic actor. It was scary how angry he really seemed to be.

And it broke my heart.

"We're in the middle of a conversation, Shanely! You can't just run off whenever they beckon!" he yelled again.

Cain slowly approached him now, trying to diffuse the situation. He was none the wiser, but it seriously helped sell this for us. *And it took some of the heat off me.*

"Maybe we should discuss this all at another time, Bastian. Let's give everyone a chance to cool off some," Cain suggested, and Bastian threw his hands up.

"Fine!" he yelled before bolting into Cade and Elijah's room. His brothers soon followed, and Cain gave me a sympathetic smile. I turned to follow Luke now, feeling utterly destroyed. Luke gave me a soft smile.

"I apologize, White Wolf. I didn't mean to interrupt," Luke said quietly.

I shook my head. "Please just, Shanely. I can't hear White Wolf right now."

He gave me sad look before nodding. "The Council can be demanding sometimes."

I looked curiously to Luke now as he guided me through the halls and away from my family. "You've been here awhile," I asked quietly, "haven't you Luke?"

He nodded as we walked the long hall. "About four years now. I've been working my way to the top since I was recruited by Paul. He was from my original pack before becoming one of our Councilmen."

"And how do you feel about your leadership changing, Luke?" I asked quietly.

CHAPTER 5

He noticed the drop in my voice and guided me to a corner. He put his hands up, motioning for me to stop.

"This spot doesn't have a camera nor does it have a listening device. They are for security purposes only, Shanely, but I understand why you have reservations over everything here."

"Luke, no disrespect, but you have no idea how I feel about this place or your *Councilmen*."

He gave me a look of alarm. "Shanely, I need you to hear from me that I support you as our new leader. I know there are many loyal to the Councilmen still, but I'm sure if they could just see your wolf, they'd realize where their alliances need to be."

I smiled to him gratefully. *I needed to hear this.* I needed to know that I still had some on my side at least. Suddenly, I had a thought. It was a risk, but he may be the only one I could ask.

"Luke, I need to ask you something before we go, and you cannot tell anyone. Please?"

He gave me a confused look before saying, "Of course, Shanely. What do you need?"

"I need you to swear it first," I said firmly, and now I really had his attention. *There was no going back now.*

"I swear it, Shanely. Not one word to anyone," he said, and I exhaled slowly.

"Where would the Council hide someone? Like if they *took* someone... Where would they put him that was hidden and secret from everyone else?"

Luke gave me a look of concern, but before he could answer me, we heard footsteps coming down the hall. My eyes widened, and I backed further into the shadows. I was afraid being caught hiding in the corner with Luke, and I didn't want to get him in trouble either. *Silas would find a way to punish him somehow, I just knew it!* Luke could see the panic on my face and dropped to the floor, yanking on my laces.

The voices grew louder, and Silas appeared around the corner. He looked startled by my appearance here, and then his eyes dropped down to Luke.

"There, Shanely! Now you won't trip! Shall we continue?" Luke said before turning around to see Silas and the other Councilmen watching us.

"Oh hello, Councilmen! We were just on our way to you all now. Is there a change in course, sir?"

"Yes, there is. Go, Luke. We can take care of Shanely from here on out," Silas said, waving him off.

I tried my best not to cringe at the thought of Luke leaving us now. I may never get my answer now, and I did not want to be left alone with these men again.

Luke gave me a soft smile, giving us all a bow, before heading down the way we came.

"Come child," Silas said, and I begrudgingly fell in step behind them. Luke's behavior puzzled me, but I was grateful for his quick thinking. It saved me from another massive headache I couldn't deal with.

"You disappeared for awhile, Shanely," Silas said, flipping through whatever paperwork he had with him.

"Being with my mate isn't a crime, Silas," I countered, and the other Councilmen gave me a look.

"As long as we still have an understanding?"

Silas looked at me through the corner of his eye. *The message was loud and clear.*

"Yes. My mate is angry with me as we speak. Anything else you need to know?" I asked, with a snarky tone.

"No, nothing else for the moment."

I rolled my eyes as he turned a corner. We walked down the stairs, and past the dining hall in the far back corner was a door to what looked like a conference room. I had yet to be in here before, but the terrible five knew the room well. They all went to their own chairs along the far wall, and I just stood there while they ignored me. I wasn't sure why I was even here in the first place.

"What did you need from me, Silas?"

Silas glanced up at me as if he had forgotten I was even here before putting his papers away. He leaned back in his chair to study me, and I stood there waiting as patiently as I could muster. *I wish I could link my mate*, I thought

CHAPTER 5

to myself. *I needed him desperately right now.* The fake fight just made everything feel off between us, and I wanted to fix it.

"You have cause quite an uproar today," Silas finally said.

"I didn't really do anything, Silas. I don't control mate bonds."

"You are a threat to the wolves, Shanely, and I don't quite know what to do with you yet."

I bristled at his comments. "Silas, the only one threatened by me is you."

His eyes narrowed, and he leaned forward in his seat.

"You need to be very careful, Shanely. You are not exactly in control here."

"Silas..."

He slammed his hand down on the table, shaking it violently. I jumped out of my skin not expecting his loud reaction as he bellowed.

"I WAS NOT FINISHED!"

It was all I could do not to walk away right now. I kept picturing Aerith and Abraham in my mind. They depended on me, and whether I liked it or not I was a distraction. Silas's full attention was on me and not my mate. I just hoped he could find Abraham soon.

"As I was saying, you are on thin ice. From now on, you are not allowed to speak freely to the packs. Anything you want to inform the packs must go through one of us. The White Wolf is just a formality, but you will not actually lead anything. We've decided you will merely be a public figure and nothing more."

My jaw dropped.

"Silas, I may not have grown up as a shifter, but even *I* know what the White Wolf means to us. You are trying to go against everything wolves believe in, and it's wrong! No wonder the mate bonds are nearly nonexistent!"

He scoffed. "We've had ups and downs before. You would know that, but you are nothing more than a child. You are not experienced enough to lead."

"I'm more equipped to rule our people than you will ever be!"

They all snarled at me, but I stood my ground. *If only I had my wolf,* I thought. *She'd make quick work of them.*

"Careful, Shanely. You have no power to decide anything. Now sit in the corner and be quiet until dinner."

"Are you serious? Why can't I go back to my mate?" I hollered loudly. "What's the point of me staying in here, Silas?"

"It's to help you get used to not needing him anymore. With that bracelet on, you don't have the issues with the bond pulling on you. It will make everything easier at the end of the week."

"I told you that wasn't happening. My punishment ends at the end of the week, and I'm going home!"

He smirked. "We'll see, Shanely. Now sit."

"This is stupid!"

I threw my hands up, storming out of the room. I wasn't going to waste time sitting in here with them. Silas sighed heavily.

"Paul send Ford in, please. We will be having an unscheduled visit this evening."

I skidded to a stop and slowly turned to glare at Silas. "Excuse me?"

"Shanely, this does not concern you anymore apparently. Go ahead and leave."

"DO NOT TOUCH HIM!"

Silas paused before gesturing to the floor. "Then sit."

I was furious, and it took everything in me not to pummel him right now. I slowly walked to the far corner and slid down the wall. With nothing left to do, I buried my head in my arms and just waited. I was stuck, and they knew it. Everything was out of my control, and all it did was infuriate me.

I didn't want to just sit back and wait for someone else to get me out of this situation. I wanted to find my brother myself, but I knew I had to trust my mate. Bastian said he would get this done, and I needed to be patient, which was not one of my strong suits.

I listened to the terrible five talk about fiances and this week's events, and before I knew it two hours had passed by, and I was bored out of my mind. I missed my mate and my family badly as the emptiness inside weighed on me.

An enforcer finally opened the door, letting in wolves from one of the London packs. They carried in the Councilman's food on silver trays, setting it down before them. I watched the five barely acknowledge them before

CHAPTER 5

they walked away. I was shocked. *How could they be so rude at the ones literally feeding them?!*

"Don't I get to eat, Silas?" I snapped at him, and he rolled his eyes.

"You girl, go grab her a plate," he barked at one of the servers. I made eye contact and mouthed a *thank you* to her. She gave me a soft nod before disappearing behind the door.

It didn't take long for her to come back. She had another tray, and she set it down in front of me. I grabbed her hand, halting her. I whispered to her, "Thank you."

She smiled wide before lifting the lid. She exposed the underside of the lid, where a piece of paper was taped to it. In big letters it said, *A is out. Looking for AB, but hang in there. I love you -B.*

My heart nearly burst with joy. My eyes were filled with tears, when I looked back at the young girl. She smiled wide before Silas scolded her.

"Go on, girl. Shanely has lessons to do."

She quickly scurried away, leaving me to my thoughts. *Bastian got our daughter out,* I thought excitedly. *She's no longer here where Silas can grab her. He did it!* My heart soared, and suddenly I felt renewed. Like a major weight was no longer pressing down on me. I ate my dinner in peace, and it was wonderful. I didn't know what half of it was, but I loved every bite. I wished I got the chance to be with everyone tonight though. I couldn't imagine what the packs thought about me now.

It was getting late, and they thankfully didn't try to teach me anything. I just had to sit there and do nothing. There was no way I was going to do a lifetime of this though. I'd go mad.

Finally, Luke came into the room.

"Ah, Luke there you are. Please take Shanely to her room before going to your shift."

I rolled my eyes. "I would prefer to sleep by my mate, Silas. You get to stay with yours, why can't I?"

"Because I said so. Now go," he replied, without looking up.

"I don't even have any of my things, Silas. The room is empty!" I gritted through my teeth.

"Well you figured it out today, so I'm sure you will be better prepared for tomorrow," Silas said, gathering all his paperwork. He growled, when he noticed I still hadn't moved.

"Shanely, I grow tired of repeating myself," Silas warned me, and I gritted my teeth in disgust.

"This way, Shanely," Luke said, and I stomped out of their presence. *At least I wasn't in the room with them anymore.* Luke stayed with me till we found my new room once more, but when he opened the door he pushed me inside rather roughly. I turned to yell at him, when I scented something that soothed me to my core.

Bastian.

He was there, and I ran to him.

"Bastian!"

My mate wrapped his arms around me tightly, and I felt him bury his face in my neck and hair. He inhaled deeply like he always does, and I clung to him.

"I didn't think I was going to see you tonight!"

"Nah," Cade said, startling me, "you can't keep us away, Baby Girl." He was sprawled out on the bed, grinning at me from ear to ear.

"Cade! Elijah! You guys are here too!"

I ran to hug them both, and when I hugged Cade he flipped me over him, and I landed dead center in the bed. Elijah jumped on the other side, crashing into me and causing me to giggle.

Bastian slowly climb up in the center towards me with a wicked grin over his face. He leaned over me like he was going to kiss me, when suddenly he dropped on top of me. He collapsed over me like dead weight, and good Lord, he was heavy!

I laughed hard, buried underneath my mate and smushed between his brothers. "Bastian! I can't breathe."

Bastian sat up, laughing before leaning on his side. "I've missed you, baby! This evening was awful."

"I know. I hated it, but they wouldn't let me leave," I replied as I played with my mate's hair. We were all squished together on the bed just content to be with one another again. *It just felt right.*

"What were you doing this whole time? Cade asked, leaning his head back on the headboard. "We were told the Council had begun the White Wolf's lessons."

"Nothing. They told me to sit down and not make a sound. Guys, they are *insisting* that I live here without you all. They just want me to be a figure head instead of their leader. Please..." I muttered, rubbing my temples. "Please tell me you found Abraham!"

"Well, it took me most of the evening to just get Aerith out. Your father hated to leave, but he and Henry left with Aerith before dinner. We snuck her out, so no one even knows she's gone. Daniel will make his way back once he drops her off, while Henry will stay with her at John's."

I sighed, feeling a tremendous amount of relief. *That was still something at least.*

"Thank you all for doing that and sending me the note. I needed to hear good news," I said, and Cade gave me a playful fist bump.

"Thank Sarah for being brave enough to deliver it," Cade said, and I made a mental note to find her once this was all over with.

"Now finding Abraham has proven to be a little trickier. Well that is until this guy found us," Bastian said, pointing to Luke, who waited patiently against the wall. He gave me a soft smile, shifting on his feet.

"Yeah, seems a certain someone asked a peculiar question. A question that made him worry about those still trying to control things," Elijah continued, and I gave Luke a big smile.

"Luke, did you find my brother?" I asked him, sitting up.

"I did, Shanely. I'm the Head of Security here, so I have access to everything. He's deep within the manor now in one of the cells below. I am so sorry, Shanely. I had no idea he was even taken. There are some on my team that are extremely loyal to the Councilmen and do orders without question. It doesn't all go through me."

I scurried off the bed to hug Luke. *I will forever be grateful to this wolf*, I thought to myself.

"Thank you, Luke!"

He grinned back at me. "Anything for the White Wolf. Now the reason I put you in this room is..."

Luke walked over to the wall next to the bed and pulled something behind the frame. We all heard a snap and part of the wall pushed in on itself.

"Whoa, a secret door!" Cade jumped up from the bed excitedly. He peaked his head in, and he was instantly giddy. "Dude, you can see the elevator here."

"No way," Elijah said before sticking his head in. "There are stairs here too! Where does this lead?"

"Everywhere. This wasn't a room originally. It was a maintenance room, but they renovated everything and covered up the door. This tunnel leads to anywhere in the manor. I figured your mate was going to have a hard time being away from you every night, and I thought I'd show Bastian and his brothers, so they can still get to you if you needed. For now, it can get us into the prison below."

Bastian patted Luke on the back. I had a whole new respect for this wolf, who had been preparing well in advance for us, and I slowly took a peek inside. It was dark, dusty, and full of cobwebs. *Yay.*

Bastian grabbed his phone, turning on his light.

"Lead the way, Luke," he said, and Luke took a step inside.

Chapter 6

It was extremely dark in here and difficult to get down the rickety steps. Bastian never let me go though and held his phone out for me to see. They all didn't need the light to see, but because of this stupid bracelet, I didn't have my wolf's sight. It seemed to take forever to reach the end though but soon we were at the very bottom. The stairs ended up at a T, and all I could see were halls going left, right, and forward.

"Alright, so these are the tunnels. We've posted signs on the wall for the new recruits, so they don't get lost down here. It's a maze honestly, but this staircase leads to the 5th floor, which is the Councilman's suite. There are other staircases spread throughout with different access points. Each floor has one as well as the kitchen, ballroom, and a separate exit to the greenhouse."

"No kidding? This could come in handy, Bastian," Cade commented, but I didn't like being down here in the dark any longer than I had to. *It was creepy.*

"Guys... Abraham?"

"Right," Luke said, pointing to our right. "Prison is this way on this level."

We followed him closely and quietly as other enforcers might be down here as well. I was trying hard not to think about all the possible mice living down in the tunnels. Soon, we stopped at a door, and he paused.

"Stay here. Let me check to see if the coast is clear," Luke said before leaving us alone in the dark and creepy tunnel.

Bastian pulled me in close, holding me as tightly as he could manage. I carefully climbed up on his feet, getting off the ground, and he turned the light towards us so I could see him.

"What are you doing, love?"

I grinned sheepishly. "I don't want the mice to get me."

He chuckled before hugging me again. "God, I've missed you. I'm so sorry this is our first Summit experience. I mean I knew it wasn't going to be pleasant, but I didn't expect it to be this."

I sighed. "I know. I promised Abraham it would be okay and look where he ended up! He's never going to trust me now. Abey was nervous about it as it was, and now he's trapped down here. I don't even know what they did to him! Does Bay know?"

"She does. She said she didn't pick up on anything being wrong. She didn't even realize he went missing until Emma did what she did with Cade. She tried to link him, but she's getting no response, and she can't see where he went now. It's just like their bond is muted somehow. All she knows is he's alive."

"I'm surprised she isn't down here already," I said as Elijah snorted.

"We barely got out of there as it was. There's security roaming the halls now, and Bay got caught. They walked her to her room, but I was able to link her to let her know what we were doing," Elijah chimed in, leaning against the wall.

"That must be so hard for her not to find him herself," I whispered, and no one answered me. We were all somewhat lost in thought, when Luke appeared through the door again.

"Let's go. I relieved the guard on duty, so it's just us now," he said, gesturing us inside. He quietly shut the door behind us, and we followed him down a dark corridor. It reeked of piss and God knows what else. The air just felt thick in this part of Summit Hall, and there was barely any light to see what you were doing. I looked to my right, and it was just empty cell after empty cell. There were so many here as if they were anticipating locking entire packs up at a time. I cringed, picturing them all full.

Suddenly, Luke stopped at a cell and hit a button on the wall. The light turned on full blast now and laying on the bed was Abraham. I bolted to the cell, when Luke caught me.

"Don't touch the bars! They're still online," he whispered, setting me down again.

Abraham shot to his feet with his arms raised, and he nearly collapsed in relief when he saw us.

"Oh thank God, Shanely," Abey said, and I felt horrible as I looked at him.

He had been beaten badly. His lip was busted, and he wore a black eye proudly. His ear even had dried blood coming out of it, and my heart just broke.

"Abey..."

"I'm alright, Shanely. Just get me out of here!"

Luke was already at the panel, swiping his card. The cell beeped twice before the door opened. I slammed into my brother, who winced. I pulled back nervously, and he just waved me off.

"It's just my ribs. I'll live," he said, giving me another hug.

"What happened?" I asked him, and he greeted my mate and brothers.

"I was jumped after talking with you two about the Blackwood pack. Everyone's eyes were on the Mate Run, and they put something over my mouth to silence me. I nearly shifted right then and there, but they stabbed a needle into my arm, and it was lights out for me. I woke up here," he said nonchalantly.

"I'm so sorry, Abe. It was my fault, I think. I accidentally tipped the Councilmen off about you being a mixer too. I wasn't thinking, and no one knew Silas has been threatening Shanely since he danced with her at the ball," Bastian said, and I could hear the shame in his voice.

Abey turned to me with rage in his eyes. "He threatened you?!"

I nodded. "At first it was with Aerith, but then he took you, and he's been using you as a way to keep me in line ever since. He's trying to separate me from everyone, Abey."

"Look not to ruin this moment or anything, but we need to hide the big guy," Luke said before looking down the hall once more.

"Come, let's get you out of here and find a way to get Bay," I said, dragging Abraham along with me.

"Did they take her too?"

The anxiety in his voice nearly broke me.

"No, but they have her somewhat locked in your room. Everyone's on lock down for the night," Bastian said as Luke led us back to the tunnels. He smacked part of the stone wall, and the door flew open. *Agh. Here we go again,* I thought anxiously to myself.

"So, where *are* we taking the big guy?" Elijah asked teasingly, and Abraham shoved him forward, making him laugh.

"Well, the first place Silas will look will be Shanely's room, then Bay's, and lastly Bastian's. So why not take him to my room?" Luke offered.

"You'd seriously hide him for me?" I asked, completely stunned again.

"Of course. No one will think to check there, and I don't bunk with anyone."

"Thank you, Luke. You are an amazing friend, you know that?" I said, and I barely saw a smile appear on his face in the light. We came back to the T spot, where the stairs to my room went.

"Okay, so this is where we split. My room is straight, left, and then up the stairs marked floor 1. It leads out into the main hall, but it's out of sight from the cameras. We can make it to my room from there. It's real close," Luke said to all of us.

"So what do I do in the meantime?" Abey asked.

"Stay out of sight, and I'll get Bay to you at some point," Bastian said, but Luke interrupted.

"Look, I know you want to see your mate, but they will be watching her like a hawk once Silas knows he's missing. It's too risky in my opinion. We need to get through Shanely's punishment, so she can shift into her wolf. Once everyone sees her wolf, they won't be able to ignore her. It's something deep within us that just knows to follow her direction. She needs to overthrow the Council first, and that can't happen until that bracelet comes off," Luke said.

"Crap. He's right, Bastian. We can't act like we know anything, and neither can she or they could just follow Bay right to him again. They won't hide him next time," Elijah said, and I fell against my mate. I was exhausted and hating every minute down here. *Or in this place altogether for that matter.*

"It's why they chose *this* punishment. It was only meant to isolate her from everyone and keep her from showing her wolf," Luke said before dropping his head. "They don't want it appearing."

CHAPTER 6

"Did you know beforehand, Luke?" I asked quietly.

"No, but I overheard Silas talking before coming to start the Mate Run. I just assumed it was because of the punishment, but I can see it's so much more. I am sorry, Shanely."

"What's done is done. Can you get a key to take the bracelet off yourself?" Bastian asked firmly.

"I can try, but usually one of the Councilmen keeps the key on hand, and you can bet which one has it this time," Luke replied, and I could feel the anger in the room again.

"Silas," Cade spat out, and Luke nodded.

"However, they told me that they want Shanely to participate in the Hunt this year. Maybe I can convince Silas to change out her bracelet for the ones we use to simply mute the bond. Then I'd have the key for it, and can meet you in the woods with it."

"Wait, the Council has more than one kind of bracelet?" I asked.

"We usually use a bracelet that just mutes the bonds and connections we have. It leaves the wolf, but what you have is much worse. It keeps everything from appearing because it mutes your animal entirely. The Council had it created a few years ago. There was talk spreading that other shifters had figured out how to silence the animal side, so they needed to have it as well."

I snorted. "Let me guess the Denmark pack supplies the Council with the bracelets and drugs, am I right?"

Luke gave me a puzzling look. "How did you know that?"

Bastian suddenly snarled. "Derek!"

All the boys were pissed, and poor Luke look so confused.

"Derek drugged me a few years ago with something that took away my animals, and my ability to use the link. He kidnapped me, and then tried to kill me. It's why we have a bounty on his head," I explained, and he looked shocked.

"We never heard about a bounty, Shanely," he said quietly.

Cade grabbed Luke by his shirt then. "What do you mean you never heard about the bounty?"

Luke pulled back, straightening himself out. "I mean us enforcers, the ones sent to execute judgment, didn't know! We were never informed of that. Because I can guarantee you that we would have went after him if we did!"

"I don't understand. Cain spoke to the Council directly," I said baffled now.

"Unless Derek and my father made a deal with the Council in exchange for their silence. It was Derek's drug, so he gets to live, the Council gets their bracelets, and my father gets rich. It's a win-win for everyone but us," Bastian spat out as Cade and Elijah looked ready to shift, they were so angry.

We stayed silent for a moment longer before Abey finally spoke up.

"Look, none of this is getting fixed tonight. Luke, can you get the key to one of those mate bracelets tonight?"

Luke gave him a look. "Yeah, I can. Why?"

Abraham lifted his arm and pulled back his shirt. He wore a thin, silver bracelet similar to mine.

"Good Lord. Okay. I'll get him back and take that off, so he can speak to Bay. You all stay out of sight and make sure you aren't in her room come morning! I'd expect a full wake up call first thing from Silas, Shanely. I'll work at getting the bracelets switched somehow so I can free you during the Hunt. Sound like a plan?" Luke asked everyone, and we all nodded.

I gave Abraham one last hug. "Stay safe, brother."

"You too. Kick some a..."

"Abe c'mon!" Luke said already halfway down the hall. Abey winked at me before following our new found friend.

"C'mon, Baby Girl. Let's get you to bed!" Cade said, giving me a nudge. I was all for getting out of these awful tunnels. If I thought the climb down was bad, the climb back up to my room was worse. Way, way worse. I was huffing and puffing by the time we made it to the top. Elijah laughed as I collapsed on the bed, my legs pulsing.

"Aww poor, Shanely!" he said, sitting next to me.

"Yes, poor me! The one who had to climb all those stairs without the help of her animals!"

"Shh! Someone's coming!" Cade said, and we all froze.

CHAPTER 6

I ran to the door, peeking through the little peephole, trying to figure out if they were coming here or not. It was two of the quieter councilmen, and they were discussing the game of golf they just watched. They made their way past my room, and I waited awhile after they disappeared before relaxing.

"Gotta love those ears, Cade," I muttered completely spent from the day. I grabbed a spare blanket and pillow from the closet, unfolding it nicely. I gave Elijah an odd look when he reached for it.

"What are you doing?" I asked, ready to fall asleep where I stood if I had to.

"Going to bed, silly. Here let me have the blanket," he asked, reaching for it again.

I pulled away. "Oh no, this is mine. Yours is over there."

I collapsed on the couch, covering myself entirely in the blanket. My whole body was crashing hard, and I just wanted to close my eyes.

"Babe, you're not sleeping on the couch," Bastian said, stalking over to me.

It didn't matter that I was dead to the world exhausted. I wasn't about to put one of my boys on the floor or the couch like this. Not after everything they've done to protect me and our family.

"You all need more rest than I do. Please after everything... it's the least I can do."

"Shanely, I'll take the couch. Cade and I just want to be here for extra protection just in case, but we're not taking your bed."

I just mumbled, too tired to continue this conversation. I could hear Bastian chuckle softly before I passed out.

* * *

I awoke sometime later completely overheated. I stirred slightly and ran right into a body. My eyes shot open, and only once they adjusted to the dark did I see my mate. I was in bed with him all snuggled up and pressed against his chest. I carefully rolled over to my other side, but his arm stayed glued to my waist. There was no moving away from him.

When I turned, I saw Cade snoring away. He was sprawled out, taking up nearly half the bed himself, making me chuckle. His mouth was wide open, and I seriously debated messing with him then. I smiled, deciding to just leave him be to sleep. My poor Elijah was on the couch with his arm covering his head. My boys were completely passed out, and I smiled again, thinking how lucky I was to have them in my life. I threw a leg out of the blanket for some relief and fell back asleep.

Chapter 7

I awoke to pounding on my door. I groaned, not wanting to get out of bed, until last night replayed in my mind and fear gripped my heart. I shot out of bed, ready to wake up the boys, when my door burst open. I panicked until I saw I was alone in my room. The secret door was shut, and my boys were gone.

"What did you do?!" Silas bellowed, with two enforcers right on his heels.

I rubbed my eyes and answered, "What are you talking about, Silas? It's..."

I looked over at the clock on the nightstand, and it said 7 am. *7 freaking am!*

"Agh, Silas. It's only 7! What is wrong with you?"

Silas was visibly shaking now and looked ready to shift. He stomped over and angrily yanked me out of bed. Now I was fully awake as he slammed me up against the wall hard. My head rebounded off the wall, giving me an instant headache. Silas's grip on my arm was so tight I could feel it begin to bruise, and I clawed at his hand.

"Silas! Let me go!"

"I don't know what game you think you're playing at, but I would think very long and hard about the consequences of your actions, young lady!"

Silas knew about Abraham, but I wasn't about to tell him anything. Playing dumb, I replied, "I already know! You'll hurt my brother or daughter, but I haven't done anything! I swear!"

Silas's eyes narrowed as he studied me carefully. He finally dropped me, turning back to the two men standing there. He shouted, "Is she *lying*?"

"No, sir. We stayed outside her door last night, and no one came in or out," the one on the left said.

I didn't know I had guards out there last night, I thought to myself. Either these two were in on Luke's plan or I needed to make a mental note of that just in case.

Silas snarled, turning back to me. He looked like he wanted to throttle me some more, but instead he just stomped away. I sat back on the bed to inspect my arm. I shook ever so slightly, feeling jittery over the whole ordeal, and the guard startled me.

"Are you alright, ma'am?"

I turned to see them both staring at me with concerned looks on their faces. I nodded, choosing to go back at my arm instead of dealing with them. I didn't know if I could trust them or not, and I couldn't risk it. There was too much at stake right now. My arm was a nasty shade of black and blue already. *Bastian was going to be pissed when he saw.*

"Luke asked us to let you know that he is detained for the morning, but not to worry. We will be escorting you to breakfast instead."

My heart stopped. *Luke was detained? Did that mean he got caught?* I wondered but mentally shook that scary thought from my mind. *That can't be it, otherwise Silas's response would have been far different.* Speaking to these two was now worth the risk, and I tried to casually get more information.

"Why is he being detained? Is something wrong?"

"Nothing for you to worry about. We'll wait outside, ma'am."

They left me to my anxious thoughts as I was now terrified for my friend. I didn't stop last night to think that Luke would be the first wolf they went after to figure out what happened. I knew Silas would come after me, but Luke was the wolf that relieved the guard last night. He just risked his life by helping us, and I couldn't help but feel sick to my stomach over it.

A thousand different questions ran through my mind. *If Luke was caught, did that mean Abraham got caught as well? No,* I thought anxiously. *Silas wouldn't have freaked out if he still had Abraham. And Luke sent these two enforcers to me, so does that mean they are on our side? Or are they entirely clueless and just members of the enforcer team?*

I groaned, realizing I wasn't going to get any answers by sitting here, so I

CHAPTER 7

quickly jumped into the shower. The hot water felt amazing, and I hated to step out and face the world again. I quickly dried myself off, when I realized I had no clean clothes. Nothing was brought here for me, and all I had left was my dirty tunnel clothes from yesterday. I groaned, wrapping myself in the towel, which thankfully came past my butt further than the robes did.

I went to the door, opening it slightly, and said, "Umm... I have no clothes, fellas."

The wolves turned to me before their faces turned beat red, and they dropped their gaze. *At least they were smart wolves,* I thought to myself. The one that spoke to me earlier stammered, "I'm so sorry, White Wolf. I can grab you new stuff."

"That would be much appreciated," I said as another voice boomed through the halls.

"Is she ready yet?!" Silas yelled at the two guards before seeing me, standing at the door in a towel and wet hair. He seemed annoyed I wasn't ready and waiting for him.

"Clearly not. I have no clothes, Silas, since you switched my room," I said sarcastically. He was not in the mood.

"Well, go get them then," he snapped back, and I gave him a look.

"Silas, I'm in a towel. Can I please just call my mate to bring me something?"

Silas narrowed his eyes before smiling wickedly. Whatever thought he just had, I knew I was going to hate. Hair stood on the back of my neck as he replied, "No. If you want new clothes so badly then go get them yourself."

"I'm not walking in front of all the packs in nothing but a towel, Silas. It's not appropriate nor would my mate appreciate it," I snapped.

"I can go get her stuff, sir," the other wolf offered as he stepped to the elevator. Silas snarled at him, and the wolf ground to a halt.

I rolled my eyes. I'm done dealing with him, and I was tired of standing here in a towel with them.

"This is stupid, Silas. I'll just put my old clothes on and go to the other room before breakfast," I replied and started to close the door, when Silas blocked it with his foot. He grabbed my wrist hard as his eyes glowed, and he yanked me towards him.

Silas whispered in my ear, "I don't know how you pulled it off, but call this a punishment for you and your mate. Let's watch him snap when he sees you like this. Let him shift in front of everyone, so I can throw him in the cell instead of your brother. We'll see how quickly you change your tune, when it's your mate stuck behind bars."

My eyes went wide as he threw me into the hall, slamming the door shut behind him. One of the wolves caught me, quickly looking away as I fixed the towel and righted myself.

"Escort her if you want or not, I don't care. Shanely, I will see you outside for the event in one hour," Silas said, storming off down the hall.

"SILAS!" I shouted, but he stepped into the elevator and was out of sight. I ran to the door, but it was locked. *This was not happening*, I thought anxiously to myself. I turned to the other two, who looked as panicked as I felt.

"Please tell me you have the key?"

"We don't, Shanely. We aren't allowed to have the master key to the rooms," the wolf replied, and I groaned.

"Can you link Luke?"

"Hang on," he replied, and I watched his eyes gloss over. We waited for awhile before he shook his head.

"I'm sorry, ma'am. He isn't answering."

"What's your name?" I asked, groaning.

"Kyle ma'am, and this is Uriah."

"Well boys... might as well be on a first name basis, dont'cha think? Can you please help get me in my mate's room without being seen?"

"We will do our best, White Wolf. We have to go to the 2nd floor and across the balcony to reach the side where your mate is staying. I'm not sure if the packs have arrived this morning already though," Kyle replied, and I gestured to the elevator.

"Well let's hurry then," I said, trying to cover as much of myself as I could. I clutched the towel so tightly my knuckles were white. We made it to the second floor no problem, but that's about when everything went to crap. I stepped out to a large crowd on the balcony and many more coming in the

CHAPTER 7

main doors below. Everyone turned, gasping when they saw me.

"Kyle, what in the world!?" I whispered, hiding behind them.

"I don't know, Shanely! Let's just move through quickly," he replied, motioning for Uriah to start clearing a path.

"Everyone move please!" Uriah's deep voice boomed into the hall.

I followed Kyle's feet, turning multiple shades of red as we pushed our way through. I could hear everyone's whispers as I passed by. They were horrified their White Wolf was wearing so little in front of everyone, while I could feel some of the male's eyes linger on my body. I clung to my towel and pressed firmly against Kyle's back. He had the decency to try to cover as much of me as he could, but it was still horrifying. Suddenly, I heard a very familiar snarl.

"EVERYONE CLEAR OUT NOW!" Bastian bellowed as he pushed his way towards me. His Alpha power hit the lot of them, and they scattered. He wrapped his arms around me, and boy was he pissed.

"Don't shift. Please don't shift!" I whispered to Bastian, and his eyes glowed gold. Cade was immediately at my other side, with Elijah behind me. The three shielded me with their bodies, making sure no one saw anything they shouldn't.

"What in the world are you doing, Baby Girl?!"

"Please just get me to the room. This is humiliating as it is," I whispered near tears, and the brothers moved faster now that most had wisely left.

My entire family stood in the halls, giving me weird looks, and I groaned. One snarl from Bastian, and all the fellas dropped their eyes to the floor. My mate opened our door, pushing me inside first. Kyle started to back away, apologizing again to us both, but Bastian grabbed him by the back of his collar and shoved him in the room with us.

"Go Shanely, into the bathroom. I'll grab your stuff," Cade said, and I took off. He didn't need to tell me twice. I could hear Bastian slam Kyle up against the wall through the bathroom door. He was not happy.

"Care to explain why my wife, *your White Wolf*, is walking around in nothing but a towel?!" Bastian bellowed, and I could hear Kyle stammering now.

"It wasn't me, sir! I swear! I'm just trying to help her..."

"THEN WHO WAS IT?!"

"Silas, babe," I shouted through the door. Cade opened it barely, handing me fresh clothes, and I shut the door again. I dressed as quickly as I could managed before making my way out.

Bastian still had Kyle in a death grip, but he turned to me for answers. "What happened?!"

"I took a shower this morning, when I realized I had nothing clean to wear. I asked Kyle to grab me something to wear from you, when Silas appeared. He was angry, Bastian..." I replied as I eyed Kyle briefly, unsure how to finish my sentence.

"He's angry because Abraham's missing from his cell!" Kyle said in a hushed voice. Bastian lifted him off the ground now, and he turned pale.

"What do you know about that, wolf?!"

"Luke sent me, sir! He's being detained and couldn't escort Shanely or help her with Silas's wrath, so he sent Uriah and I to take care of her. You can trust us, I swear!"

Bastian looked back to me, and I nodded. "He was livid, Bastian, and this was a punishment. Silas threw me out of my room, and it locked behind me. He was hoping it would be enough to make you snap and shift in Summit Hall, so he could throw you in the cell instead."

"Whoa, Bastian look here," Elijah said as he zeroed in on my arm.

"It's a handprint," Cade said snarling, and Bastian finally dropped poor Kyle.

My mate inspected my arm, and I could see he was fighting the shift badly now. I leaned forward, giving him a kiss. Anything to help him. His face softened as he rested his head on mine.

"It's fine, Bastian. My arm will heal, and my embarrassment will die," I said quietly, trying to reassure him. He pulled me into a firm hug, and I gently rubbed his back.

"Nearly the entire wolf population just saw you in nothing but a towel. Silas nearly got his wish today," Bastian whispered. I pulled away, kissing him again.

"But you didn't. You have incredible self control, Mr. Fenrir," I replied, smirking at him. He grunted before turning to Kyle. My mate stared hard at him, and I could see he was still struggling with his wrath. The wolf wisely stared at the floor, waiting for my mate to release him. I believed Kyle after everything he just did for me.

"I promise you, Bastian. Kyle and Uriah were complete gentlemen the whole time. They both tried very hard to keep me covered and out of sight all without looking at me," I said with a chuckle.

Kyle rubbed the back of his head nervously, and my mate walked towards the young wolf again. Kyle tensed, I'm sure bracing to be thrown up against the wall again, but Bastian simply extended his hand.

"Thank you for trying to protect my mate and for adverting your eyes. I'll tell Luke what you did for Shanely as well. Your boss will be proud. Now go ahead and report back. I'll escort my wife from here," he said in his Alpha tone. I melted right there. I missed my mate so badly, and I loved it when he used his bossy Alpha voice. Kyle quickly shook his hand and left us alone.

"This is seriously getting ridiculous, Bastian. We need to get that bracelet off Baby Girl now, so we can end this. Dad will be here today as well," Cade said, leaning against the wall.

Bastian snarled at that thought, stomping back over to me. He took my hand, inspecting my arm once more before answering his brother. "I know, but I'm still waiting on Luke. He's been detained all morning."

"Let's just try to reach out to the packs at breakfast. We at least have Shanely with us today," Elijah said before turning me slightly, "Here."

He ripped the sleeve off of my T-shirt before doing the same to the other side.

"What are you doing, Elijah?" Bastian asked.

"I'm letting the packs know that Shanely isn't being treated well here. It won't be safe for her to stay at the end of the week with those hurting her," Elijah replied, tossing the sleeves in the trash. I kissed his cheek.

"You are brilliant, Elijah."

He smirked, giving his brothers a knowing look. "Oh, I know. It's just nice to hear it out loud sometimes."

I laughed, and Bastian hit him. Elijah pushed him back playfully, and it was good to see the brothers act like old times. I let the boys lead me to the hallway where the rest of my family waited for us. I gave everyone hugs even though I was still embarrassed. I hug Bay longer though, and I could see her stress and worry.

"He's okay," I whispered ever so cautiously into her ear. She sighed but said nothing further to me about it.

We all walked somewhat in silence towards the dining hall. Everyone grew quiet the minute I walked in the room. I gave everyone a sheepish smile as my mate pulled me along to the breakfast line. Honestly, I wasn't that hungry, but Bastian loaded my plate for me anyways and set me down at a corner table with our family.

I waved to Garrett and Eliana as they passed by us. I waved at anyone, who looked my way for that matter. Most didn't want to make eye contact with me after this morning though. I sighed. This was humiliating, and I pushed my plate aside, resting my head on the table.

"Can the earth just swallow me up whole? Just put me out of my misery, please," I muttered as Bastian rubbed my back.

"Heads up," Elijah said quietly, and I looked at what new dilemma was coming my way.

Emma entered the dining hall. with her new tiger mate right behind her, and they immediately sought me out. I sunk in my seat until our eyes met.

For the first time in my life, she didn't look at me with hate. She skipped the line entirely, making her way to me instead. My boys were rigid, and she could clearly see she was not welcome. First thing I noticed though was her scent had changed. *Blackwood had dropped her from the pack*, I thought to myself. *Emma was a rogue now and was only here because of Wes.*

"Shanely? Can I sit for just a moment?" she asked in such a quiet voice that I almost couldn't hear her. I debated letting her but finally caved, motioning to the seat across from me.

Cade immediately shot up as she sat down next to him, making his way to stand behind me.

She looked sad as he moved away, but she gave him a small nod in understanding. Her mate sat down next to her instead, and I could see he

CHAPTER 7

was still his normal, grumpy self.

"Hello, Wes," I said, greeting him.

"Hi, Miss Shanely."

"So what do you need, Emma?" I asked, leaning back in my chair. My arms crossed my chest, and I waited to see what she could possibly have to even say to me.

"Look Shanely, you have every right to hate me right now, but I wanted to say I'm sorry for everything. I was hurt and envious of you, and it made me a very bitter person. I know this doesn't make up for what I've done, but I *am* sorry."

It was surprising hearing Emma actually apologize for something. *A first really.* But it still wasn't enough though because she hurt my child and put her at risk yet again. I wasn't sure how to handle her honestly, and I wish I had my wolf to rely on. Sadly, I was stuck with just me.

"You know you hurt a child, Emma? Not just Bastian and I, but you hurt Aerith and put a target on her back with that little stunt you pulled on Cade," I said rather gruffly.

She winced as her mate looked at her hard. *He was not happy with her either it seems,* I thought to myself.

"I know, and I'm sorry. When Wes and I mated, I finally felt the love and warmth I had never received as a child. It's no excuse, but it's what fueled everything. My dad was always so upset with me when I didn't mate with Bastian, and then when you came along and started changing the McCoy pack, he blamed me even more. I always felt so inferior to you, and I jumped at the chance of their offer of a mate bond. It was very wrong, and I really hope one day you can forgive me," she said, and I motioned for Octavia to come closer.

"You heard everything?" I asked her, my eyes never leaving Emma.

"Every word, Cuz. She's being honest and no bad intentions," Octavia replied, digging back into her plate.

I slowly nodded my head, processing everything she had said. I looked to my mate now, who didn't look so convinced.

"Which one of you made the decision to apologize?" Bastian asked, and

Wes leaned forward.

"I knew what happened with Emma prior to all this, but I discovered the rest after the bond formed. My streak is loyal to you and Abraham. Emma wanted to right the wrong, and I insisted she apologize the next time we saw Shanely. We needed to fix this *immediately*, but you've been gone for awhile," Wes answered.

"I can scent the rogue smell coming from you. I'm surprised you haven't been escorted from the Hall yet," I said to Emma.

She looked back down at the table. "Blackwood dumped me when I refused to reject my mate. I'm allowed to stay because of Wes."

"And you plan to live with Wes?" Bastian asked, and she nodded.

"I may not belong to a pack, but I figured it didn't matter. I have him, and that's all I need," she replied, squeezing his hand tightly.

"Wes," I said, pulling his attention away from Emma. "Abraham is tied up at the moment, but you are required to talk to Bay before you bring Emma to their lands. I understand you are in a tough spot, but Emma has done some horrible things to multiple people. She may have to be on some restrictions if she is to live there until she can prove that she won't repeat those mistakes again," I said, giving him a firm look.

You could see the struggling with wanting to defend his mate but understanding that they were both in a bad spot because of her actions. He slowly nodded before starting to stand up. I held my hand, halting them both.

"I apologize for this because I am not normally a cruel person, but my hands are tied with the Council. Emma, if you truly are sorry then you will publicly admit your wrong doing to the entire pack," I said, and her eyes went wide.

"Shanely, I don't want to humiliate her," Wes said firmly, and Bastian stood up.

"It's her cross to bear, Wes," Bastian said firmly as he started to address the entire pack here in the dining room. I stopped my mate from speaking.

"Not here. Later when the Council is present too. You better stay close to our family Emma for the rest of the Summit. You're a rogue now, and there is only so much I can do *until* I take over. If your answers are anything

CHAPTER 7

but truthful, then I'll make sure you are never allowed to join another pack again, and you can guarantee Bay will not allow you on streak lands either. Do we understand one another?"

She nodded solemnly, but Wes was livid. *I liked Wes*, I thought to myself, but there was nothing more I could do for him right now. I watched Emma surprisingly try to calm him. Emma agreed with our demands and would follow along, accepting the consequences of her actions.

"It's the only way you and I can have a life together, Wes. These are my consequences, and I can take it. I promise you, Shanely. I'll prove to you and everyone else that I can be a different person."

"Thank you for your apology," I said softly, and she gave me a smile.

"I am sorry to you guys as well," she whispered before they left us alone. Cade whistled.

"Well, that was unexpected," he said, helping me to my feet. The horn blared, letting us all know it was time to head outside.

"Seems like Wes ended up being the best thing for her," Bastian chimed in.

"I think it gave her what she desperately needed. She's no longer trying to get in your pants, babe," I said, winking at him. Bastian smirked, smacking my backside.

"Cheeky mate," he whispered, and we followed the large crowd outside. It was beautiful out today, and I realized how much I missed my wolf.

"I need a run," I said quietly, and I saw my mate give me a sad smile.

"Not much longer, love. You're halfway done with the week, but hopefully Luke has some ideas to swap out the bracelets today."

I nodded softly, and we tried to interact with as many packs as possible. I listened to many Alphas vent their stress and worries to me over the mate bonds not appearing or adjusting to other shifters being around. We tried to help everyone the best we could, and while some seemed genuinely relieved, others just had a hard time believing we could fix anything at all. Suddenly, a loud buzzer sounded through out the yard, and Bastian gave his brothers a confused look.

"What's that one mean?" I asked. I hadn't heard this one before.

"The Council has finally graced us with their presence. The event is starting up," Bastian replied, his eyes roaming the yard before us.

"I thought the Hunt was happening later this evening?" Cade asked as Bastian nodded.

"Seems like they're changing things again," Elijah said as my boys surrounded me. We slowly made our way closer to the large crowd forming at the stage when I stopped. *I couldn't face them right now*, I thought as my the anxiety in my stomach rolled. *I couldn't stand to see Silas again.* I was so overwhelmed as it was... I just couldn't handle it. Every time Silas was around, he separated me from my mate, and I wasn't ready to let him go today. I *needed* Bastian.

Bastian felt me pull back and slowed to a stop with me. His face soften, seeing my internal conflict. He motioned to his brothers. "Go ahead, and see if Cain knows anything. I'll hang back with her."

They nodded, giving me a moment alone with my mate.

"I don't know how much more I can handle, Bastian," I muttered, and his face softened. He pulled me under the shady spot of the large oak tree.

"I know my love, but if Luke has managed to get us a way to swap that bracelet for the other, then we might able to finish what we started today instead of the end of the week. You can do this, Shanely. You were chosen to lead, and I know you can handle anything they throw at you."

I leaned into his embrace. "It bothers me so much that this is how the Council behaves. I don't even understand how they managed to get into power like this in the first place. And to just sit back and watch our people suffer like this? It's just unbearable, Bastian."

Bastian pulled back, gripping my chin. He forced me to look in his eyes before answering, "It's because you're the White Wolf. You've found your wolf, Shanely, and ever since you agreed to try to be *her*, you have just taken over and known what to do. You didn't even talk to me or your uncle about the Blackwood pack. You just went there and handled it all by yourself. You were meant for this. It's why the hypocrisy and lies bother you so much. Because these are your people, Shanely. You are changing, baby. And it's amazing to be here to watch it all."

CHAPTER 7

I stood on my tiptoes to kiss him. *This man was truly amazing, and he always knew what to say to pick me up when I was down.* I deepened the kiss, feeling greedy. I felt like I haven't really kissed him since we got here, and boy was it long over due. It seemed Bastian felt the same way because his grip around my waist tighten, and I felt him slowly back me up against the tree. I was in heaven, missing my mate like crazy. There was no one around but the two of us, and I was thrilled. I needed him, and he needed me.

A highly irritating voice came over the speakers, interrupting the two if us. My little piece of heaven came crashing down around me then.

"Don't you think that's a little inappropriate to be kissing our White Wolf like that?"

We broke apart to see Silas looking at us with disgust. The crowd parted enough that I could see the rest of the council members up on their make-shift stage, and everyone stared at us. It was humiliating to say the least. I glared at Silas, but Bastian stepped around to cover me.

"Seeing how she is my mate," Bastian growled, "no, I do not."

Silas snorted in response. "That is *if* she's your true mate."

"Excuse me?" Bastian asked gruffly. He stalked towards the stage, with me running to catch up. *What is the world were they up to?* I thought to myself. Silas pulled the microphone closer so everyone could hear.

"I said *if* she really is your mate. Besides young man, she is our White Wolf, which means we come first. If you really are bonded to one another, then you need to understand that fact and always step aside when required," Silas said as cocky as ever. Everyone started whispering, and I felt Cade and Elijah's presence move behind us again.

"Shanely is my mate! We share a bond, and it's strong! She wears my mark just as I have hers, and we already share abilities. Not like it's *any* of your business, Councilmen," Bastian snapped back angrily. He clenched his fists together, and I stepped behind him slightly. Anything to hide away from their prying eyes.

"Well, I'm sure you won't mind proving it then? We've changed the Hunt this year to test out if you two are really bonded. Who knows maybe the White Wolf's true mate is among us? Maybe her real mate is Xavier? Then it would make sense why our wolves feel so strongly about her staying here with us."

Bastian practically roared. The packs scattered away as he barred his teeth, gripping my hand tightly. Cain moved through the crowd quickly, while I just stood there baffled. *Like seriously?* I thought to myself. *This was their grand plan?* Trying to say Xavier was my mate was just plain ridiculous. They were seriously grasping at straws now, but a thought made me shudder. *They wouldn't say this unless they felt confident they could prove it. The question now was how? How were they going to spin this lie?*

"You will not touch my mate!" Bastian shouted as Cade and Elijah encircled me. I was pressed firmly against Bastian's back by his brothers. They each had a hand on my shoulder, glaring ahead to Silas and the rest of the sleazy old men.

"Are you seriously trying to force Shanely to mate with Xavier? He's twice her age!" Cain shouted.

"Oh, of course not! You all with your tempers, blowing everything out of proportion. See this is what I mean folks! The White Wolf belongs to everyone! She belongs to the entire world of wolf shifters, and the McCoy pack seems dead set on hogging her. I merely suggested that maybe her true mate is here and isn't actually Bastian. It would be unfair to everyone if we didn't make sure Shanely wasn't told a lie and had a mating forced upon. I mean there's the whole incident this morning with her running around in nothing but a towel. Seems like she would have more respect for her mate than to do something like that, so maybe the bond isn't really there for her," Silas continued smugly.

I shot around Bastian. "It was your fault that I had to walk the grounds with just a towel on, Silas!"

The crowd started up again all talking at once, when Silas bellowed loudly in the microphone.

"I did no such thing! I was with my enforcers this morning, handling a security issue. I am very disappointed in you both. Your reactions only prove that you are ill equipped to rule our people. You can't even keep a level head!"

"You know very well why he's reacting this way, Silas. All mates behave

CHAPTER 7

this way, but it's even more for him because she is the White Wolf! Their bond is unlike any other, plus you know how simple it is for the mate bond to connect for wolves. Your ridiculous plan is full of holes, Silas," Cain countered, crossing his arms angrily.

"If their bond is so strong then prove it in our game. Only Shanely will go out in the woods today. All eligible single men, and of course Bastian, will enter the course. The first one to find her must really be her true mate then."

I opened my mouth to chew Silas out further, when Bastian clamped his hand over my mouth to silence me.

"Done. I'll play your stupid game, Silas!" he bellowed.

Silas smiled at the two of us before turning to the crowd. "Everyone take an hour for lunch, while the course gets set up! We'll have the Hunt right after!"

The packs split in different directions then, all giving me looks as they went, and my whole family came to encircle us. I was freaking out.

"Bastian, why would you agree to this?! You know he has something up his sleeve because we freed Abraham," I cried out in a huff.

A thousand worst case scenarios ran through my mind as I began to pace back and forth, but he gripped my chin, halting my freak out. I looked up in his eyes, seeing nothing but confidence and warmth.

"Shanely, if I didn't then I'm afraid of what everyone would think. You are *my* Fated Mate. I can feel your heart beating in my chest. I'm confident that I'll find you first, besides Luke mentioned trying to get you out of that bracelet during the Hunt. We were playing regardless, baby."

"Bastian, I've never even played this game before. What if we just walked in a trap? You know Silas is going to go after you, so Xavier can find me first!"

"No one is ever going to take you away from me. Okay, baby? I will fight them all if I have to, but you are *mine*," my mate said firmly. I just couldn't shake this awful feeling thought. Deep down something was wrong.

"You got this, Bastian," Elijah said, slapping his back.

I groaned as his brothers gave me the same pointed look as Bastian had. *Silas was going to hurt Bastian*, I thought to myself. *I just knew it.* The boys seemed determined to play though. Even if I thought it was a trap.

"No one runs any interference. If they suspect cheating, it will look just as bad. Promise me, okay?" Bastian asked, looking at his brothers. They were frustrated but both nodded at the command. I just rolled my eyes. *This wasn't right*, I thought to myself.

Luke finally graced us with his presence, and my eyes widened when I saw him. *He looked rough*, I thought to myself.

"Cade, Elijah, Bastian, Ryder. You all will be participating in the Hunt event. This is for wolves only," Luke said in a formal tone, looking only at Caleb. "Give me your arms."

"I didn't want to play anyways," Caleb muttered, and I stuck my tongue out at him.

The boys obeyed, and Luke shot something in each of their arms. My eyes went wide.

"It's just the tracker. It comes out after the game," Bastian answered softly.

Luke turned to me. "Your turn."

I pulled my arm away. *No thank you*, I thought to myself, but Bastian looked at me with a pleading expression and gently took my hands in his. He gave me a soft smile saying, "It's just a pinch. I promise."

Luke shot the tracker into my arm, while I was distracted with my mate. I shrieked, ripping my hand back. *Just a pinch, my butt!*

"Good Lord, that hurts!"

Luke gave me a soft smile. "I'm sorry. Rules are rules."

He glanced around briefly before looking to Bastian. He muttered quietly, "I'm sorry it took me so long. You all are right. They aren't playing fair here, so just stay on your toes boys. They are watching me like a hawk right now, so I wasn't able to find out anything more. I'm sorry."

"Are you okay, Luke?" I asked, and he nodded.

"I'll be fine, Shanely. Nothing that won't heal, I promise you," he said, and my heart hurt. "Now listen closely. Silas informed me that Shanely is to receive the mate bracelet today. He is removing the inhibitor himself."

"What? Why would he do that voluntarily?" Cade asked confused. "Why

CHAPTER 7

would Silas come up with this idea *himself?*"

Luke's eyes glossed over before he snapped back to us. "I don't know. He wouldn't tell me anything more except to bring it down today. Silas suspects me as it is, but stay on your toes, and I'm sure you will be fine. I'll find you in the woods after it starts."

Luke left without another word, and my anxiety went through the roof. Bastian hugged me close and rubbed the back of my head. *God, he felt good,* I thought as I leaned further into him. I just wanted to run. Run and never look back but I knew the cost if I did. I knew the trouble it would cause, and I forced my feet to stay put.

"Something's wrong, Bastian," Elijah stated, looking around as if we'd be attacked at any moment.

"What are we missing, guys? Why would Silas want to switch the bracelets?" Bastian asked quietly.

"I don't know, but heads up, brother," Cade said, and we turned to see another one of the Council's enforcers approach us.

"White Wolf? It's time to go."

Bastian gritted his teeth. "The game doesn't start for 45 minutes."

"Rules are rules. The Council wants her placed in the arena now."

"She hasn't had anything to eat yet," my mate countered.

"It's fine, Bastian. I'm not hungry anyways," I said softly. "Just find me fast, okay?"

Bastian kissed me hard before letting go. "The game won't take long, I promise."

I let the enforcer lead me to the table where the Councilors sat. My feet feeling like lead with every step.

"There's our White Wolf!" Silas said excitedly. *Something was different with him,* I thought to myself. *He was livid with me this morning, but now he seemed genuinely happy and excited. What was I missing?!*

"Here, child. It's in the rule book that the females wear this to mute the bond, so we shall switch out the inhibitor with this one. Just for the game, mind you. We like to stick to our rules though."

"What game are you playing, Silas?" I asked him, and he looked almost hurt.

"Oh, you and your imagination! Extend your wrist, Shanely."

Ignoring my gut feeling, I extended my wrist for him to switch the bracelets. He snapped the new one on first, and then clicked off the other one. A rush of adrenaline coursed through my veins, and I wobbled on my feet.

"There! Now you will have access to your wolf for the game, so your true mate can find you. Nothing will be hidden from the men playing today!" Silas announced loudly.

Suddenly, I felt woozy, and everything was just quiet inside my body. I tried to look within, but I still couldn't find my animals. Not my bear or my wolf. *Something was wrong.*

I opened my mouth to explain that I didn't have my wolf back, but I couldn't get the words out. Everything shifted weird in my vision, and bile rose to the back of my throat. Something was very wrong with this bracelet, and I wanted it off *now*. I went to tug on it, when a sharp pinch pierced my skin, and my eyes widened.

"Take her to sector 5 for this years run," Silas said to the wolf.

"Are you sure, Councilor? That section..."

Silas cut him off. "It's meant to be a challenge, Nick. Now go."

Nick nodded before pulling me into the woods. I was honestly having a hard time putting one foot in front of the other. I turned around to look for Bastian, but everything swayed so badly that I couldn't focus on where my mate was. I couldn't differentiate who was who.

"What's the matter with you? Can't you walk straight?"

I couldn't respond. Everything in my body felt heavy, so I tried hard to just focus on my feet. Nick babbled the whole time. About what I had no idea, but he was oblivious to me and my dilemma. That or he just didn't care, I don't know.

He held me up by my arm, and we somehow made the long walk to a beautiful waterfall. It was loud and powerful, but Nick seemed unphased by it like he'd been here all the time. Every sound pounded against my head though, and I stumbled again. *This was very wrong and not a mate bracelet at all*, I thought as I staggered on my feet. I was still alone in my body and

CHAPTER 7

about ready to pass out.

Nick led me to the left of the falls, and we were able to sneak in behind the waterfall from there. A small cave was hidden behind it, and it had a drop off inside the cavern. A large post was along the back wall, and Nick pulled me to it. You couldn't see anything from outside, and I got why this was a hiding place for the games.

"I was told to leave you here, ma'am. Oh, and the Council wants you handcuffed to the post here," he said. A large chain was bolted into the post, and he reached for it.

"Don't worry, White Wolf. You'll be safe the whole time."

Suddenly, that freaking bracelet stabbed me again as he bent my wrist to attach the cuff. My wrist burned against my skin, traveling up my arm towards my chest. I groaned, but Nick didn't seem to notice. He didn't seem to hear anything past the falls. *Something was seriously wrong with me, and he didn't once notice.*

"I'm sorry, Miss. The game seems crazy for sure, but it's safe here. We plugged the hole way up in the ceiling a long time ago so no water can get inside the cave, and the handcuffs just makes sure Bastian actually finds you and not you just stumbling around into him or someone else. The males *must* be the one to find you. The girls aren't allowed to move around," he explained. The room started to spin as he attached my hand to the post, and I leaned against the wall to keep from toppling over.

"Don't be nervous, Miss. No one doubts your bond with Bastian," he said with a smile as he looked around to see if he was missing anything. *The irony in that,* I thought to myself. "Alrighty then. I guess I'll head out then. Oh! Last thing, in case of emergencies just..."

I couldn't hear him anymore. The pain inside my body thundered loudly, pulsing as it traveled through the blood in my veins. *This was wrong, so very, very wrong.*

Nick's lips were moving, but everything was muffled and distorted. I tried to speak, but my body felt so heavy. Bile burned in the back of my throat, and I prayed Nick would notice something was wrong.

But he just smiled sweetly and patted me on my shoulder before heading back up the make-shift stairs.

Please... please stop, I begged inside my mind. *Please see something is wrong!*

Nick didn't stop though. He just left, and I was alone.

Before I knew it, I passed out.

Chapter 8

I woke to the sound of water everywhere. The rushing sound of water echoed loudly in the cave, and I rubbed my head as I slowly sat up. My arm felt full of pins and needles from dangling above my head, and I quickly pulled it down as I opened my eyes slowly.

What happened?

Suddenly, my eyes widened as I took in the room. Water flooded the cave from above, and I realized I was already laying in about a foot of water already. I scurried to my feet, dripping wet, and panic filled my chest. *The cave was filling,* I thought as my heart thundered in my chest. Water was pouring in fast, and I was handcuffed to a freaking post...

I had to get out.

I pulled hard on the chain, feeling that God awful stabbing feeling when I pushed against the bracelet, but the chain wouldn't budge! A wave of nausea hit me, and I groaned, leaning against the wall to keep from puking. *What did they do to me?!*

"Bastian!!" I screamed, but I couldn't imagine anyone hearing me over the sound of all that rushing water. Despite the water pouring in from above, there was still enough water going down the falls at the mouth of the cave. My heart continued to race as the reality of my situation hit me. *I was alone... My boys may not be able to save me in time.*

Rage burned the blood in my veins as I searched for a way to unlock the chain. *I assumed they would mess with Bastian, but I never would have thought they'd actually try to kill me!* Silas must be really desperate if this was his plan now.

"When I get my hands on you…" I gritted through my teeth, pulling on the chain again. My wrist burned again, and I tried to ignore it.

The water was just past my waist now, but I forced myself not to watch the rising water. I pulled on the chain again, injecting more of that poison in me, and the room began to sway. I growled. *If I passed out again, I was sure to never wake up*, I thought as fear quickly began to replace my anger. *Nick said something to me about emergencies, but I don't remember!*

"Please someone help me!" I screamed again. I tried slipping my wrist out of the cuff, but it was on there so tight. I couldn't get my hand through it, and I nearly sobbed when the water reached my chest. The drop off was way above my head, and I'd drown before anyone ever found me.

"Agh, Silas!" I screamed again.

I was struggling to move with this much water, and my feet would slip as I tried to pull myself free. Water went up my nose, and I cough to get it out, but soon it pushing past my chin. *There was nothing I could do to stop it,* I realized and took my last deep breath before my head went under. I tried searching for my wolf as it was my last hope of getting out of here alive. I had broke Abraham's bracelet, so maybe I could break through this one, but no matter where I looked, she was still gone.

My eyes widened as I looked around. *This was it,* I thought to myself. *Silas had won.*

I was going to die.

Suddenly, someone dove in the water behind me. They were followed by another, and my shoulders sagged in relief.

It was Bastian!

And Luke.

Bastian pulled me close before planting his mouth on mine, trying to give me air to breathe as Luke yanked on the base of the chain. It wouldn't move. Frustrated, he grabbed the chain. We yanked on the chain together, but it still didn't work. My vision turned gray as Luke looked to us with fear in his eyes. Bastian snarled.

Suddenly, Luke started digging in his pockets as Bastian pulled on the chain again. The post shifted slightly, but I was out of time. My lungs burned, and

CHAPTER 8

I couldn't help but release what little air I had left. Luke waved his hand in Bastian's face, and he grabbed my wrist, yanking it towards him.

Luke put the key in the bracelet, and that awful cuff fell off. All at once, my shifter abilities came back to me in full force. The rush would have knocked me over if I wasn't already floating in my watery grave. My eyes turned red instantly, and Bastian and I pulled hard once, snapping the chain in two.

My mate grabbed my waist and shot for the surface. I gasped for air as Bastian swam the both of us to the side. Cade and Elijah shot through the falls, sliding to the edge and reached for me. The triplets hauled me up and out, putting me safely back on the ledge. I coughed and sputtered as my lungs expelled all the water it just held, while Bastian hauled himself out of my grave. Everyone shouted back and forth as I struggled to calm my rapid heart. *I almost died. Silas almost killed me...*

Bastian picked me up, and the five of us left the cave. He set me back down outside to look me over before turning to Luke.

"Thank you, Luke."

Luke nodded still trying to catch his own breath and looked at me. "I'm so sorry. I knew something was going on but nothing like this. I would have never let you play if I knew."

"It's okay. I don't think Nick even realized what was going on either," I said softly, trying to calm down and keep myself from shaking further.

"I doubt it. Nick can be pretty oblivious most days, but he's good at following orders. That chain has a safety on it, and we plugged that hole a long time ago to leave the cave safe and dry for the Hunt. The safety had been welded shut, which is why you couldn't break it."

"Someone must have opened the hole after Nick left. I passed out right after he left me, and when I woke up there was so much water. It came in so fast Bastian..." I replied, unable to stop the fear from coming through my voice.

My whole body began to shake, and my mate pulled me in close. *How many close calls can I take before one of them actually succeeds and kills me?* I wondered.

"What was with that bracelet? It's way different than any of the bracelets we usually use," Cade asked as they each inspected it. "What's with the needle here too?"

"I've never seen it before. I just assumed they made a more decorative one for the White Wolf," Luke replied.

"It was just another inhibitor but way worse. Look at my wrist," I said, showing them. My shifter abilities were beginning to take over, but the cuts were still there. "That needle kept stabbing me over and over, making me so incredibly sick. It burned every time it pierced my skin, and it's why I passed out. I didn't get my wolf like Silas said I would. He tried to kill me because he knows he lost his control over me."

Elijah swore, and I could hear Bastian's anger when he spoke, "Give that to me."

Luke handed it to him, and I saw Bastian's eyes glow as he crushed it. He dropped the pieces on the ground.

"Never again, Shanely," he whispered.

Luke grabbed all the pieces. "I'll dispose of the rest, so no one else gets it," he said, pocketing the pieces and then he grabbed his phone. "The game is still happening, and so far we have no other wolves are in this immediate area, but we need to move. I can guarantee Xavier is the one that's supposed to find you, so he will be here soon."

"Yeah, once I'm good and dead," I muttered.

"So, he can play a grieving false mate," Elijah stated.

"If they can't control Shanely, then the only thing left for them to do is kill her. She's the only real threat to them, and they'd have to keep their positions if the White Wolf is gone," Bastian said, and I exhaled slowly. The adrenaline was wearing off, and my rage was returning. Now that I had my wolf back, I was ready to move. I am not tip-toeing around them anymore.

"We need to go though. You all still have trackers, so Silas can see we're all together. I'm the only invisible one here," Luke stated.

"Luke go. Get back and pretend you never left. Actually, go get Abraham. I'm taking over right now, and I'll need him present," I said as I stood up, wringing out my hair. "Coming boys?"

"Thought you'd never ask!" Cade said, bouncing on his feet.

CHAPTER 8

"Let's end this," Elijah said, completely ready to go. Bastian kissed my forehead, giving me a firm look.

"Are you sure you're okay?" he asked softly.

"I'm more than okay. I'm angry, and I'm ready to deal with Silas right now. No longer will I wait for the crowd to come to my side. I'm taking over tonight, and I want this tracker out!"

Luke nodded. "I'll remove them myself tonight. I'll see you there."

He shifted and ran the opposite way back to Summit Hall.

"Ready to run with your White Wolf, boys?"

Cade cried out excitedly. "Oh yes, Baby Girl! We're doing this in style!"

He shifted followed by Elijah, with Bastian shifting last. I scratched behind his ears before shifting myself. *Man, it felt good to be back in my wolf form.* I realized this was the first time I got to be my wolf with the Fenrir brothers all together. *It's a shame our first run was for this though,* I thought to myself.

I nuzzled them all before Cade yipped at me. He seemed impatient and was waiting for me to move first. I howled loudly, letting the packs know I was coming. Let Silas panic, knowing his impending doom was looming over him. My wolf was eager to get her paws on him, so we all took off. My boys kept up with me just fine, and they'd each brushed up against me as we ran through the woods.

I could feel the other wolves from the game nearing the four of us, so I opened up my connection to see every wolf shifter at the Hall. I wanted to make sure no one was attempting to leave before I was ready.

The wolves participating in the Hunt could sense their White Wolf presence, and everyone left the game, running back to Summit Hall. It didn't take long for me to see the gates, and the crowd that had formed. Silas was there front and center, and he was pale. As white as a ghost and looking terrified. *He had ever right to be,* I thought to myself. *This wasn't the outcome he thought he was getting today.*

Everyone gasped once we crossed the gates. They were finally seeing their White Wolf for the first time. I barred my teeth, and they all quickly exposed their necks in respect to me. I slowly turned to the Councilmen and snarled viciously. Silas was quietly pushing the other four down the stairs. The pathetic man knew he lost and was trying to escape!

I howled, alerting everyone, and Bastian answered my call. He bolted into the crowd who scurried far away from him. He blocked the Councilmen from leaving the stage. They all paled and backed up. *I don't think they realized how large my mate's wolf was. The true beast they had been poking all week.*

I snarled at the Councilmen again. They looked between my mate and I nervously before they pushed Silas forward. He glared at them before addressing everyone.

"Well congratulations, Bastian. It seems you are her mate..."

I growled loudly, and I pushed my Alpha power out to everyone. I wanted everyone to feel it and not question me with what I was about to do.

"No need for that White Wolf..." Silas tried to say, but he was forced to his knees by Luke and Abraham.

Bay bounded the stage, relieved to see her mate. Whatever drug they gave Abraham looked like it was still in his system still as not all his wounds had healed. It reminded me of what Derek gave me all those years ago, and I couldn't help but snarl again. My heart went out to him, and I gave him a grateful nod for his help today. I sent a hive message to everyone with the link.

"Silas, I have had enough of your arrogance and deceit, but this was too far! You tried to kill me during the Hunt! Your own White Wolf!"

My family snarled and growled as they pushed forward, glaring at the Councilmen. They filled the gaps in my defense, making sure no one else would try anything. The pack demanded answers as everyone began shouting angrily.

Silas's eyes widen, and he stared at me with a cold, harsh glare. I could see his mind was reeling as he glanced at Xavier, who was currently being pushed forward by my Uncle Cain.

"Shanely, you are mistaken. We would never try to harm you!" he finally said.

"Liar! The bracelet you gave me was not like the ones normally used in the Hunt. It was like poison to my wolf! And then you maneuvered everything so I'd drown in the cave before Bastian could ever find me!"

CHAPTER 8

"Is this true, Silas?" Garrett shouted, stepping forward from the crowd.

Everyone began shouting loudly again. Loud enough my ears hurt listening to it all. Even the ones that didn't care for me as much were appalled by their Councilman's actions.

"She's lying! I never would have tried to hurt her!" Silas tried to counter.

"Silas also had his enforcers jump me! I've been sitting in a cell, drugged with whatever they gave me, until Shanely and Bastian rescued me last night!" Abraham bellowed as Silas glared at him.

"Why would you take the tiger, Silas?!" someone in the crowd asked.

Abey grinned wickedly as he hopped off the stage. "I'm glad you asked! It's because Shanely is my sister! We share the same mother, making me a mixer as well!"

Everyone was startled by that revelation.

"I'm proud that I'm a mixer! Silas and the rest of your Council have used me against Shanely so they could control her! Haven't you all notice that she acts funny whenever your Council is present!?" Abraham cried out.

They all started murmuring amongst themselves again just as a voice from the back came out. One I hoped to never hear again.

"Everyone! Calm down! Since when has the Council ever done something like this?" Liam shouted, shushing the crowd. He walked forward, with his pack following closely behind him. My whole body recoiled as I saw him approach. I tried to keep my composure, reminding myself that I belonged here. *I was not an abomination nor was I a mistake to Bastian.*

"You're saying the White Wolf is lying?" someone in the crowd countered.

Liam raised his hands, and my anger reached a whole new level when Derek walked through the pack. He had the audacity to smirk at me, and my body shook with fear. My mind flashed back to the moment he strung me up to die in the woods all alone. I saw the same smirk then that was on his face right now. I had no idea what a trigger that one look alone was for me, but it shook me to my core.

I froze, unable to look away from the man as my heart raced, when I felt Bastian's love pour into me through our bond. *He was with me,* I thought to myself, and I forced myself out of that awful memory. I forced myself back to the present, knowing I couldn't fall down that rabbit hole again.

"Listen, all I'm saying is Shanely is new to all this. I think her perception is a bit off is all. She has made up many stories of perceived slights," Liam said condescendingly.

That did it.

I shifted back now and yelled, "Perceived slights? That man standing behind you also tried to kill me and my unborn child! Yet you defend him simply because I'm a mixer!"

The crowd gasped, and Derek shifted on his feet. The smirk gone and uncertainty lie in it's place.

"This is what I'm talking about people! Derek and Shanely had a disagreement years ago, and she and my son put a bounty on his head over it! It's why he was forced to join my pack! This is really getting out of hand now, Shanely."

Bastian snarled as he stalked towards Derek and his father. Derek looked uneasy and backed away, but Liam was either insane or trying to die because he stood firm. He could see Bastian's wolf had changed, but Liam didn't care.

"That's a lie! Derek deserves death because of what he did to my niece! We've been waiting on the Council to take care of the issue, and they told us they were *investigating.* That was years ago!" Cain shouted.

"He beat her, sliced her with a hunting knife, and then hung her up to die in the middle of winter! She was barely conscious when we found her!" Cade shouted back. Everyone had shifted back except Bastian. His ears were back, and his teeth barred.

The crowd shouted further, demanding answers. It was hard to hear everything going on, but my eyes were locked on Derek's. *He was going to pay for his mistakes,* I thought. *There was no getting away from me now.*

"See everyone! Shanely is just confused, and her family would clearly do anything for her. Even lie! Maybe this is all because she isn't a full-blooded wolf? She seems to have twisted everything and caused such a mess for us. Our Summits have never been this chaotic before. This is why we never mix shifters! It only harms our kind!" Silas shouted.

CHAPTER 8

"Luke," I hollered over everyone, and the group quieted down. "Were you or your team ever informed of the issue we had with Derek?"

"We were not!" Luke spoke boldly, silencing the crowd of wolves. Cain gritted his teeth as he glared at Silas.

"Silas, care to tell everyone why you chose to spare Derek despite what your law says should happen? I mean rules are rules, right?" I asked, and he glared at me, refusing to answer.

"No?" I said, stepping forward. "Alrighty then. I guess I'll answer for you. Derek discovered how to strip shifters of their animal forms like the bracelet I was punished with this week. He sold them to the Council here in exchange for his life! All while Liam sat back getting rich."

"This is nothing more than a he said/she said situation. There is no proof, mixer," Liam snarled.

"See for yourself! I still have the scars from Derek!" I shouted as I pulled my jeans up. My two long scars could be clearly seen on my legs, and the crowd looked shocked.

"Derek sliced me, so I could bleed out or attract some kind of animal. He tried to kill me because things were changing with our pack, and he blamed me for it. But these changes needed to happen! It's why I was chosen to be your White Wolf! Don't you all see? My mother risked everything to protect me, Abraham, and Caleb. She gave her life for us! We were meant to mix with one another. Not hate everyone that's different from us. Aren't you curious as to why you aren't finding mates anymore? It's because they aren't wolves!" I bellowed. The crowd gasped as Silas snorted.

"This is nonsense everyone! I'm sick of these lies!" Silas shouted angrily.

"They aren't lies!" Emma shouted. She gave me a small smile before stepping forward with her mate. Derek's eyes widened, when he saw her holding hands with one of Abraham's tiger enforcers.

"I stupidly made a deal with Silas in exchange for a forced mating," she said as everyone processed this new revelation. "He needed information, and I wanted a mate. I gave him what he needed to know about her daughter being a half-breed in exchange for them forcing Cade to mate with me. They wanted a mating between wolves, and I just wanted to belong to someone. I wanted to hurt Shanely because I was jealous, but it was *wrong*. Silas threatened to kill Aerith by handing her over to the Division, forcing Shanely to do what they wanted."

The crowd all started yelling angrily at the Councilmen, who looked very pale. They were losing this battle with our people, and they knew it.

"How could you, Emma!? How could you mate with a tiger of all shifters!?" Derek yelled, and Wes stood protectively in front of her.

I was proud of Emma though. We never saw eye to eye, but what she did here today was incredibly brave. *Credit where credit is due*, I thought to myself. *She did well.*

"Derek are you seriously telling me that you would have your daughter spend a lifetime alone with no mate and no children simply because your hate and prejudice is more important? All shifters are special! They all matter, and they are not our enemy! Our enemy is the Division, and they are very powerful!" I bellowed, but Derek just shook his head angrily.

He needed dealt with, I thought to myself as I turned to the Council. *It was time to end this.*

"I hereby remove all five of you from our Council," I snarled, pointing my finger at the ones who had led the wolves astray for so long. "I banish you from the Summit pack, and you are permanently barred from *ever* joining a pack again."

The Councilmen shook violently as their Alpha power left the five of them and slammed into me. It caught me off guard as my power grew exponentially. My eyes glowed red, and I held my breath as the last of it drained out of them and filled my core. The thick, nasty stench of rogue permeated the air the second they were disconnected from the pack. They were left with nothing but their hate and wickedness. It was vile, and I struggled not to gag as it filled my nose.

Everyone recognized the smell immediately and knew exactly what it meant. They couldn't conceal it anymore, and no one would ever trust them again.

"What did you do!?" Silas shouted angrily, clutching his chest.

Bastian shifted back finally and shouted, "She stripped you of your Council

CHAPTER 8

title. You have been rejected, Silas. You all are merely rogues now. Wolves without a pack, and we don't allow rogues at Summit hall. Do we, Silas?"

Rage filled Silas's eyes, and I couldn't help but smirk at him. He played this game stupidly and lost. But then he clenched his fists together tightly, and I knew it wasn't over.

"You little…" Silas snarled as he hopped down off the stage. "I challenge you, Shanely Fenrir!"

"Silas!" Cain yelled, but I stepped forward, grinning wickedly.

"With pleasure, you prick."

Silas snarled as he shifted into his gray wolf. I shifted as well ready for this fight. Bastian roared, stepping towards the two of us, when Cain blocked him.

"MOVE, CAIN!"

"Bastian, I can't! He issued a challenge, and she accepted! There's nothing either one of us can do now! I'm sorry," he said to my mate before turning to us. "The challenge is to the death."

Brilliant, I thought to myself before I charged forward. I let my wolf get her own vengeance for once. There was nowhere for him to escape to as the packs quietly formed a circle around the two of us, and Silas clashed against me. I could smell his vile breath as his jaw snapped, trying to grab my neck, but Silas wasn't trained to fight. He was sloppy and arrogant, and it was easy to slip away from his powerful jaws.

I connected on his right side with my claws, just barely getting out of the way of his bite. The scent of blood filled the air as it began to coat his fur. It wasn't enough to drop him though, but that was okay. I wasn't ready to end him just yet.

Silas attempted to bite down on my front paw, but I twisted around, grabbing the back of his neck. He left himself wide open, and I began to shake violently like the boys taught me. He bucked hard, trying to break my hold on him, but I refused to let go. The rage I've felt the last few days burst forward as each and every threat he's made came to mind. I shook harder and harder until I heard the snap. His body went limp, and I dropped him at my feet. I turned back to the group, who watched in silence. I shifted then.

"Anyone else?!"

No one dared to move, let alone speak. Their silence showed me where they stood on the matter. I looked to my mate, who gave me a proud look. He made his way to me, taking my hand now.

"Bring Derek forward," I said to my brothers.

Cade and Elijah nodded before making their way towards their father's pack. Derek paled and started to run, but Caleb blocked his escape.

"I don't think so, Derek," he spat out as Cade grabbed his arm. The Fenrir brothers dragged him over to Bastian and I, while Derek fought against them. Liam's eyes went wide, but he did nothing to stop his sons as they hauled one of his pack members forward. They forced Derek to his knees in front of me, and Cain volunteered to stand behind him.

"Now Liam," Bastian commanded. I looked to my mate, but his focus was on nothing but his father. Cade and Elijah started to make their way to their dad, when Bastian hollered.

"Not by you!" Bastian bellowed. "My brothers take your rightful place by our side."

They barred their necks before stepping behind us.

"Abraham and Caleb! Will you bring my father forward? I want non-wolves to participate in this trial," Bastian said coldly.

"With pleasure," Abraham said, cracking his knuckles.

Liam was stubborn, I thought to myself. He didn't try to run like Derek did. He just glared as Caleb and Abraham grabbed him by his arms and hauled him forward. They pushed Liam to his knees in front of us, when Bastian turned to my Beta.

"Cade? Bring Emma forward," Bastian said quietly.

Emma paled as she staggered back in shock. Even I was surprised, but Bastian held firm, and Cade obeyed. Wes snarled as he approached, but Emma put her hand on his shoulder.

"Wes, it's okay. I deserve the punishment," Emma said, gaining her composure. My eyes widened as she began to walk forward all on her own, but Wes yanked on her hand, stopping her. My stomach twisted watching them. *This didn't feel right.*

CHAPTER 8

"Wes, please…"

Wes looked broken as he slowly let her go. Emma walked with her head held high, willingly getting on her knees with the other two. I turned to Wes who shook, fighting to control the shift. He turned to me then, and my stomach churned even more. Regret and fear filled his eyes, and I struggled with the guilt eating at me so badly that I had to look away. *I will never forget the look on his face.*

"Derek," I said, turning my attention on the wolf who deserved punishment. "For trying to kill another shifter and an unborn child, you will be sentenced to death. Death at the hand of your Alpha, Bastian."

Bile rose to the back of my throat as he paled. I had never pronounced judgment before, and I wasn't sure I ever wanted to again because Derek's eyes went wide, and he started stammering uncontrollably.

"Listen now," he said with a shaky voice. "I think we can work something out? You didn't even die so am I to be punished for something that technically didn't happen?! Liam, you promised to protect me!"

"So you admit it, Derek?" Garrett said, his voice strong and firm. He stepped forward out of the crowd. "You admit you tried to kill Shanely?"

Derek rolled his eyes. "What do you all want me to say? She was changing things she shouldn't be messing with, and it was all against the law! It wasn't like I knew she was the White Wolf back then!"

"And that makes it any better? She was still a shifter! She was carrying a pup!" Garrett snarled. My eyes widened when he turned to the crowd, tossing his hands in the air. "I stand with Shanely! I don't want *any* part of these wolves. They are the reason for the war, and they are the reason why we have so much violence now! Shifters taking advantage of other shifters. Killing one another simply because they have a different animal! I rather merge under one ruler with all the shifters united than to *ever* be associated with them again!"

Garrett stood behind me, and his wife and family followed. With that one bold stand, more and more wolves started to stand behind me. To my amazement, everyone began chanting, "I stand with the White Wolf!"

"I stand with the White Wolf!"

Just over and over again, everyone shouted their support. I stood in awe just watching as the majority chose a side. They chose *me*.

"I stand with the White Wolf!" Bastian's mother shouted above the rest, and my eyes widened when I found her pushing her way to the front. She came right over to me, grabbing my hand tightly as she said, "I am *so* sorry, Shanely."

"Michelle! You are my mate! You cannot abandon me for that abomination!" Liam shouted, but my eyes were glued on my mate's mother. She turned and barred her teeth at her mate.

"You're the abomination, Liam. I don't understand how you can't see that," Michelle said quietly.

Bastian followed his mother as she took her place behind the two of us. I felt anguish seep through our bond before the rage returned, and he turned back to Derek and his father. He slowly started pacing back and forth. As if standing still was too difficult to do, and I watched my mate carefully. Turmoil filled his eyes as he debated his father's punishment. I waited patiently though. *This was a decision he needed to make himself,* I thought to myself.

"Where did I go wrong with you? Look at the mess you've become," Liam snapped, shaking his head in disgust.

"According to Pack Laws, harboring a fugitive means a life sentence. You are hereby stripped of your Alpha status and will remain at the prison here at Summit Hall. Along with the rest of the Council members until your White Wolf is able to determine your involvement with the plot today," Bastian said gruffly.

Liam clutched his chest his eyes wide in disbelief as the Alpha power left him. "You're not the White Wolf."

"Nope, but she's my mate," he replied before kneeling until he was eye level with his father. "We share abilities, remember?"

Liam's eyes widened as Bastian walked my way. He held my hand again, tightening his grip on mine so tightly it actually hurt, but I never let go.

"Abraham," I said quietly, "can you bring me the collars you made?"

Abraham ran off towards the manor in his tiger form, and it didn't take long to see him reappear with a bag in his mouth. His glorious white tiger sat near my feet, hissing at the three before us.

"I made sure Abraham brought a few of these just in case, and it looks like I was smart to plan ahead," I said, pulling one out of the bag. "I don't trust you all, so I am removing your ability to shift. Being a shifter is a privilege, and none of you deserve it."

I passed the collars to Abe's enforcers, and Darryl and Henry started putting them around each of the Councilman's necks. Devastation filled their face, but then there was Liam. His face was stoic as his wolf was taken. He just stared at the ground, and for the first time in his life he had no crappy comment left to say. Henry motioned to Derek then, but I shook my head.

"There's no need for him," I said quietly.

Derek shook violently as he snapped. "You whore!" he shouted. "You have no right to do this! You are destroying what it means to be a wolf! I should have made sure you died before I left you in those woods. I should have..."

Bastian took two steps and snapped his neck. Derek's eyes rolled to the back of his head as he landed on the ground, and my stomach churned as I stared at the crooked head on his body.

Liam's eyes widened, and I could smell the stench of fear in the air. I think he's finally understood how powerful his son had become, I thought to myself before my eyes drifted over to Emma. She looked ready to puke and kept her eyes firmly on the ground. *This wasn't fair to her.*

"Octavia?" I asked, and my cousin stepped forward. "I want you apart of the questioning. I want to know everyone's involvement."

"Question my father as well, Octavia," Bastian snarled. "I want to know if he had *any* involvement with Derek's attack on Shanely years ago."

"I didn't!" Liam shouted. "I only allowed him in after everything happened."

Abraham hauled Liam on his feet, and Bastian stalked towards him. Bastian had a good few inches on his father, and he towered over him, getting close enough that their nose were nearly touching.

"We shall see," Bastian snarled, "won't we? I promise you, *Dad*. If you had any involvement in Derek's plan or knew of it beforehand and did nothing to warn us... I will kill you myself."

Color drained from Liam's face before his eyes drifted back to Derek's body. *He finally had the good sense to stay quiet,* I thought as Bastian stalked towards me. I could feel the anger rolling off him in waves. His rage filled my core, and I knew this was too much for him. This was becoming way too much. I met him halfway, and he hugged me close, inhaling my scent for a moment before reluctantly letting me go.

I turned to Luke, motioning to Derek's body, and he immediately motioned his enforcers forward. They picked up Derek and Silas and hauled them away. I watched Emma exhale then, and I gave Bastian's hand a squeeze. *It was time to deal out her punishment.*

"Emma," I said, and her eyes met mine, "you have admitted to willingly putting a child in harm's way, while also trying to harm your White Wolf. Those actions are deserving of punishment according to Wolf laws."

She cringed, dropping her head shamefully, and I sighed. *I didn't want to do this anymore,* I thought to myself. My eyes drifted to Wes, who started pacing the moment I said his mate's name. Abraham tried to help his enforcer, but Wes wanted none of it. His gaze was on me solely.

I turned to Bastian, and he gave me a nod.

"Listen to your wolf. We will stand by what you decide."

I closed my eyes as my wolf pushed her feelings towards me, and I was surprised on how forgiving she could be. *But it was the right call,* I realized, feeling a weight lifting off me. I turned to face Emma once more.

"You also stood bravely before everyone and told the truth. You were ready to defend your White Wolf, and you willingly stepped forward to accept punishment. I feel like that was worth something. So for your punishment, you will continue to remain a rogue without the protection of a pack. Your actions from here on out, whether they are good or bad, will tell every shifter you meet if you have truly changed by your scent alone."

Her eyes widened in surprise as my command struck her, and Wes ran to her. He picked her up off the ground, holding onto her tightly.

"Thank you, Shanely," she whispered, and I gave her a small smile. I turned to my Uncle Cain. Silently begging him to take over. *I couldn't do this*

CHAPTER 8

anymore.

Uncle Cain gave me a nod before turning to the crowd around us. "Everyone! Please see Luke, and he will get you all set up with rooms here. We're going to cancel the rest of the events for today. We will still have our planned ball tonight. so please join us for that. Shifter law is swift and brutal at times, but it doesn't mean we won't enjoy the rest of our time together," he said loudly before turning to us. "We'll take care of Derek and deal with these wolves, but we all need to discuss some things before dinner."

Bastian pulled me away before Cain even finished speaking. I was thoroughly exhausted from this whole day, and my sticky, wet clothes clung to me. We must not have been moving fast enough though as Bastian hauled me into his arms and carried me straight to our rooms.

I didn't fight him on it.

I just wanted this day to end.

Chapter 9

Bastian moved through the manor quickly, heading straight for our room and slamming the door shut behind us. He promptly went to the bathroom to ran a bath for me. I just stood near the sink, shaking as everything that just happened replayed in my mind.

I had finally done it.

I had officially taken over. Silas was no more, and neither was Derek. All my enemies were gone, and they were *never* coming back. A relief unlike any other washed over me, and I let go of the tension that had been building since we first arrived. Slowly, I stripped down to my undergarments and turned towards the mirror. My eyes widened when I saw my reflection.

"My hair!"

"Shhh..." Bastian said as he rushed towards me. Tears filled my eyes as he said, "Sweetie, it's okay. You're still beautiful."

"When did this happen?!" I cried out as tears ran down my cheek.

He kissed my forehead before pulling me further into his arms. I couldn't take my eyes off my new look though.

"When you banished the Councilmen," he said softly. "You changed then."

My reddish brown hair had turned completely white. My skin looked paler to compensate the drastic color change, and I just looked *different*. So unlike myself.

"I've changed completely, Bastian. I don't even look like me anymore!"

"I think you look beautiful, Shanely. You are finally who you were meant to be. You are perfect, my love. In every way."

He kissed my shoulder slowly all the way to my neck, and I just leaned into

CHAPTER 9

his embrace. I shut my eyes, refusing to look at my reflection anymore. *I just wanted my mate.*

Bastian's lips trailed my jawline, and my sadness melted away. It had seemed like forever since I had any alone time with my husband, and I needed him now. I turned, letting him kiss the other side of my neck, when there was a knock on our door. I groaned in frustration.

"Bastian..." I whined.

He sighed and buried his face in the crook of my neck like he always does when he was stressed out. I felt him inhale deeply then. "I know, Shanely. It won't always be like this. You need to warm up anyways."

Bastian left me at the sink to shut the water off. I pouted and leaned against the bathroom counter. "I was warming up, Bastian," I said, giving him a pointed look. He smirked and pulled me closer to him.

"Take a bath and rest. I imagine tonight will be a lot. Just enjoy the peace for the moment, and I'll see to whoever is at the door."

Another knock happened, and Bastian smacked my butt as he left.

I groaned and climbed inside the tub. *He was right about one thing though,* I thought as I laid back. *The warm bath water seriously helped my aching body.* I tried to shut my brain off, but it was hard with this abundance of power within me now. It would take some getting used to, so I sat up and decided to practice using the pack locator ability, while I soaked in the tub. I opened the bonds again, and this time I could feel the entire wolf population like ribbons connecting everyone to me.

Every pack was different, and the wolves who belonged to them matched them. It was easy to see who belonged where, when I realized the packs all had their own unique color.

The Amber pack looked like the color amber, which was fitting, and the Blackwood pack were black. I looked for my own pack, and McCoy's were white. Made sense since I was the White Wolf, and I came from there. I looked at my own color, which was a mixture of white and dark gray. Almost like Bastian's wolf, who had a lot of dark, smoky gray in its fur. I saw the Denmark pack huddled together with Michelle and realized the smoky gray color came from them. I looked for Bastian then, who was deep in the castle now, and his color was the same as mine.

Must be a blend of us then? I thought to myself. I assumed Bastian was in the dungeons now since he was so low in the castle. He was with other wolves that were white, which probably meant Cain, Ryder, and possibly Ash and Aspen were with him along with Elijah and another wolf with a gray color.

Pulling away from Bastian, I noticed a wolf with a white color standing outside my door. I focused harder and could sense it was Cade. *My Beta never left my side,* I thought smiling. I wanted to try this out with Aerith when we got home. I was tempted to see if I could reach her from here, but I was too exhausted to even try it.

I found Bay easily in her room. I couldn't see Abraham as he wasn't a wolf, but she came up clear and bright. Her color was still white as she technically never left the McCoy pack, but she now had an orange swirl mixed with her. *Was that because she was mated to a tiger?* I wondered. I decided to look at Johnny now, and sure enough his was white but with a brown swirl instead. *We were all mixed matings,* I realized. *So wolves with a different shifter for a mate had a unique swirl to them. Interesting...*

As I backed away from Johnny, I noticed another with a white swirl in their center. I froze when I realized who it was. *My father...* I thought as I sat forward in the bath. *And that color... it was from my mother.* I struggled to keep my heart from racing. *Did this mean she was still alive? Wouldn't her color die with her if their bond was really gone?*

I couldn't take it anymore and slammed the bonds shut, removing Dad from view. I went entirely under the water now, trying not to think about everything or get my hopes up when it came to her. I honestly had no idea, and there was no one I could ask about it. There has never been a White Wolf before, so I will never get answers to those questions. I just had to wait and see.

I stayed in the bath until my skin shriveled up, and the water ran cold. I put on my robe before I decided to mess with my hair. I dried and styled it, but it was rather difficult getting use to the color. I applied a small amount of makeup then. I didn't want to go over the top tonight but wanted to look

CHAPTER 9

nice.

No matter what I did though, I just felt miserable every time I looked in the mirror. I couldn't adjust to my new look and felt too different and not exactly myself anymore. My vivid green eyes stood out like a sore thumb on my face, and my hair looked much like Abraham's. *Almost like twins honestly.*

I sighed and forced myself away from the mirror. *I had once looked like my mother, but now it was all different.*

At least I was alone the whole time, and I was thankful for it. I didn't want to deal with anything anymore. I was ready to leave this place for good and just go home. Get back to our life there. I felt like I had done enough in helping the wolf shifters, but I knew I couldn't just take off like I wanted to.

The afternoon had passed before I heard a small knock on the door. I slowly made my way to greet whoever was there, even though I was tempted to ignore it entirely. I opened the door to find my brother Abraham standing there with Cade.

"Hey," he whispered, and I opened the door wider to let him come in. Cade waved hello as well but chose to stand guard outside my door.

"Hey, thanks for helping us today," I said quietly.

"It's no problem really. Actually, it was rather fun for me," he said as he motioned for me to join him on the couch. I chuckled, collapsing on the soft cushions.

"It's been a long and eventful day, that's for sure."

Abraham stretched and then kicked his feet up on the coffee table. He was a big guy, so he didn't fit very well on the couch with me.

"Tonight will be interesting," he replied once he was comfy.

I grabbed the blanket from the back of the couch and bundled up in it. "Yeah, no kidding. I'm really tempted to just sneak out the back door though."

He gave me a look. "You need to finish this, Shanely. You've changed everything today. All shifters are going to start blending together after this. I mean aren't you the White Bear as well? You'll probably be their Queen too!"

I rolled my eyes. "Their prophecy is different, Abey. It just a marker for great change, which technically has already happened. They don't have a formal World Council like the wolves do. They simple manage their own clans. Actually, I think the Wolves are the only ones who have a council like this."

"That's because the vast majority of shifters in this world are wolves, but either way things are changing. It's not a bad thing though. We just need to be prepared for every possible scenario. Make sure that our future little ones like Aerith have a safe life to grow up in. You can do this, Shanely."

I sighed, rubbing my face. "I know, Abey, but it's overwhelming. I mean everything's changing so fast. Now that I'm not as angry as I was earlier, I'm kinda freaking out. I mean look at me! Even my hair looks different. I have all this power, and I don't know what to do with it. I haven't even gotten the chance to shift into my bear in such a long time either. Balancing out time between the two is hard enough, plus trying to raise Aerith and be there for Bastian and my family. It seems like I'm everyone's enemy or I'm always needing rescued. I feel like I'm just blundering along, barely getting by."

Abey gave me another pointed look, and I groaned, knowing I was just complaining.

"I'm just as afraid as you are, Shanely. I'm tired, and I miss my mate dearly. I'm ready to just go home, but every time I try to bail, I think of our mother. At least *you* get to watch your kid grow up. She gave up everything for us, and other shifters will go through the exact same scenario until we make something good out of her sacrifice. We already did the hard part. Now we just got to finish this," he replied.

Mom. I hate that Aerith will never know her grandmother, and my father will forever be without a mate. All because of the laws separating us, and the horrible shifters that were stuck in power. Now I'm here, and I have the chance to make it better, and all I want to do is run because I'm overwhelmed. *I'm pathetic and selfish.*

"You don't like when I'm right, do you?" Abey replied, smirking in his corner of the couch.

I playfully punched his arm. "Hush you!"

He laughed, rubbing his arm. "Look, Shanely vent away. You always have

CHAPTER 9

me as your brother and a member of your council to unload all your stress and anxiety on. Just promise me at the end of the day, you keep getting back up. You dragged me into all this, so don't bail on me now."

I rested my hand on his as I said, "I promise, Abey. Can I tell you something crazy though?"

He nodded casually, and I sighed.

"This will sound nuts, but I've seriously been wondering if mom's alive."

Abraham frowned slightly. "I know Dad has never felt the bond snap, but it's probably because she was stuck with that bracelet still on her when she died. Our mom's gone, Shanely. She would have come back by now if she was still alive. You made the call to every wolf in the world when you shifted, right? There's no way she wouldn't have come forward to see what was going on or at least check to see if it was safe to come back. She wouldn't just stay away."

"I know, but because I'm the White Wolf, I can see everyone and which pack they belong to. I noticed that while Bay and Johnny are still apart of the McCoy pack, they are different than the others. Like Bastian and I, they each have a swirl of another color running through them. Bay's is orange, while Johnny's is brown. When I looked at Dad... He has a white swirl around him. If mom was really dead then that connection would be completely gone, wouldn't it?"

I was grasping at straws, I knew that, and Abraham honestly looked uneasy the longer I went on about it. I leaned back in my seat again. "I told you it was a crazy idea."

"I just don't know what to say, Shanely. If she's alive, why hasn't she ever come back? Wouldn't she check to see if it was safe or if things have changed at all? And how would we ever find her?"

I shrugged. "I don't know, Abey. Maybe ask Dad? Start with places he might think she'd go?"

He gently tussled my hair. "It would be worth anything to find her again. I'm sorry you lost your normal look though. I know Dad said you looked like her."

I gave him a weak smile. "It's okay. It will grow on me, I suppose."

"I mean you looked just like me now other than the eyes, so I say it's an improvement," he said with a muffled laugh. I punched him in his arm as Bastian walked through the door. He gave us a small smile before disappearing into the bathroom.

"I think I better go. He doesn't seem okay. And besides Bay's been having a hard time accepting her mother being back in her life. I should go find her before dinner."

He stood up and kissed my cheek before leaving me to my mate. I walked in the bathroom and found Bastian in the shower. I grabbed the dress I was planning to wear tonight and started to finish getting ready.

"You okay, Bastian?"

He was quiet for a long time before he finally responded, "I was with my father."

"Bastian, you should have come to get me. I could have been there with you for that," I replied.

"It's okay. You needed to relax a moment, and you'd catch your death if we didn't warm you up. I felt better knowing you weren't going down there anyways."

I stared at his dark silhouette, feeling awful my mate shouldered the task of dealing with Liam alone. But soon, my thoughts turned scandalous as I watched him continue to shower. *Too bad it was all foggy from the steam,* I thought to myself.

"I can feel you staring, mate," he growled, causing me to blush as I turned back away.

"Hey," he said, sticking his head out, and I turned to face him. Water dripped down his face from his hair, making my stomach do a little flip. "I didn't say it was a bad thing. You could join me if you really want to help me feel better."

I chuckled softly as heat filled my cheeks. *He still made me weak in the knees even after all these years,* I thought to myself. *I was madly in love with him, and that would never change.*

"Aren't we supposed to go to dinner soon?"

"You're the White Wolf. No one will start without us. Join me, mate?" he

CHAPTER 9

asked, extending his hand out to me.

"Bastian, I'm dressed already!"

"Mate... Don't make me beg," he replied, his voice turning husky and deep as his eyes glowed red. I unzipped my dress, and it fell to the floor.

"I'd never make you beg, Bastian."

Chapter 10

Bastian escorted me to the main ballroom after our little escapade in the shower. We were running a little behind schedule, but it was nice not having such a heavy weight on my chest as I walked down these halls. As we came around the corner to the doors that led to the ballroom, I noticed everything looked different than it had before. The back stage was empty except for the band that played soft, relaxing music, and all the lavish decorations were down. The room was decorated in a simple yet elegant design.

Everything was gorgeous and white. None of the blue and gold shiny things that the Council previously used, and my heart warmed at the incredibly sweet act my wolves did for me. *They decorated everything to honor me tonight,* I thought as I looked around the room. From the white roses to the stunning white linens covering each table, the room was beautiful, and it felt like I had entered one of the many balls I had read about in those fantasy books Bastian bought me.

Whoever did this must have worked very hard to get it done in time, I thought as I looked around. I was grateful they put the band on the stage as well. I didn't want anyone up on a pedestal, especially me. They left the microphone up though for us to speak to the crowd later, but other than that there was no room left up there. *No one would be exalted here, and that was just how it needed to be.*

The whole room smelled absolutely divine, and everyone seemed to be way more relaxed than at the first ball. It was weird. It felt like an eternity had passed since we first got here, even though it had only been a few days. I looked at Bastian, who wore his suit so nicely and smiled. A solid black tux,

CHAPTER 10

with a red and gold tie that looked incredible on him. My Bastian would be turning heads tonight.

But he was all *mine*.

Bay put me in a red sparkly dress to show off my Alpha status, with simple black heels. She tried to push higher ones on me, but I didn't want to embarrass myself tonight by face planting because of the shoes I wore. We both knew at a certain point I'd be kicking off my shoes altogether, so what's the point in killing myself in the meantime. I had to restyle my hair because of my second *shower* with Bastian, so I simply dried it and let my natural curls run a muck because of the lack of time. It still took some getting used to seeing white hair instead of my reddish brown, but I kept reminding myself that it was just hair. Even though it still bothered me.

Everyone clapped their hands as we entered the room, and we made our way to our table. I blushed and waved as we passed by, but I really wanted to have everyone just move on and enjoy themselves tonight. They all looked so grateful though that I had to admit it felt good knowing we did that. We changed their lives for the better, and now was the time to celebrate.

"It's okay, baby. Just smile and wave," Bastian said chuckling. "That's what I plan to do. We can eat first before..."

Suddenly, Bastian stopped dead in his tracks, and I spun around to look past him. His mother was seated at our table with the rest of our family.

"What is she doing here?" he gritted out. I squeezed his hand, trying to calm him.

"She left your father and publicly supported us. I know it doesn't excuse all her behavior or choices, but we should hear her out first, Bastian. She isn't your dad."

His jaw locked as he nodded but didn't say anything more about it. My hand felt empty when he let me go to approach the table, and I couldn't help but wonder if I crossed a line just now. Our family stood to greet us, and I tried to smile like nothing was wrong. Even if it felt like it.

"Cain, I need you to switch tables with us," Bastian demanded firmly.

Cain gave a small smile. "Sure, Bastian. I'm sorry she insisted on sitting there. There wasn't much to persuade her otherwise."

Bastian nodded once before turning to me. "I will hear her out, but not tonight."

I sighed, and let him move our things to where he wanted us to be. Then he very loudly addressed the crowd. "Will Garrett and Eliana Thompson please join us at our table? Your support this afternoon was brave and appreciated by me and my mate! You spoke up and were the first ones to do so. We'd like you to dine with us tonight, and please bring your boys as well!"

The room erupted in applause as Garrett and his family stood up from across the room proudly. I looked to Bastian's mother, and her dejected look was hard to stomach. She clapped along with the others, and I couldn't help but feel sorry for her. I didn't blame Bastian for doing what he did, but this whole thing would turn into a mess if we weren't careful. Regardless, I wanted my mate to know I supported him. *He* needed to be okay with accepting Michelle. Not me.

"Bastian," I whispered in his ear as the family made their way over. "I did not mean to push you or back you in a corner. I only meant to suggest hearing her out before casting judgment, *when* you are ready."

His face softened, and he kissed my forehead. "It's fine, Shanely. I'm not mad at you. I just... I can't deal with her right now. She went back with my father before. She gave up knowing my mate and daughter for all those years ago. My childhood was one thing, but standing with that man while he insulted you both is another. It's hard to stomach right now."

"I know. All I meant was that we don't know her side of the story. She may not have agreed on a lot of things."

"She didn't try to stop them though," he replied with a snarky tone. I gave him a pointed look.

"She may have in her own way, but we won't know until we speak to her. Your father was a bully, and I wonder if it wasn't just to you kids. Some people are strong in different ways is all. Just give yourself time and talk to her when you are ready. She is completely alone now and has been cut off from her mate."

"Bastian! Shanely! Thank you for inviting us to dine with you!" Garrett said loudly, pulling Bastian and I from our conversation. The fellas shook

CHAPTER 10

hands, and I gave them all hugs. Cade and Elijah greeted them as well, and they sat on either side of Bastian and I. Cade winked at me before kissing my cheek.

"Hey, Baby girl."

"Hi, Cade! Thank you for guarding me outside my door this afternoon."

"Of course. I'm your Beta now, so if Bastian isn't around then I will be. I let you have your peace and quiet, but I stayed close enough to watch. Elijah stayed with Bastian during his tasks this afternoon too, but between you and me... I get to be Beta to the better Alpha anyways," he replied with a wink.

Bastian was in the middle of helping the family get settled at our table, but he rolled his eyes at Cade anyways.

I giggled, and then smiled at Elijah, who stuck his tongue out at me. *I really was lucky to have them apart of my family*, I thought to myself. Cade stretched his arms out, adjusting the sleeves on his shirt, when I noticed his arm was wrapped. I gave him a funny look before looking at Elijah. *His arm was wrapped too!* My eyes widened as I looked at my arm, finding a small red glow just under my skin.

Panic surged through me as I grabbed my Beta. "I forgot my tracker, Cade!"

"Shh..." he whispered as he patted my leg, "it's okay. We can take that out later tonight."

"No!" I cried out in a hushed whisper. "Please just take it out now. I don't want it in any longer."

Anything that connected me to the old Council needed to go. Cade's face softened when he realized how frantic I was feeling over it.

"Okay, okay, okay," he said as he took my hands in his. "Settle, Shanely. I'll take it out, but it's just deep enough that it might get some blood on you."

Bastian's eyes darted back and forth between us and our company, but Garrett and his mate were so excited to be here they were talking up a storm and none the wiser to what was happening with me. My mate reached under the table and squeezed my leg. I relaxed a bit from his touch, and he didn't remove his hand, while Cade helped me.

"Please Cade, just be quick. I can't stand the idea of it still being in me. I'll use this to help stop the bleeding," I said as I grabbed my napkin. My eyes pleaded with his. "I don't want anything connected to those men."

He sighed but nodded anyways, grabbing his napkin as well. "Fine, but use this to cover your lap. This might hurt since we aren't able to numb you first, and I don't have my knife on me right now. I'll have to use my nail, alright?"

I nodded fervently, not caring at all where we were or what he was about to do. "Just do it, Cade. I *need* it gone."

Then Cade did something I had never seen before. He partially shifted. I have seen some with extended nails or canines before, but this was the first time I'd ever seen a part of the wolf pull through, while the shifter remained human. *It must take a tremendous amount of self-control to hold the shift like that,* I thought to myself. His claw extended, and my eyes widened, seeing how sharp it really was.

"Okay hang on, Baby Girl," Cade whispered.

Our guests continued to talk, while my eyes were glued to Cade. I appreciated that Bastian kept them distracted because I didn't want to disrupt anything. I just needed it gone.

Bastian squeezed my leg again as Cade quickly sliced my arm above the tracker. I gasped at the pain it surprisingly caused, but Cade held my hand firm. He never let me go.

"Are you okay, Shanely? Wait... Is that blood?" Eliana asked, sniffing the air.

"I'm fine!" I stammered as my arm throbbed. "I just needed to take care of something super fast, and I didn't want to leave everyone. Please, do not worry!"

Cade dug his claw into my arm a bit more, which hurt like the dickens. He did good though and pulled the tracker out fast just like he promised. Bastian quickly covered my arm with my napkin, pressing firm on the wound. Cade shifted his hand back to normal and cleaned the blood off before placing the tracker in front of me.

"There. It's out now," he smiled at me. I returned the smile, grateful to my best friend and Beta.

"Oh, the tracker! I don't blame you, sweetie. I'd want that out too!" Eliana

CHAPTER 10

said sympathetically.

"I'm sorry I did this right now. I had forgotten it this afternoon, and when I noticed Cade's arm... I just couldn't stand it being in there for another moment."

"It's fine! We're not bothered by it at all, and honestly you can do whatever you want! You're the White Wolf," Eliana replied as she smiled at us.

"Well, I don't want to make anyone uncomfortable either," I replied as Bastian put his arm around me. I pressed the wound on my arm, hoping to help it clot faster until my shifter abilities kicked in, but honestly the pain was gone already. Confused, I looked under the napkin, and my eyes widened.

"Whoa, Baby girl!" Cade said excitedly. "You're healed already!"

Bastian grabbed my arm, inspecting it closely, and all that was left was a blood smear.

"I didn't know I could heal so fast," I replied as Bastian rubbed his thumb over where the mark should have been.

"Perks of being the White Wolf, I suppose?" Elijah countered, and Bastian just leaned over to kiss me. I blushed and leaned further into him, needing the comfort he always gave.

I picked up the tracker, examining this tiny device that blinked slowly. It was so tiny, no bigger than a grain of rice, yet I hated the stupid thing. My blood boiled, thinking back to earlier today, and I dropped it on the ground. I slammed my foot down on it, snapping it in two. I picked up the pieces and dropped them on the table.

Members from one of the European packs cooked dinner for everyone and served us all tonight. I thanked each sever as they came by, making sure they knew how much I appreciated them, and they smiled at us in return. I learned that they came from Romania, and the meal they made was something called sarmale, which was stuffed cabbages and polenta. They called it something else, but I butchered the word trying to repeat it. They laughed, while I turned multiple shades of red and told me not to worry. Many don't even try, so it was nice to see their Alpha give it a go. Despite being embarrassed, I was genuinely excited to meet this pack. I've never been out of the US, and they invited me and Bastian to come visit them soon. They wanted to show us around their home, and I loved that idea.

Actually, seeing all the pack's homes sounded incredible, and I made a mental note to bring it up to my council. *Maybe we could travel here and there occasionally?*

Dinner was delicious, and I was completely stuffed before dessert even came out. It was then my uncle eyed me from the other table and motioned to the stage. I had briefly forgotten this part and narrowed my eyes to him. *I hated public speaking,* I thought as anxiety rolled in my stomach. Cain gave me a firm look back, and I finally caved. I groaned, looking up at the ceiling for my last few moments of peace.

"Let's get this done, I guess," I said with a sigh.

He nodded before excusing ourselves from our guests and guiding me to the stage. Everyone seemed to quiet down as we walked up the stairs, which only made this even more awkward. *Please don't trip,* I anxiously thought to myself. *For the love of God, don't trip...*

Bastian stepped in front of the microphone first, and I about sagged with relief.

"Welcome, everyone!" he said with a smile. "I'd like to say a few words before I turn it over to your White Wolf, if you all don't mind?"

The audience applauded, and I could even hear some chuckle in the back. My gaze drifted to Michelle, who watched her son closely. She made eye contact with me and smiled before turning back to Bastian. Her smile didn't reach her eyes, and I knew it was forced. I felt bad for the situation, but I truly didn't know how to handle it.

"Shanely and I cannot express how grateful we are to receive your support. Our old ways and customs would have insisted we never accept a shifter like her, but you all saw past all those stupid laws and gave her a real chance. You stood up for her against our old Council and defended her when we really needed it. It was brave, and I personally thank each and everyone of you. We..." Bastian said, pointing between him and I, "cannot do any of this without you! We are here for all shifters, and we are stronger because of it!"

The room thundered with the applause of everyone. They promptly stood,

CHAPTER 10

cheering us on, and I beamed back at Bastian. I didn't expect a response like this, but then he stepped aside and extended out his hand. *The microphone was all mine now,* I thought as the anxiety in my chest grew. I wasn't angry like the first time I took the mic and addressed the wolf shifters. I wasn't even sure *what* to say, especially after Bastian's speech. *He knew exactly what he was doing. I, on the other hand, did not.*

Bastian raised his hand, and the crowd quieted for me. I swallowed hard.

"Hello, everyone! As Bastian said we are very thankful to you all. I know firsthand that change can be intimidating, but I also know that we can make the change together. I would have been lost without the support of my mate and family, when I found out I was a shifter. They helped me through everything that has been thrown at me, and I know that if we stick together, we can get through this too!"

Everyone applauded the two of us again, and I sighed contently. It felt good to have their support, and just like that, my nerves faded away. I continued, "No more will we fight with other shifters. It doesn't matter where you find your mate now! It will be honored, and it will be viewed as special. No more will *anyone* live in fear!"

Bastian looked at me proudly, and I couldn't contain my toothy grin. *This right here was worth all the crap we dealt with these last few days.* Everyone genuinely seemed happy and hopeful, and I finally felt like I did something right for once. And that felt *good*. I looked to Abe, who winked. *I did this in my mother's name,* I thought to myself. *And it felt like I could breathe again.*

Bastian took the mic again. "Everyone, please enjoy the rest of the evening! Tonight will be our last night here! We're cutting the Summit short to return home to start preparing for the changes yet to come. We will announce a new Summit event to happen later this year to make up for this one!"

Bastian took my hand and led me down the stairs and straight to the dance floor. I smiled as I wrapped my hands around his neck as the music started playing.

"A new Summit?" I asked.

"I thought since the World Council will no longer live here that we could make this the official hall for a brand new all inclusive Summit Event. Make this the official Headquarters for shifters as a whole. I think it will be a good step forward, don't you think? We have more than enough room here too."

I rested my head against his shoulders saying, "I love that idea, Bastian! Thank you."

"Oh course, Shanely. We do this together," he replied softly.

More and more couples joined us on the dance floor, and I smiled watching everyone. *They actually looked happy tonight*, I thought to myself. There was no pressure or anyone looking over their shoulder, and it made my heart swell with pride.

In this moment, I felt renewed and *ready* to be the White Wolf.

II

Part Two

"Sometimes, I still struggle to understand why the bonds chose me to be Shanely's mate. My mistakes were grand, my experience little... but one thing's for sure, I would die for that girl. I'd take a bullet for her again and again. Whatever I needed to do to keep her safe."
— Bastian Fenrir

Chapter 11

"So how do we go about this?" I asked, leaning forward on the conference table.

My family and I made it home safely a couple weeks ago, and it took a little bit to fall back into our normal routine. We grabbed Aerith as soon as we were off the plane and sort of isolated ourselves for a little while. I know we have a lot on our shoulders and plenty to do, but I needed space. Bastian made sure to give it to me too.

I wasn't the only one either.

It seems my aunt and uncle were enjoying *retirement* as they disappeared into the woods the week we arrived home. I decided to leave them for now. Let them just enjoy being mates and nothing else for awhile. They've shouldered most of the responsibility for years. This was the least I could do.

I left Luke as Alpha of the newly appointed Summit Hall pack, and they were required to stay there and keep the place running year round. They also were to act as enforcers and security during any and all events and to keep the prisoners fed and locked up. He seemed honored to be given the title of Alpha, but I was just glad to have another real friend.

With the help of Octavia, we went through the Alphas currently in charge. It took time, but the Alphas were more than happy to come to McCoy land to see me. I went to some of the local packs, but Bastian insisted for now they could come to us, and we could visit more packs later once things have settled down.

Luke kept most of the wolves that he worked with before, minus a few who sworn fealty to the fallen Council. They received their punishment for what they did to Abraham and are currently sitting next to their precious Councilmen in the cells beside them.

I asked the packs before we all left if anyone would be willing to live here at Summit Hall under Luke's direction, and we had a surprising amount of wolves volunteer. A mixture of both men and women, all without mates, left their old packs to join the Summit Pack. Luke would train them in time for the next event. It was all coming together rather nicely.

I only had to remove a few Alphas, replacing them with better shifters that would uphold the changes we were putting in place. No more would packs be run with hatred or violence. I can't force non-wolf shifters to accept it, but my wolves were going to. It was smooth for the most part, but some encounters ended rather roughly. Cade only had the chance to prove his loyalty to us more, and his quick thinking saved me.

Again.

Now, my council sat with me and Bastian at our conference table, trying to figure out how to reconnect the shifters again.

"First things first; we need to let the rest of shifter kind know we've abolished the old laws amongst the wolves. Hopefully, they will all agree to the new ways as well," Bastian replied.

"There are so many shifter kinds though. How do we reach them all?" Cade asked.

"I've told my streak already. We spread by word of mouth and start with the leaders we do know," Abraham suggested.

"Maybe start planning the next event already. Formally invite the shifters who are willing to put aside old feelings of hate to join us for the week event," Bay countered.

"I like that idea. Invite them to our hall, and we can plan events to try to smooth over issues," I replied.

"We should have a day where their leaders can talk to us personally about issues though. Might show a measure of goodwill if we have something in place beforehand. Wolves have continued to be the most prosperous, and seeing how we are the largest shifter kind out there, many look to us as those in charge. If we can hold a conference with the leaders then maybe we can

CHAPTER 11

make them feel more equal to us rather than beneath us?" Bastian added.

Elijah nodded saying, "Maybe we should create another World Council like in the old days. One from every shifter kind and give them all a voice."

"That's brilliant, Elijah!" I cried out excitedly.

He smiled and wiggled his eyebrows towards Cade, who rolled his eyes and pushed him playfully.

"Maybe we could also plan a mating game again? For single shifters to see if their mate is among the group. Having those bonds happen between shifter kind will help smooth everything as well. It's also an exciting thing to see someone find their mate," Ryder chimed in, and we all agreed.

"What about the Division? They are used to things being one way. Do we inform them of our new system?" Abraham asked, and everyone groaned.

"Sorry, but someone had to bring them up," he replied with a laugh.

"I wasn't thinking about them. I'm afraid to get them too involved with our plans. I vote to let them continue thinking nothing has changed. The less they know the better," I said solemnly.

"I don't know, Shanely. We need to be cautious with them. What if they find out and decide we're now a threat because we've been quiet," Bastian countered, and I sighed nervously.

"But what if we tell them how things are going now, and they decide we're a threat anyways. Right now, they know the shifters are divided. If we merge everyone together, wouldn't that look like our numbers are tripling and be a threat then too?" I replied.

Bastian and I slowly looked to one another. *This was the first time we really were on opposite ends over something,* I thought quietly. *I didn't like it.*

"Dang. Two very good points," Elijah muttered.

"So what do we do? The year visit is almost upon us," Bay asked.

"Let's vote, I guess," I suggested, and everyone nodded.

"All those in favor of telling the Division what's going on raise your hand. If you rather keep it quiet for now then keep your hand down," Bastian said, while raising his own hand. I kept my hand down. I hated being at odds with him, but I was scared to have *anything* to do with the Division. Telling them just felt like a bad idea.

Elijah raised his hand, while Cade did not, but I figured they'd be split being our Betas. Caleb left his hand on the table, making it 3-2. Abraham raised his though, along with Ryder, while Johnny kept his hand firm on the table. He looked to me with a nod, and we all then turned to Bay. She was sitting at the end seemingly lost in thought.

"You're the deciding vote, Bay," I said patiently. We weren't in a serious disagreement or anything, but this was a big decision. She looked up at me briefly and then to Bastian.

"I'm sorry brother, but I vote with Shanely."

She touched the table, signifying her choice and tipping the vote in my favor.

"Alright we say nothing for now, but I think we may need to periodically take the vote again if circumstances change," Bastian said, and we all agreed.

We parted ways shortly after that with our plan in motion. The boys were to locate the leaders of the other shifter kinds and invite them to Summit Hall towards the end of the year, which wasn't very far off. All while us girls planned the events. No one would mention anything to Calvin, the Division's Head for our area, during his next yearly visit, which was coming up in a week.

I waited patiently as everyone else filed out of the room before standing up to meet my mate. "I'm sorry, my love. I don't like when we don't agree on things."

He pulled me in close and kissed my forehead. "I know, Shanely, but it's part of being in a leadership role. We're not always going to agree, but we took a vote, and I'll honor that. I still think we need to be extremely cautious though. I don't want to give them any excuse for going to war against us."

"I don't either. I'm afraid of pulling them into our plans too fast or too soon. I'm just scared, Bastian. I'm trying so hard to keep my warnings from coming true, but truth be told, I don't know what to do."

Bastian rubbed my back as he sighed. "Let's just take it one day at a time. We don't know how our future will go, so the best we can do is just stay together and take it slow."

I nodded before I let him lead me home. Uncle Aspen brought Aerith back

CHAPTER 11

shortly after we got home from her lessons. He's been trying to help her reach her inner wolf but said it was hard to get her to focus today. She was still pretending we were still at Summit Hall, dancing the night away. I sighed, and thanked him anyways. *It was fine though,* I thought to myself. *I was a slow shifter, so maybe she's just taking her time as well?*

We ended up spending the next few days at the cabin, planning the Winter Summit Event for all shifters. Bay, Alana, and Octavia all came over to help me plan the event. We thought we'd ask the wolf packs to each take a night to prepare food and serve everyone in the dining hall, and then the following year we'd extend it to everyone to share a night. We went over a special dancing game for those to find their mate, since it's all different between shifter kinds, and we also planned a race outside along with a winter carnival for the families.

We were having a ball planning the week long event, and even Aerith chimed in with some ideas. She wanted a bonfire, which I thought was a great idea. It would be pretty this time of year and a fairly inexpensive way to have fun.

Abraham had already reached out to the other tiger streaks and sent the invite, while Caleb did the same for the bears. I was finally going to meet my cousin Noah as he informed Caleb that the Russian Clan would be attending this year. Four years into this family, and I was finally meeting the last known family member I had, well that I knew of. Abraham and I kept quiet about my suspicions with my mother, but I knew he was looking for her too.

Before we knew it, the time came for Calvin to stop by. I was a nervous wreck, but since Bastian and I were now the Alpha pair, it was our responsibility to meet with him. *The perks of being Alpha just kept coming.*

Now that Cade was my Beta, I had a stronger connection to him, and I could sense him anywhere at all times without needing to use my Alpha power. It was oddly comforting and convenient, seeing how it didn't require me to concentrate like I had to with everything else. I was working on it, and I'm hoping over time it wouldn't be such an effort to use my power.

"Cade?"

"What's up, Baby Girl?"

"Calvin will be here within the hour. Can you step away from work?" I asked, knowing full well my nerves pulled through my voice.

"Of course!" he replied. "I'll tell Elijah too. He's working today as well."

"Oh shoot. I didn't mean to ruin your day at the shop."

"Nah, don't worry about it. It's slowing down, and Brody is here with a few others. They can finish up the last couple jobs we have. I'll grab Elijah and meet you at the lodge. Is Bastian with you or do you need a ride?"

"Bastian is with me, but thank you," I answered. "We'll just see you then."

"Okay, Baby Girl. I'll see you soon."

I felt the disconnect and turned to my bubbly four year old.

"Well Aerith, daddy and I have a meeting we have to attend to. Do you want to go to Grandpas today?"

"Yes! I want to see the baby! Can I mommy?"

"I don't care if Alana doesn't mind. I'm not sure what she has planned today, but let's call Grandpa."

I dialed my dad's number as Bastian walked in the room. His hair was still wet from his shower, and he grinned at me when he caught me staring. I rolled my eyes, when my father answered.

"Hey, Shanely!"

"Hi, Dad! How are you?"

"Oh, I can't complain," he said softly. "Just working around the house today. Nothing too special. Whatcha need?"

"Well for starters, I'd like to have you over for dinner sometime soon! I feel bad we haven't seen much of each other lately."

"I know, kiddo. Perks of being the Alpha, right? But I'd love that! We need to catch up. I've been wondering how you're handling everything," he replied.

"I've been doing okay. Some of it has been good, while others not so much. Speaking of the not fun things I get to do, we have Calvin coming in for his visit today," I replied with a groan.

"Ah, yeah. I kind of wish Cain and Cassia still ran those to be honest," he replied.

"Me too, but I was wondering if Aerith could come over for a while? I don't want her at the lodge while he's here," I asked.

"Sure. Do you need me to come get her?" he asked.

"No, Bastian and I can drop her off. Thank you, Dad! We really appreciate it. I know she will be super excited," I replied as Aerith beamed and ran to grab her shoes. Bastian chuckled before following after her.

"Well, it's not a problem," Dad chuckled. "She will be good company today. I'm home now, so bring her over whenever!"

"Okay, we will see you soon!" I replied as I disconnected our call.

"Hurry, mommy!" Aerith hollered from the other side of the house.

I giggled before making my way to them. It was a fairly quick drive over to my dad's but not nearly long enough going back to the lodge. I groaned as I stepped out of Bastian's truck. We were a few minutes early but cutting it kind of close.

I followed Bastian inside, where Cade and Elijah were waiting already. I greeted my boys before taking the head chair next to Bastian's. We didn't have to wait long before one of our enforcers led a skinny man into the room.

He gave us all an odd look before taking his seat. I studied Calvin, and I could see Patrick was the opposite to this man, other than the eyes. Calvin was skinny and short, with a dark mustache and pale skin. Patrick was tall and broad compared to his dad, and I couldn't tell if Calvin had any hair under that massive sheriff's hat. His dark eyes just stared ahead at Bastian and I.

"Where's Cain?"

"Cain is no longer the Alpha of McCoy pack. We have become the next Alpha pair, so you will be dealing with us from now on," Bastian spoke with confidence.

Calvin snorted, crossing his arms in a huff. "Is that so? Well when did this all happen, and why were we not informed before today?"

I gave him an odd look as my head cocked to the side. "It only just happened, and we planned on letting you know today during our annual meeting. It wasn't necessary to inform you the moment the switch happened."

"And you are?"

"Shanely Fenrir, and this is my husband and mate, Bastian," I replied before gripping my mate's hand.

Calvin didn't seem to happy with me, and he stared harshly at the two of us. His gaze lingered on me a moment longer than I felt comfortable with, and I shifted in my seat. He finally spoke, "Shanely. I've heard your name quite a bit lately. You're not exactly who I pictured though."

"And who did you think I was?"

He gave an odd grin. "No one in particular, but you do look oddly familiar. Have we met before?"

"No, you have not," Bastian answered for me.

"Huh," he muttered as a sly grin crept up his face. "Must be my mistake then. Since you both are new to this I will let this one slide, but you are to inform me of any changes the moment they happen. We clear?"

I bristled at his tone. "I know that I am new to this, but I was never told we needed to include you in all of our dealings. Have there been any human deaths as a result of a shifter attack?"

Calvin glared at me. "No, there has not."

"And has any wolf shifter willingly shifted in front of humans, alerting them to our kind?" I asked again. My questions were clearly agitating him, but I didn't care. I would not allow us to get bullied simply because we're new.

"No, your pack has not done anything like that."

"Aren't those our two laws with the Division? That's what these meetings are for, correct? To make sure we understand not to break those laws. Well we've kept them, so I don't think it's necessary to fill you in on every little detail of our lives. You do not *own* shifter kind. We merely live amongst one another, and we are doing our part. That's all you need to know," I snapped back before sucking in a breath.

What did I just do? I thought as my eyes widened. I felt Bastian squeeze my thigh under the table, but I refused to look at him. *I just royally messed up by opening my big mouth.*

Calvin studied me a moment before smirking softly at me. "I see. My son mentioned you were a fiery one. I shall inform the Division of our meeting then. It was nice to meet you two, and I'm sure we will be seeing each other

CHAPTER 11

again *real* soon."

With that, he stood abruptly and left us. The moment the door closed I let my head fall to the table with a loud thunk.

"Why didn't someone stop me?!"

Bastian laughed loudly, rubbing my back as I wallowed in my massive mistake. *He constantly needed to do that lately,* I thought as I gently hit my head on the table. Repeatedly.

"You are a force to be reckoned with, Shanely. There's no stopping you when you get like this."

"I just pissed off our Division Head! I don't know what came over me!"

"He didn't seem too thrilled when he left guys," Elijah said nervously.

"No, Calvin just seems fixated on Shanely like his douche bag son," Cade chimed in.

"What's done is done. Let's just lay low and see what comes of it. We technically didn't break any laws, so we will try not to stress unless we need to," Bastian said as he reached for my hand.

"C'mon, love. I think you could use a run," he said, and I gladly took it. *He was right,* I thought. *I did need to run.*

"You two coming?" Bastian asked his brothers, and they grinned.

"Heck yes, we are! Let's run with our White Wolf, brother," Cade said as he bounded from the room. *It was good to see his goofy side again.* Since joining our council and becoming my Beta, Cade's been more serious than ever, and I missed my best friend.

We all ran after Cade, laughing as we bolted from the lodge, and shifted the second we stepped in the woods. I felt the earth beneath my paws as I bounded on ahead, letting my stress and anxiety go, and the brothers pushed themselves harder to catch up. I smiled, feeling a tiny bit smug, when a black blur collided into me. *Bastian.*

He was the only shifter that could truly keep up with me, and soon we were wrestling. His brothers quickly joined in on the fun. It's funny how much wolves loved to play and needed constant companionship. Such big and scary creatures couldn't live without their pack and family.

I nipped at Elijah, who was quick to get away. He and Cade disappeared into the brush, only to pop out somewhere else in an attempt to get me. Cade managed to tackle me once, and he scared the living daylights out of me when he did. I scurried to my feet, determined not to get caught again, and I watched the two of them closely.

Bastian brushed against my side and started to show me what they were doing. Soon, our playful game became a tactical exercise, and the boys began teaching me different ways to track someone stealthily. Bastian stayed as my teammate, and we were honestly getting pretty good at catching Cade and Elijah.

I pounced on Elijah, tackling him to the ground, and his poor wolf looked exasperated with me.

"Ow, Shanely," he muttered through the link.

I laughed as I lowered my front half and wagged my tail, waiting to see what he would do now.

"I'm getting the hang of this," I replied. I *loved* tracking with my wolf, and I felt like I could do this all day.

He snorted, shaking his fur all grumpy like. "That's only because Bastian spoiled our fun and taught you how."

I stood up on all fours, barking at him. *He can't seriously be mad I beat him again, can he?* Suddenly, he bolted forward, tackling me. I landed on my back as he stood over me with a wolfy grin. I gave a low growl before pushing him off.

"You big cheat," I said.

He howled before rolling over lazily.

"Aww, did I hurt Shanely's feelings now?"

I barred my teeth, glaring at him. *He so did not just say that!* I growled again before clashing with him. The sparring continued on, and it wasn't long before Bastian and Cade had joined back in. Soon, I sprawled out on the ground, rolling around on my back, while the brothers continued to fight.

The snarls sounded vicious, even though they were all playing. I stretched out my wolf's muscles and watched from the sidelines. *I would never get used to this feeling,* I thought as I sighed happily. *I absolutely loved every second I spent in my wolf's skin.*

CHAPTER 11

I pitied those who could not do what I could.
Life just seemed so dull without my wolf.

Chapter 12

My Uncle Cain had finally made his way back to the lodge as we were having problems finding some of the other shifter leaders. He and my Aunt Cassia had spent a few weeks in their wolf form, just enjoying the break from running the pack. They came back with a new zeal and looked refreshed. Honestly, it only made me wonder when Bastian and I could take a vacation like that.

Cain helped us contact the rest of shifter kind, and we managed to invite everyone to the Summit Hall. We even got in contact with the descendants of the original shifters that met with the Division all those years ago, and I made sure they were coming too. We wanted to get as many as we possibly could to help change the world for shifters.

The event was coming up quickly, so it was becoming a mad dash to get it all done in time. We weren't there that long ago, but we were confident we could get everything ready by then. The fall weather was turning colder, and soon snow would be here. We had everything in place now that my uncle came back to help, and we got a surprising amount of shifters to agree to attend. Some didn't respond, and a few outright said no, but like Bastian told me before... Baby steps.

The months went by as quickly as the snow fell, and it was December before we knew it. We were all at the lodge, gathering everything we were taking to the event at the end of the week, when we heard a howl outside. Brody appeared out of the woods. He was hauling in his wolf form, and he shifted as he skidded to a stop.

"Police are on their way up now, guys," Brody exclaimed in between

CHAPTER 12

breaths.

Bastian glared down the drive. "Why are they here?"

Brody shrugged and said, "I don't know. My patrol saw them on the outskirts of our territory, and I came straight here."

"You did good, Brody," I said with a smile. "Go ahead, and make your way back to your patrol. Don't be seen."

He nodded and left the way he came.

"Aunt Cassia? Can you take Aerith inside?"

She nodded and her and Alana went inside with the littles.

"Shanely, you should go inside as well. We don't know if it's Patrick," Bastian suggested.

"Patrick's going to be the Division Head for our area at some point, Bastian. I'm Alpha, and I can't hide from him."

"Oh yes, you can. You can hide from him for the rest of our lives, baby. I just..." he replied but was cut off when the car came into view on the drive.

"No hiding her now," Cade snorted as the brothers stood in front of me.

Patrick stepped out of the vehicle once it stopped with his father in the drivers seat. I narrowed my eyes. *What in the world were they doing here?*

Patrick's eyes darted back and forth nervously like he was uptight just being here for some reason. *What was he looking for?* I wondered as I watched the two make their way to the front of the vehicle. Patrick finally saw me standing behind the Fenrir brothers, and that's when he noticeably settled down. He glared back at Bastian, who was a whole new level of tense.

"Well hello, shifters! You all aren't busy, are you?" Calvin hollered, and my eyes went wide. *He called us for what we were in front of his son,* I thought to myself. *That's why Patrick looked so nervous.* I looked at Bastian and then to his brothers as my anxiety rolled in my stomach. *This was not good.*

"What? Not going to talk to us now?"

"He shouldn't be here, Calvin," Bastian spoke up finally.

Calvin shrugged in response. "Well since that little one is changing the game on your end, I decided to change it on my end too. I've decided to overseer you shifters with the help of my son now. Shanely, you remember Patrick, don't you?"

I glared between the boy's shoulders but refused to speak. Anger welled up inside me because this was all my fault. I mouthed off the Calvin in the first place. My hands tightened into fists.

"He knows everything?" Bastian asked, his eyes flashing with anger.

"Yeah I do, Bastian. Makes a lot of sense why you all act so weird. I couldn't put my finger on it until my Dad finally told me about you freaks," Patrick answered back. The boys snarled in response.

Calvin tsked at us. "Careful now. You don't want to threaten a human, now do you?"

Patrick smirked as Bastian began to shake where he stood. I could feel his rage come through our bond, and I gripped his hand in mine. *This was turning from bad to worse.*

"Calvin, you and I both know that was against your own rules. Shanely and Bastian didn't do anything wrong during your last meeting, and you know that," Cain said firmly.

"Like I said Cain things are changing now. The Division isn't as strict as it used to be, so we're allowed to handle our territory as we see fit. I'm changing things, starting with my son. Oh, and I'll be having monthly meetings instead of yearly. I want to make sure you all are staying within the law," Calvin clapped back. Now I was pissed.

"No," I snapped.

"No?" Calvin questioned. "You're not in a position to be saying no, little one."

"Well, I just did. You will not harass my family, Calvin. We will stay with our yearly meetings unless someone in the Division contacts me further. Now you can get off my land," I snapped, pushing past the brothers. Bastian gripped my arm, letting me know I was far enough.

"C'mon Shanely, don't be like that. It won't be all bad, I promise. Now you get to see me once a month," Patrick said, smirking as he leaned on his police cruiser.

"Whether you all like it or not, this *is* how things will go. I'm running the Division for this area, so I suggest getting used to it. It will be easier on everyone," Calvin said as he reached for his door. "Let's go, son. We will see

CHAPTER 12

you all next month."

Patrick slowly got back in the passenger's side, winking at me before his dad backed their cruiser up. I clenched my fists at my side, feeling my animals trying to shift. I was angry. So angry that I caused this new problem in the first place. *We had enough on our plate already*, I thought as my eyes flashed red. Bastian tried to pull me in, but I pushed away.

"Let's just finish packing. I want to leave a few days earlier than we planned," I said, causing Bastian to frown. Suddenly, the idea of being inside that lodge felt too much. I needed to shed my skin and run, and I took a step towards the woods.

"And where are you going?" Bastian asked.

"Away. I need..." I sighed, throwing my hands up. "I just need to get away."

I shifted into my bear and took off in the woods. I ran for awhile, just needing to stretch my legs and let go of my rage. I knew I shouldn't go far since it would be dark soon, but I was just so furious! I stopped near the creek bed, pacing back and forth angrily. *Calvin was just as annoying as his son, and they think they can just waltz in here and change everything like this! I don't think so*, I thought angrily to myself. I was so lost in my own thoughts that I didn't see the large shadow coming up behind me.

I heard a chuffing sound and jolted around to see Bastian coming through the trees. His dark fur stood out like a sore thumb against the snow, and I felt stupid that I missed him. His large gray bear calmly strolled up to me before nudging me with his snout. I stomped away and chuffed back at him. *I wasn't mad at him*, I thought to myself. *I was more mad at myself than anyone really. It was my stupid mouth that caused all this in the first place.*

Bastian laid down on the ground, waiting patiently. *This man was a saint.* I was taking my anger out on him, and I knew that wasn't fair. Shifting back, I slowly made my way over towards him and plopped down. He stayed in his bear form, looking out into the woods while I stewed in silence. Bastian at least managed to find the one area where the snow was mostly gone, but I really didn't care if I sat in snow. I was already overheated as it was, and with my anger the cold air felt good.

"I'm sorry, honey," I whispered to him. He looked at me but said nothing. I sighed and leaned further into him, knowing he was waiting for me to go on.

"I'm furious with myself. I mouthed off to Calvin, causing all this to happen. I don't know what I'm doing as Alpha. I don't know where to push things or when to back off. I'm making a mess of everything, and I'm sorry. I should have never taken it out on you."

I put my head on my knees, and after a moment I could feel Bastian shift back. He sat behind me, with his legs on either side as he wrapped his arms around my waist.

"Shanely, it's okay. I'm not mad at you. You spoke up with conviction, and honestly, I agreed with you. I don't want to be under their thumb anymore than you do, but I'll let you in on a little secret though," he said, leaning in close. "I don't know what I'm doing either."

I turned abruptly to look at him and said, "You always seem so sure though. You were trained to be Alpha Bastian from an early age."

He snorted. "Yeah, well being trained and actually being Alpha are two totally different things. Plus, we're not just Alpha to our pack only, but the entire wolf community and everyone else by extension. It's a lot to handle, and I have no idea what I'm doing either."

"You just seem so confident though. I feel like I'm a mess all the time," I replied as I leaned against him. He laughed loudly now, and I playfully elbowed him.

"I may *act* confident, but I worry just as much as you do. The only thing that keeps me rooted is you. I know that as long as you are by my side, I can handle anything thrown at us then."

I smiled before giving him a small kiss. "I'm sorry I ran away, Bastian."

"Everyone needs to get away for a moment. I just wasn't going to let you go alone," he replied before kissing my jaw line and trailing down my neck. Goosebumps followed everywhere his lips went, and Bastian continued to kiss the back of my neck and down the other side.

"Bastian..." I groaned, but he didn't stop. He quickly scooped me up and turned me around, so I straddled him. His lips found mine, and I could feel

CHAPTER 12

his tongue push hard against my lips, begging to be let in. We haven't kissed like this in so long that I had forgotten how badly I missed it.

I let him in as I ran my fingers through his hair, pulling him closer. I could feel his hands on my waist just under my shirt, when I finally pulled away.

"Bastian... the patrols are going to discover us and get an eye full if we don't stop," I whispered softly. My lips were swollen already, and he gave me a wicked smile.

"I don't see any patrols near us, do you?"

My lips slowly turned up into a smile as I scanned our area. *Bastian was right... No one was near us.*

"You have that ability too?"

He nodded his head. "I do, and right now, I think my mate needs some time to relax."

Bastian slowly kissed just behind my ear down my jawline, sending shivers up and down my spine. All my stress and anxiety left me with each and every kiss he gave.

"Here?"

His eyes flashed gold, and I heard his wolf pull through his voice as he said, "Right here, my love. It's where our animals prefer to be anyways, and I need you now, Shanely. I don't want to pass up a moment to have my wife."

My eyes flashed, causing him to growl before he kissed me again.

Chapter 13

We pulled up to Summit Hall, where Luke was the first one down the steps to greet us. The rest of the week prior passed by with no more issues from Patrick or Calvin thankfully. I actually felt pretty good during the last couple days, which I think had a little something to do with Bastian's help in the woods. I blushed, thinking back to that night and quickly pushed it aside to greet my friend. Although, I'm sure Bastian heard what I was thinking.

"Luke! It's good to see you!" I said as I gave him a hug. He smiled back at me before shaking Bastian's hand.

"Alphas! Glad you made it safely! Come on in, we can show you to your new rooms before the rest of shifter kind gets here."

It was surreal walking into this place again. It looked so different inside, and I was glad as I wanted nothing to remember my first time here. Luke guided us up the stairs and to the 5th floor, explaining everything his pack had been up to since we left last time. He was excited to show off all the changes.

"It's weird coming down this hall again, but I love all the changes you've been making. In such a short amount of time too!" I said as I turned in a full circle, taking everything in. We passed by my old room, which was now a security room. The corners of my mouth rose slightly.

"This used to be the Council's wing, so we decided as a pack to give it to you. There are plenty of rooms for you and your entire council as well as the major leaders in the other shifter races. We thought we'd give you all this wing, and then we've divided the floors and wings between the shifters. We thought this year we'd put all shifter kinds together instead of just mixing everyone up. Might make them all feel better being with their own kind for now," he replied excitedly.

"That's really considerate, Luke. I feel bad taking this nice wing though," I said as we made it towards the end of the hallway.

"No please, don't feel bad! We are all happy to have someone that actually deserves it to be staying in these rooms. This room here is yours, Alpha."

Luke opened the last door on the left to the most gorgeous suite I had ever seen! *It was like a small house in here!* I thought as Aerith ran on ahead and into one of the rooms on the right. *As if she's been here before.*

"We renovated that room for her in particular," Luke said just as she squealed loudly.

I followed her inside to find her climbing the bunk bed and sliding down the slide attached.

"Mommy look at my room!" she squealed before going up again. I was in awe as I looked around. *They seriously out did themselves.* Her room was an adorable soft yellow with plenty of toys and stuffed animals. She had her own TV set up in the corner, with a pink tent off on the other side.

"Luke, this is amazing! You did this for her?"

"Well, our princess needed a room to match!" he grinned, and I hugged him again.

"Thank you, Luke. This just made her day," Bastian said as he clapped his hand on Luke's shoulder.

"We wanted this stay to be perfect for everyone. We're all excited for this Summit Event."

"Us too. We can't thank you enough for doing all this and for being the Alpha here. I know it's not all fun and games," I said quietly, and he gave me a small shrug.

"Someone has to, and I'm glad I can take that off you guys," he replied.

"How is it going?" Bastian asked quietly. My mate had been tense all week, and I know it's because of his father in the prison below.

"Easy for the moment. The council men don't really speak honestly. I think we killed the head of the snake the last go around."

"And my father?" Bastian asked, and I picked up on guilt through our bond.

"Your father..." Luke replied, his voice trailing. "Well he's struggling a tad, but he's not a problem we can't handle."

I furrowed my eyes at him. "Struggling how?"

Luke shifted on his feet. "He's having a hard time as a human. The disconnect... It's driving him crazy in moments, but we can handle it. I would advise not mentioning we have a prison here though. Might send the wrong message."

"Wasn't planning on it," Bastian said a little gruffly before leaving the room abruptly. I sighed. I hated that my mate was hurting like this. *His dad really hurt him more than he ever did me.*

"Forgive him, Luke. He's under a lot of stress and hearing about his father isn't easy."

Luke nodded understandingly. "I get it, and no offense taken. I'm your Head of Security here, so I just needed to advise you about it. However you and Alpha Bastian decide to go about it is entirely up to you. Summit pack supports you 100 percent."

"Thank you, Luke. Will you see to it that my council members find their way to this floor. We brought many things to contribute for the event too, and Bay has the schedule. Everyone will arrive between tonight and tomorrow, and I want things to go as smoothly as possible."

He nodded before replying, "Of course, Alpha. I'll make sure it all gets done."

Luke quickly left the room, leaving me with my brooding mate. I walked through our living room and into the other bedroom across the way. It was decorated in ivory white and gold colors, with a king size bed in the center. We had our own TV as well, and a luxury sized bathroom with this shower\tub combo in the center of the bathroom. I had never seen a shower like this before, but you stepped down into it, which allowed for the tub to fill up a certain way before meeting with the rest of the floor. The shower head was up high in the ceiling, and I'm assuming acted like rain when it was turned on. *Fancy*, I thought to myself.

I found Bastian in the bathroom, unpacking our bags before making his way back to the bedroom. I let him pass, patiently waiting for him to find his voice. *What Luke said about his father bothered him, and he just needed a minute,* I thought to myself. He was lost in his own head now, and I just watched my sexy mate work through it. He always did and would come back to me sooner or later. Bastian had begun unpacking our clothes, when he finally caught me staring at him from the doorway. I smiled as he sighed, collapsing on the bed.

"I'll apologize to Luke," he finally said, covering his face with his left arm. I plopped down and laid back against him.

"I wasn't saying anything, baby."

"I don't know why it bothers me, but it does. I know he doesn't deserve his wolf, and he's the one that put himself in that prison, but I don't know. The thought of him going crazy because of the disconnect to his other half.... It's hard. Especially when it was *me* who sentenced him."

I sighed and snuggled in close. "Bastian, no one would blame you for feeling bad about your dad's situation. I love that you're compassionate and feel for those even when they're in the wrong. It's why you're the perfect Alpha."

Bastian leaned into me now, his face pushing further into my neck. I could feel him inhaled deeply, calming his wolf, and I rubbed the back of his head. I absolutely loved when he buried his face in the crook of my neck, and I'm glad it was a comforting thing for his wolf. *He could do this anytime he needed.*

"I love you, Shanely. I can't tell you enough how much I appreciate you."

Aerith came bounding into our room, climbing up and over us. She giggled up a storm as she plopped down on Bastian's chest. "Daddy! Uncle Cade and Uncle Elijah are coming up!"

He tackled her, and she squealed before the two started wrestling. I quickly hopped off the bed to avoid getting squished.

"Is that so? I didn't hear anyone knocking," he said as he tickled her.

"They're coming! I can hear them!"

I eyed her funny as Bastian slowed down. "You can hear them? How do you know it's them?"

She shrugged. "I don't know, daddy. I just know where they are. They smell like Uncle Cade and Uncle Elijah. I can hear them walking to us down the hall."

"She's improving, Bastian. I think she's a shifter after all," I said quietly. I studied my daughter, but she gave no indication she had an animal or even that she belonged to the McCoy pack. She had no color when I looked at her with my ability yet she was doing all these things. It didn't make sense other than that she had a wolf and was just shielded like John said.

"Does this mean I'm like you mommy?" she asked, climbing on her dad's back.

"Maybe, honey. Do you feel a wolf or bear inside you?"

She shrugged again. "I don't know. I just feel like me."

A knock sounded on our main door, and Bastian scooped Aerith up. "C'mon. We can figure this all out later."

I followed him out of our room, and Bastian went for the door. Sure enough, in walked his brothers.

"Hey, Little One!" Elijah said, grabbing Aerith from his brother. He tossed her in the air before setting her down on the couch.

"I told you they were coming!" she cried out as she jumped up and down on the couch excitedly.

They gave us an odd look, and we briefly explained.

"Whoa, that's a bit improvement then," Cade replied, scratching his head.

"She must be shielded like John said. Maybe we will get to see her wolf this week since we will have so many shifters here?" Elijah wondered.

I shrugged as my stomach started feeling a bit woozy. I sat down at the table behind the couch and let the brothers talk about the week ahead. Aerith insisted they see her room, and I waited while they explored our suite, feeling more and more queasy as the time passed.

"Luke's already unloaded everything, and his pack is finishing setting up the welcome mixer. Our council all have their rooms on this floor with us, while Cain and Cassia are staying with McCoy pack. The wolves are getting our old floor on this side to make things easier. So all wolf shifters are on the second floor in the west wing, while the bears are on the second floor of the east wing," Cade explained.

CHAPTER 13

He and Elijah went on to fill me and Bastian in on what shifter was assigned each floor, but I was half paying attention. My stomach churned, and breakfast rose to the back of my throat more than once. *Great...* I thought to myself. *The last thing I needed was to be fighting a bug while we were in the middle of the biggest event for shifter kind.*

"We have plenty of wolves arriving as we speak, and a few streaks have arrived as well. Everyone is kind of keeping to themselves for the time being, but it would probably be a good idea to have you guys present during the mixer, since you're the ones changing everything. We have the welcome dinner already in motion, and then first thing in the morning we are to meet the descendants of the original Shifter Council. Hopefully make things feel more official," Elijah explained, and Bastian nodded.

"Shanely, do you think your dad can watch Aerith?" he asked. I nodded slowly, and he cocked his head to the side.

"Hey baby, are you okay? You look a little pale," Bastian asked as he knelt by my side. He immediately started inspecting me, placing his hand on my forehead to check for fevers, but I waved him off.

"Yes, I'm fine! Why don't you take Aerith to his room now? I can meet you in the main lobby after I freshen up a bit," I replied, giving him a weak smile.

He frowned slightly. "Okay, I can do that. Will you be okay though?"

"Of course! Go, I'll only be a few minutes behind you," I said as another wave hit me. I took in a deep breath, hoping to contain my breakfast for at least a few minutes longer. Bastian scooped Aerith up off the couch before turning to Cade.

"You will escort her then?"

"Yup! Elijah will go with you, and I've got Baby Girl."

Bastian nodded and leaned down to kiss my forehead. "I'll see you in a little bit then."

Elijah waved goodbye and left with Bastian right on his heels. I exhaled deeply and steadied myself by the table until I heard their footsteps fading down the hall. Cade was staring at me, watching me closely as my mouth watered and bile rose to the back of my throat. *This wasn't passing...* Before Cade could say anything, I bolted to the bathroom.

I had barely made it to the toilet before I emptied my stomach. Cade got a front row view to me losing the contents of my stomach again. *I've got to stop throwing up in front of them.*

"Baby Girl," Cade whispered, when I finally stopped heaving. I slowly stood and rinsed my mouth out before looking for my toothbrush.

"I am so sorry, Cade. I don't know what came over me."

He watched me from the doorway as I started brushing my teeth to rid my mouth and breath of the awfulness that just came out of me. He gave me a moment to finish up before coming over. Cade picked me up abruptly, setting me on the counter to check me over. I gave him a look as he felt my forehead and then each cheek.

"You're not running a fever or anything. Did you feel sick earlier?"

"No," I answered truthfully. "It just came out of nowhere, but I'm sure it's nothing. Probably just jitters over the Summit. Everything needs to go smoothly otherwise I don't see us blending anytime soon."

I hopped off the counter before choosing to sit on my bed instead. I wanted to make sure I wasn't going to puke again, but I needed to get out of Cade's prying eyes. He sat next to me, and I just tried to pretend like it never happened. Because honestly, I felt way better now than I did a moment ago.

"Well, we should keep an eye on you. If you get sick again or start to feel worse then we need to take you to the pack doctor."

"I'll be fine, Cade," I said, nudging him. "Just promise me one thing?"

"What?"

"Please don't tell Bastian I just got sick," I asked quietly. I knew he wouldn't like my request, and sure enough, I got a stern look from my Beta. *But I had a good reason.*

"Shanely, I don't want to get in the middle of you two like this," he said, giving me a pointed look, "besides he *should* know, so he can keep an eye on you too."

"I know, and normally I wouldn't hide it, but he's got a lot on his mind, Cade. It's not easy being Alpha over everyone *and* dealing with those in the prison here. He's having a hard time with your dad especially," I said as Cade

CHAPTER 13

gave me an understanding nod. "He's already stressed, Cade. I just don't want to worry him because my nerves got in the way."

Cade gave me another pointed look, but it softened, and I knew I had won. "Alright, but if you get worse then I'm telling him."

"Deal," I smiled gratefully. I leaned on his shoulder, giving myself a few more moments before I left to face everyone. But my mind was in a thousand different places at once.

My stomach churned, thinking about the events coming up and meeting with the descendants, but I didn't think it was so bad that I made myself sick over it. Then again *everything* was riding on me being able blend everyone together smoothly. I had years of hatred and mistrust to weed through, and while I was technically the Head of the wolves, I wasn't really anything to the other shifter kinds.

All these thoughts were making my head spin.

And it was not helping my stomach feel any better.

Chapter 14

Cade and I made our way downstairs and found Bastian, Elijah, and Luke all standing by the railing. I looked over the rail to the main floor below and saw a plethora of shifters filing in. The Summit pack was checking everyone in like a hotel would and directing shifters to their rooms. Bastian's eyes lit up when they found mine, and he gave me a quick kiss.

"There you two are. I was getting anxious," he whispered in my ear as Cade starting whispering to Elijah. I eyed them closely as Elijah's face flashed with concern before he immediately turned to me. *Crap*, I thought to myself. *I asked Cade not to tell Bastian, but I think he just told Elijah.*

"Yeah, I just wanted to freshen up before meeting everyone. When's dinner happening?"

"In about an hour. Most of the shifters are arriving today with the exceptions of a few coming in the morning. We thought we'd have a later dinner tonight to make sure to give everyone enough time to get settled in," Luke replied.

I nodded and rested my head against Bastian. I looked to the Fenrir brothers, who were both looking at me with concerned. *They needed to stop it before Bastian noticed.*

"Cade? Did you just tell Elijah?" I asked through our link.

"You said not to tell Bastian, but Elijah's fair game. I feel better with more eyes on you anyways, Shanely."

I rolled my eyes and pulled Elijah into our conversation now.

"Okay, listen up, you two. I am completely okay. Stop staring at me like I'm an injured puppy. I don't want this event to turn into everyone constantly watching

CHAPTER 14

me just because I threw up once," I said firmly. Luke chattered on about the mixer.

"Shanely..." Elijah chimed in, giving me a look, *"we want to make sure you are alright. You don't just get sick like that for no reason."*

"Exactly what I said," Cade butted in. *"That's not normal for you, Shanely."*

"I'm okay, really. I promise I feel fine right now! I just don't want to upset Bastian. Everything's weighing on him heavily right now."

"Fine, we won't tell anyone else," Cade said, his eyes flashing red, "but I'm your Beta and certifiable best friend, so I'm going to do what's best for you no matter what."

Elijah nudged his brother. "Hey, I'm her best friend too! But seriously Shanely, even though I'm not your Beta, I'll always act like it. You're our sister, so your health and safety come first."

I chuckled softly. "And I can't thank you two enough for that. You both are my best friends, but I promise you it was a fluke thing."

They didn't look too convinced, but they nodded towards me, subtly ending our conversation. I watched from above as families came in with their littles, who were excited to be somewhere new. It made me smile seeing them run about and play. *This is what we were doing this for,* I thought to myself. *This was worth a little stress.* After a few more moments, Bastian lead me down the hall towards the dining hall.

Dinner smelled amazing, and I found our friends from the Romania pack back in the kitchen once more. *Everyone was in for a treat tonight,* I thought to myself. Bastian led me to behind one of the serving tables in the back and tossed me an apron. I grinned, turning to face the room as shifters of all kinds starting filing in eager to eat.

The Romanian pack brought out the food in large pans while Bastian, Cade, Elijah, and I helped the pack serve food for tonight. We greeted all sorts of shifters, and this was the first time meeting some of them for me. Mountain lions, panthers, and foxes were the ones I recognize, but Bastian and Elijah helped me with the others. We had a few anacondas present as well as crocodiles, lions, and even elephants. They insisted they wouldn't shift inside, and I nearly snorted at that. *Imagine a herd of elephants running a muck through the house? Imagine any shifter running amuck through the house...*

We mostly had wolves, bears, and tigers here though. As we filled the plates of everyone here, I leaned over to my Beta and asked, "So why are the other shifter numbers so low?"

Cade replied, "It's difficult to pass the ability on for some. Bears, tigers, wolves, and African Lions almost *always* pass the ability to shift onto their young, but for all other shifter kinds, it was rare to pass the gift."

I frowned slightly, scooping another pile of food onto a young wolf's plate. "So most of their children..."

"Don't have an animal to shift into," he answered, giving me grim smile. "It's a bummer but not much can be done, so their numbers were very low. You won't see aquatic shifters here either. They hate land and prefer to stay in their animal forms in the water."

My eyes widened slightly as I filled another plate. *It was so interesting learning about other shifter kinds*, I thought to myself. *I finally felt like I was fairly knowledgeable when it came to shifters, but it seems I still had so much to learn.* I scooped the last portion in my tray and pulled it from the holder.

"I'm going for a refill!" I hollered to the line, but everyone was too busy to notice. Smiling, I headed back into the kitchen.

As soon as I walked in something sour filled my nose. My stomach churned as bile rose to the back of my throat. *God, what is that?* I thought as I covered my nose. I looked near the waste bins, but they weren't very full, and I didn't see anything rancid in there. I followed my nose, trying to find the source of that awful smell, but when I opened the fridge...

The putrid smell hit me like a ton of bricks, and I held my breath. Inside were trays and trays of some kind of fish. They were mashed into some sort of dish with lots of lemon and dill, but it was just awful. *It had definitely gone bad*, I thought as saliva filled my mouth, and I just couldn't take it anymore. My eyes watered as I ran to the garbage bin with my hand over my mouth. I heaved into it, gripping the sides of the bin roughly, when two hands gently grabbed my hair.

They pulled it aside as I continued to evacuate my stomach. Nothing but bile rose, burning my eyes as it violently left my stomach. *God... this sucked.*

CHAPTER 14

When I was finally done puking my guts out, the mystery hands gave me a towel, and I quickly cleaned myself up. I turned to find Cade standing there with concern in his eyes again.

"Shanely... What is going on?"

"That fish smells awful, Cade. We can't serve it," I said, motioning to the fridge. He gave me an odd look before walking to the fridge and opening it. I quickly covered my face with the towel as he inhaled deeply. He shut the door.

"It smells alright to me."

My eyes narrowed. "Cade, it's rancid. Don't you smell that?"

"No, I don't," he said, crossing his arms, "and this is twice in the last couple hours that you've gotten sick. Something's not right."

Bastian walked in, carrying two empty trays.

"Hey, Baby. What are you doing with the towel?"

I quickly tossed it aside and tried to just hold my breath instead. He refilled his pans and looked back at me, waiting on an answer, but I didn't have an answer to give him. *He had enough on his plate, and if he thought I was fighting a bug or something, he would bench me for the whole Summit.*

And I couldn't do that. I had to make sure everything went smoothly for him too.

Cade crossed his arms, waiting on my answer too, and I nearly scowled at him. His eyes bore into my skull, and I forced myself to look away.

"Oh, nothing. I just wanted Cade to make sure the fish was alright. It just smelled off to me is all," I quickly replied, and Cade rolled his eyes.

"Okay, well let's make sure it's good then. We can't afford people getting sick at dinner," he winked at me as he checked the fridge too. I held my breath, while Cade studied me closely.

"It smells alright to me," Bastian replied before grabbing his pan again.

"That's what I said too. I *also* said Shanely looked a little off tonight, and I suggested maybe she grab something to eat and take a break. Don't you think that's a good idea, Bastian?" Cade asked, and I glared at him. He stuck his tongue out at me as Bastian walked up behind him.

"Babe, don't push yourself. If you're wore out then you need to take a break. Are you sure you're doing okay though? You didn't look great back in our room either," he said, setting his pan down and feeling my forehead. He looked concerned as he inspected me all over, and guilt ate me up inside. *This is why I didn't want to tell him anything,* I thought to myself. *I didn't want to be another reason for stressing him out this week.*

"I'm okay, my love. I can finish serving with you guys," I replied as I gently pulled away. The idea of food wasn't too appealing to me anyways.

"No, baby. Just grab a plate, and take a break. We can finish up," Bastian insisted as he pushed me out the kitchen doors.

"Bastian, I'm really okay..."

"Please take a break and eat something. I can't have you down and out this week, baby. I need you, Shanely. If I'm going to make it through any of this, I need you to be okay," he replied, giving me a pleading look.

I caved then. "Alright. I'll eat a little something."

He grinned back at me. "That's my good girl. Now c'mon."

Bastian guided me down the line, filling a plate quickly. Elijah gave me a funny look, but I didn't say anything. I already knew Cade was filling him in as we speak. Bastian led me to where my father, Caleb, and Abraham sat with Bay and Aerith. Someone from the Romanian pack called Bastian's name, and he quickly set my plate down, giving me a kiss on my cheek before running back into the kitchen. I felt horrible not being there to help anymore, but I could see Cade watched me from afar. I didn't even get a step in before his link came through.

"Don't even think about it, Baby Girl. You eat and stay off your feet or I'm telling Bastian."

I stuck my tongue at him before turning to my family, but they were looking at me funny too.

"What's wrong?" I asked nervously.

Caleb scrunched his nose. "I'm not sure. Does she seem off to you, dad?"

My father inhaled deeply. "Yeah, she does. Are you feeling okay, Shanely?"

I shrugged. "I've been a little nervous about everything, but I'm alright."

"What's going on?" Abraham asked.

"I don't know, she just smells different. I can't figure out what it is," Caleb

CHAPTER 14

answered. Abraham scented me too, and I playfully pushed him away.

"She smells normal to me. I mean she could use a shower, but she doesn't smell like anything out of the ordinary," he replied with a laugh. I punched his arm before returning to my plate. I really wasn't hungry, but I picked at it anyways.

My father shrugged. "I don't know then. Glad you are able to eat with us though."

I smiled as I bit into a roll. "Me too. I've missed you guys."

Caleb shrugged before giving me a playful look. "I see you nearly everyday."

"Fine, I missed dad," I replied, making my father laugh. I took another bite as I could feel Cade's gaze on me still. As long as I munched he wouldn't tell Bastian, so I forced myself to eat something. I really didn't want to make anything worse for my mate.

I caught up with my dad and brothers and talked to different shifters eating near us. The evening seemed to be going on rather well all in all. Suddenly, Bastian's voice filled the room, and when I turned I saw him at the microphone. I smiled, and he winked at me before continuing.

"Welcome, everyone! We're so happy everyone could make it for this year's Shifter Summit Event!"

The room thundered in applause, and my mate let everyone go for a moment before raising his hands high. I shoveled the last of my roll in my mouth as the room continued to cheer.

"My Fated Mate and I would like to warmly welcome everyone tonight. We know word is spreading fast amongst the shifter world, and ever since we discovered that my mate was not only the White Wolf but also the White Bear, we knew that we wanted to make big changes for the benefit of all shifters. Shanely, will you join me?"

My eyes widened. I had no idea he planned to call me to the front tonight, and my cheeks were currently stuffed to the brim of buttery bread. Abraham and Caleb laughed hysterically as everyone's eyes turned to me. My mate extended out his hand, and slowly got to my feet, trying to chew my bite quickly. I gave my brothers a death glare, who only laughed harder.

Please don't trip, I thought to myself as I walked between the tables. *Or choke. God, that's all I needed to make this night perfect, the Heimlich.* Bastian grabbed my hand and turned back to the crowd with a smile. I tried to turn away slightly, covering my mouth with my hand so I could chew without everyone seeing, and I could still hear Abraham and Caleb chuckling in the back. *Pay back was in their near future.*

"For too long, we've had hatred amongst shifters simply because of the animals we are, but Shanely could see something we could not. She gave the wolves a new perspective and blended us with the bears and tigers in our area. Now that we are the Alphas over all wolves, we want to extend that same mentality to the rest of shifter kind. We are abolishing the law that says shifters can't mix! We are abolishing the law that says shifters cannot mate with other shifters not of their kind! Mates are sacred, and we plan to treat them as such," Bastian said loudly in the microphone. Surprisingly, a great amount of cheering came from the crowd, but as my eyes drifted around the room, I could still see a whole lot of uneasiness on many faces. *Just like when we first met the wolves in the last Summit*, I thought to myself.

I finally swallowed the massive chunk of bread before grinning at my mate bashfully. He shook his head, chuckling to himself before pulling me into his arms.

"Not everyone seems okay with this, Bastian," I said through the link.

"Baby steps. Just try not to choke, love."

I smirked at him as he continued on.

"No events have been planned for tonight, so just relax and enjoy yourselves! We have activities and events planned for the whole week for everyone to enjoy though, but if you have any questions or concerns, please bring it to Luke's attention. He is the Head of Security and Alpha of the Summit Hall pack. He will help you as well as Shanely or I! While most of our meals will be right here in this room, tomorrow night will be our first scheduled ball, with the very special mate dance event. All single shifters are invited to participate for that event. So enjoy tonight, and remember, this whole event is to forge new friendships and make alliances!"

Everyone clapped once more as Bastian led me back to our table. I smiled, feeling lighter than before as we approached our family. We sat down, and I pushed Bastian my plate, no longer hungry. He didn't seem to notice I had basically only eaten a few bites and the roll off it as everyone started congratulating him on his speech and talking about the week coming up. I barely got a word in as everyone was busy all talking at once. I didn't mind though. Everyone was real excited for the Summit this year, and *that* made me feel good.

The rest of the evening went by fairly well, and I met so many new people. Other than Cade watching me the whole night, it was pleasant. We said our goodbyes after dinner and called it night somewhat early. I refused to admit it, but I did feel off. I was afraid I caught a bug before we came, and I was hoping it would be gone by morning. *My shifter abilities should help me fight it off fast, I would think.*

Bastian, Aerith, and I spent the last of our evening in our room, watching a movie together. I got to snuggle with my family, with no problems or issues, and it was perfect. Just perfect. That is until Bastian was called back down to the prison below. He cringed as he stood up to leave and a scowl replaced his smile. My shoulders fell as we put his shoes on, I hated seeing him so stressed, and I knew seeing his dad down there wasn't going to help him any.

"I can go, Bastian," I said, sitting forward on the couch. "Just because Luke sent for you doesn't mean I can't handle what needs done."

Bastian laced up the other boot saying, "No, Shanely. I don't want be down there myself, but I *certainly* don't want you down there. I'll just go see what the problem is and come back to you."

I sighed. "Bastian, we are a team. I'm the White Wolf and I..."

"Please, baby," he whispered softly. Bastian stood tall, walking towards me and gripping my chin firmly. "Please just stay far away from the prison below. If you really want to help me, stay right here where I know you'll be safe."

His soft lips met mine, and I knew he wasn't playing fair. But it was hard to think when he kissed me again. Far rougher than the first time, and I dug my hand in his hair.

A knock sounded, and Bastian pulled away, resting his head briefly on mine.

"I'll be back soon," he whispered before giving me one last kiss and disappearing out the door. I slumped on the couch, missing him already.

Chapter 15

I awoke under a mess of sticky sheets the next morning. *Bastian must have carried me to bed because I know I fell asleep on the couch waiting for him*, I thought. I looked over to Bastian, who slept like a rock besides me. *I wonder when he got in last night.* Suddenly my stomach churned again, and I barely managed to get to the bathroom in time before I got sick.

Thankfully, I didn't wake Bastian, and I quickly brushed my teeth to rid my mouth of the awful taste of bile and leaned against the sink. *What in the world was wrong with me? I must have some sort of bug or maybe it was a touch of food poisoning? That would explain the randomness*, I thought before turning on the shower. Water fell from the ceiling, mimicking rain, and I closed my eyes as the water ran down my body. I stayed in the warm water until my fingers felt pruney before forcing myself to get out.

I actually felt refreshed and fairly good once I had dried off and wrapped myself in one of the robes here. *Maybe I was finally getting past this bug*, I thought to myself. I left the bathroom as Bastian was just waking up. He rubbed his sleepy eyes, smiling as he looked at me.

"Morning, my love."

"Morning, baby," I replied, giving him a kiss. "Go take a shower, Bastian. I'll drop off Aerith to my Aunt Cassia real quick, and then we can head to our morning meeting."

Bastian groaned. "I forgot about that. I was hoping we could skip breakfast and spend the morning in bed. I missed out last night."

His wicked grin made my heart flutter, and the thought of spending the morning in bed was amazing. *We haven't had a chase in awhile*, I thought to myself, and I could see what was on his mind. Now that I had my wolf, I was able to actually give him a real chase, but we had no time for that this morning.

I gave him a devilish grin in return. "Bastian, you know we can't skip this meeting. Now go on and get cleaned up or we'll be late."

"Then let's be late, and you can join me. How does that sound?"

He wrapped his arms around my waist and gently kissed across my shoulders towards my neck. He knew my weak spot, and he was using every play in the book to get me to change my mind, especially when his hands ran up and down my thigh.

"Babe, we can't. You and I both know Luke will be looking for us in the next few minutes, and I really don't want to be interrupted with something like that," I said as I gently pulled away.

His face fell, and I hated to disappoint him like this. I wanted nothing more than to stay with my mate. All these Alpha responsibilities were wearing on us both, and I missed him. *We always ended up going in two different directions it seems,* I thought to myself. A vacation kept coming into my mind, and once we got home, I was going to look into it.

Bastian looked disappointed, and it killed me. I hated the look of rejection he couldn't help but make.

"Alright, but you owe me," he replied before swatting my butt.

"Hey, how did it go last night?" I asked, and I saw his face darken.

He just grumbled not really answering me, and my heart sunk.

"I'm sorry."

"It's fine," he said, kissing my cheek. He headed off to the bathroom then.

"I can feel you watching me, mate," he said with a forced laugh. He was changing the subject, so I let him.

"What? Can't help my mate is incredibly sexy," I replied in a cheerful voice, watching him disappear behind the bathroom door. *I needed to help him relax today,* I thought to myself.

I sighed, going through the dresser for my clothes for the day. I grabbed my dark jeans, and my white dress shirt. I wanted to look nice but not so formal, so I grabbed my black waist band. I fastened it just under my chest, and I

CHAPTER 15

quickly straightened my hair. I almost always had it curly, but I decided to let it be straight for the day. It's funny how something a simple as straightening my hair made me look like a whole new person.

I left our room and made my way to Aerith's room. She had a big day yesterday too and was still passed out asleep in her bed. I gently woke her up and got her ready for the day. It didn't take long for that extra burst of energy all children seemed equipped with to kick in though, and I put her in jeans and a cardigan since we were going outside later today. *Our coats would be downstairs already, so this was perfect for now.* I heard someone at the door, but Bastian grabbed it.

"Luke's here, love. I'm heading out with him. Have Cade walk with you and Aerith this morning okay, baby?"

"Bastian, we'll be okay. Just going down the elevator," I replied.

"Just humor me."

"Alright," I said, caving again. *"I'll knock on his door. Now go, and I'll see you soon."*

I felt him kiss my cheek through our link, and then the door closed. I waited for Aerith to brush her hair and officially be ready for the day before grabbing my shoes. I grabbed her an apple off the counter, and we made our way to the door.

We entered the empty hallway, and I listened in at Cade's door. He was snoring so loudly I could hear him through the door. I didn't have the heart to wake him, plus I didn't want to answer any *How are you feeling?* questions. He would just fuss over me, so I let him be.

"C'mon, baby. Let's just let Uncle Cade sleep. We can find Aunt Cassia ourselves, right?"

"Right! We're smart! We can find her."

Suddenly, I had an idea. "Why don't you try finding her like you did your uncles yesterday?"

She jumped up and down excitedly. "Oh! I can do that!"

We followed down the hallway to the elevators on the left. I opted against the stairs once the room began to sway slightly, churning my stomach all over again. Once inside, we pushed the number 2 button and began our descent. Aerith shot out of the elevator the second the doors opened. Her little nose wiggling all around as she focused on her task at hand, and I wish I had brought my phone. *I would have taken a video to show the others,* I thought as I followed her down the hall. I knew my Aunt Cassia was in room 215, but I was curious if Aerith would be able to find her. She slowed down near 210 and carefully went to each and every door. She paused before settling on 215.

"This one, mommy. I can smell Aunt Cassia, Uncle Cain, and someone else."

I smiled wide. "You got it right, baby. Good job! Go ahead and knock."

She knocked on the door rapidly. Cain answered it and scooped her up quickly.

"We've got adorable visitors, Cassia!" he bellowed before ushering us in the room.

Their room was slightly smaller than ours was but still nice and spacious. I smiled at my aunt, when Michelle suddenly came around the corner, and I stopped in my tracks. Bastian had been so busy with me and our new position that he really hasn't had much of a chance to talk with his mom. I didn't want to get in the middle of this, and I didn't know if he'd want me to leave Aerith here now.

"Hi, Shanely. It's nice to see you again," Michelle said sweetly before sitting back down at the table.

"Hello, Michelle. I'm sorry, Aunt Cassia. I didn't realize you would be busy this morning. I should have called," I said sheepishly.

"No, no, I'm not busy at all. I was just catching up with Michelle here. We were good friends before... Well before everything happened. Do you need me to watch Aerith?"

"Well... I don't want to interrupt. I can ask my dad too. I just have a meeting this morning, and I can't take her with," I replied apprehensively.

"I can help Cassia watch her, if you want?" Michelle offered. "I mean it would be nice to get to know my granddaughter after all."

"Oh, that's a lovely idea!" Cassia said with a warm smile. "We can all hang out in here until it's time for breakfast."

I opened my mouth, when my uncle stepped in between to pass Aerith off

CHAPTER 15

to my aunt.

"Shanely, we're late for that meeting actually. Better get a move on," Cain said, nudging me along.

I frowned, looking back at the table where my daughter sat on her aunt's lap. *Surely Aerith would be fine here, right?* Cassia was the one watching her after all. Cain pushed me towards the door again, and I sighed.

"Okay, just stay here if you don't mind? I'll come grab her before the activities start. Aerith be good and listen to Aunt Cassia," I said, and she gave me a nod. Michelle looked a little dejected by that and guilt ate me up inside. *I don't know how to handle her,* I thought to myself. But I didn't want to cause undo pain on anyone. Not even Michelle.

"And have fun with your grandmother," I said, tugging on Aerith's curls softly. "This is daddy's mother, Michelle."

"Shanely," Cain said firmly, tapping his watch as he gave me a pointed look.

Aerith looked at the woman sitting across the table and gave a little wave. I don't know if I just made a mistake, but Michelle just looked so excited, giving me a grateful smile. I reluctantly followed Cain out the room, feeling off about the whole thing. *I hope I made the right decision.*

My uncle led us to the elevators, and we went all the way to the main floor. Not far from the ballroom was a grand conference room, where our meeting was scheduled to be held. It was the same room I was unfortunately stuck in with the old council actually, but that was the past. I was excited for the now.

The tables were laid out in a circle against a main table. Bastian and Elijah were already sitting at the head table and every seat was filled minus three. Luke and his enforcers were scattered across the room, and I followed my uncle before taking my seat next to Bastian.

"Bastian, I need to talk to you..."

"Shanely, you're late!" Bastian whispered before quickly turning to everyone. Nervous energy rippled through our bond, and my shoulders fell. *I can tell him about his mother and Aerith after this, I suppose.* Cade was the last to enter, giving me a stern look before sitting next to me.

Cade leaned over and whispered, "You went without me this morning. We will be talking later, Baby Girl."

Great... I thought as I rubbed my face. *I've pissed off two out of the three Fenrir brothers.* I felt an intense stare coming from my left, and I turned to find Elijah giving me a stern look too. *I guess make that three...*

Sighing, I rubbed my temples, hoping to clear this headache that was creeping in. My vision swayed ever so slightly, and I tried to sit as still as possible to keep myself from throwing up.

Bastian stood then and greeted everyone. "Welcome, everyone! Each and everyone of you is a direct descendant of the original Shifter Council along with a few new additions. Shanely and I both appreciate you all coming so without further a due, I hereby start the first meeting of the Shifter Alliance."

I looked around the room as everyone gave a short round of applause. I couldn't get a great read on everyone, but I was grateful Bastian was running this meeting today. *I didn't think I had it in me to do it.*

Bastian sat back down and settled in his chair. I tried to sit up a bit more, so I didn't look like such a slouch, but I just felt awful. My stomach churned from worrying how Bastian would take his mother watching Aerith with Cassia, and this freaking headache that came out of the blue was driving me insane. Cade glaring at me didn't help any either.

"To begin, we realize that there are not as many shifters as there was once before. As Shanely and I announced earlier, we want to abolish the laws stating shifters couldn't mix. We are hoping it will increase the number of mates found and thus helping out our population issue. Does anyone object to this?"

The man directly across from us spoke.

"The issue is merely ours. Wolves tend to breed like rabbits, and that's why you and your mate own the majority share with the alliance. You really don't need our vote," he replied coldly.

"What's your name?" I asked, and everyone turned to look at me.

"James. I'm in charge of the only African lion pride in the world," he said in a softer tone. His hazel eyes softened, and I gave him a smile.

"It's nice to meet you, James. While the largest kind of shifters are wolves, it doesn't mean we aren't seeing issues with finding mates. Besides, it's

CHAPTER 15

clear that Bastian and I are trying to show you all that we value your opinion. We understand the tension that fills the room. These problems are not going away overnight, but they *can* go away in time. So we are asking; Do you have an issue abolishing the law officially, and will you be okay with your pride finding mates, whomever they might be?"

Bastian gave me a proud smirk before moving his eyes back to James.

"I do not have a problem. I would like to see improvement for my pride, and this seems like the best bet."

"Anyone else?" I asked.

No one said anything in objection, so I continued, "Luke will make sure everyone receives an official document stating the change. Abolishing the law brings forth new issues though. We will still need rules," I said firmly. "Problems need to be handled within the groups involved. I vote for serious matters, or matters that no one can agree on, to be brought forward to *this* council. Anything else can be handled within. Raise your hand if you agree."

Everyone raised their hand, and I exhaled slowly. *That wasn't so bad,* I thought to myself still eyeing the trash can in the corner.

"Any mating will be allowed no matter what shifter kind is involved. It *must* be honored. That being said, it is up to the groups involved to decide who moves where. Agreed?"

Everyone raised their hand again. *This was going fairly smoothly,* I thought as Bastian signed off on the slip of paper before passing it to me.

"One last thing, I want to bring to our attention. The Division is becoming an issue with our pack lately, and they are trying to exercise authority they do not have. I move that all issues with the Division needs to be brought before this alliance. Agreed?"

Half raised their hands. *Shoot... I jinxed myself.*

"What's the issue for the half that did not raise their hand?" Bastian asked.

A panther woman spoke up now. "Why should we be involved with the Divisional problems of wolves? We are a much smaller group, so why rock the boat, so to speak."

"Because what if you start having problems with the Division? Wouldn't you want help or guidance?" Bastian growled, commanding the room's attention.

She shrunk in her seat a little. "Well... We *are* smaller. We don't have the resources to go against them."

Bastian scoffed now. "So what because the wolves have more numbers, we're just supposed to sacrifice ourselves at your beck and call?"

She glared at him now, and my wolf snapped angrily at the disrespect. "No..." the panther snapped back, "but you and your mate are two prophecies in one. You have tremendous power, and we can all feel it. It's why you are at the head table, and no one is pushing for it. You have the numbers and power to help out the smaller alliances."

Bastian stood, leaning forward on the table with his arms spread wide, and I felt his anger trickle through our bond. He seemed fully in control, so I sat back and let him go. *He didn't need me here.*

"Let me make something *clear* to everyone. Shanely and I put this group together because we want to help us as a whole, but we will not be the only security here. If this is to work, then we all must be a team together. It's us against the Division. I will not sacrifice my pack or the wolves as a whole to protect all of you if you refuse to assist anyone else," he snarled.

"But if we stick our necks out for you and then it backfires on us with our own Division Head, what then?" the panther snapped back. *Lord, this girl...*

"Then we help you. Don't you get it? The Division likes that we are divided because it's easier to control us. If they keep us small and divided then they can slaughter us all if they choose to. But if we work together *and* look out for one another, then we will become a real threat against them. I'm not saying start a war, but if one comes up then I want to know we can sure as heck finish it!" I cried out as I sat forward in my chair. My wolf snarled angrily, making my head spin even worse. Keeping her at bay was making me feel awful.

"It makes sense, Esme. This isn't going to work if we don't all start playing fair and trusting each other," Abraham countered, and I turned to him. *I didn't even know he knew her,* I thought to myself, but she hesitated for a moment. Trust with her wasn't going to come easily, I realized.

"Fine. Bring all Division issues to the Alliance. We deal with them

CHAPTER 15

together," she finally replied.

I smiled at her. "Anyone else disagree?"

No one said a word, and I let out a deep breath. I leaned back in my chair grateful the meeting had gone fairly alright.

"Alright then. Everyone has our numbers, so we can always stay in contact from here on out. I say let's end here and go finish up breakfast before it's over with," Bastian said, and everyone nodded and started filing out. I stayed behind with my mate and brothers. We slowly made our way out the room, letting the others get further ahead of us.

"Good lord, I wasn't sure how that meeting was going to go," Elijah muttered, letting out a deep breath.

I nodded, feeling my stomach churn again. Maybe I just needed to eat something? I wondered as we made our way down the hall. Cade continue to eye me funny but didn't make a big deal over it. *As long as I acted fine, he'd have nothing to worry about.*

"I know. I've been freaking out about this meeting all week," Bastian grumbled as he grabbed my hand. The dining room was just ahead, but it wasn't until we got to the door when I remembered Aerith.

We stepped inside, and I turned to Bastian. "Wait... I need to pick Aerith up in Cassia's room."

He snarled loudly though, and I jumped hard. His eyes weren't on me but at something directly ahead. I peeked around him to find Aerith in Michelle's arms, eating food at the table. My Aunt Cassia was nowhere to be seen, and everyone stopped to look at my mate.

Crap.

He turned to face me. "Did you know she had Aerith?!"

I sighed then. "Yes, I did. It's not exactly..."

My mate's eyes widened as he stepped back like I struck him, and my voice trailed off. He had this look of betrayal on his face, and that about broke me.

"Bastian..."

"You left her with that woman?! Even after knowing how I felt about her, and that I wasn't ready to let her back into *our* lives, let alone our children's!"

My brows furrowed as guilt filled my chest. "Bastian, that's not what happened. I left her..."

Bastian had stopped listening and stormed away from me. My mouth dropped as he left me standing there in shock. *My mate has never talked to me like this before*, I thought as my heart began to break. *He's never once treated me like this.*

Cade was at my side, glaring ahead at his brother. I watched Bastian take Aerith from Michelle without a word before stomping passed us and out the door.

Elijah grabbed his hand to stop him. "Hey! Chill out, man."

Bastian yanked his arm free. "Don't, Elijah. I'm taking my daughter to our room. Then I'll know she will be safe at least."

He left without another word, and I was left humiliated in front of everyone. Why did he do that? Why didn't he give me the chance to explain? My mind ran amuck as I staggered on my feet. Tears filled my eyes as I turned to my Beta.

"Oh, Baby Girl..."

He reached out for me, but I stepped away. I didn't want anyone to comfort me. *Bastian was the one who did that, but he didn't want to be around me right now. He didn't want me.* It was my own fault. I knew he'd feel funny about it, but I didn't think he'd blow up like this over it.

Then I felt it.

Bastian closed our bond, and that just about *broke* me. My wolf and bear whined inside over the loss of our bond, and I felt utterly alone as I clutched my chest. Suddenly, this place just felt suffocating. I couldn't stand to be around everyone's prying eyes, and I couldn't go to my room. I just wanted to be *anywhere* but here.

"What's his problem!?" Elijah snapped, but Cade ignored him. My Beta was hyper focused on me as I took another step back.

"Shanely... Whatever you are thinking right now, don't do it. You still aren't feeling well, are you?"

My eyes shot to his angrily, but I was so done with this. I was so done with *everything*. The last thing I wanted was to cry in front of everyone, and arguing with my best friends wasn't something I could handle either. My eyes drifted to the door, and my wolf pushed me forward. She wanted to run.

"You two are not to follow me. You are to stay away from me until I say," I said quietly, letting my Alpha power out. Their eyes went wide as my command hit them in the chest, and I backed further away.

Cade's eyes flashed red with rage "Shanely, don't even think about taking off right now. Remove this command right now!"

He tried to step forward but was forced down by some invisible force. Elijah was the same way, and now that I was confident they could not follow me, I ran. I turned around and ran right out the side door that led outside. I took off across the yard and ran as fast as I could into the woods. I shifted into my wolf and ran to the only place I knew around here.

I ran to the waterfall.

Only when I heard the falls did I finally stop. I shifted back before collapsing and puking my guts out. The shift had been the final straw, and I couldn't hold back the nausea.

"Shanely!" Cade bellowed. *"Come back right now, and I will deal with my idiot brother! Baby Girl, answer me!"*

I shut down the link and all my bonds then. I made sure I was invisible before I finally let myself cry.

Chapter 16

I stayed at the waterfall for the rest of the day with no one but my thoughts to keep me company. I vaguely heard some of the festivities going on outside Summit Hall, but no one came in my direction. I knew they wouldn't. Bay and I planned this event together, and no one would be coming this way. I was alone here.

For hours, I was alone.

My stomach let me know I had skipped lunch a long time ago, but honestly I didn't care. I was sick of throwing up anyways. I wished it was summer though. I'd love to swim in the creek and clear my head, but it was just a frozen tundra out here. Despite the chill and my lack of coat, I refused to go back, and I shifted into my fur when I needed warmth.

Anger flooded through my veins as I thought about this morning. I couldn't believe my mate had spoken to me that way. *I wasn't trying to force him into anything with his mother, and where was my aunt?!* Guilt hit me hard then. Bastian wasn't okay with his mother. I knew that. Even thought Aerith was fine, I should have just said no and taken her to my dad.

My heart hurt just thinking about it, but I couldn't get it out of my mind. I couldn't get what he said or the way he looked at me out of my head. The longer I stayed out here, the worse I felt too. My head pounded against my skull, and my body felt jittery from the lack of food.

Bastian never came for me either. *That* just about killed me because he always came for me. *He always found me.*

A branched snapped behind me, but I knew who it was without even looking up. I could smell a tiger.

CHAPTER 16

"Shanely! Good God, there you are!" Abraham shouted after shifting back. He yanked out his phone and dialed a number. "Hey, I found her! Yeah, I'll bring her back just let Caleb know. Yeah, yeah... I'm moving, Cade."

He snapped his phone shut before kneeling down to where I was sitting. I shifted back as he got close.

"I'm not ready to go back, Abey," I said firmly.

"Shanely, your brothers and I have been looking everywhere for you! You can't just take off like that and binding Cade and Elijah?? What were you thinking?"

Anger flooded all my senses, and I abruptly got to my feet. "I was thinking my mate yelled at me in front of everyone, and I needed space! I was embarrassed, Abraham! Bastian's never talked that way to me before, and he's acting like I did this on purpose to hurt him when really, I was backed into a corner by his mother and my aunt. I did what I thought was best, and I tried to tell him before that stupid meeting!"

Abe's face softened as I paced the snowy ground before us. Tears filled my eyes as I went on, "Abraham, I can't do this. I can't be the White Wolf if *this* is what it will do to my mate and our bond. If the stress destroys my bond with Bastian, I think I'll die. I just can't Abey..."

He looked at me with sorrow in his eyes, and he hugged me tightly. I lost control of my emotions as I cried into his chest.

"He didn't even look for me, Abey," I said between sniffles.

Abraham sighed. "Shanely, I don't even know if he knows you've been missing all day. He's refused to leave his room. He and Aerith have spent the whole day together *alone*. Cade and Elijah sent me and Caleb to find you since they're grounded. No one thought you'd come back here though."

I pulled away. "It's pretty despite the memories; besides I didn't know where else to go."

"Look, I don't know what's going on with Bastian. Everyone can tell he's shouldering a lot on his plate, but so are you. I think he's just wound up tight being here. His dad is losing his mind in the prison below everyone's feet, which is not a pretty sight, let me tell you. And now his mom, who has never stood up for him before, wants to be grandma? Yeah, I'd be pissed too, but not at you. I think you just got the brunt of his anger today even though it was meant for someone else."

"Still doesn't excuse the way he spoke to me," I replied frustratedly. My wolf huffed in agreement.

"No, it does not, but that's something you need to say to him. Just try and give him some slack though. I mean he's never done something like this before, and you have also done some not so great things in the past, am I correct?" he asked, and I lowered my head in shame.

He sighed, rubbing my arm. "I don't mean to make you feel worse, just to remember he's hurting right now and clearly not in his right mind. Bastian loves you more than anything, Shanely, and I think he'd be beside himself if he knew you ran away like this. He's just too wrapped up in his own head at the moment, but your mate almost never misses a beat when it comes to you," Abey replied as he started dragging me along back to Summit Hall. He then gave me his hoodie, which I was grateful for. He wrapped his arm around me once I got it on, and we walked slowly through the snow.

"I don't know why I'm so bothered by this because you're right. I've done plenty to be ashamed of in the past, but it's like my emotions are all over the place lately, and I'm just hurt. He hasn't checked in once, and he's never needed space from me like this before. He's never even closed our bond before," I muttered, wiping my eyes again. "It's *killing* me and my animals. How are we supposed to fix this now? The ball's about to start, and everyone stares at us as it is. I don't want them to see us divided like this, but it's hard to do anything under all this scrutiny."

"Let's just handle one thing at a time, okay? First things first, you need to unlock Cade and Elijah. They've been blowing up my phone all day trying to find you. It's driving me crazy," he replied, rolling his eyes.

We stayed in silence after that, walking through the snow back towards everyone. I dreaded each and every step, but soon the gates to Summit Hall came into view. Cade and Elijah were stalking behind the metal gates, with their hands on their hips. I gulped.

They did not look happy.

"Shanely! Thank God, you're okay!" Elijah shouted but was soon pushed

CHAPTER 16

back by an invisible force the closer I got to them. Cade was seriously trying to fight it as well, but he was stepping back too. By the way their faces twisted and their eyes furrowed, it must be painful.

"Baby Girl, take off this stupid command right now!"

"Cade, Elijah... You are both free of the command to stay away from me," I replied. They took in a deep breath before Cade slammed into me.

"Don't you ever do that to me again! Do you hear me?"

"Cade! I can't breathe!" I said as I struggled under his tight grip before he finally let go, and Elijah hugged me far more gently.

"We're just glad you're okay," he said, kissing my forehead.

"Yeah, well at least I have you guys to look for me, right?" I said sarcastically, and Abey's words rattled through my mind again. I cut my snarky tone saying, "I am sorry I made you all worry. I just needed a moment to myself, and I couldn't go to my room."

I looked at the floor, and I could feel their anger from here. It was thick in the air, but honestly my own frustration was starting to match theirs again. *What in the world was wrong with me?*

Cade's phone rang, and he snarled when he saw who was calling. He sent them to voicemail and took my hand.

"C'mon, Baby Girl. We have a ball to go to tonight."

Elijah's phone went off now, and I had a feeling I knew who it was. He hesitated as it rang and looked at me. Cade must have known what he was debating and grabbed his brother's arm saying, "Oh no! Let him freak out for a while. I had to all day because of his temper. You ignore that call, Elijah!"

"He is her mate, Cade. And I'm his Beta. It's not right to ignore it. I mean how would you feel?"

His phone stopped ringing, and he missed the call anyways. Suddenly it dinged, and Elijah read the message.

"Look he is freaking out now! He said Shanely shut their bond, and he can't find her," he said, showing us the text.

"Look, I'll let you all handle Bastian. I'm going to find Bay, but please Shanely don't run off again. Just hide in my room if you need to," Abey said, giving me a kiss.

"Thanks for everything, Abraham," I replied as Cade and Elijah both gave him a grateful nod. He left the dining hall, leaving the three of us alone.

"Elijah, let him stew. He needs to see how bad he's messed up. Bastian's locked himself in his room all day and has no idea that we couldn't find Shanely since this morning! Do not respond! I'm her Beta, and I said no!" Cade snarled out, and Elijah slowly put his phone back in his pocket, gritting his teeth the whole time.

"Guys, can I change in your room? Please?"

My question interrupted their argument, and they both softened when they turned to me. I was just ready to get this night over with, and I was already feeling like crap. I hadn't had anything to eat either, so my body felt really weak and off.

"Of course, Shanely. Let's just get her ready for tonight. Bastian will be finding us any minute anyways," Elijah countered, and they led me down the hall and to their suite.

Cade was fuming mad the whole way up, while Elijah just looked stressed. I hated they were stuck in the middle of us, but I wasn't ready to fight with Bastian right now. We were late for the Ball as it was, and everyone was excited for the Mate Dance. I didn't want to ruin everyone's night because I was fighting with my mate.

Cade opened their door, and I walked inside their room. It was nice and cozy. Not as big as my room with Bastian, but still a good size and perfect for the two of them.

"Hang on a minute," Cade said before leaving us alone. I sat on the bed and leaned on Elijah, while we waited for Cade to return.

"I'm sorry, Shanely," he said quietly before wrapping his arm around me.

"It's not your fault, Elijah. I know your brother is overwhelmed by everything, and I have no room to talk. I just... He shut our bond. He didn't even look for me. Bastian always looks for me, Elijah."

I sniffed, trying not to cry again, and my brother-in-law just held me close. He had no words to comfort me though, so in silence we sat. Cade came in a few moments later with my makeup bag, and the dress I had chosen for tonight. He gave me a soft smile as he handed everything to me.

CHAPTER 16

"Bastian and Aerith weren't in their room, so I grabbed your stuff," he replied, handing me everything.

"Thank you guys again. I don't know what I'd do without you," I replied, giving them a weak smile.

"We are always here for you, Baby Girl," Cade said.

"Go change. We'll dress out here, and we can walk you down," Elijah chimed in. I nodded and entered their bathroom.

I took a moment to myself before daring to look in the mirror. But nothing compared me for what I saw. *God, I looked awful!* I thought as I looked in the mirror. I had deep, dark circles under my eyes, and my face was red and blotchy from crying. I immediately started applying makeup. That was a *must*. I was glad he brought the whole bag because I needed everything tonight. I added more than I usually used to hide some of that awfulness away before fluffing out my hair. I didn't have time to shower or style it, but I honestly didn't even care tonight. I felt as awful as I looked.

I put on my long black evening gown and then my heels. My dress was gorgeous, but I had picked this dress with Bastian in mind, but now it just didn't seem so special anymore. Nothing felt right with the two of us at odds. I left my clothes and bag in their bathroom before knocking on the door.

"Can I come out now?"

Elijah laughed. "Yeah, we're ready."

I entered their main room and smiled wide. *All the girls were going to be going crazy for them during the Mate Dance,* I thought to myself.

"Wow, Shanely! You're gorgeous!" Elijah said as he spun me around. I smiled wide, and Cade noticed.

"It's good to see that smile again, Baby Girl. Shall I escort you, Milady?" he asked, holding out his arm.

"Thank you both for everything. Did Bastian... stop by?" I asked quietly.

Cade's eyes flashed red as he said, "No, he hasn't. I wouldn't have let him in anyways."

A part of me was relieved that I didn't have to face him right now. I was terrified he was still angry with me over what happened, and I didn't think I could take seeing that look he gave me earlier. The other part of me was crushed, again. *Why hasn't he found me?* I thought to myself. *He can clearly see Cade and Elijah's bond and had asked them where I was. Wouldn't he come here at some point to see for himself?*

"Let's go, I suppose," I said, making my way to the door.

Elijah opened it, letting us all out into the hall, when Cade snarled loudly. I stepped out to find Bastian exiting the elevator in his tux. He looked good in his simple yet elegant black tux but his eyes... They looked nearly feral and full of panic. That is until he saw me, then relief washed over his face, and he started rushing over to us. Seeing him rattled me though. My stomach rolled as I braced myself against the wall.

"Oh my God, Shanely! I've been looking everywhere for you! I..."

Cade decked him before he finished his sentence. I gasped, and Elijah stepped in front of me, blocking me from my mate's view.

Bastian was back on his feet abruptly, his eyes flashing red as he snarled, "What was that for?! Are you out of your mind, Cade?!"

Cade shook out his hand like he was ready to go again. "Nah brother, but you have been."

Bastian barred his teeth, stepping forward and into Cade's face as he snarled, "Back off, Cade. Step aside from *my* mate!"

The Fenrir triplets snarled at one another. Cade and Bastian barred their teeth, and my eyes widened. *I had never seen them fight like this before.* But it was getting loud in the hallway, and anyone else running late would most definitely hear. Embarrassment washed over me as the two brothers continued to argue.

"So, now you want to act like her mate?! Seriously Bastian, after the way you treated her this morning?" Cade snapped back, pushing Bastian further away.

Bastian lost some of his fury as his eyes sought mine. "Cade, I know. I messed up alright. Shanely, I'm so sorry for taking my stress and anger out on you."

"Not good enough, brother," Elijah said, shaking his head. Bastian glared at him now.

"I know that, Elijah! If you'd move out of my way, I can try to fix things

CHAPTER 16

with my Fated Mate! I've been looking everywhere for her! Shanely, please open up our bond," Bastian pleaded with me.

An overwhelming sense of guilt ate at me, but I kept the bond shut, not ready to open it just yet. I don't know why I couldn't open it, but my hurt was the only thing I could see in this moment. He seemed crushed when I wouldn't listen. Tears welled in my eyes, and to make matters worse, doors started opening up behind the brothers. Ryder and Johnny emerged, assessing the situation, and I watched Johnny tell Alana to wait there. *Great, more people to watch this between my mate and me.*

My body shook, feeling weaker by the second, but Cade wasn't done letting Bastian have it. He rolled up his sleeves, barring his teeth again.

"Oh, you've been looking everywhere?" Cade snapped.

"Yes! And you two haven't picked up your phones! Why didn't you tell me you had my mate?" he bellowed back. Ryder and Johnny stepped closer.

"How long?" Cade asked, crossing his arms.

"What?"

"I asked how long were you looking for her?!" Cade growled. "Are you deaf and dumb tonight, Bastian?"

Bastian snarled again, shoving his brother, but Cade just pushed right back.

"As soon as I realized she was missing! What is your problem, Cade!? Let me pass now!"

"My problem!? HA! My problem is I've been looking for Shanely since you blew up on her in the dining hall *this morning!*"

All the fight left Bastian then, and he looked to me.

"What?"

"That's right, brother. You're too lost in your own temper and problems to even notice that your mate ran off this morning. She used an Alpha Command on Elijah and I to stay away from her and then shut the bonds down tight. I had to send Caleb and Abraham to look for her because Elijah and I couldn't leave Summit Hall! It took us *all* day just to find her Bastian, and I had no idea if she was okay! No idea if she was even alive! We found her the minute you finally realized she even closed her end of the bond and wasn't even here.

So no, your apology isn't good enough. You screwed up today, Bastian, and you are so lucky Abraham found her and not something else!"

Bastian looked sick when I dragged my eyes to his. "Shanely... I didn't know. I just needed space to process everything, and I stayed in to be with Aerith. I spent the day with her... I didn't know. Why did you run away?"

Cade scoffed, but I answered, "Why do you think, Bastian?"

He looked dejected. "Shanely, I'm so sorry for everything. I..."

"It's fine, Bastian. I can take care of myself. I didn't need you to rescue me today. Clearly, you have enough on your plate, and I don't want to be another thing you have to deal with or worry about. Now please guys, let's make our way to the ballroom. Everyone's waiting on us."

Once the words left my mouth, I heard how harsh they were. Even my wolf seemed startled by my temper, and that was saying something. *What is the matter with me?* I've never been this unstable before, but I couldn't stop the words from coming out of my mouth or the anger from rising. I wanted to make amends with my mate, but I was crushed by the fact he didn't even *notice* I was gone.

I shakily made my way passed the brothers, needing a minute to get my emotions under control before fixing this with my mate, and my legs wobbled with every step. Bile burned in the back of my throat, but I kept moving my feet. I just wanted to get the event started so I sneak back to my room.

Bastian reached for me but dropped his hand when Cade whispered something harsh to him. I didn't stay to listen. I *couldn't* listen to any of it anymore. This was all too much to bear, and the more stress I felt, the worse my head hurt. I passed Ryder and Johnny, who gave me weak smiles, and I saw Alana standing at her door. She opened it up for me, but I knew I couldn't take it.

"Shanely wait!" Bastian called out to me, but I made my way down the stairs, wiping away the tears that were forming again. I didn't want to be stuck in an elevator with all of them anyways.

Ryder quickly caught up to me as I reached the ballroom doors. The sudden overwhelming scent of all the different shifters combined hit me like a ton of bricks, and I swayed on my feet. Ryder caught my arm, looking concerned.

CHAPTER 16

"Hey, are you okay?"

I shook my head no and gave myself a second more to adjust. "No. No, I am not, but you are not allowed to tell Bastian anything you may see going on with me."

I hit him with a command, and his eyes widened.

"Shanely, why did you do that? What's going on? Is it more than the fight?"

I could hear the Fenrir brother's footsteps closing in, but I didn't want to discuss this in front of them either. "I don't want to be another thing he has to deal with. Not right now."

"Shanely, he's your mate. He's supposed to care for you," he responded.

I saw Bastian making his way down the last flight of stairs before I pulled away from Ryder. I entered the main hall alone, and everyone clapped as I walked through. My family looked concerned, and even my uncle mouthed, *Where's Bastian?*

I looked ahead and didn't answer him. I wasn't about to give anyone any indication that I wasn't my old cheerful self. We were a united happy family, and no one would know anything different.

I could feel Bastian eyes on me the whole time as I made my way up the stage to the mic. Bastian had made it to the door along with his brothers. My mate said something, but when Ryder tried to answer he just opened and closed his mouth repeatedly. Ryder gave my mate a frustrated look, while the Fenrir brothers suddenly looked to me. They were all confused, but Cade's was the only one who's eyes flashed with worry. He immediately pulled Bastian back, and I knew right then he was telling him I was sick.

"Cade and Elijah," I said through our link. "You are not allowed to tell Bastian how sick I've been. You are not allowed to discuss my health with my mate at all."

Cade's jaw visibly snapped shut, and they both glared at me. Bastian went from them to me, narrowing his eyes as he tried to sort out the issue. I realized then everyone was still watching me, while I just stood there looking like an idiot. My cheeks turned a deep shade of red before I grabbed the mic.

"Good evening, everyone! I hope you've all had a wonderful day today!"

Everyone applauded as the brothers and Ryder made their way to our section. Bastian was heading straight towards me though, but I didn't want him to catch up. I didn't want to hash this out, and once he caught me, he wouldn't let me go. I felt miserable and just wanted to be left alone. It was mine turn to hide away, and I had every plan to start this thing and then disappear.

"I would like to start this evening with what everyone's been so excited for... the Mate Dance!"

That got everyone's attention then, and it forced the brothers to a halt. My family looked at me unsure what was going on. We had planned to do the dance after dinner, but I needed to get through this part, so I could leave.

"Bastian, will you please help the DJ find the right song?"

He frowned before turning to the opposite side of the room where the DJ was set up. Bastian smiled to everyone, but his feet were like lead with every step.

"Okay, so every single eligible shifter please make your way to the dance floor. The song will play, and when you hear this chime," I said before ringing the bell on the table, "turn to your right and change partners! Now remember every shifter is different when it comes to finding their mate, so if you get a strong feeling like you're sure they're the one, then ask them how they discover their mates. You might just need a little extra nudge like the tigers do. I'll spill their secret though. They need a kiss to be able to tell!"

Everyone giggled as my vision blurred, and I blinked rapidly to clear it. When it finally did, I found Cade glaring at me as he walked to the end of the stairs and crossed his arms. He knew very well what was going on and blocked my way out.

"Please be respectful though and leave your kiss to their hand or cheek!" I said, scrambling to figure out how to get passed him now. "And remember have fun!"

Everyone started to make their way to the floor, but Cade and now Elijah still blocked my path. They were waiting for me to come off the stage with no intention of participating. I did the only thing I could think of. I forced them to.

CHAPTER 16

"*Cade, Elijah, and Ryder. You are hereby required to participate in the Mate Dance.*"

Cade looked furious as his feet moved towards the floor. I could see Ryder's eyes go wide as he rushed to talk to Johnny, who just looked at him like he was crazy, but his feet were moving whether they wanted to or not.

"*SHANELY! Remove this command right now!*" Cade bellowed in my ear.

"*Whatever you are about to do, don't even think about it! You are not well, and you need help!*"

Both were shouting at me through the link, so I closed the bonds with them too, silencing them. The moment I did, my chest felt heavy, and I swayed slightly on my feet. A kind wolf came to my aid as I tried to walk down the stairs, and I forced a smile to my lips. *I just needed to sleep this off*, I thought to myself. *I needed space to figure this out, and when I've had a moment then I'll talk to Bastian and his brothers.*

Two girls approached the brothers, and I watched them begin to dance. Nausea struck me in waves, and I made my feet move a little faster. Worry knitted my brow, but I kept moving. *I just had to get to my room, and then I'd feel better...*

I walked on the opposite side as my family, who were oblivious to what was even going on, but that was okay. I didn't want them involved anyways. I stayed far away from Bastian and his brothers and even managed to dodge Cade, who tried to dance with his partner over towards me. I walked past the crowd on the floor and out the door.

I stumbled to the elevator, unable to take the stairs this time, and somehow made it inside without anyone stopping me. But as I walked off the elevator, everything started to spin hard. I felt for the wall and carefully made my way to my room.

Ten more feet.

That's all I had left to go as I inched along the wall. But I felt so sick, and for the first time since it all started, I was genuinely worried. Something was wrong. Something was seriously wrong.

I took another step towards the door, reaching for the handle to my room, when suddenly my vision finally went black.

And I fell...
Landing in complete darkness.

Chapter 17

I groaned, reached for my head as it pounded against my skull. *What in the world happened?* I thought to myself. It felt like my brain was ready to burst through my skull and explode all over the place. Moving felt unbearable, and my stomach churned as I looked around.

I wasn't in my room. My eyes narrowed as I remembered reaching the fifth floor, but I don't remember actually getting into my room. I tried to sit up, when something tugged on my arm. *There was an IV in my left arm,* I realized. *What was that doing here?*

My eyes adjusted to the dark a bit more, and I realized we were in the med bay. As I glanced to my left, I found a dark silhouette, sitting in chair. Their head was all the way back, leaning on the wall for support, and they were passed out asleep. It was too dark to tell who it was, but as I tried to sit up further the room swayed again. *God, I felt horrible.* All my muscles hurt, and bile rose to the back of my throat. *Please no...* I thought to myself, begging my body not to throw up again. I had barely reached for the bucket next to my bed in time before I started retching. *That* woke up the person in the corner, who bolted over to me.

"Shanely? Oh, thank God!" Bastian's voice bellowed as he smacked a button on my bed. It chimed as he held my hair back, while I continued to empty my stomach. Or tried too at least. There really wasn't anything left in me.

The lights were on instantly, and the door slammed against the wall as multiple people filed in. *Yay... another audience to puke in front of,* I thought. I lost what little energy I had left when I finally managed to stop. I fell back against the bed and turned to face my mate. My eyes widened as Bastian looked as haggard as I felt. Dark circles were under his eyes, and he still had the busted lip where Cade struck him. I have never seen my mate look like this before. He usually healed pretty quickly, especially for smaller cuts and bruises, but right now he looked as if something was draining him. *What was wrong with him?*

"Shanely?" a voice I didn't recognize said. I turned to find a wolf in a long white coat smiling at me. "I'm Dr. Henley, the doctor for the Summit pack. It's good to see you're finally awake."

Dr. Henley seemed like a kind man with soft eyes and a warm smile. He put two fingers on my wrist, checking my vitals, while his eyes glowed gold. *He must have an ability,* I thought to myself. Cade, Elijah, Ryder, Abey, Bay, my father, and Caleb all hovered at the end of my bed anxiously. *The whole gang was here...*

"I had to stop the rest after this lot barreled through, but the rest of your family is waiting outside," Dr. Henley said with a chuckle.

"What happened?" I asked groggily. Bastian's eyes filled with pain.

"I found you collapsed outside our room. I tried to reach you, but you bolted so fast after announcing the Mate Dance that I couldn't catch you in time. Our bond was closed too, so I tried to follow your scent, but it's been difficult to track lately. I am so sorry, my love. My heart broke when I saw you like that. You were so pale and weak, and I've been terrified ever since I brought you here."

Bastian went to reach for my hand but hesitated. Things still weren't right between us, and he held back. I hated this drift between us, but everyone was watching. I didn't want to bring up our fight in front of them, so I tried to focus on what was going on with me and Bastian by extension. Because whatever was happening was draining him too. Normally, my shifter abilities helped me heal and rather quickly ever since I unlocked my wolf. I haven't had the bond closed for very long, but I felt drained and weak like it had been closed off for months. *Why?*

"How long have I been here?"

"For 2 days," Cade answered solemnly.

CHAPTER 17

What? I've been unconscious for two days...

"Listen how about we get the patient healed and back on her feet, and then you all can hash everything out, alright? I have some things I'd like to discuss with them, and I can't do that until we get her strength up," the doctor said, alarming me and Bastian.

"What do you need to discuss with us? Is something wrong with her?" Bastian asked nervously. The doctor gave us a small smile that was anything *but* comforting.

"Let's heal her first and you by extension. Now Shanely, I can tell you have the mate bond closed. I need you to open it."

I gave him an odd look. "What does that have to do with anything?"

"It has *everything* to do with why you feel so bad right now. It's draining Bastian at an unusually fast rate as well, and it will only get worse if you don't open it. If you open the bond and touch your mate, then he can help heal you quickly."

"It's only been closed for a few days. It shouldn't be this bad *this* fast. Something else is going on," I replied insistently.

"There is, but I can't get to that part until you heal yourself. You're too weak right now, Shanely, and keeping your mate bond closed like this is wrong. The two of you are destined to be together, and you cannot shut out the other one for long anyways," Dr. Henley said.

Bastian looked at me, waiting patiently, but his face soon turned to hurt when I didn't say anything or open the bond. Tears filled my eyes, and the last thing I wanted to do was hash this in front of everyone.

My father spoke, "C'mon, let's give them a moment. Bastian can ring the bell when she's healed."

The doctor nodded in agreement and ushered everyone out. "Remember, Shanely. You need him as much as he needs you."

With that the doctor left, leaving me alone with my mate.

Bastian sighed, looking more broken than I have ever seen him before. He grabbed the chair along the back wall and brought it near my bed. He gently took my hands in his, rubbing his thumb over mine. I knew I was being ridiculous. I had no room to talk, and I shouldn't hold this against him, but I just couldn't stop how I felt. As silly as it was, I needed to talk before opening our bond.

"Shanely, I was wrong. I honestly don't know what came over me. When I saw Aerith with my mother, my wolf took control and saw nothing but a threat. Then when you knew about it... It just killed me. I thought you deliberately set this up to push my mother and I together, and I snapped. I took all my angry I had with my parents out on you. Please, forgive me. I feel horrible that I spoke to you that way. I'm so sorry, mate."

"You closed your bond that day too," I replied, still wallowing in my misery.

Bastian dropped his head saying, "I did. Nothing will excuse my behavior, but I was so scared and angry that I took Aerith and hid from everyone. I was just overwhelmed by everything, baby. I didn't purposely close yours first. I just shut everything down all at once, and I spent the day playing with Aerith and thinking. I realized how in the wrong I was, but when I opened the bonds up, I found everyone *but* you. You were just gone, and I panicked. I took care of Aerith, and Luke forced me to get dressed before I could look for you. I tried calling and texting everyone I could think of, but no one knew where you were. I couldn't locate you nor could I scent you. My brothers weren't answering, and my mind raced with all the worse possible scenarios."

"I was hurt, Bastian. I was embarrassed that you snapped at me in front of everyone, and then when my brother finally found me, you still hadn't noticed I was gone. I felt like you didn't care," I said as the tears finally fell down my cheek.

"Oh, Shanely..."

Bastian gently wiped away my fallen tears before kissing my cheek. "You have no idea how badly I care about you. I love you, Shanely, and I never would have left you out there if I had known. I promise you; I will never close our bond like that again. I swear to you. Please forgive me, baby. Please open our bond," he begged, leaning his head against mine.

I missed my mate, and I hated being separated from him like this. Abey's words came to mind now, and I thought back to all my mistakes. I realized how harsh I was being. I had lied to him more than once, trying to do what I thought was right. This was the first time he had ever spoken to me like that,

CHAPTER 17

and I did not like him begging me to open our bond. He deserved forgiveness and love. Not my knee-jerk reaction to hide and run away. I was being stupid, so I slowly opened our bond.

Well, I tried to open it gently, but the rush of emotions and connections hit me like a ton of bricks and just flooded the gate wide open. We both felt like it sucker-punched us in the gut, and we struggled to catch our breath.

And then there it was. Bastian's heart began beating in my chest once more, and now that our bond was fully opened, his touch soothed my body. My muscles relaxed and stopped hurting, while my dizziness left. I felt stronger all of the sudden and no longer sick like I was.

Bastian kissed my forehead, and I could see the dark circles under his eyes had faded with his normal color returning. He seemed like he was feeling better too.

"Thank you, Shanely. I am still so sorry. I should have never treated you like that. I promise that I will never react like that again," he leaned down to kiss me, and I let him. He was gentle with his kiss, but I craved more.

I craved him.

"Bastian? I was wrong too. After everything I've done in the past, I had no right to close myself off to you like that. I shut our bond down, and I hurt you too. I really didn't mean to leave Aerith there with Michelle. She was just there and..."

"Shanely, it's okay. Your Aunt Cassia found me while you were in here. She explained she put you on the spot, and your uncle was practically forcing you out the door. She also said she made the mistake of not listening when you asked for them to stay put until we came to get her. She didn't think anything of it at the time, but she overstepped taking her to breakfast with my mom. She was there in the cafeteria but had stepped away for a moment when we walked in."

"I still should have put my foot down and taken her to my dad's or something. I don't want to put you in a spot you aren't ready for with your mother, Bastian. I'm here to support you too."

He sighed, bringing my hand to his lips. He gently kissed my hand before saying, "I should have talked to her a long time ago honestly. I've been holding onto this anger for so long... I just wasn't ready to deal with it. Then being here, while my father is losing his sanity in the prison below and watching her act like nothing had ever happened was just too much. I don't know. I just couldn't handle it, so I shoved it aside, but look where it landed us. It *nearly* broke you, and I'd never forgive myself if something happened to you because I was a coward and ran from my feelings. I can't even begin to imagine what would have happened if I hadn't found you when I did. I didn't even know you were feeling so sick."

I sighed, knowing it was my turn to confess. "Yeah, well that was my fault. I assumed it was just nerves and stress over this week and being the White Wolf, so I made sure not to bother you with it."

He gave me a pointed look.

"Shanely... I want to know if something's going on with you. I like taking care of you, and you are never a burden. Not to me. Not to my brothers. Not to any of us. Got that? Don't push me out of the loop when it comes to your health," he replied, pushing my white hair off my face.

"You have been so stressed lately that I felt silly giving you something else to worry about. It just started getting worse as time went on, and then when I closed the bond it progressed quickly."

"Wait a second. How long have you been feeling sick?"

"Since we first arrived. Cade found me throwing up the first morning here," I said sheepishly. Bastian gave me another look.

"Is that what they were trying to tell me at the ball? That you were feeling ill?"

I nodded slowly. "Ryder caught me from falling over before we walked inside. I commanded all three not to tell you. I'm sorry."

"You gave them an *Alpha Command* not to tell me?" he asked, pinching the bridge of his nose. "Shanely, why would you do that? What if I hadn't gone to look for you that night?!"

"Hey, I was mad at you then, and I didn't want to be a burden. I still don't. I was managing it up until that night at least."

Bastian sighed as he dropped his head. He gave himself a minute before looking at me firmly.

CHAPTER 17

"Okay, no more. We can't do this to one another. Promise me that you won't keep secrets from me, and I promise never to speak to you like that again. I will never close our bond like that either, but please don't shut me out, Shanely."

"I promise, Bastian. Can we just start over? Forget this all happened?" I asked before kissing him softly. He grinned wickedly.

"I'd love nothing more."

Bastian gripped the back of my hair and pulled me close. His lips slammed into mine, and a rush of emotions filled my core. I could feel his joy, his love, and his happiness flood our bond. And I knew he could feel mine too. His touch was greedy, and I soaked up everything he gave me. My animals finally hummed in contentment like everything was right with the world again. His hands stayed tangled in my hair before he begrudgingly pulled away. We were breathing heavy by the time he rested his head against mine.

"I love you, Shanely," he whispered.

"I love you too," I replied.

We stayed like that a moment longer before I convinced Bastian to help me to my feet. He tried to insist I'd spend one more night here in the medical wing, but I was anxious to finish the Summit. I had missed so much as it was.

I swayed a little bit as I got my bearings, but now that Bastian and I were connected again I felt pretty good. He brought me clothes Bay had brought down earlier for me and then helped me change out of the hospital gown. He pushed the button though before I could object.

"Shanely, we need to know what's happening with you. I don't mind that you want to get dressed, but I can't leave without knowing all the facts."

"Babe, I feel pretty good. I think he was just trying to scare me into opening the bond quickly," I replied, pulling my hair into a ponytail. *I seriously needed a shower, and that was my first order of business when we got back to our room. Maybe if I played my cards right, I could convince him to join me.* I smiled wickedly at that thought.

The door swung open, and while I expected the doctor, it was Cade instead. His eyes went straight to my bed, which was now empty before he found me standing in front of the mirror.

"Baby Girl! What are you doing up?" he asked as he plowed into me. He pulled me into a bear hug before pushing me back towards the bed.

"Cade! I'm okay! I'm ready to go back to our room."

"Oh no, you aren't! You need to go back to bed until the doctor comes in. You've..."

Cade's teeth clattered as his jaw snapped shut. Anger filled his gaze, and he put his hands on his hips.

"Shanely, please lift this command right now," he demanded. "I cannot keep it a secret anymore."

My lips pursed together. *I had forgotten I hadn't lifted my command.* Everyone piled into the room now, which was good because I could lift Elijah's and Ryder's command as well.

"Cade, Elijah, and Ryder. You are hereby free of the command I gave you to keep my illness a secret from my mate."

The three of them rubbed their chest in relief.

"Thank God!" Ryder exclaimed.

"Please don't ever do that to us again, Shanely," Elijah said as he hugged me.

"Have you told Bastian yet?" Cade asked, giving me a pointed look.

"She did, and we promised never to keep secrets from each other again amongst a few other things," Bastian spoke up, joining our group.

Cade gave him a sharp look out of the corner of his eye. "Are you two okay then?"

I nodded. "We are, Cade. Bastian and I are good."

Bastian wrapped his arms around me, kissing my cheek. He turned to his brothers then saying, "Thank you all for watching over her. I messed up big time, and you made sure she stayed safe. I can't thank you enough."

Caleb and Abraham gave him a nod, while Elijah insisted it was his honor to keep me safe in his absence. Cade, however, studied him longer before extending his hand.

"I'm sorry for being so harsh, brother, and for busting your lip. It's hard to explain, but my wolf was heavily involved that night," he replied, crossing his arms.

CHAPTER 17

"We made the pack anyways, so whatever was driving it, I just appreciate you being there," Bastian replied.

Pack? What did he mean by that? I opened my mouth to ask him about it, but my father spoke instead.

"It's because you are my daughter's Beta," my father chimed in before reaching out to hug me. He kissed my cheek. "I'm so glad you're feeling better."

"Why is that?" Cade asked.

"You already have the sibling bond between you, and it's not just between normal siblings. It's more because you are triplets. Then you add the fact that you have become best friends with Shanely and are as close to her like you are her own brothers. When she made you her Beta, it added an extra cord between you. You have this increased desire to protect her like Elijah has with Bastian. You protected her that night, even from her mate, because your wolf felt like he needed to," he responded as the doctor walked in.

We all mulled over that interesting tidbit before Cade grinned at me. He stuck his tongue out at me, making me giggle.

"Wow, everyone's in here again. Alrighty then. Well, it's good to see you up and moving around, Shanely. Bastian, you look better too!"

"Yeah, you were right. I just needed to open the bond up. I'm ready to head back to my room now and what's left of the week's activities," I replied, reaching for my bag on the bed.

"Well hold on, Shanely. We still need to discuss some stuff. Maybe we should speak in private?" the doctor asked, giving my mate and I a look. I cocked my head to the side.

"Doc, I'm fine. It was just nerves and closing the bond for too long. I really just want to go now."

He laughed now, giving me an amused look. "Yeah, no. It's more than that, Shanely. You're pregnant."

My jaw dropped as everyone froze.

"She's what?" Cade finally spoke. I looked at Bastian, who had zoned out entirely and looked pale.

"She's pregnant. It's why she's been feeling so sick. Then when she closed their bond, they stopped relying on one another, so it drained her faster. Actually, by the speed she dropped so quickly, I'd say she's pregnant with twins or triplets," the doctor said matter of factly.

"Oh my God, catch him!" Elijah shouted as I watched in horror as my mate dropped to the ground.

Chapter 18

I paced back and forth, waiting for my mate to wake up. He was the one lying in bed completely unconscious, while I was nervously pacing the room. *I can't imagine how Bastian deals with this,* I thought to myself. *I did not like being in his shoes.* The doctor made everyone minus Elijah and Cade step out to give us some space after he collapsed. My mate was fine. Unconscious but fine.

It was getting close to dinner by now, and everyone would soon be going out for the bonfire planned for tonight. We were only here for a couple days more before the event was officially over, and Bastian and I had barely spent any time with anyone other than our immediate pack. But I couldn't think about that right now. My mate came first. Bastian had been unconscious for the last 10 minutes, and it was freaking me out just watching him lay there. I focused on his heartbeat for comfort, which was steady. *That* was the only thing keeping me sane.

With nothing to do but pace the floor, I thought of everything the doctor said. *I was pregnant.*

Pregnant.

With possibly twins or triplets. The doctor said they must be strong shifters because they are draining me faster than normal pregnancies would. He gave me vitamins to help keep my levels where they should be, and some things I can eat or drink to build up what essentials I'd need to keep them alive and fortify myself. The more I was able to keep in me the better I'd feel, but I just couldn't wrap my head around it. I couldn't wrap my head around the fact that I was carrying Bastian's child. My *mate's* child. A small smile would curve on my lips every time I thought about it. *But what would Bastian think?* He fainted after all.

Elijah looked stressed, tapping his foot as he watched his brother, while Cade sat in his chair with his hands over his head. Not a care in the world.

"Shanely, come sit. You're going to burn a hole in the floor with all that pacing," Elijah muttered, patting the chair beside him.

"I can't sit still, Elijah. What am I going to do? I'm barely juggling the responsibility of being the White Wolf as it is. With the alliance *and* the Division problem, how am I supposed to carry a baby? Let alone two or three?"

"You can do this, Shanely. You can handle anything, I'm sure of that!" he replied, trying to settle me.

"But at a certain point I won't be able to shift! And I'm pregnant in my warnings, Elijah!"

Cade finally sat forward and sighed. "Baby Girl, sit."

I looked at him exasperated. "I can't, Cade. I'm freaking out here! Even Bastian's freaking out. He's never fainted before guys. Does that mean he doesn't want this kid? Is he not ready for them?"

I was rambling by this point, but the thought of Bastian not wanting these kids just about killed me. Tears filled my eyes, and I quickly tried to wipe them away.

"Babe, I want this kid. I'm one hundred percent ready to be a dad. *Again*."

I turned around to find Bastian slowly sitting up. He rubbed his face briefly before I plowed into him and hugged him fiercely.

"Bastian! You *fainted*," I said, burying my face in his neck. "God, I was so scared."

His scent was the only thing keeping the tears from falling. I inhaled deeply, trying not to fall apart. Bastian gently shushed me as his brothers left the room.

"I'm sorry. It was overwhelming, and I didn't mean to. I think it was just too much after just getting the bond back," he said, chuckling.

"Bastian, how can you laugh right now? I'm pregnant in my warnings! What if they are coming true? And how can I do everything and carry these

CHAPTER 18

little ones?"

He pulled back, forcing me to look him in the eye, and gave me a happy grin. "I can laugh because it's funny. I did the typical guy finds out he's going to be a dad move. Like in all those girly movies you've made me watch. I just never expected to do that yet here we are. I didn't expect the doc to say that you were pregnant, let alone with more than one baby, but I am ready, Shanely. You are an amazing mother already, and I'm so excited to meet our newest additions. Your warnings are just that, a warning, and I'm not living our life in fear of a what if."

I leaned against Bastian as his joy trickled through the bond. It was so strong that it was hard not to smile. My own terror was slowly subsiding.

"I'm afraid, Bastian," I said quietly.

"Well then, I'll just have to be excited for the both of us then. That is until you realize I was right all along, and then jump on board the happy train," he replied, laughing. I playfully smacked him, and he pretended to wince.

"Right all along, eh?"

He smirked before setting me on the floor, "C'mon, babe. Let's go celebrate!"

Bastian practically drug me out of the room, where our family was still waiting. His smile was wide, when he saw everyone.

"We're pregnant!"

The room erupted in cheerful shouts and applause. We were swarmed, and the group congratulated me and teased Bastian for fainting in the first place. Bastian insisted we celebrate at the bonfire tonight, and everyone split in different directions to get ready. I took Aerith in my arms, and while she clung to me, she seemed so excited at the idea of getting another sibling. She also seemed quiet, and I wondered what was going on in her little mind.

"Are you sure you're okay, baby?" I asked once we were alone in our room.

"I missed you, Mommy. Daddy said you were really sick, and I couldn't see you for awhile."

"Aww baby," I said as I gave her a big hug. I had no idea she was so worried about me. I figured she'd be off playing or something. Not even aware of what was going on.

"Mamas alright. I wasn't feeling good because that's what happens when you're carrying a baby. It was all normal," I replied as Bastian sat down on the couch next to us. Aerith put her hand on my stomach.

"So, mommies get really sick when they have babies?"

"They can sometimes. Your brother or sister is in there growing right now," I replied, watching her little brows furrow.

"Brothers. There are two boys, Mommy. One is going to be a very big wolf, and the other will be a grizzly like Uncle Caleb and Papa."

"She did this with Alana too, remember? She was right about it then," Bastian said as he rested his hand on my stomach too.

"So, you see two boys in there Aerith?"

She nodded. "Yeah. I'm going to have brothers, Mommy."

She smiled softly before cuddling close to Bastian and me. My thoughts swirled around what Aerith proclaimed. *This must be an ability*, I thought to myself. A small smile curved on my lips. *Sons. I was going to have sons.* A twinge of worry rattled through me then. I had only ever been a mom to a baby girl. *How was I supposed to raise a boy let alone two?*

Bastian checked his phone saying, "C'mon, you two. Let's grab our coats and blankets and make our way down to the bonfire. It was Aerith's idea after all."

Her bouncy self came back as she squealed before running into her room. I laughed, watching her go. "Well, that seemed to perk her up. Oh! I completely forgot to ask, but what happened with the mate dance?"

Bastian grinned wide. "It was a huge success, Shanely. We had a large number find their mates during that dance including your Uncle Aspen. The rest I think you should see for yourself."

Relief washed over me, and I quickly grabbed my jacket. I was so excited to meet Uncle Aspen's mate and see who else had gotten paired up. *He deserved a mate, and I was glad he finally found her,* I thought to myself. If the dance was a failure, then I don't think blending everyone would have worked out so well.

We left our room, Bastian and I hand-in-hand, and made our way to the stairs.

CHAPTER 18

"Your uncle's mate came from the Russian clan actually," Bastian said with a grin. "She came with Alexei and your cousin Noah, I guess. They nearly missed the ball too, but they made it just in time."

"I'm so glad," I replied as we walked down the stairs. I smiled to the Fenrir brothers waiting for us. "Aspen has been waiting a long time for this."

Cade seemed to be back to his normal self as he plowed into Bastian and I, but Elijah seemed off. I wasn't sure why, but whenever I looked at him, Elijah just seemed tense. Uptight almost. I couldn't figure out what was going on with him now, and I sighed as we walked to the back doors.

The bonfire was already lit and the event in full swing as we walked out. *I had to give the fellas credit*, I thought to myself. *Luke and his enforcers did a good job with the set up.* They had heaters set up every so often to help keep the smaller shifters warm, and a large banquet table was set up filled to the brim with snacks.

We laid our blankets out by a family of lions, whose kids were already covered in sticky s'mores. Aerith's eyes grew large, and Elijah volunteered to get her one. She hopped on his back, and I watched the two of them head over to the snack table.

I nudged my mate. "What's going on with Elijah?"

He shrugged. "I don't know, Shanely. I've been a little preoccupied with you."

"He's been acting weird ever since the whole fight between you two honestly," Cade chimed in. I opened my mouth, when Caleb walked over with a brute of a man that looked a lot like him.

"Shanely! There you are! I want you to finally meet your cousin Noah. Noah, this is my sister, Shanely," Caleb said as he helped me stand up.

Noah extended his hand out. "It's a pleasure to meet you. I've heard a lot about you from my dad."

I blinked in surprise. *His thick, Russian voice was not what I was expecting, but I guess that would happen if you lived in one place for a long time.* I shook his hand as I studied my cousin. Noah was way taller than Caleb, with thick, dark, wavy hair. It was long on the top and short on the sides similar to my boys, and he definitely took care of himself. His large arms were a testament to that.

"It's great to meet you too, Noah," I said, smiling. "I've heard a lot about you as well. This is my Fated Mate, Bastian, and his brother and my Beta, Cade. The other brother is with my daughter now."

Noah shook their hands as well before eyeing me a little funny. He stepped closer, scenting the air before frowning slightly.

"Everything okay, man?" Bastian asked him.

"Yeah, I apologize. Just something smelled off with you, Shanely. I can't figure it out," Noah replied sheepishly.

I laughed. "Ah, yes that would be the twins I'm carrying."

"Wait, twins?" Caleb asked excitedly.

"I can't scent your pregnancy though. You just scent... Somewhat odd," Noah said baffled. I shrugged not really knowing why that was the case either.

"No idea. Maybe it's because one son will be a wolf and the other a bear? I have no idea really. Oh, and Aerith told me what I was having. Two boys," I said, smiling to my brother.

"Wow. Well, congrats you guys!" Caleb said, giving me a hug.

"Wait what? She told you?" Noah asked. Confusion knitted his brow, and I couldn't help but chuckle.

"My daughter Aerith. She, somehow, can sense the gender and animal of babies still developing. She nailed your sister's pregnancy right on the head. Is this the first time you've met your nephew?" I asked.

He gave a weak smile. "I was unfortunately stuck in Russia when she gave birth. This is the first time Alexei has allowed the clan to leave the Mother Land. Tommy looks just like my father though. He seems sweet."

"Yeah, he's pretty perfect honestly," I said with a small laugh.

Noah rubbed the back of his head. "Between you and me... The little guy terrifies me."

"Wait what? You afraid of babies?" Cade said with a laugh, and Noah gave him a pointed look.

"I'm not good with littles, alright. They always fuss and are so delicate, and they smell," he said as he visibly shook his large shoulders. "I'm just

CHAPTER 18

not good with them. Once they're older, it's easier to bond with them."

I laughed hard at my cousin then. He was well over 6 feet tall with broad shoulders and defined muscles. I'm sure his grizzly was a sight to see too yet *babies* scared him.

"Oh c'mon! I would have not said anything if I knew you'd just laugh at me," he said exasperated.

"I'm sorry! I promise I'll stop, it's just so funny. You're a scary shifter that's afraid of babies. Just not what I expected you to say is all," I replied, giggling into Bastian's chest, trying to stop.

Noah scoffed, "Yeah well..."

Soon he was laughing too. "I give up, Shanely."

"Aww, don't worry Noah. We won't tell anyone," I said with a big smile.

My Uncle Aspen arrived at the bonfire then with a petite woman hanging on his arm. I gave Bastian a curious look, but he just winked at me. The older woman looked sweet, and Aspen was soon waving us over. I said my goodbyes to my cousin and made my way over to meet my new aunt. Her name was Delaney, and boy was she incredibly shy. Delaney's thick Russian accent made it a little hard to understand her, but my uncle quickly interpreted for her and made up the difference for her shyness. *It's funny how both my uncles found mates who were the exact opposite of each other.*

We all were having a genuine time together at the bonfire, and I was glad we didn't miss this. Bastian made sure to mix the vitamins in a smoothie for me, and it was seriously helping my nausea.

Elijah was oddly quiet during the whole event, sticking close to me and Bastian instead of mingling with the others. I noticed he kept getting distracted, watching everything going on around him and scenting the air every so often. I frowned and nudged my mate. It was so bad that everyone had to repeat themselves around him. He finally gave up trying to talk to anyone and just crashed on our blanket that was spread out under the heater. My heart fell, just watching him struggle for some reason, and I couldn't take it anymore. I asked Bastian for a s'more and plopped down next to Elijah. *It was time to figure this out.*

"Alright spill. What's going on?"

Elijah frowned. "Nothing's going on. What are you talking about?"

"Liar. You're not here tonight, so what's up? Is something bothering you?"

Elijah sighed, clasping his hands together. "I don't know, Shanely. I'm just having a hard time focusing is all."

"Any reason why?" I asked.

I nudged him when he didn't reply.

"Elijah. Just because I chose Cade as my Beta, doesn't mean I don't look at you like my best friend too. You're my family, and I'm here to help if you need it. Let me do what I can to help you out for a change."

He gave me a pointed look before slowly grinning. "I've always wondered how you two made that choice honestly."

"Bastian made it actually. He chose you first, and I couldn't think of anyone other than you or Cade."

"I know you and Cade are closer though. I just wanted to make sure you know I love you just as much as he does," he replied.

"Oh, Elijah!" I said, leaning into him. "I know that. You're just as much my best friend as Cade is. Cade is special to me, but so are you. Did you think that I preferred Cade over you?"

"I just wanted to make sure you knew I'm here for you too. That's all," he said with a cheesy grin. I smiled wide at him.

"Elijah, I have never once doubted that. If I could have two Betas, then I'd tell Bastian he'd have to pick someone else," I said as my mate plopped down next to me.

"Who am I picking?" Bastian replied with a tray of s'mores in hand. I took the one with the most chocolate on it, grinning wickedly at my mate.

"Betas. I was saying if we could pick two then I'd get your brothers, and you'd have to find someone else," I replied before taking a big bite.

Bastian laughed loudly. "Oh, I figured. I already know they'd abandon me and choose you if given the choice."

Elijah laughed and just shrugged. "Well, can you blame us? Shanely's amazing."

Bastian looked at me with this adorable grin. The flames from the fire bounced in his eyes and just looked mesmerizing. I felt his love come through the bond, and I hoped he could feel mine too. "Nah, I don't. I prefer it that way. Better chance of keeping you safe."

Elijah snorted at that. "That is the truth!"

I slapped him playfully. "Hey now! I'm not that accident prone."

They both laughed at me like I had just said the most ridiculous thing ever, so I just ate my s'more in peace, seeing how there was no arguing with them on that. *They did kind of have a point.* We all quieted down, watching the fire roar on.

Elijah finally broke the silence. "Guys, I do need to discuss something."

Cade plopped down next to him abruptly. "What are we talking about?"

I shook my head. *I had no idea he was even nearby,* I thought to myself. He smirked before tousling my hair. I swatted his hand away, and Elijah rolled his eyes. "I need to discuss something, and I thought I'd ask them since they've been through it."

My eyes went wide, wondering if he was asking what I was thinking. "Elijah, what's going on?"

His eyes slowly shifted to mine. "What did it *smell* like when you guys first scented one another?"

Bastian stopped mid-bite. We both looked at him in shock.

"Guys, c'mon. I'm freaking out here," he said quietly.

"You scent something that's connecting to your wolf?" Cade asked in a completely serious tone.

Elijah nodded slowly. "I think so. I've been getting small whiffs of something every so often, and I can't figure it out, but my wolf is obsessed with it."

"Whoa, Elijah... Your mate may be here then," I said as I scanned the yard.

"Don't make it obvious, Shanely," he hushed at me, pushing my head down.

"Wait why?? Don't you want to find her?" I asked him, lowering my voice to a whisper.

"I do, I do, it's just... I'm afraid. It's more than likely a non-wolf, which isn't the issue, but what if she won't move to the pack? I cannot leave the McCoy pack, so am I to stay weakened because my mate won't join me? And how am I supposed to live with that? I have commitments and responsibilities, and she also has to be okay with all of us. I'd do anything for your mate, Bastian, and I know you all will do the same for me and mine, but what if she doesn't like that? It's a different situation with us because most don't deal with mate bonds like we do," he said before collapsing on his arms. "What if she makes me choose?"

Cade whistled, while Bastian rubbed the back of his head. Neither brother knew what to say to him, and my heart broke for Elijah. *He was so afraid of being rejected for one reason or another that he was willing to not even try to look for her now*, I thought as my shoulders fell. I have *never* seen him scared like this before, but I wouldn't be his sister or best friend if I didn't try to talk some sense into him. *He was being ridiculous anyways.*

"Elijah, look at me," I said quietly.

He tilted his head to the right to meet my eyes, and I gave him a firm look. "Go find your mate. Those are all scenarios that may not even happened, and if she has issues with you caring for me the way you do... Then you will stop."

All three boys turned to me.

"Shanely, no. That's not going to happen," Elijah countered.

"Yeah, we're triplets, Baby Girl. We have this agreement between us. We are drawn to protect our brother's mates no matter what. We're just extensions of one another when they can't be there. It's why Elijah and I protect you the way we do. Our wolves *demand* it. Our wolves were basically the same until Bastian bonded with you, but we couldn't change that even if we wanted to," Cade chimed in.

Bastian grunted in agreement, but I shook my head. *They weren't getting it from her side*, I thought to myself. *That is if she even had an issue with it in the first place, which I highly doubted. Their mates will be perfect for them, which means they will also be okay with me too.*

"Guys look. Elijah's right, she's probably a non-wolf. Wolves get the bond between twins and triplets, and their mates understand too. I get it, and I'd do anything to make her comfortable in this with us, but if she's not... If this is too much, then maybe we give her space. Let her come to terms with

CHAPTER 18

things on *her* time. Mates come first, that's all I'm saying."

They all sat quiet for a moment.

"Nah, I don't like it," Elijah said finally.

"Me either," Bastian replied.

I sighed as Cade smirked at me. "Looks like you're stuck with us, Baby Girl."

"Well, you're looking for her tonight, Elijah. My boys aren't scaredy cats, are they?"

They all looked playfully offended as Bastian spoke, "Name calling, are we mate? You know that means I'll..."

He didn't get to finish that sentence as a loud gunshot sounded through the air. Blood splattered across my face as Bastian flew backwards, hitting the hard ground behind us.

I screamed as I saw the blood soak the snow around him.

Bastian's eyes were closed.

Chapter 19

Chaos.

That was the only way I could describe what was going on. I stared at Bastian's fallen body as blood poured out of his chest. I prayed for it to stop and for him to open his eyes. I prayed for me to wake up from this horrible nightmare because that's what this had to be.

A nightmare.

I'd wake up in my bed any second now and tell Bastian all about it, while he wrapped his arms around me to comfort me. It was the only thing that made sense.

But he didn't move, and I didn't wake up.

Elijah roared in my ear, but I couldn't make out what he said. I could barely focus on the screams in the air or the sound of rifles going off. He yanked on my arm to get me to move, but I refused to leave Bastian's side or even look away from his fallen body. I felt our bond waver, and it made me cry harder. More shots sounded, and I felt bullets whiz by my head, when Cade finally dove over me. We slammed to the other side of Bastian, and he covered my head with his body. It snapped me back to reality.

"Shanely, we've got to move now!" Cade yelled as he hovered over me. We slowly sat up, trying to stay low as everyone ran around us. Most had shifted and were looking for the source of all these bullets, while others were trying to find safety.

Nowhere felt safe though.

I looked back at Bastian, and my heart fell. *I couldn't leave him. I won't go inside and leave him out here alone to die.* My wolf snarled at the thought, and

CHAPTER 19

I turned to my Beta.

"Take him!"

"Shanely, you first!" Cade shouted, covering my head again.

"No! Take him! My bond is *wavering* with him!" I bellowed. "He's dying, and he needs to go to the doctor now!"

Cade covered me again as more shots fired. I couldn't breathe as my bond with Bastian wavered again. *It was fading.* Cade snarled, "We're stuck in the open, Elijah! Where is this coming from?!"

"I don't know! But we need to move now!"

They weren't listening to me. They were wasting precious seconds that Bastian desperately needed. *There was only one way I could make them listen,* I thought as anger welled inside. They were *saving* Bastian. I used my Alpha power now and hit them with a command.

"Elijah, Cade, you are to protect your brother at all costs. Save him and take him inside to the doctor now!"

They glared viciously at me as Cade shifted off me.

"Shanely, remove this command now!" Cade bellowed loudly, but it didn't stop his body from moving towards Bastian.

"I'm so sorry, but Aerith is still out here, and I can't carry him. I won't leave him. He has to live! Do you understand me?! *He has to live!*" I shouted, watching the brothers each take an arm. The rage in their eyes quickly turned to utter panic and terror as they moved further from me.

"Please tell him I love him! I love you guys too," I said before sprinting off in the chaos. I couldn't look at Bastian otherwise I think I'd fall apart. *They could carry him inside, while I found my daughter.* I trusted them to do their job, while I did mine.

They did not agree though.

I could hear their wolves roar over the chaos and gunfire, and I knew they may never forgive me for this. I had never heard a roar like that from either of them before and guilt ate me up inside. I felt horrible forcing their hand like that again, but I refused to let my family die because they tried to save me first. *It can't always be me first.*

They'd save Bastian, and as long as I could feel his heart beating in my chest, I knew he was alive. Right now, I needed to find my daughter, and I wasn't leaving that job to anyone but myself.

Everyone ran towards Summit Hall as the guns continued to go off, dropping shifters as I passed by. Pain flooded my senses as my wolves dropped from my connection. I stumbled, forcing myself to close my bonds entirely so I could focus. Tears filled my eyes as I ran faster. Shifters were pushing and shoving one another, not knowing which way the bullets were coming from. I tripped and fell on the ground hard near the main fire but thankfully managed to land on my hip instead of my belly. I rolled on my side, screaming when I saw what I tripped over.

Uncle Aspen.

I scurried away from his lifeless body, as tears filled my eyes. My fallen uncle laid there with his eyes wide open. I covered my mouth in shock as I saw another lifeless body beneath him. *His mate... He tried to shield her.* My heart snapped in two, and I forced myself to look away.

I needed to find Aerith now! My stomach twisted at the thought of finding her lifeless body somewhere in the mix of this mess. I shifted into my wolf, who senses were far better than my own, and searched for my daughter.

I sniffed the air as I ran through the crowd, but I couldn't pick up her scent over the stench of fresh blood. I leapt over a fallen wolf, when I finally spotted her across the yard. Aerith was underneath the snack table by herself, and I bolted over to her.

"Mommy!"

I shifted as I slid to a stop. I don't know how she managed to find herself alone, but it didn't matter now. *She was alive, and we were getting out of here!*

"Come here! We've got to go now!"

I reached for her, when suddenly I was knocked to the ground. She screamed as my arm burned from an unbearable pain that rattled my left shoulder. I slowly rolled in the snow, trying to catch my breath in the midst of the pain. I looked down at my arm as blood trickled through an open wound. *I'd been shot... again.*

I inhaled deeply and forced myself to get up. But then just like that, the bullets stopped and everything got quiet. I scanned the woods, knowing

CHAPTER 19

that whoever attacked us was still out there. I wasn't sure why the gunfire stopped, but I wasn't sticking around to find out. I reached for Aerith again, pulling her close to me. My left arm was useless now, but it wasn't going to stop me from getting her to safety.

"Stay close to me. Okay, baby? And if anything happens you run like mad to our room, alright?"

She nodded her head as her tears continued to fall, and I made sure to cover her as we made our way through the mess. I tried to shield her the best I could, and I prayed she didn't focus on the bodies lying on the ground. We made our way around the fire, and that's when I saw my knights in shining armor.

Cade and Elijah's wolves were running swiftly through the snow, when they spotted us. They shifted back to their human form as they met us, and without a word, Elijah grabbed Aerith from me while Cade grabbed me. He immediately scented the blood on my arm, snarling viciously, and the brothers took off towards the main hall. The attack seemed over with, and while I was grateful, I was also completely confused. *Who would do such a thing and then just leave like that? If this was to annihilate shifters, why let most of us go?*

We made it safely inside the dining hall, and I looked around the room. It was crowded, with everyone freaking out from what just happened. Some were crying hysterically, and many were bloody and wounded. The enforcers were trying to assist those in need, but it was just as chaotic in here as it was out there.

"Let me down, Cade," I commanded, and my Beta glared at me.

"I cannot believe you, Shanely," he snarled, and my eyes widened. Cade carried me to the back table, with Elijah hot on our heels. He grabbed a rag from the serving station before tearing off my coat. He was not in the mood, and I might have pushed them too far tonight. I had never seen my Beta look like this before.

Cade examined my arm, which was already starting to heal before covering it with the rag. Aerith clung to Elijah, and I listened to him softly sing to her. Both were livid with me, and I knew I needed to fix this with them. Bastian's heart still beat in my chest, so I turned to his brothers.

"Cade, I'm sorry I used the command again, but I am not sorry that I made you save your brother first. I was not about to leave him in that field to die, and I couldn't carry him. I needed to find Aerith and..."

"YOU DON'T GET TO MAKE THAT CHOICE FOR ME!" he bellowed, causing others to step aside. The room quieted with his voice, and I leaned backwards nervously. Cade had never lost it like this before. *At least not with me.*

"I'm your Beta, *your brother!* You don't EVER command me to leave you in the middle of a gun fight!" he bellowed, jabbing his finger in my face. "We would *never* leave our brother to die, but if it came down to it, all three of us are in agreement. IT'S YOU BEFORE US!"

My eyes widened, and this time I kept my mouth shut. Cade's eyes were red and downright scary looking. *Cade was every bit of an Alpha just like his brother,* I realized. The goofiness aside, Cade was strong and terrifying when he *wanted* to be. *And I pushed him too far tonight.*

I opened my mouth to say something, but no words came out. *What could I honestly say though?*

I messed up by giving them the command, but I didn't mean it with ill intentions. I just wanted to save my mate, my daughter, and them by extension. *That's why I chose the path I did,* I thought. *But was it the right path?*

Cade was breathing heavy, daring me to try and defend myself, but I wouldn't challenge him. He was right, so I barred my own neck, trying to apologize to his wolf.

Soon, the room grew noisy again as everyone scrambled to help the other. Our alliance leaders stormed their way through the crowd, and I could see they were heading our way, with my family right behind them.

"Is this what you meant when you wanted to blend shifters together or were you just trying to eliminate us lowly shifters to make more room for the wolves?!"

It was that panther woman again, and she was seething mad. Cade took two steps, getting in her face as he snapped.

"Watch it, Panther! Shanely was shot as well as her mate and my brother. Why would she stage an attack only to nearly lose her Fated Mate?!"

CHAPTER 19

Elijah snarled behind her, causing her to freeze. The Fenrir brothers were not in a patient mood, and she could see it.

Despite the feral look in their eyes, it still didn't stop the group from arguing with one another. I was beyond emotional though. I needed my mate. I needed to fix this with my brothers, but I certainly didn't need to deal with this. I stood on the table Cade sat me down on and whistled loudly.

"EVERYONE SHUT UP!" I shouted, forcing the room to a quiet. I used just enough power to command attention before snapping it back in.

"Now where's Luke!?" I asked, and I saw him push his way through.

"I'm here!" he said through the crowd.

"It's good to see you, friend. Send out the Summit Hall team now. Scan the woods and surrounding area. Make sure we aren't going to see a secondary attack and find out who did this! My alliance leaders... I promise you that I had nothing to do with this, and I will stop at nothing until we figure out who's behind it! If you want to make yourself useful then send your best trackers and stealthiest shifters with Luke. Bring me answers! Until then, I want everyone into the main ballroom! It's the inner most room, and we can be safe there if we are attacked again! Cassia! Gather up a team with Cain and start setting up a healing station there. Anyone with healing abilities follow my aunt! Someone get food, water, and blankets! Absolutely, no one other than the security team is to go outside! Now move!" I shouted, causing everyone to scatter.

Cade glared at me, ready for round two, but he'd have to wait a moment as someone else came running into the room. Uncle Ash looked around the room frantically, rubbing his chest as he searched for his twin. Cade followed my line of sight, when the tears fell from my eyes. He softened slightly and let me hop off the table. I walked towards my uncle then.

"Uncle Ash?"

"Shanely!" Ash cried out as he rushed towards me. "I can't find him. I felt a snap, but it must be wrong. I can't find him!"

My heart broke, watching my serious uncle fall apart at the seams. Ash was panicking. He wouldn't stop rubbing his chest or searching the room. My heart broke further as I reached out to him.

"Uncle please..."

I couldn't even find the words. My voice fell as I pictured Uncle Aspen's face again. His wide opened eyes that were void of any life left. His mate clinging to him.

Ash looked down at me before he finally lost it. He howled in despair before his wife grabbed him.

"I've got him, Shanely. He will be okay," she said through her own tears. I nodded before going back to my boys.

I collapsed in Cade's arms. "Please take me to my mate, Cade. You can yell at me some more there."

He gave me a pointed look before guiding me to the hospital wing, where more chaos ensued. *At least this was more of a controlled chaos,* I said to myself. The doctor and nurses knew what they were doing as they ran from bed to bed. They were completely full, and some shifters looked like they were barely holding on. I cringed and held Cade's hand tightly as he took me to the back room where I was just hours ago. I looked through the glass, and my whole body tensed up. Dr. Henley had Bastian on the table with his shirt off, and his hands inside his chest. *There was so much blood. Bastian looked so frail... So broken.*

I lost it.

I lost it right there, and Cade pulled me away from the door.

"Shh... Shanely, it's okay."

I buried my face in his chest and sobbed. Elijah's eyes flashed with worry, and he quickly walked to the left where the waiting room was.

"Where's daddy? I want daddy!" Aerith shouted, and she started to cry too. I wished I could hold her in my arms, but my left arm was useless still. The pain was nothing compared to Bastian. I'd give anything to take this away from him. I'd trade places with Bastian in a heartbeat if I could.

Elijah whispered something in her ear before taking her further into the waiting room. Cade stopped one of the nurses and asked for a few supplies. She handed them to him and took off to another patient. Cade guided me to one of the chairs near Elijah and Aerith. He sat in front of my daughter, blocking her from my view, while Elijah flipped the TV over to cartoons.

CHAPTER 19

"Let me see your arm," he asked, his voice numb of any feeling.

"Cade, I'm fine..." I tried to say, but he gave me another murderous glare.

"Shanely don't even think about arguing with me right now," he snapped, and I shut my mouth. *I had really stepped in it now.*

I took my sweatshirt off all the way and stayed in my black tank top. Dried blood coated my arm, and I could see the wound was already starting to close. He cleaned up my arm before inspecting the back.

"Looks like it went clean through," he mumbled. I nodded not really caring.

He put some sort of cream on it, which stung a bit before wrapping it in a bandage. He threw away the bloody mess before sitting back down.

"Thank you, Cade," I whispered, and he nodded slowly. I watched as he rested his face on his fist, staring at the door where Bastian was. Both Cade and Elijah's eyes were glued to the door.

We sat in silence for a moment, listening to the sound of cartoons playing on the TV for what felt like forever. Hours passed by with no word. Nothing. No one even came in or out of that room, but at least I had Bastian's heartbeat still. It was off but still beating. I couldn't stop the tears from falling as I waited for news. I tried to keep it quiet from the boys. I had done enough and didn't deserve the comfort they would give, regardless of how angry they were with me.

Dr. Henley's nurse finally came out of the room. She scanned the area quickly before running over to us.

"He's going to be okay! The bullet missed his heart, but the Doctor said it was good you got him in when you did. He's lost a lot of blood, but now that Doc has managed to close the hole and stop the bleeding, his shifter abilities are kicking in. I'm not sure when he will wake up, but the doctor is almost done with him, and then you can go in."

She took off as fast as she came, and I felt like I could breathe again. Cade and Elijah visibly relaxed too, and we all took a deep breath. I turned over to look to the brothers and sighed. Neither would look at me, and I exhaled slowly again. I needed to fix this between us, and now that I know Bastian was okay, I could think straight. I slowly stood to my feet and faced them both.

"Cade? Elijah?"

Cade raised his head to look at me, while Elijah peeked over Aerith's head. She was fast asleep in his arms, my poor baby.

"What is it, Shanely?" Cade asked, and I noticed that he didn't use his nickname for me. He didn't call me Baby Girl. He just looked spent and overly exhausted. Cade has never looked this bad before, and I felt awful for giving them an Alpha command.

"I'm sorry. I put you in a horrible spot, and I forced you to do something you did not want to do. I was trying to save my family and keep the two of you from running back and forth into all that gunfire, but it was wrong to do it the way I did. I never want to force you like that again. I see that I took it too far tonight, and I'm forever sorry."

They studied me for a moment before Elijah spoke up. "Despite me being pissed with you about it, you probably did save Bastian's life tonight. Don't you ever pull a stunt like that again though."

I nodded solemnly. "I am sorry, Elijah. I was afraid..."

"And we weren't?! I just watched my brother get shot in the chest, Shanely. I was terrified!" Cade snapped back, causing Aerith to shift in Elijah's arms.

"Quiet dude. Don't wake her up!" Elijah snapped back, but Cade's eyes were on mine. He stood to his feet and stalked towards me.

"I was scared to death when you commanded me *yet again* to walk in the opposite direction of you as you ran through gunfire!" he whispered angrily. "I get needing to find Aerith, but you should have carried Bastian in with Elijah and let *me* find her. It's my job to protect you when Bastian cannot! You are *my* responsibility even more so as your Beta, and you just took that away from me! Again!"

Cade hovered over me; his eyes filled with fury and fear. I never really noticed how tall Cade was or maybe it was simply because I was in the hot seat now, but I held my breath, waiting for the verbal lashing to continue. But then his eyes filled with tears, which only killed me more. *None of the brothers ever got teary-eyed, let alone actually cried.*

Yet Cade cried now.

CHAPTER 19

"What was I supposed to tell my brother if you died tonight? That I failed to protect you. That I failed to protect his twins," he said, his voice shaking with emotion now. I instinctively hugged him, whether he wanted it or not, and I could feel his anguish through the bond somehow.

Cade wrapped his arms around my waist and held me close. I stayed like that until he was ready to pull away. I didn't think about all that when I commanded him. I just thought of saving Bastian and finding my daughter.

"You were shot, Shanely," he whispered, and guilt ate me up inside. He finally pulled back, and I saw his eyes red with tears.

"You're right, Cade. I am so sorry I took away your free will. I promise I *never* will again."

I glanced at Elijah, who's face looked grim, before going back to Cade.

"Cade, Elijah? I command you to never obey another Alpha Command from *anyone*. You will never give up your free will again," I said before snapping my Alpha power back in, and they inhaled deeply.

"Shanely..." Cade whispered. His face looked utterly shocked, and I put my hands up defensively.

"I'm sorry! I couldn't prove to you how sorry I was without using my Alpha powers, but it was for the last time, I swear!"

Cade barreled into me, hugging me tightly. He squeezed me so hard I couldn't breathe. I laughed softly and hugged him back.

"Thank you, Shanely. I didn't even know that was possible," Cade replied before grinning at Elijah.

Elijah smirked back at us. "Only you, Shanely. Only you would defy all shifter rules and figure out things we never even knew were possible."

I gave them both a cheesy grin. "Just don't tell anyone, okay? It will be our little secret."

Cade laughed before playfully pushing me. A weight lifted off my shoulders now that we were back on good terms again. We waited awhile in the waiting room, hoping the doctor would let us in soon. Luke found us sometime later, and I sat forward in my seat as he came over.

"Whatcha find Luke?" I asked.

"My team has found nothing but this," he replied, handing me a piece of cloth. It was from a white camouflage jacket, and I scented it. I got nothing from it, and my eyes narrowed.

"So, you've got nothing to go off of?" Cade asked, his eyes narrowing.

"Other than footprints that led to the road, all we found was small specks of blood," Luke went on. "Scents like a human, but the trail disappeared from the road. Whoever they are, they were quick."

A low growl emitted from my throat as I stared at that cloth. *The only human I knew capable of this was back home in Washington.*

"I have patrols set up around Summit Hall, but it's been clear so far. We'll keep at it," Luke said as I handed him back the cloth.

"Thank you, Luke," I said softly. "Please inform the Alliance leaders that I want a meeting with them first thing in the morning. And start working on getting everyone home safely. I'm stopping the Summit early."

He gave me a firm nod before turning to the room where Bastian lay. "How's he doing?"

"He'll live," Elijah answered gruffly, and I leaned over to squeeze his hand.

Luke nodded once. "I have a team gathering the bodies outside. We'll make sure everyone goes home with their loved ones."

I cringed, thinking about all those I lost. The pain I felt when my wolves were disconnected from me. The youngest death was a 17-year-old male from the Romanian pack. My heart broke whenever I searched for his bond. Luke waved goodbye and made his way back upstairs.

Abraham, Bay, and Caleb made their way down with Ryder, Johnny, and Alana right behind them. Other than a few scrapes they were all okay. I was grateful everyone was alive. *Well almost everyone.* Caleb said my aunt had yet to stop crying since she felt the break but refuses to stop helping upstairs. They stayed with us for a while until Alana had to return to Tommy.

Johnny nudged me gently as Alana stood. "Want me to take Aerith? She can bunk with Tommy."

"Thank you," I answered, placing my hand on his arm. "I think that would be better for her actually."

He gave a soft smile, and I turned to kiss her softly. Johnny then took her from Elijah's arms, and I watched Elijah stretch, bringing blood flow back to

CHAPTER 19

his hands.

"Brody, I need you standing guard outside Johnny and Alana's door," I said through the link. "You are to protect my daughter until I come for her."

"Can do, Alpha."

I smiled softly to myself, feeling better about her leaving. *It's what Bastian would do.*

Elijah stood and offered to grab us food. Abraham and Ryder went with, leaving the rest of us to just wait. What surprised me though was Michelle. She came flying into the room, looking utterly frantic before finding us. Bay graciously filled her in on Bastian's condition before sitting her down in the corner with her. I wasn't sure what I should say to her, but I just couldn't handle it right now. The nurse talked like he was nearly done, but the doctor was taking forever to emerge. My anxiety was through the roof, and no matter how many times Cade tried to get me to sleep, I just couldn't close my eyes.

All I could see was Bastian getting shot. That image would forever be burned into my memory, and I slumped against my Beta, trying to push it from my mind. Finally, Dr. Henley stepped out of the room and met us halfway.

"Shanely, Cade, and you must be Bay. I'm sure Elijah's around somewhere, but you will have to fill him in later," he said to us. Michelle looked dejected again but said nothing as the doctor continued, "Bastian is out of danger. I stayed around for a while to make sure his own abilities kicked in and stayed in, but he's been stable for the last hour. However, due to his condition, I'm only allowing two to stay with him. Everyone can come back when he wakes."

"Thank you, Dr. Henley," I said, and nodded before leaving to check the main ballroom. Most of the patients here were stable enough for him to leave. Elijah and the boys passed the doctor on their way in, and my brother-in-law looked to me for answers. We quickly filled them in, and a look of relief washed over his face.

I turned to the group then. "Thank you all for being here with me. Having you here helped me get through this. Thank you, Elijah and Cade, for saving him as well. We'd all be lost without you."

Cade pulled me in and kissed my forehead. "Nah, Baby Girl. It was all you."

I smiled, letting myself enjoy this momentary peace. Cade insisted on going wherever I went now, so Elijah volunteered to stand guard at the door with Abraham and Bay in the waiting room. Surprisingly, Michelle sat back in her seat to wait as well. I figured she'd go back to her room to get some rest, but she stayed put.

I gave everyone a grateful smile before making my way to my mate's room. I was grateful my Beta was with me though because I was afraid to see Bastian like this. I was afraid to see him so broken and hurt. He was always my strong savior, my protector, and seeing him fallen like this wasn't easy.

It was hard to move my feet at first, and Cade had to gently push me into the room. My eyes widened. *Bastian looked rough.* His chest was all bandaged up, and they had put a small oxygen tube by his nose to ensure he got a good amount. My heart broke. Not even 24 hours ago *I was in this bed. What would have happened if I was too stubborn and refused to open the bond?* I thought as my guilt plagued me. *Bastian would be dead right now if he was as weak as he was earlier.* I vowed right then never to close the bond because of a stupid fight.

Cade finally forced me to move my feet to the couch and threw a blanket over me.

"Go to sleep, Baby Girl," he whispered, hitting the light switch on the wall. The events of the day weighed heavy on my chest, but somehow, I managed to fall asleep.

Chapter 20

I awoke to a bright light coming from the above windows and shining directly on my face. Cade and I had somehow managed to sleep next to one another on this tiny couch, but I was not where I was when I fell asleep last night. I had started curled up on the side closest to Bastian, but Cade had sprawled out the length of the couch, tucking me into the safety of the inner couch, with his arm over me. *He must still be jittery from last night because his grip dug into my arm*, I thought to myself. My head was on his chest, and I was cozy and warm where I lay. It was probably why I was able to sleep for as long as I did honestly. My animals and I felt safe with Cade.

I looked to my mate, my heart seizing when I saw him still unconscious in the hospital bed. *I was hoping he'd finally be awake by now.* What I didn't expect to see was Michelle, sitting in the chair opposite to us, looking haggard and sleep deprived.

"I see you're awake," she said without taking her eyes off Bastian.

I slowly slipped out of Cade's grip and took the chair next to her. Cade simply rolled over in the couch without waking.

"I didn't expect you to be in here," I replied softly.

She looked to me briefly. A snarky tone came forth as she said, "He's my son after all. I won't stay away while he's like this."

I bristled at her tone but shook off her snarky comment, trying to look at it from her point of view. *It can't be easy being in her position*, I thought to myself.

"I didn't mean you aren't *allowed*. Just that I didn't expect you to be here."

She sighed, rubbing her face. "I'm sorry. I'm just tired is all."

"Michelle... Look I don't want to get in the middle between you two, but I have to ask. Did you ever try to protect your children from Liam?"

She glared at me, and I wasn't trying to be rude or insinuate anything, but if I was going to try to help them make amends or frankly allow her to be a grandmother to my kids, then I needed to know.

Her face softened as she looked to Cade and then back at Bastian. "I did try, Shanely. It wasn't easy with Liam, and I quickly learned the less I got involved the better it was for them. Liam punished *them* when I got upset with how they were being treated. They got extra training or disciplined whenever I involved myself in Liam's affairs. All because Liam thought they needed a stern hand to grow up to be tough Alphas. I learned that if I didn't speak, they'd get the lesser of two evils."

"I can't imagine being mated to someone like Liam," I whispered, and her face fell. *She just looked so sad,* I thought to myself. *So broken.*

"He gave me them, so for that I'll always be grateful," she said softly as Cade stirred some. He stayed asleep though, and I turned back to Michelle.

"You need to hear them out because they are angry, but I think in time they will forgive you."

She looked at her feet nervously. "I know I did wrong, Shanely. I'm trying to make up for it, and I'm paying for it dearly. I mean Bastian looked feral when he saw me holding Aerith. I don't even know if I will ever have a relationship with *any* of my family again. All because I was afraid of my mate. I really did try to be a good mother to them though."

She looked nearly in tears, when I took her hand in mine. I said softly, "You did an incredibly brave thing by leaving your mate and standing up for us before. They will see it in time, but Michelle? I think you will make a wonderful grandmother."

Michelle held her breath, trying to gain control of her emotions before she finally dabbed her eyes dry. I gave her a soft smile. *I truly meant every word too.*

"Thank you, Shanely. I needed to hear that."

I smiled. "Of course. I never wanted Bastian to give up on you, but I've been letting him work through his feelings himself. It just takes time, and

CHAPTER 20

he has a lot on his plate."

She nodded. "Yes, he does, but that's where you and his siblings come in though. You all help each other out, it seems. It's interesting the way they share you."

I laughed at that, causing Cade to stir again. I quickly covered my mouth before whispering, "Well, Bastian doesn't share me in every way. I'm his mate only, but the brothers have this strong connection to one another which extends into the mate bond. At least that's how they've explained it. They'd do anything for me, and when Elijah and Cade find their mate then it will be same for them too."

"And you're okay with that? I mean would you be okay with Bastian sleeping on the couch next to his sister-in-law like that?"

"Well to be fair I fell asleep on the other side of the couch, but honestly if roles were reversed, and it was Cade in this bed with Bastian watching over his mate for him then no. I wouldn't be mad. I know without a shadow of a doubt who Bastian's heart beats for, but they look out for the other's mate when they themselves can't. I'm extremely close to all three brothers, but in very different ways."

Michelle seemed to mull that over for a moment before responding, "Those boys have always been extremely close. Ever since they were little, they refused to be separated and had to share everything. I just never thought they'd share mates like this."

She smiled wide, making me laugh again. This time it woke Cade up, and he shot forward in a panic. He patted all over the couch, throwing off the blanket.

"I'm over here, Cade," I said, waving my hand at him.

His sleepy eyes found my voice, and he relaxed against the couch. Cade slowly sat up, rubbing his head before he noticed his mother in the room with us.

"Mother," he said, acknowledging her.

"Hello Cade," she replied, smiling at him. I gave her a wink, keeping our conversation between us.

Elijah walked in now with coffee in hand and stared hard at Bastian. This hit him just as hard as it hit me, but he quickly tore himself away from his brother and looked around the room. His eyes settled on his mother. "I wondered where you went to."

"You were sleeping, and I didn't see the harm in checking in," Michelle replied casually.

Elijah grunted but said nothing more to her. He handed me one of the coffees and asked, "How you doing, Shanie?"

"Shanie?" I asked inquisitively as I took a sip. *God, it was good,* I thought to myself. He even made sure to add the creamer I liked with a dash of cinnamon. He *remembered.* Elijah just shrugged before giving me a dashing smile. He passed the last cup to Cade, who nearly downed the whole thing right there.

"Cade gave you a nickname, so I figured you should have one from me too."

I grinned wide. "Shanie... I like it, Elijah. And I'm okay. I actually just woke up."

"You sleep alright? I know that couch ain't comfy," he asked before sitting down on it. Michelle snickered in her seat, making me laugh.

"I did actually because I ended up sleeping on my Beta instead of the couch," I said, laughing harder.

Cade looked at me funny. "Is that why my back is killing me?"

The four of us laughed then, and for a brief moment I was able to forget about what happened last night. The momentary relief was short lived though as Dr. Henley and Luke walked in the room, silencing us all.

"Well Bastian looks like he's healing well! I'd say he should be waking up sometime this morning," Dr. Henley said cheerfully after checking on Bastian's bandages. I smiled and walked to the other side of Bastian bed. I ran my fingers through his hair as Luke spoke.

"The alliance is ready to go in the conference room, Alpha. We need to start escorting everyone home and address the leaders soon. Everyone's getting restless," he said, and I nodded, looking down at my mate. The idea of not being here when he woke just about killed me.

"I can't leave him though. He can't wake up alone," I whispered, looking to Luke. He gave me an understanding look, but I saw it in his eyes. *There was nothing he could do. I was Alpha. I had to go.*

"I'll stay, Shanie," Elijah said calmly. I turned and gave him a weak smile. "I'm his Beta anyways. I can't get my wolf to leave him like this. I promise I'll find you the moment he stirs."

I sighed, knowing there was no arguing this. *We ruled together for a reason.*

"C'mon, Baby Girl," Cade said as he stretched. "I'll stay with you, and we'll be back before you know it."

I leaned over and gave Bastian a kiss.

"I'll be right back, my love."

I didn't know if my link would reach him, but I had to try. I followed Luke and Cade out of the room, leaving the love of my life in the hospital bed. I passed an exhausted Abraham and Bay in the chairs next to the door. Abraham gave his mate a kiss before joining us. Bay stayed behind, and I hugged her before leaving the hospital wing all together.

"Luke? Can you send a link and put two enforcers outside Johnny and Alana's room please? Brody is going to need a break. Oh, can you also send more to relieve Bay as well? She's exhausted and needs to sleep. Please make sure to have the enforcers bring breakfast up for Johnny, Alana, and the kids too. I don't want them leaving their room right now," I asked, and he nodded before his eyes glazed over a bit. I turned to Abraham then.

"Abey, you can skip the meeting today. You're exhausted and need to crash with Bay."

"Nah, Shanely. I'll be okay for a while longer. I'll take a nap afterwards," he replied. I gave him a look, but he just tussled my already messy hair. *Brothers.*

I sighed, giving up on trying to convince him and followed Cade and Luke down the hall.

"Johnny?" I said through the link.

"Morning, Alpha. Little One is still asleep."

"Good. She needs all the rest she can get. Listen, I'm meeting with the Alliance members now, but I need you to sit this one out. I need you to stay in your rooms and watch over my daughter and nephew please."

"Sure thing," he replied. *"Are you going to be alright? You're not going alone,*

are you?"

"No, Cade is with me as well as Luke and Abraham right now. I'm going to pull who I can, but I need to make sure our kids our safe first," I said as we walked up the small flight of stairs.

"I agree. Don't worry, Shanely," Johnny said firmly. "I'll protect them."

"I know you will. I'm sending two more enforcers to guard your door, and they will bring you all something to eat so you don't have to leave," I explained."

"Got it. How's Bastian?"

"He has yet to wake up, but he will live. Elijah is staying close by."

"Good," he said relieved. "Well keep me posted please."

"Will do."

I ended the link as we made our way to the main foyer. I stopped momentarily at the ballroom and sighed. It was a mess, but it looked like everyone was at least escorted back to their own rooms. Far more comfortable than sleeping on the floor in here. I made a mental note to help clean before I left today.

We entered the room to find the leaders already in their seat. Caleb was here too and stood when we walked in.

I leaned in as we passed saying, "He's not awake yet but still good."

He relaxed and nodded as I stood by my chair. Ryder gave me a small wave, and I waved back.

"Good morning, everyone. I cannot tell you how sorry I am that this happened to us," I said. Cade tried to get me to sit, but I shook my head. I was too jittery to sit right now.

"Who would do such a thing?" James asked, leaning forward on the table.

"How do we honestly know you weren't behind it?" Esme muttered under her breath.

My eyes flashed red. *God, that stupid Panther again*, I thought to myself. I don't know why she didn't like me, but this ended *now*. My power poured into the room as my anger rose, and I realized it affected more than just wolves as *everyone* winced. I tried to funnel it more so at her, but I was angry and exhausted. Esme looked somewhat worried as our eyes locked on one another.

CHAPTER 20

"Let me set the record straight because this is the *second* time you have accused me of being behind this. The ones we lost last night were mostly wolves. My own people were the ones that died! And if I was planning on killing you and your kind, I wouldn't use a gun. I nearly lost my mate and was shot in the process of saving my daughter, but you already knew that. We had this exact conversation last night! Do I need to remove you and place someone else from your kind to take your seat?"

I forced my Alpha power back, releasing the room of the uncomfortable pain, and Esme tightened her hands in fists. My eyes narrowed. *She was still pissed*, I thought as my wolf snapped within me. *Well, guess what panther?! So am I!*

"Actually, that's a brilliant idea. Go ahead, panther," I said, putting my hands on my hips.

"Go ahead and do what?" she asked with a clipped tone.

"Go ahead and call whomever you would choose to take your place. Who in your claw would you feel would be a wise choice for the seat."

She looked alarmed as she sat forward. "Are you replacing me?!"

I mulled my answer over carefully, trying to reign in my anger. I cannot have her bucking every decision we make, nor could I keep dealing with her accusing me or Bastian when things went wrong. I looked around the room though as the other leaders looked concerned as well. *If I just straight up replaced her now, they all might start feeling like we'll just get rid of any who do not agree with us*, I thought. *I can't have that either.* They need to feel valued and apart of everything otherwise we won't be able to smooth things over. We won't become a community of shifters, and any attempt at trying again will be squashed.

I decided to go a different route despite my angry wolf snapping within me.

"Not yet, but I feel like your seat needs to be split in two. You are too hot-headed and have accused me on intentionally harming shifters more than once. I'm done dealing with it, so go ahead and think. Call them here now otherwise I choose, and you may not like who I pick."

She gritted her teeth, but her eyes still glossed over. I turned back to the group.

"Back to the issue at hand... We have no idea *who* would do something like this, but my enforcer found this," I said, taking the piece of fabric from Luke and tossing it on the table. Everyone inhaled deeply.

"It smells like wolves and faintly like something else," James commented to no one in particular. I nodded in agreement.

"You're going to pick up on the scent of wolves because his team found it, but the other scent is too faint."

"So, we have no leads other than this scrap of fabric?" the panther asked sarcastically.

"We scented human blood in the woods," Luke chimed in. "A minute amount though. The scrap of fabric was practically on top of it. So, this could be from our attackers, or it could have belonged to the hunting party we escorted off our land a few weeks ago."

My eyes narrowed. "You didn't tell me that."

Luke shrugged. "It's happened before, but it's rare. My team went through double checking the perimeter fence and fixed where they got through."

"It wouldn't surprise me one bit if this was Patrick," Caleb said, redirecting the whole conversation. Cade snarled at the sound of Patrick's name but said nothing further.

James looked to him briefly before asking me, "Who's Patrick?"

"He is the son of our Division's Head for our area. He's obsessed with Shanely and has been a trigger for her warnings," Cade snarled as he started pacing the room. I sighed, watching my Beta struggle with his wolf.

"You're a seer?" the elephant leader asked.

I nodded as Abraham interjected loudly, "I told you we should have killed him a long time ago!"

"He's a human, Abey! We don't kill for no reason either, and up until this point, he's just been annoying and pushy. Besides, we have no proof it was him," I countered, cocking my hips to the side.

"But things started changing before we came here," Caleb countered.

"How so?" James asked as the door opened.

A girl around my size walked in, and my wolf perked up at the sight of her.

CHAPTER 20

She felt oddly familiar, but I couldn't put my finger on it, and her scent was one my wolf recognized. I turned to Cade, who looked like he felt the same way I did. He gave me a look as my wolf pushed against my skin.

"Shanely meet my sister, Emersyn. Emersyn, Shanely," the panther said in a clipped tone, and my eyes widened.

Emersyn looked a lot like me just opposite in color and with long, straight, dark hair instead of my curly white. Her small nose and thick, full lips fit her round face perfectly, and she had an adorably small number of freckles on her nose and cheeks. I looked to Cade again, who shrugged.

It was *weird*.

"Esme, what am I doing here?" she asked nervously.

"I invited you. You and your sister shall share the seat on the alliance for now. It's nice to meet you, but for now your sister can quietly catch you up," I replied as Cade took over.

"If it was Patrick then I'd bet anything he was the one to shoot Bastian. Out of everyone there last night, *Bastian* was the one who took the first hit," he said angrily.

"But that would mean this was a direct attack from the Division. We didn't break any laws, so they have no grounds for anything!" Abraham shouted.

"Tell me, Shanely. What's been different with your Division Head?" James asked again.

"Well, for starters, he told his son about us early on. They're working together now, and Calvin said the Division itself has been too laxed with all of us, so they're changing things. Instead of meeting yearly, he wants monthly check ins. They want to be informed of our every move, and I said no. It seems to have started things between us, but I can't believe they'd do something like this!" I replied.

My stomach twisted though. *What if I was wrong? What if it really was Patrick who attacked us?* But going down that path meant getting closer to my warnings and to war. *And I just couldn't do that.*

"Who else could it be though, and who would resort to guns instead of their own shifter abilities? Guns are not the shifter way. They are *human* weapons. Honestly, everyone think because we were all there. Does anyone else have a target on their backs?" Caleb stated.

No one spoke then, and my heart sank. I know everyone thought it was Patrick and the Division, but I was hoping for an answer to a problem I *could* solve. I didn't trust Patrick one bit, but I didn't think he'd be dumb enough to try and kill Bastian and the rest of shifters kind like this. *This can't be the beginning of my warnings.*

Can it?

"So, what are we going to do?" Emersyn asked, pulling everyone's attention back.

She was definitely more on board with the whole teamwork idea, and I was grateful. *She seemed more suited to this job than her sister did.*

"I don't know yet, but that's why we're here, right? To figure this out," I said, finally taking my seat.

We deliberated for a while longer before coming to the conclusion that we needed to find out if this was an attack on the whole of shifters or just a vendetta on me and Bastian. In the meantime, Luke was going to sweep the area again and check the local airports. See if anyone we knew took a plane out of here.

Everyone was to return home today, and they were to get back in touch once they got there and could see what was going on their end. Emersyn made the suggestion to send a few people from each group to our pack lands as extra security, especially with Bastian down and out. I was surprised by her suggestion but extremely grateful when everyone readily agreed. The alliance, other than Esme, was more than willing to help us. Everyone was sending at least two people to stay on McCoy land in case we were right and came home to a trap.

"Shanie!" Elijah bellowed through the link. "*Bastian's awake!*"

My heart stopped in the middle of the meeting. I abruptly stood up, silencing the group.

"I'm so sorry, but my mate's awake. I need to go," I said before taking off out of the room.

Cade was hot on my heels, but I didn't slow down. The others could finalize everyone's departure, and the rest of the details needed. Right now, my mate

CHAPTER 20

was awake, and I needed to see him.

Chapter 21

I flew into the room to find Bastian trying to get out of bed.

"Elijah, move! I need to find Shanely," he growled as Elijah pushed him back down.

"You can't! You were shot yesterday! I sent her a link so just give her…"

"Bastian!" I cried out as I flew into his arms, knocking him back against the bed. He grunted, and I backed away, feeling entirely stupid. "I'm so sorry…"

Bastian pulled me back with such force it nearly took my breath away. He growled, "Don't you dare move further away from me. I'm fine as long as you stay right where you are."

I relaxed against him before finally losing my grip on my emotions. I cried hard as he held me tight. Never once letting me go. I could hear Cade say he was glad to see him awake, but other than that no one spoke. Bastian's brothers stood near the door, giving us as much privacy as their wolves allowed for the moment.

"Bastian, I was so scared! When you got hit, I just… There was so much blood," I barely choked out.

"I'm okay, baby. And apparently, it's all thanks to you. Elijah told me everything," he said with as much gentleness as he could muster. His wolf was still close to the surface.

"I did what I thought was best for everyone," I said, dropping my head in shame. I knew I was going to have to tell him about the Alpha command.

"He filled me in on that part too, but seeing how you permanently freed them from being bound again, I won't yell at you," he replied with a low chuckle. My eyes widened in surprise.

"Really? I thought I'd get an earful from you about that."

"I heard Cade already gave you an earful. Twice," he said, raising an eyebrow towards his brother. Cade smiled sheepishly, shrugging his shoulders.

"What? I just channeled my inner Bastian," he replied, causing us to laugh. Bastian winced as he chuckled, clutching his chest from the pain, and my shoulders fell.

"You jerk," he snapped back to Cade.

"Well, I'm so glad you're okay. I wish you had my healing abilities though. My gunshot wound is nearly gone now," I said as Elijah made a face.

"Wait, what!? You were shot!?" Bastian asked as he yanked me forward. It didn't take his wolf long to find the wound, which was just a faint mark on my shoulder now.

"I thought you knew," I said confused.

"Elijah seems to have left that part out," he said as he glared back at his brother.

Elijah ran his hand through his hair, while Cade scrunched his nose.

"Well... Elijah and I both agreed last night to not freak you out even more than you'd already be once you woke up. We found her and Little One as soon as we dropped you off and brought them both back to safety," Cade finally said. Bastian cocked his head to the side as he gave me a sharp look.

"Okay, now I'm pissed. Shanely, what were you..."

I kissed him before he could finish that sentence. I held him firm until he relaxed somewhat against me before I bravely pulled away.

"That's not fair," he whispered. I batted my eye lashes, trying to soften his anger.

"I'm okay, Bastian. We're all okay..." my voice trailed off as I thought of Aspen. My heart hurt all over again, and I laid against his shoulder. "Well, almost everyone. Everyone except my Uncle Aspen. He didn't make it, and neither did his mate."

Tears filled my eyes again, and he wrapped his good arm around me.

"Shh... I know, Shanely. They told me about your uncle. How's Cassia and

Ash?"

"Ash has shut down. Losing your twin is... hard. He won't let anyone but his mate nearby. He took Aspen's body along with his mate back home already. They left sometime in the middle of the night," Elijah answered, and I looked back to him. *I didn't know that.*

"Cassia is managing. She's asleep right now. I think the task of healing the injured helped her last night," Cade continued, when a knock on the door interrupted us.

Cade opened it, and Elijah went rigid. Emersyn walked in, giving us a small smile. She inhaled deeply before her eyes narrowed slightly, and suddenly Cade and I knew *exactly* what was going on. We immediately turned to each another, grinning like banshees.

Emersyn walked further into the room, and Cade started waving his arms around like crazy behind her. Elijah barely looked his way as Cade mouthed the word *Mate!* over and over excitedly. Elijah shook his head sternly before burying his face in his hands. Emersyn looked around the room, giving Cade an odd look, when her gaze settled on him. His hands were way above his head, so he pretended to stretch, giving her a nonchalant smile.

"*Smooth, Cade.*"

He just winked at me as Emersyn spoke up.

"Hi. I'm sorry to interrupt, but I wanted to give you the list of who was staying at the McCoy pack. I also wanted to introduce myself to your mate as well, seeing how my sister and I will be joining you from our claw. I can come back later though," she said quietly as she handed the list to me. I scooched off Bastian's lap, setting my feet on the floor. Bastian wrapped his arm around my waist, warning me not to go any further.

"No, you're fine. Emersyn meet my mate Bastian, and behind you is the other triplet, Elijah. You already know Cade," I said casually.

She turned to look at Elijah, and I swear sparks filled the air when their eyes locked on one another. Emersyn suddenly began to stammer, "There are three of you? Oh well... It's nice to meet everyone. I'm going to get packed, so we can join you on your flight."

She flew out the door before anyone could stop her, and Elijah finally

CHAPTER 21

exhaled the breath he had been holding. He slumped against the wall, putting his head in his hands.

"My God man, go after her!" Cade shouted, opening the door. "Did you not see my hand gestures, dude?!"

Elijah glared as he stalked over and slammed the door shut again. "Back off, Cade! You don't get it."

"What's there to get, brother? You found your mate! Even Shanely and I felt something in that meeting today," Cade hollered. "Why won't you go?"

"Don't either of you recognize her?!" he hollered back.

I shook my head, and Cade looked bewildered.

Bastian finally spoke, "She's the daughter of the Chief of that panther claw a couple hours south of us. That's Emersyn Whitlock."

Cade swore, but I was still confused. I turned to Bastian and asked, "Wait, who?"

"Emersyn Whitlock. Their family is actually from Denmark. Her family lived not far from our father's pack, and while we were never allowed near them, our father treated them harshly. He managed to drive them out of their land and then bought it on the cheap. Dad bankrupted them, and they were forced to leave the country. I only know where they live now because of Cain. Their dad has been sick for the last... What 5 years now? And Esme's been running things ever since. Emersyn's the baby of the family," Bastian said, and I exhaled slowly.

"Good lord. No wonder you're afraid, Elijah," I replied, and he glared at me.

"I'm not afraid, Shanie, but this isn't good. It's one thing having her sister on the council and seeing them once a year, but now this? They hate the Fenrir's, and I don't *blame* them. What am I supposed to do? Just walk up to her dad and say hey, remember me? I come from the wolf pack you hate, and I'm here to mate with your daughter. No wait... I can make it even worse, hang on," he snapped, gesturing as he spoke. "I'm actually *the son* of the man that drove you out of your home, stealing it from you on the sly, and I'm here to marry your daughter and take her away from your family and claw. Yeah, that's going to work out really well."

"Actually, Emersyn's apart of the council now," I said sheepishly, twiddling my thumbs.

"What?" he asked in disbelief.

"Her sister kept insulting me, so I made her split her seat with someone else from her claw. Emersyn was whom she chose. I didn't know anything about all of that though," I said guiltily.

"You didn't know, Shanely. I was hoping to smooth things over this week with them," Bastian said, rubbing my arm.

"Well, we still can once we get home! Then you will see there is nothing to be afraid of Elijah," I said with a big grin. Elijah narrowed his eyes to me uneasily.

"Shanie.... What are you up to?"

"Shanie? That's a new one," Bastian muttered, but I shushed him

"Nothing Elijah, but for the record I think you're being crazy!"

He rolled his eyes. "Okay, let me just say this now because I have a feeling it needs to be said out loud. No one is allowed to tell her I think she's my mate. *No one* will pressure her or me into diving headfirst into this. Are we clear?"

"Umm... I believe I'm the Alpha, thank you very much. I should have given you a command to find her before freeing you," I said sarcastically, hopping off the bed to grab Bastian's clothes. He growled softly the moment I stepped away, and I gave him a look. He grunted and laid back down. Someone brought him some new things and thankfully took away the bloody set. *I didn't want to see those clothes ever again.* Elijah just smirked at me.

"Well, aren't I just thrilled you freed me before this happened then?"

"Alright, enough you two. Cade, go get me out of here. Elijah stand outside and make sure no one else comes in, and Shanely... You get your sexy butt over here and help me get dressed. I want our pack and clan ready to go to the airport in 1 hour. Let's move," Bastian demanded. His brothers rolled their eyes, laughing as they made their way to the door.

"He seems back to his bossy self," Elijah muttered as he left the room.

"Yeah, well make sure she's actually getting you dressed and not the other way around, alright?" Cade smirked before ducking out the door as Bastian

CHAPTER 21

threw something at his head.

I laughed at the three of them. Bastian winced and clutched his chest again. I sighed and said, "Alright, easy now. You're still healing."

"Not that slowly. I'll be good as new by the end of the week," he replied, taking off his gown and sitting on the bed in nothing but his boxers. His chest was still bandaged, and my heart stilled. I was frozen, staring at where I knew the bullet hit him.

"Hey baby... It's okay. Here help me put on my shirt first then you don't have to see it," he said as he carefully lifted his arms. I helped him pull the black t-shirt over his head and down his body, feeling awful as he winced in pain. It did help having the bandage covered honestly. Now he just seemed like the same old Bastian, even though he was still so injured.

I was slipping his feet in his jeans when he whispered, "Was my mother here?"

I looked up at him and then shimmied his pants to his knees. "She was, Bastian. For the whole night since they brought you in. When I woke up, she was here in the room already. She stayed until some point this morning, but I don't know when she left since I was at the meeting."

Bastian mulled it over before slowly getting on his feet. I pulled his pants all the way up before zipping them up and snapping the button. He already wore socks, so getting his shoes on was the last step.

"I want to believe her baby, but it's hard not to think back to everything growing up. She never said a word to any of dad's decisions. She *never* said a word when he removed the birthright and threw us all away."

I sighed, hesitating as I tied his shoes. "She did, Bastian. She told me at first, she was against a lot that happened to you guys growing up, but when she disagreed your father took it out on you guys. You'd get extra work or a harsher punishment, and she learned that staying quiet meant you got the lesser of two evils. It's not right, but I think she thought she was doing everything she could for you guys."

"She told you that?"

I nodded and continued on tying his shoes. "This morning she did, but please know that I won't force you to talk to her. You decide when you're ready for that step."

I kissed his cheek, but it apparently wasn't enough as he yanked me close, capturing my lips. He spread his legs, and I stepped between them, fitting perfectly against his body. Bastian was perfect for me, and he quickly deepened the kiss. We were lost in each other. He needed me as badly as I needed him.

Cade suddenly pushed his way through the door and cleared his throat.

"Seriously guys? I was only gone 5 minutes."

Bastian broke our kiss, glaring at his brother. "God Cade, just wait till you find your mate. I'm going to give it right back!"

Cade just laughed at the threat, but I knew my Bastian was serious.

"C'mon lovebirds. We've got a flight to catch," Cade said, extending his hand to Bastian.

Bastian groaned, but we tugged him along anyways. Seeing him move around, smiling, and holding my hand… That was something I didn't want to take for granted.

Never again.

Chapter 22

The flight home seemed shorter this time around, but I was glad to be going home. Well half of me was. The other half was nervous about what I'd find. I had filled Bastian in on what Luke found in the woods and who we suspected to be behind it all, and he was fuming mad the entire flight home. Everyone could sense it too. They stayed far away from the brooding Alpha.

Aerith, however, was oblivious to his dark gaze and temper. She clung to Bastian from the moment we picked her up from Johnny and Alana's room. Thankfully, no one else from McCoy pack was harmed severely, but we still lost enough. Enough that a lot were heading home to grieve. Our first Summit ended in disaster, and I couldn't help but shoulder the blame.

Luke was already starting to add extra defenses around Summit Hall to keep out everyone who wasn't invited, whether they were human or shifter. I never thought it would come to this, and that was my mistake to bear.

Emersyn and her sister flew home with us, causing a very difficult ride for my poor Elijah. He was distracted and tense the entire flight. At one point, he even took my sweatshirt and buried his face in it. I nearly laughed when he did, but the murderous glare he gave me shut me right up. I've been prodding, trying to see what she smells like, but he won't tell me anything. Well, other than to hush.

The sisters stayed further to the back of the plane, and I kept trying to sneak peeks to see if she was struggling too, but Elijah dug his nails into my thigh, forcing me to stop. He was seriously giving me a bruise though.

And Elijah was the first one off the plane when we landed.

Other than the two panthers, we had James with his version of a Beta, Mark.

Both were light hair males with the typical dreamy blue eyes. They were tan southern boys with their pride hailing from Texas.

Then the Elephant King sent one enforcer Khalan, who was incredibly quiet. He had dark, spiky hair with bright green eyes and a tattoo on his left shoulder. He reminded me a lot of that popular vampire movie, although he looked more like the pack than the *cold ones*. He was shorter than most the guys here, but he shifted into one of the largest animals we had. The King's herd was very small, so they could only spare one, but I appreciated it, nonetheless.

We had two anacondas as well. Twin sisters, Nathara and Havu. They were gorgeous identical twins with dark skin and kinky curly hair. I didn't know much about them, but their leader said they were the best he had available. Their combat skills were left to be desired, but they were swift and stealthy, which is exactly what we needed.

Lastly, we had one leopard named Harley, but everyone called her Scout. She volunteered her stealth skills before we left the Hall, and I gladly accepted. She was a little quiet, but she seemed to study everything and everyone. Processing everything before she ever spoke or made a move. She had shoulder length, blonde hair with nearly jet-black eyes. They were honestly incredible, and I tried very hard not to stare at them. After she caught me staring for the millionth time, she explained that they were naturally very dark, and that she usually wore special contacts when going around the public to keep people from freaking out over it.

It wasn't an army, but the shifters that came were apparently good at what they did. We didn't want it to look like we were building an army at pack lands anyways. I was grateful for the help, even if it was small.

The drive back didn't take long, and we set everyone up at the lodge. Bastian kicked up the security, and we had way more teams and patrols coming and going. Caleb went home to work with his uncle on scouting the town for us. Many cops got drunk on the weekends at the Den when they were off duty, so they were going to start seeing if anyone would talk about Patrick or his father. Anything to indicate that *they* were actually behind this. If it wasn't them then I had no idea who attacked us.

CHAPTER 22

My aunt left shortly after returning home to find Ash. He and his mate never came home, and I knew they were deep in the mountains. Cain felt horrible for leaving in a time like this, but Cassia mentally wasn't here. She was lost and grieving Aspen too. No one even had a chance to really get to know his mate, and now we never will. He got only a few days with her. It wasn't fair, and I only ended up angry when I thought about it. I told Cain to go ahead and to take their time. They needed to heal, and I could deal with the pack. It was my responsibility anyways.

I was glad to be home though. Elijah went straight to his room, locking it before anyone could follow him. He wasn't holding up very well either, but Bastian said to give him time. We all began to unpack and settle in, when I heard a knock on my front door. I opened it to find my cousin standing there.

"Hello, Shanely," his deep voice rumbled through the house.

"Noah. Come in! Come in!"

He walked in, and I saw he brought a large bag with him.

"I wasn't sure where you would like me to be, but I am planning on staying here in America with my family. I peaceably left my clan in Russia, and I am rejoining my father's clan. Until we deal with those who attacked us, I want to stay here on pack lands to offer my services to you and your mate."

I was surprised, giving him a genuine smile. "You switched clans to help us?"

He smiled softly saying, "You are family, and my family is in danger. Our cousin Alexei agrees that I belong here with you. I was always meant to take over for my father anyways. I'm just moving up my schedule."

Bastian walked around the corner, cocking his head to the side as he said, "Noah? What a nice surprise! What are you doing here? I thought you'd be on a flight back home by now."

"He's switching clans, so he can stay here and help us," I said with a big smile. I crashed into Noah, hugging him. It surprised him, but he gave me a hug back as I said, "Thank you, Noah."

"Absolutely. Now where would you like me?"

"Here of course," Bastian said, gesturing to the house. "We have two spare rooms now, so take your pick. You're family, so I'd be honored if you'd stay with us."

Noah smiled, nodding his head as he replied, "Thank you, cousin."

Bastian led him up the stairs to one of the spare rooms, while I went in to make dinner. We might all be zonked from the flight home, but it doesn't mean we need to eat junk. Unfortunately, I didn't expect us home so soon, so I was limited in my options. I pulled out a large pack of ground beef and threw it in the defroster. *No one can complain about a burger, right?* Soon, the whole house smelled delicious and that finally pulled Elijah out of his room. We were all hanging out and enjoying dinner, when my phone rang. Caleb was on the other line.

"Hey, Caleb! We're making burgers if you want to just stop over. Noah's here," I said, holding the phone with my shoulder as I cut up Aerith's burger.

"I wish. Listen Shanely, I'm at the bar time with Octavia, and the cops here are pissed that a certain someone bailed on all his shifts this week. They're also mad because daddy covered his butt and then yelled at the ones who complained. They all got stuck with extra paperwork and double shifts, and boy are they pissed."

"That can't be a coincidence, right?" I asked grimly. The room could hear my shift in tone, and everyone quieted down.

"It could, but unlikely. I mean what are the odds that Patrick would take a vacation the same time we're attacked? Patrick was MIA all week, and daddy's been covering up for him, but there's more," he said.

"What?"

"Patrick just walked in with two guys I have never seen before. He's introducing them as the fellas he trained with in Texas."

"They're probably from the Division then," I commented. Bastian slowly stood to his feet. No longer interested in his meal.

"He's been telling his fellow coworkers that he's been promoted and is bringing in a new team. He looked right at me when he said it though," Caleb said. I could hear the worry in his voice, and even I was nervous now.

"Caleb, call someone else to work tonight. Now. Just bring Octavia home," I commanded.

"Shanely, I can't just run because he's here. This is my bar, and I won't

CHAPTER 22

hide from him," my brother countered.

"Caleb, I think he's sending you a message because he knows you're a shifter. If we're right and Patrick was behind this attack, then you and Octavia are alone in the bar with him. It isn't safe."

Suddenly a loud commotion interrupted us, causing me to jump. I heard Caleb swear and a whole lot of shouting before the line went dead. I dropped my phone in a flash before bolting to the door.

"Shanely, wait!" Bastian hollered, grabbing my hand. I tried to yank my hand away, but he had a death grip on me.

"I can't! Something's happened to Caleb. I have to go!"

"We will, but we can't just take off like that. Give me a minute," he said before he zoned out.

"Bastian, I don't want to wait. He could be hurt right now!"

Brody jumped on my deck, shifting before walking inside.

"Go, I've got Aerith," he said, sitting down next to her.

"Thanks, man. Alright, now we can go," Bastian said as he made his way to his truck.

"How did he..."

"Brody's on the team that stays by our house. He was right outside," Bastian said, opening my door. He winced slightly as he hopped in the truck. I hopped in next to him, slamming the door behind me. Cade jumped in the driver side, and Noah and Elijah were already hopping in the back.

"Bastian, you shouldn't go! You're healing still!"

"Like I'm letting you walk out that door without me. I already know if I try to make you stay, you'll just find trouble getting there yourself anyways. Now drive, Cade!"

Cade floored it as we hauled the truck to the Den. I just prayed Caleb was okay, and that we'd make it in time.

Patrick better not lay a finger on my brother.

Series Order

Shifter Series
Shifter Awakened
Shifter Prophecy
Shifter Deliverance
Shifter Sacrifice

Nightlocke Series
Realm of Darkness
Island of Horrors

Bonus Chapter

Cade

God, I was going to kill him, I thought as I tightened my hands into fists. *This time Bastian's gone too far.*

I glared one last time at my deranged brother stalking down the halls and turned to Baby Girl. The look on her face... It broke something in me.

Tears filled her eyes, angering me all over again. My wolf snapped within me. He wanted to rip Bastian a new one too. We were supposed to protect her. *Even from her mate.*

"Oh, Baby Girl..." I said, reaching for her, but she promptly pulled away. I frowned. Something's been going on with her lately, and this wasn't helping any. With all the weird bouts of sickness, and now this dull look in her eyes, I was genuinely concerned for my best friend. And then I felt it. Bastian closed his bonds, breaking her heart even more.

Shanely put her hand to her chest as her mind raced. I could see it. She had never been good at hiding her emotions, and Bastian's never closed his bonds before. Not even growing up did he do that, but he chose *today* to be a prick. I snarled again, pulling the attention of everyone around us.

"What's his problem!?" Elijah snapped, but I ignored him. Shanely looked panicked almost, and her eyes darted from one person to the next. *She's overwhelmed.*

"Shanely..." I said sternly, "whatever you are thinking right now, don't do it. You still aren't feeling well, are you?"

Anger flashed on her face, and she began to blink rapidly. She was losing the fight over her emotions, and I felt awful. *I need to get her out of here,* I thought to myself. *Out of being the center of attention but somewhere safe.* My wolf pushed hard to protect her, but what was I supposed to do when it was her mate that caused all this distress in the first place? What was I supposed to do when I didn't even know what was wrong with her health?

"You two are not to follow me," she said quietly. "You are to stay away from me until I say."

Her Alpha power hit me square in the chest, wrapping around my wolf abruptly. My eyes widened as I realized the command she gave me. Gave us. *What she was about to do...*

My wolf roared inside.

"Shanely, don't even think about taking off right now," I yelled loudly. "Remove this command right now!"

I lifted my foot but was yanked down to the floor again. Pain erupted in my body just thinking about following Baby Girl. Elijah's eyes widened when he tried to move too, and I barred my teeth.

But Shanely's gaze looked so broken, so hurt. I don't even think she saw me right now. She definitely didn't hear my wolf's snarl. Closing their bond seemed to really rattle her, and for the first time in my life, I didn't know what to do. All I knew was that my wolf wanted out to protect her.

But then she bolted, and I couldn't go after her.

We rushed outside the moment that command lifted, but she was long gone by then. I made it to the wall before it forcefully came back, and I snarled loudly.

"Shanely! Come back right now, and I will deal with my idiot brother!" I bellowed through the link. *"Baby Girl, answer me!"*

Nothing but radio silence, and rage filled my chest as I paced in front of the gate. But when she shut down her bonds, I officially *snapped*.

"God, I'm going to cave his face in when I see him," I snapped, hitting the gate. You could see my breath it was so cold out here, and I worried for my sister. Even with her wolf she shouldn't be out here, especially with how she felt.

"We should get Bastian," Elijah said firmly, and I snarled again.

"This is his fault!" I bellowed, pacing back and forth where the invisible line was drawn.

"He can find her though," my brother countered, and I barred my teeth.

"So can I," I snapped, pulling out my phone. I dialed a number.

"Cade, he's her mate," Elijah said, putting his hands on his hips. "We need to let him know."

I scoffed as the phone rang. "He closed their bond. He doesn't want to know."

"He closed *our* bond," Elijah countered, his voice laced with irritation.

I rolled my eyes. "He closed theirs too. Or did you miss the look on her face when it happened?!"

Elijah's shoulders fell. He simply stared at me, so I rolled my eyes again and began to pace.

"Why are you calling me?" Abraham said as he picked up the phone.

"I need you," I snapped. *I was in no mood for games.*

Abraham paused a moment before asking, "What's going on?"

"Shanely took off," I explained. "Put an Alpha command on Elijah and I not to follow her too, so grab Caleb and meet us outside. I'd rather keep this between us if you don't mind."

He sighed. "Yeah, sure. He's already with me so I'll see you in a few."

The line went dead, and I shoved the phone in my pocket. It was pissing me off that I couldn't go after her myself. *God anything could be happening right now*, I thought as anxiety rolled in my stomach. *What if she fell sick again? What if she stumbled in the frozen lake and is about to drown? What if a wild animal...*

"Stop," Elijah said, stepping closer to me. "You're going to drive yourself crazy thinking about all the what ifs."

"It's my job to protect her," I said, glaring, "and I'm stuck here with you."

"Gee thanks," he muttered, and I rolled my eyes.

"Not what I..."

"I know what you meant," he said, and the two of us grew quiet again. After a moment, Elijah said, "Why in the world would Bastian snap like that?"

I snorted, resuming my pacing. I managed to have found the dirt under all this snow by this point. "No idea, but I could care less because no matter what's going on, Shanely didn't deserve this," I said angrily.

Elijah gave me a long look.

"Bastian has never once treated her this way," he said, putting his hands on his hips again. "He's the kind of guy *I* aspire to be when I find my mate, Cade. Something's up."

Sighing, I stopped pacing. I leaned on the massive gate then saying, "I don't know. He was pissed Aerith was with mom."

Elijah didn't respond for another moment. The two of us mulled over the issues with that woman too. *She left with our father*, I thought as anger welled up inside again. *Left with that man after everything he's done to us over the years.* Taking the birthright from Bastian was wrong. Ousting Shanely because she's a mixer was even worse, but harboring Derek after he tried to kill her...

That was inexcusable.

Footsteps sounded behind us, and I turned to find Abraham and Caleb coming out the side door.

"So which way did she take off too?" Abraham asked as he approached. "Her bond is closed."

"No idea," I answered in a huff. "The command wouldn't let us move until she got further away. This is the line."

"Did you inform Luke?" Caleb asked, and my eyes widened. *Why didn't I think of him?* I turned to Elijah, who's eyes glossed over.

"We are now," he said, stepping closer, "but this needs to stay quiet. With all eyes on us, the last thing we need is everyone seeing a chink in our armor. Fixing these issues won't work if they think the King and Queen are at odds."

I scoffed again, kicking the snow as I stewed in silence. Deep down, I knew he was right. All the hard work they've done will amount to nothing if people see all this, but something's going on with her, and I was more worried with her being out there all alone. I turned to Caleb then.

"Look, this part needs to stay amongst us," I said firmly. They each gave me an odd look, and I sighed heavily. "Shanely's been getting sick lately. Like a lot. She doesn't want everyone to know, but something is going on with her."

"What do you mean?" Abe asked, his deep voice rising with worry. "No one told us anything."

"Well I'm telling you now," I said in a huff. "I need you to find her and find her quickly. It's bad enough she's running around out here with no coat, but if she has another episode..."

"Just find her," Elijah said for me. I gave him a grateful smile as he turned back to the two. "Luke is sending out a team to scour the front towards the river. You two get back here since we're grounded."

"That means the waterfall, the meadow, and the area we use for the Hunt," I said, giving them a look.

They nodded, and Caleb opened the metal gate.

"I guess I'll take the meadow and this side of the Hunt," Caleb said as Abraham blew out an exasperated breath. "I doubt she'd go back to the Falls after last time."

"We should check just in case. I'll start with the Hunt and make my way there," he said stepping through. My wolf whined inside as the door shut behind them. *It should be me going after her,* I thought as guilt ate me up inside. *I was her Beta after all.*

"I've got my phone," I said, shoving those awful thoughts away. "Call me as soon as you find her."

Another nod, and the two disappeared in the woods. I gritted my teeth as I stood there watching. After a minute, I pulled out my phone.

"We should head inside," my brother said, and I barked out a laugh. He glared at me. "What?"

"You go inside if you want then," I snapped. That guilty feeling struck me again, knowing I was taking my anger out on the wrong brother. I sighed and turned to him. "I'm sorry. I just don't wanna go inside."

"They are going to find her, Cade. But we have a castle full of nervous shifters that need guidance too," my brother said firmly. *Always the smart one.* "If Shanely and Bastian aren't around, it falls to us."

He was right. I should take care of everything for Baby Girl since she wasn't here, but the idea of walking away right now just killed me. I felt like such a failure as I stared at the snow covered woods.

"Alright," I finally said, accepting defeat. "Let's just get this done, so I can be here when they bring her back."

My brother nodded, and I drug my feet back inside. The morning meal was done and most shifters were meandering about. Elijah dealt with the questions and instructions, while I checked my phone every two minutes.

"She's not up front," Luke's link came through, and I sighed again. *Where would she go?* I wondered.

Every step around Summit Hall just felt wrong. Elijah handled everything, and I honestly wondered how he did it all. I could feel his worry through the bond, but the dude was a rock. I was unraveling with every hour that passed and no luck in finding her. It didn't help that *both* of her animals were white. *Maybe they overlooked her somehow? Maybe she just blended in?*

I dialed Abe's number as I walked down the long dusty tunnel beneath Summit Hall. My wolf snapping at me every minute I was here and our Alpha was missing.

"Dude, I'm looking," Abraham snapped as he picked up the call. "I can't do that if you call every other minute."

"Sorry to be a nuisance, dude," I snapped as I shoved open the hatch to the greenhouse, "but I need an update. Have you found her?"

"Cade, I would have called if I had," he said in a low tone. "I've just cleared my half of the Hunt. I'm making my way to the falls now."

I groaned as I took in the empty room. "You're just now clearing the Hunt?!"

"It's a big area, Cade!" he snapped, and I took a deep breath. "You're the one that wanted to keep this quiet. Luke's got the front, town, and handling security here at Summit Hall. It's just Caleb and I back here."

"I'm sorry," I admitted genuinely. I made my way back to the tunnels. "I'm just worried. I've barely been her Beta, and I've already lost her. She's been sick too, and I'm just stressed."

Abe sighed on the other line. "You're doing fine being Beta, Cade. Maybe it's time to get Bastian?"

I scoffed, feeling every bit of my anger rising again. "Not happening."

"He's her mate..."

"My brother shut their bond down, Abraham. He's been locked in his room all day, and frankly this whole issue is because of him," I snapped angrily. "He's been a crap mate today, and I don't feel like dealing with his moody butt."

Abe sighed again. "Bastian doesn't act like this. Not with Shanely, so figure out how to deal with your brother because I can guarantee Shanely is going to need him after this. They're mates, Cade."

I paused in the dark tunnel at the crossroad. I should go straight. Back to Elijah and the mountain of work left to do, but left would take me to the prison cells, where my wretched father currently sat. My blood boiled as I stared down the hall.

"Cade?"

"Aren't mates supposed to love one another no matter what?" I asked, not really sure where that question came from. "Aren't they supposed to treat one another with kindness and respect. Not yell or act so harsh with them."

Abe didn't say anything at first, and I pursed my lips together, feeling silly I even asked. I don't know why it bothered me or why that question rolled around in my head all the time. But it did.

"Just forget..."

"Mates make mistakes, Cade," he said finally. "No one is perfect. Just because you have a mate doesn't mean you don't mess up. Your brother messed up, but it doesn't make him a bad mate. In fact, it's infuriating how great he is. Makes the rest of us look bad."

Guilt crept in as Abe chuckled at his own joke. I stared down the tunnel though. *It was weird seeing Bastian mess up like this,* I thought to myself, and I didn't know why my wolf was so angry with him over it. He was the one I tried to be like. *If he messed up this bad; what hope is there for me?*

"Do you think..." I started but quickly shook my head against it. "Never mind. Just find her, Abe. Please."

"I'll call as soon as I find her."

The line went dead. My feet turned left before my mind even caught up. Something was gnawing at me, and maybe it was why my wolf was so angry. Maybe it really wasn't Bastian, but the behavior who reminded me so much of a man I wanted to forget. I hit the tunnel switch, and the door creaked open.

I stepped into Summit Hall prison, forgetting how awful it smelled down here. How dark and disgusting it truly was. We didn't have many down here, and I knew which cell to go to.

"Beta Cade," a wolf said as I approached his station. "I didn't expect to see you here now."

"Take a break, wolf," I said, giving him a look. "Take a five minute break."

His brown eyes studied me a moment before he stood. "Make him pay."

The wolf enforcer left his desk and meandered up the stairs. His comments made me feel sick, but I shoved that feeling aside and moved to the cell at the far end. I stopped at my father's cell.

"Never thought I'd see you again," Liam muttered.

His back was too me, and I noticed he had yet to touch his plate of food. Bright red scratches surrounded the collar on his neck, and his hair was disheveled and messy. *He looked small sitting in that cell,* I thought solemnly.

I took a steadying breath saying, "Yeah, well I didn't plan on coming down here ever again."

"Then why are you here?" my father asked as he turned. His dull eyes reminded me of Bastian's, when Silas removed him from the packs. I blinked, shoving my brother's face from my mind's eye.

"I have a question, and you're going to answer me," I said, crossing my arms.

Liam scoffed and turned back away from me. My wolf bristled at his blatant disrespect, but I forced him to ignore it.

"Did you ever love mom?" I blurted.

I don't know why I needed to know, but I did. Fear crept in that I inherited more of my father than I thought. My anger was getting to the point it was hard to control. Ever since I accepted the weighty honor of being Shanely's Beta, things have spiraled for me. Seeing Bastian snap under the pressure made me afraid I would to act like that to my mate too someday.

Liam slowly turned, raising an eye as he studied me. "Did you come down to add insult to injury, Cade? Is it not enough that I'm barred from my wolf, stuck in this God forsaken cell, that you had to remind me that *my mate left me?!"*

My eyes widened, and I took a step back. Liam stood, coming as close to the bars he could without touching them. I held my breath as he glared at me. That very familiar glare I knew so well.

"You've got some nerve, Cade," he muttered, his nostrils flaring. This would be the moment he'd punish me. This is where I'd receive some sort of ridiculous punishment for asking a simple question, and I instinctively cringed.

But nothing happened.

I slowly looked at my father. *He was so frail now,* I thought as I truly studied him. I stood eye level with him and something finally dawned on me. *Why I let this man mess with my head is beyond me...*

"Mom left you because you treated her horribly," I said with a clipped tone. "She left you because you pushed all her kids away for some puke who didn't deserve to live according to *our laws!*"

His eyes widened as I slowly approached the cells, feeling the hum of electricity that ran through them.

"I asked because I needed to know if there was any part of your wolf that actually *loved* his mate," I sneered, "but I should have known better. I can't tell you how utterly relieved I am to know that neither my brothers nor I took after you."

For the first time in my life, I saw my words strike my father. Something I said actually rattled him, and I honestly didn't know how to take it. I turned on my heels, admitting this was a stupid idea in my head, when I realized something else.

I turned to my father one last time. "Do you realize the life you gave up just for that power and money?"

My hands gestured to the guests around us.

"The people you sided with are all here with you," I said quietly. "Is it everything you thought it would be?"

Liam turned in a huff and sat back down on his cot. I shook my head, feeling worse than when I came down here.

"You don't have a mate, Cade," my father said, and I stilled. "Nor do you have kids, so don't come whining at me for things you know nothing about and maybe *never* will."

My face fell. I was grateful that prick's back was turned because I couldn't keep the hurt from spreading across my face. I turned and stalked to the hidden entrance once more, cursing myself left and right for coming down here in the first place. *This was a waste of time,* I thought angrily.

But my father's words continued to haunt me as I made my way down the dark tunnel. I didn't have a mate yet, and maybe I wouldn't get one. *Maybe I wasn't meant to have a mate...*

I shoved my hands in my pockets as I continued back to my brother, feeling a little sorry for myself. My mind drifted back to Shanely. *I couldn't even keep her from running off,* I thought to myself. *And if she were hurt right now...*

Some mate I'd be.

Shoving the heavy door to Summit Hall open, I found myself face-to-face with Elijah.

"What?" I asked.

"I thought we were doing this together," he said, crossing his arms.

"You don't need me, Elijah," I said as I shoved past him. My wolf was just aggravated, and I didn't have it in me to listen to him berate me over visiting Liam, so I lied. "Besides, all I did was check the greenhouse."

Elijah gripped the back of my collar and yanked me back. His eyes flashed red, and I stilled. His wolf rose to the surface as he stepped towards me.

"I have that same desire you do in finding her, Cade. You took off without me, which isn't fair. We may have to do this crap, but it doesn't mean I rather do this than look for Shanely."

My jaw opened, but I promptly closed it as a group of panthers walked by. Elijah stiffened as they made their way around us, and I sighed.

"I'm sorry," I said quietly. "I didn't think you'd care or anything, and my wolf was itching to move and look for her. I wasn't trying to bail on you."

He shook himself off before shrugging. "I just don't want you thinking I don't care, Cade. I'm worried sick over her too. It would be you and me scouring the woods if it weren't for this stupid command. I'm just trying to do something useful, while we're stuck waiting."

BONUS CHAPTER

Suddenly, my phone rang.

I sagged in relief as I answered it. "Talk to me, Abraham."

Bonus Chapter

"Hey, I found her!" Abraham said from the other end of the line.

I exhaled loudly. "Bout freaking time! Bring her..."

"Yeah, I'll bring her back," he said annoyed with me already, "just let Caleb know."

"Just hurry up!" I hollered.

"Yeah, yeah... I'm moving, Cade."

The line went dead, and I shoved the phone in my pocket. My feet were flying down the halls, with Elijah right behind me. Suddenly, Bastian opened his bond.

"I'll let Caleb know," my brother said as we ran towards the dining hall, ignoring our idiot brother. Most of everyone were already making their way into the Ballroom for tonight's event. We were seriously behind now.

The two of us rushed outside, and I bounced on my heels, watching for her to appear. The woods were empty, and my wolf snarled within me. I couldn't get control of his temper today, and that bugged me.

"Just settled down," my brother said, his eyes firmly fixed on the woods as well. "They'll be here any minute."

"What if she's still mad and put a command on Abraham too?" I snapped. God, my wolf was becoming annoying with how anxious he was getting.

"You're overthinking this," he said, and I shot him a glare.

"No, I'm not!" I snarled. "I'm thinking pretty clear, Elijah. How am I supposed to do my freaking job if she commands me to do the opposite every time! How am I supposed to keep her safe? And if I can't keep *her* safe, then how will I be able to..."

Shanely's honey scent filled the air, and I turned, searching for her.

"Cade, finish that sentence," Elijah demanded, putting his hand on my shoulder, but I shrugged him off.

"Let it go," I snapped. I put my hands on my hips and stalked back and forth behind the gate. Suddenly, they appeared.

Shanely was currently swallowed up in Abraham's massive hoodie, but other than that she seemed alright. My wolf snapped angrily again. *He was mad at her too.*

"Shanely! Thank God, you're okay!" Elijah shouted. He winced, taking a step back, and soon I felt it too. The sickening command hit my skin as Shanely drew closer. I ground my teeth, trying to stay put, but I couldn't take the pain anymore and staggered backwards.

"Baby Girl," I shouted angrily, "take off this stupid command right now!"

"Cade, Elijah..." her soft voice said quietly, "you are both free of the command to stay away from me."

I exhaled as the pain suddenly stopped, and I rushed towards her. I wrapped my arms around her and squeezed.

"Don't you ever do that to me again!" I hollered. "Do you hear me?"

"Cade! I can't breathe!" she said, squirming under my grasp. I reluctantly let her go, and my brother walked over to hug her.

"We're just glad you're okay," he said, kissing her forehead.

"Yeah, well at least I have you guys to look for me, right?" she muttered, and that burning rage filled my chest again. "I am sorry I made you all worry. I just needed a moment to myself, and I couldn't go to my room."

She looked to her feet, and it was all I could do to not pummel my brother now. I couldn't stand the thought of her feeling so hurt by my own blood. I tried to shake off the intense frustration, but then my phone rang. It only made things worse.

I snarled when I saw Bastian's name appear on my screen. I knew I should answer it. He's probably realizing Shanely's bond is gone, but my wolf was just mad at him. I didn't want to make this easy for him for some reason. It was nothing to send his call to voicemail, and I took Shanely's hand in mine.

"C'mon, Baby Girl. We have a ball to go to tonight," I said, dragging her towards the door.

Elijah's phone suddenly rang. When his eyes slowly drug to mine, I knew what he was about to do. I grabbed his arm saying, "Oh no! Let him freak out for awhile. I had to all day because of his temper. You ignore that call, Elijah!"

"He is her mate, Cade," Elijah said firmly, "and I'm his Beta. It's not right to ignore it. I mean, how would you feel?"

His phone stopped ringing. I knew we should answer the call, but I couldn't shake this aggression. *We were only in this mess because of his screw up.* I looked over to Shanely whose peaked skin and sullen eyes broke me. She was feeling sick again. Elijah's phone chimed.

"Look, he is freaking out now! He said Shanely shut their bond, and he can't find her," my brother said, and I snorted.

"Look," Abraham said, interrupting us all, "I'll let you all handle Bastian. I'm going to find Bay, but please Shanely, don't run off again. Just hide in my room if you need to."

Abraham kissed his sister's cheek as she said softly, "Thanks for everything, Abraham."

"Elijah, let him stew," I said as Abraham disappeared from view. "He needs to see how he messed up. Bastian's locked himself in his room all day and has no idea that we couldn't find Shanely since this morning! Do not respond! I'm her Beta, and I said no!"

Elijah gritted his teeth but put his phone away.

"This is wrong."

"I don't care."

"Guys, can I change in your room? Please?"

We both turned to her. Her hands were tightly wound together and tears had formed in her eyes. She desperately tried to clear them, and I just felt awful for her.

"Of course, Shanely. Let's just get her ready for tonight. Bastian will be finding us any minute anyways," Elijah muttered, and I squared my shoulders. *My brother and I were going to be having a conversation alright.*

My fists stayed clenched the entire walk to our rooms. Never once did we cross paths with my brother. Shanely's pace was slow, and I couldn't figure out if it was because she didn't feel well, or if it was because of what happened with Bastian today. She just wasn't bouncing back like she normally does though. It was stressing my wolf to no end that something big ailed her. It was our job to fix, but I honestly didn't even know how.

I opened the door to my room instead, and she walked right in. I didn't want her to get blindsided if Bastian was waiting for her, and I slowly put my finger up.

"Hang on a minute," I muttered before leaving her with Elijah.

I stewed the entire way to their room and opened the door without knocking. Elijah and I each had a Master Key, and it was about to pay off. But to my dismay, Bastian wasn't around. I poked my head in Aerith's room, noticing her dress was missing for tonight. I walked to the Master bedroom and found Shanely's dress hanging on the hooks. Bastian's stuff was gone too.

"Managed to get ready for the ball before looking for your mate," I muttered as my wolf snapped within me. My eyes flashed gold, and I bit down on my lower lip. I've been close to shifting all day, but I couldn't afford to now. *I* needed to handle this with my brother. Not our wolves. And then afterwards, I needed to figure out what was going on with Shanely and find out why she was so sick.

My wolf snapped his jaws at me, and I sighed. I'd been gone too long already. I rushed to the bathroom, grabbing every bag that looked filled with makeup or hair supplies, before grabbing her dress and shoes. It didn't take me long to get back to my room again.

Her head leaned on Elijah's shoulder, and she just looked so sad. I gave a soft smile, hoping to get one in return.

"Bastian and Aerith weren't in their room, so I grabbed your stuff," I said quietly. I handed her everything, and she stood.

"Thank you guys again. I don't know what I'd do without you."

And there it was. A smile finally.

"We are always here for you, Baby Girl," I said, and my wolf chirped in agreement. *He was insanely proud of his job as Beta.*

"Go change," Elijah said, pulling me from my thoughts. "We'll dress out here, and we can walk you down."

She slipped into the bathroom, and we scurried to grab our own tuxes then. I dumped my hoodie and kicked off my sneakers before unzipping the stupid bag that held everything.

"Was Bastian really not there?" Elijah asked quietly.

"He and Aerith had dressed and gone already," I answered firmly. He said nothing, so in silence, we got ready.

I pulled my pants up, tucking in my white shirt, and fastening the clasp. I looked in the mirror to work my tie, when I realized how awful my hair looked. I had been running around all day worrying over Shanely, that I didn't realize how messy it had gotten. I ran my fingers through my hair before grabbing my jacket. It would have to do.

Not like I had any mate to impress anyways.

"Can I come out now?" Shanely's meek voice came through the door.

My brother laughed. "Yeah, we're ready."

"Wow, Shanely look at you! You're gorgeous!" Elijah said as he spun her around. Shanely relaxed, smiling wide as she twirled her dress. I exhaled deeply. *She finally seemed like herself again.*

"It's good to see that smile again, Baby Girl. Shall I escort you, Milady?" I asked, holding out my arm. I knew eventually this had to come to a head with Bastian, but I wanted to give her a good moment until it came.

"Thank you both for everything," she said, when her smile fell. "Did Bastian... stop by?"

She just looked so broken all over again, and my blood boiled. Sighing, I said, "No, he hasn't. I wouldn't have let him in anyways."

Her brows furrowed as she processed that. I couldn't quite tell what was going through her mind other than hurt. *She was the White Wolf,* I thought to myself. *She should have every bit of confidence to search for him herself. To chew him out like he deserved, but she just folded her arms across her chest and retreated further from us.* I didn't like that.

"Let's go, I suppose," she said quietly.

I led the way, walking into the hall first, when I heard the elevator slowly coming to our floor. I knew who it was before the doors opened, but I couldn't contain the snarl that escaped my lips when I saw my brother walk out.

BONUS CHAPTER

His eyes were frantic until they saw Shanely. I saw her shrink behind Elijah slightly, and my vision turned red.

"Oh my God, Shanely! I've been looking everywhere for you! I..."

I took two steps and swung. My wolf pulled through as I connected with Bastian's jaw, and he dropped.

My brother shot to his feet, and I felt his wolf surge to the surface. His eyes were red too, but I didn't care. He may be stronger, but this is a fight I would *not* lose.

"What was that for?!" he bellowed loudly. "Are you out of your mind, Cade?!"

I shook my hand out, adrenaline pumping through my body harshly. "Nah, brother," I said, with more control than I expected, "but you have been."

He got in my face, but I didn't back away. I stared right in his eyes, knowing his wolf would hate the disrespect.

"Back off, Cade. Step aside from my mate!"

I barred my teeth, and he did the same in return. The three of us snarling so loud, it rattled the walls.

"So, now you want to act like her mate?!" I snapped, pushing my brother further back. "Seriously Bastian, after the way you treated her this morning?"

Bastian's gaze moved past me to Shanely. His eyes softened some as he looked at her.

"Cade, I know," he said, his tone calmer than before. "I messed up, alright? Shanely, I'm so sorry for taking my stress and anger out on you."

"Not good enough, brother," Elijah said, and I smirked. Bastian only glared at his Beta.

"I know that, Elijah! If you'd move out of my way, I can try to fix things with my Fated Mate! I've been looking everywhere for her! Shanely, please open up our bond," Bastian pleading.

Johnny and Ryder emerged behind Bastian, quietly assessing the situation.

"*Stay put,*" I said through the link. "*This is between us.*"

Bastian's eyes flashed with hurt then. Shanely hadn't opened the bonds with anyone yet. It pissed me off that he thought he'd get it back so easily.

"Oh, you've been looking everywhere?" I snapped, unable to keep my temper and wolf at bay.

"Yes! And you two haven't picked up your phones! Why didn't you tell me you had my mate?"

Johnny and Ryder took another step closer.

"How long?" I asked, crossing my arms. His eyes narrowed as he went from me to Shanely.

"What?"

"I said, how long were you looking for her?! Are you deaf and dumb tonight, Bastian?"

My brother snarled, shoving me back, but I held my ground. I was ready to swing again.

"As soon as I realized she was missing! What is your problem, Cade!? Let me pass now!"

"My problem!?" I scoffed, eyes widening. "HA! My problem is, I've been looking for Shanely since you blew up on her in the dining hall THIS MORNING!"

Bastian's face fell. He turned to Shanely utterly lost now.

"What?"

"That's right, brother. You're too lost in your own temper and problems to even notice your mate ran off this morning," I snapped. "She used an Alpha Command on Elijah and I to stay away from her, and then shut the bonds down tight. I had to send Caleb and Abraham to look for her because Elijah and I couldn't leave Summit Hall! It took us *all* day just to find her Bastian, and I had no idea if she was okay! No idea if she was even alive! We found her the minute you finally realized she even closed her end of the bond and wasn't even here. So no, your apology isn't good enough. You screwed up today, Bastian, and you are so lucky Abraham found her and not something else!"

I was breathing hard by the end of my outburst and could feel everyone's eyes on me. Bastian looked sick as he struggled to comprehend the truth.

"Shanely... I didn't know. I just needed space to process everything, and I stayed in to be with Aerith. I spent the day with her..." he muttered. "I didn't know. Why did you run away?"

I scoffed, pacing the floor between them. *God, the thick headed...*

"Why do you think, Bastian?" she asked quietly.

"Shanely, I'm so sorry for everything. I..."

"It's fine, Bastian. I can take care of myself. I didn't need you to rescue me today. Clearly, you have enough on your plate, and I do not want to be another thing you have to deal with or worry about. Now please guys, let's make our way to the ballroom. Everyone's waiting on us."

My eyes widened as I turned to look at Baby Girl. *Maybe she was more angry than I thought.* Her brows furrowed as she slowly made her way towards us. My brother reached out to stop her, but I cut in and blocked his way.

"Don't even think about stopping her," I gritted through my teeth. "You've done enough today."

Bastian dropped his hand, and I stood in his way as Shanely made her way down the hall. I didn't know why I couldn't get a grip on my wolf, but he was just so angry. So furious right now that I let guide him me in this. Something changed with us the moment I became her Beta, and maybe he understood what it was and why. *I was just done ignoring him.*

"Shanely wait!" Bastian said, shoving past me as she disappeared into the elevator. Ryder was already moving down the stairs, and the rest of us followed.

"Shanely, why did you do that? What's going on? Is it more than the fight?"

I heard Ryder's voice from the top of the stairs, and I made my feet move faster. *Something was wrong,* I thought. *I knew Ryder and... Something wasn't right.*

I hit the landing, and my eyes narrowed on Shanely and Ryder. He looked freaked, but she bolted again. She was so fast I couldn't catch her.

"What did she say to you?" I demanded, and Ryder gave me a frustrated look.

"She said..."

Ryder's jaw snapped shut. Hard enough his teeth clattered. He cleared his throat and tried again.

"She said…"

Again it slammed shut.

"Is something else going on?" Bastian asked, and my eyes widened. My wolf whined inside as I turned to Baby Girl. *She was having another episode,* I thought to myself. *She was sick.*

I pulled on Bastian's arm, letting go of my anger long enough to tell him, when I heard her voice.

"Cade, Elijah. You are not allowed to tell Bastian how sick I've been. You are not allowed to discuss my health with my mate."

My teeth rattled as my jaw shut just like Ryder's. Rage boiled my blood as I turned to Baby Girl. Her cheeks flushed as she grabbed the microphone.

"Good evening, everyone! I hope you've all had a wonderful day today!"

"What is going on?" Bastian asked, and my jaw locked. I turned to Elijah.

"What are we going to do?"

"I don't know."

Bastian took off, crossing the room towards Shanely. I followed Elijah and Ryder to our family's section. *Maybe I can cut her off on this side if Bastian has that side?* I thought to myself. I had to catch up to her and forced her to remove this command.

Again.

I could hear her heart racing from here, and she swayed on her feet just standing there. *This was bad.*

"I would like to start this evening with what everyone's been so excited for…" she said smiling, "the Mate Dance!"

I ground to a stop. *We weren't supposed to do this dance until after dinner was served.* I narrowed my eyes to Elijah then.

"Bastian," Shanely said, "will you please help the DJ find the right song?"

I could feel Bastian's hesitation and worry through our bond, but he smiled and obeyed her request.

"I know you're pissed, Cade, and you have every right to be," Bastian said firmly, *"but stop helping Shanely escape me. I just want to fix this."*

"I'm not part of this! Not this time," I bellowed loudly through the link.

Bastian had reached the DJ table, when his eyes settled on mine.

BONUS CHAPTER

"Okay, so every single eligible shifter please make your way to the dance floor. The song will play, and when you hear this chime," I said before ringing the bell on the table, "turn to your right and change partners! Now remember every shifter is different when it comes to finding their mate, so if you get a strong feeling like your sure they're the one, then ask them how they discover their mates. You might just need a little extra nudge like the tigers do. I'll spill their secret though. They need a kiss to be able to tell!"

"Then what is going on?" Bastian asked.

The stupid command kept my link blocked every time I tried to form the words. Bastian narrowed his eyes, but it didn't fix anything. I turned, glaring at Baby Girl. *This was wrong,* I thought angrily. Commanding me to stay away and ignore my wolf's instinct with protecting her *was wrong.*

I turned and stood directly in front of her with my arms crossed. There was nowhere for her to go now, and Elijah took up position from the other side of the stage.

"Please be respectful though and leave your kiss to their hand or cheek! And remember have fun!" Shanely said, and the dance floor quickly filled with shifters eager to start.

Shanely wasn't feeling good. Honestly, this was the worst I had ever seen her look. I tapped my foot, waiting for her to come down the stairs, when I heard her voice in the link again.

"Cade, Elijah, and Ryder. You are hereby required to participate in the Mate Dance."

My wolf roared. Like an invisible force picked my feet up and pushed me forward, I left Baby Girl on the stage and blended in with the crowd of shifters.

"SHANELY! Remove this command right now!"

She shut me out, and my eyes widened.

"Do you want to dance?" a small girl asked me. *A timid primate,* I thought as I watched Shanely carefully walk down the stairs, but a sweet girl who didn't deserve my snarky attitude. My hands wrapped around her waist as the music started.

The primate talked incessantly as I tried to guide her to the side. Shanely moved quickly through the crowd, and I swore under my breath.

"I'm sorry?" she asked, frowning. "What did you say?"

"Nothing!" I blurted, shaking my head. "I'm sorry, I'm just preoccupied."

Shanely was gone, and I gritted my teeth. I turned, finding Elijah and Ryder looking as worried as I felt. But until this freaking song ended, we were stuck.

"*Find her, Bastian. Now!*"

My brother was already moving towards the door but looked downright afraid as he rushed out of the room. I bit down on my lip to keep myself from snarling as the song played on. *Please*, I thought to myself, *please let her be alright*.

Bonus Chapter

Cade

Elijah and I bolted from the ballroom the second that song ended. Ryder was hot on our heels as we raced towards the stairs. Pure terror came from Bastian's bond before we finally heard the link.

"*Help me.*"

"I am *sick* of Alpha Commands!" I yelled.

"Call Cassia!" Elijah yelled, and Ryder's eyes glossed over.

"What is even happening?" he hollered as we rushed to the 5th floor.

"Shanely's been feeling ill since arriving," I stammered between breaths. "We don't know why."

A loud snarl rippled down the hall as we made it to the 5th floor. Bastian held Shanely in his arms, leaning against the wall like he couldn't carry her. My breath caught in my chest as we skidded to a stop.

"Don't just stand there," he snarled. "*Help* me."

I rushed towards them, and Bastian let her go into my arms. She was unconscious with dark circles appearing under her eyes. I turned to my brother, but it was then I noticed him too. Bastian looked *weak*. I have never seen him struggle like he was now, but whatever was going on was draining him fast. *Even the mark from where I struck him stayed.*

"What happened?!" I shouted.

"I don't know," Bastian said as Elijah put his arm under his. "I found her collapsed outside the room."

"Cassia's on her way!" Ryder said as he smacked the elevator wall. He held the door as I carried Shanely inside.

"Why is she like this?" Bastian asked, and I couldn't even open my mouth because of that stupid command. The three of us stayed silent as the elevator went to the first floor.

Bastian scoffed. "I know you're all pissed with me right now, but Shanely is my mate! I deserve to know if something's going on with her other than our fight."

No one said a word, and I was beginning to feel awful for my brother. I may have been a jerk to him today, but I didn't want to keep *this* from him. I gritted my teeth, clinging to Baby Girl. My wolf raged inside, and it was a struggle to stop him from shifting. Bastian's gaze settled right on me, but I couldn't look him in the eye.

The doors opened, and the three of us rushed our Alphas to the med bay.

"What happened?!" Cassia hollered as she rushed towards us, with Cain right behind her. The Summit Hall doctor stormed into the room from the back.

"Luke said there was an emergency?" he said, and I turned to Ryder.

"I thought it would be a good idea to tell him too," he said, and I gave him a grateful nod.

"I found my wife collapsed outside our room," Bastian said, stumbling forward. "I don't know why."

"Well you don't look too good yourself," the Doctor said. He motioned us to the back room. I laid Shanely on the bed, gently moving her white hair aside.

"I don't feel good," my brother said before pushing me aside, "but something's wrong with Shanely. Help *her*."

The Doctor sighed. "Does anyone know what could be going on?"

Ryder, Elijah, and I all looked to our feet. It was killing me inside, but I couldn't open my mouth. Anger radiated down the bond from Bastian, but I didn't look at him. This was just a mess.

"Alrighty then," the Doctor said before snapping his fingers. "Let's get her hooked up to fluids and see what's going on. Shall we?"

The room began to move, and everyone was ushered out. Bastian stood just outside the door, watching the doctor insert an IV on Baby Girl. I had to admit, it was hard to watch.

Elijah slowly approached our oldest brother.

BONUS CHAPTER

"She'll be okay, Bastian."

Bastian scoffed. "No thanks to you."

My nostrils flared as he stormed over to the waiting room.

"That's not fair," Elijah said, following him. I kept my feet firmly planted where I was at. I just felt like a puke, and Bastian wasn't wrong in being upset over this. I just couldn't tell him why.

"Oh, it's not?" Bastian snapped as he collapsed in the chair. He glared at the three of us. "You three know what's going on with my mate yet you won't tell me! And for what?! Because you're mad at me?"

Elijah snarled. "You screwed up today, Bastian! Your behavior put us in this spot in the first place, but it isn't why we aren't saying anything."

"Then why?!" Bastian bellowed.

"Lower your voice," Cassia scolded, her heels clicking as she approached. "This is our medical facility, and we will not turn this into a shouting match."

"Explain what happened now," Cain said, putting his hands on his hips. Guilt wrapped its way around my heart, and I dropped my head.

"I messed up and snapped at Shanely this morning," Bastian said, dropping his own head. Shame trickled down our bond then, but I still couldn't look at him. I was her Beta, and my actions didn't help her any. My eyes slowly drifted towards the small glass window to the room she lay in.

"She bolted, Cain," Elijah continued. "It took us all day just to find her too. But..."

His jaw snapped shut, and he groaned, rubbing his face. Cain narrowed his eyes.

"Look I get I messed up, but Shanely collapsed!" Bastian went on as he paced the room. "I need to know what's happening to my mate and these three *refuse* to tell me."

Suddenly, my eyes widened, and I bolted to Shanely's room.

"Cade?!" Bastian yelled, but I slammed the door in his face.

"What are you doing, sir?" the Doctor asked. Bastian yanked on the handle, but I held it tight.

"An Alpha command was placed on myself, Ryder, and my brother Elijah," I said as Bastian hit the door. "We were commanded not to tell him what's wrong with his mate, but no one said anything about you."

The Doctor gave me an odd look. "Who would do that?"

Bastian slammed his fist on the door, and I glared at him through the window.

"Cade! Open this door right now!" he hollered loudly through the link.

"Elijah, shut him up!" I snapped, and I saw my other brother step in between. I turned to the Doctor then.

"She did," I said, pointing to Shanely. "Look, it's all been a God awful mess today, but Shanely's been throwing up off and on since she got here. Her nose has been extra sensitive too, and she's been weak and just off from the get go. These two have been fighting all day today too, and I thought it was just her mood, but then she collapsed and well..."

The Doctor slowly nodded his head before turning to the nurse. "Do a blood drawl please. Do you know if their bond's open?"

"He closed it this morning and opened it sometime before the ball," I answered before sighing. "She shut her bond down to everyone shortly after. As far as I know their bond is still closed on her end."

The Doctor pursed his lips together. "Thank you. You did good, Cade. Go ahead and head back out. I'll wrap up what I need, and then I'll allow her mate in. We'll get this sorted out."

I gave him a grateful nod before stepping back out. Bastian was in my face before the door closed.

"What is your problem?!" he bellowed angrily. The dark circles under his eyes getting worse. My shoulders fell, and I pushed past him. I slumped into a chair and buried my head in my hands.

"Just let it go, Bastian," I muttered quietly.

"Why are you shoving me out after one mistake?!" he snarled, "I already feel like a puke, Cade. You really feel the need to do this?!"

I shot to my feet angrily.

"Because that one mistake hurt her!" I yelled back. "You didn't see her face, Bastian! And you know what?! That's the kind of crap our father would do to our mother!"

Bastian's eyes widened, and he took a step back. He promptly shut his bond off to me then.

"That was low, Cade," Elijah snapped, stepping between us. Guilt ate me alive, and I sighed, rubbing my face.

"I'm sorry…"

"Don't," Bastian said. He walked over to the far end of the waiting and sat down.

My wolf whined inside me. It felt like he was scratching at the spot where Bastian's bond used to be. I took a step towards him saying, "Bastian…"

Elijah blocked me. He pointed to the other side saying, "You can sit over there."

I groaned and stormed to my own seat. I slumped down, and the room grew quiet. No one said a word to either of us, and I had to sit there being the odd man out from my brothers. Elijah sat next to Bastian, and their eyes would gloss over every so often. I knew they were using the link so I couldn't hear. I dropped my head low and waited. Waited for anything really.

I don't know what was wrong with me, but if I couldn't get a handle on it, I was going to ruin every relationship I had.

***

I awoke to a dark room and slowly straightened in my seat as I looked around. Elijah was asleep in the chair next to Shanely's door, but Bastian was nowhere to be found. I moved silently towards her room, finding my brother with his head on her lap through the small window on the door.

"You better fix this, Cade," Elijah muttered quietly. He cracked an eye open to glare at me.

"I thought you were asleep," I said quietly.

"I can't sleep," he answered, leaning back in his seat. "Bastian's health is getting worse, and Shanely hasn't woken. My wolf won't let me sleep with them like this."

I pursed my lips together as I looked back to them. My heart hurt seeing them like this, and Elijah sighed.

"Cade, you've always blundered your speech growing up, but usually you're not wrong," he said, and I dropped my head. "Just drop the temper and talk to him. He feels bad enough."

I sighed and slowly pushed the door open. Bastian lifted his head, and my eyes widened slightly. *Elijah wasn't kidding,* I thought as I stared at my brother. *He looked awful with his dark sullen eyes and pale skin.* My shiner was still present too, and I narrowed my eyes. He's an Alpha. Mate to the White Wolf. He should be healed already.

"Hey," I said softly. "How's she doing?"

Bastian gently rubbed Shanely's cheek. "Doc said the fluids he gave is helping. He expects her to wake soon, but we don't know when."

I nodded as I went to the other side of her bed. I leaned against the back wall as silence filled the room.

"I'm sorry," I said, trying to get over all this pent up nervous energy. "I shouldn't have compared you to our dad."

Bastian leaned back in his chair. "You weren't wrong though."

"No, I was," I said. "You made a mistake, but it doesn't make you him."

"Doesn't it though?" he asked, his eyes never leaving Shanely. "I don't know why I did it either. I was just so stressed about proving myself to all these shifters who are still so leery of us and with dad losing his mind in the prison below..."

Silence filled the space between us.

"I paid him a visit," I muttered, and Bastian slowly turned to me.

"You did?" he asked. "Why?"

I shrugged. "I was angry. Angry with you, angry with Shanely for commanding me to stay away from her, angry at him still, I suppose. I just wanted to know the truth, I guess."

"The truth about what?" he asked quietly.

"Mom," I answered honestly, "and us really. I just... I don't know. I've been feeling like a failure since taking up the Beta role, and then when you did that, it just threw me for a loop. You're the sort of man I want to be and..."

"If I behaved that poorly, where does that leave you?" he finished, and I nodded my head slowly. Bastian sighed, leaning forward on his knees to look at me. "Cade? You have got to stop comparing me to you. We are *minutes* apart. I may be your older brother, but you are just as much my equal."

"I haven't found my mate," I said, admitting another fear I've been holding onto, "and I want to do a good job being Beta, and I want to be a good man. I'm trying to figure this out, Bastian because I'm sick of being the screw up."

"You're not a screw up," he countered, and I shot him a look.

"Out of the three of us, I'm the one *no one* comes rushing too," I said, shoving off the wall. "You're the strongest, and Elijah's the most level headed. Shoot, I don't even know why Shanely asked me to be her Beta. All I seem to do is lose my temper and screw up."

Bastian sighed and walked around the bed to me. "Shanely picked you because you are worthy of the position. You were her first pick honestly."

I smirked, gently giving her hand a squeeze. "Really?"

He nodded. "I had a hard time choosing between you and Elijah honestly, but I knew how close you guys are. You guys have just gravitated to each other since we met her really. All I knew was I wanted my brothers in the Beta roles. I would have respected Shanely if she chose another, but she wanted you, and I got my way regardless."

Bastian grinned wide as I chuckled. "Gotta love, Baby Girl."

"Look, you were right earlier," he went on, "and I needed to hear it. I don't ever want to behave like our father. If I'm getting out of line, I fully expect you and Elijah to step in."

I grinned. "That I can do."

He laughed, but my smile fell. I slowly turned to my brother. "You'll do the same for me, won't you?"

Bastian gave me a wide grin then. "Absolutely. Although, out of the three of us, I don't see you needing to be corrected, Cade. You always took after mom anyways."

The corners of my mouth rose as we watched Baby Girl sleep. Her wolf was strong, and whatever was going on we would fix together. I may never find my mate, but it didn't matter. I'd be here for Shanely and Aerith, for Bay and her children, and any kids and mate my brother Elijah had too. Liam was a stain I was removing from my family line. None of us would *ever* behave like him. That much was proven with just how far we went to take care of them not only physically but also emotionally.

I was *here* for my family. No matter what.

The Doctor stepped in and smiled. "I need to check over our patient here. Can you step out, Cade?"

I gave him a nod as I made my way to the door. My wolf barred his teeth though, and I sighed.

Enough already, I told myself, but he still seemed agitated. Knowing he wouldn't quit until I pacified him, I turned to my brother and asked, "Can we talk again later? There's more, I guess."

Bastian nodded. "Yeah, of course."

His attention had shifted to the Doctor at Shanely's side. I gave a soft smile and made my way to the door. My wolf may still be pissed over the events of the day, but I was glad to be okay with Bastian again.

My wolf snapped his jaws as I left the room again, and I rolled my eyes.

We can fix the rest later.

www.ingramcontent.com/pod-product-compliance
Lightning Source LLC
LaVergne TN
LVHW091714070526
838199LV00050B/2398